DETOUR

A CREEKWOOD NOVEL

A. MARIE

Editing: Sarah Plocher, All Encompassing Books
Proofreading: Julie Deaton, JD Proofs
Cover Design: Murphy Rae
Formatting: Champagne Book Design

PLAYLIST

Music plays a big role in my writing. You can find the full playlist on Spotify

Everything Is Everything—Ms. Lauren Hill
Young, Dumb, & Broke—Khalid
Ain't No Rest For The Wicked—Cage The Elephant
Heathens—Twenty One Pilots
Pretty Girl—Maggie Lindemann
Issues—Julia Michaels
Sorry Not Sorry—Demi Lovato
Taki Taki—DJ Snake Ft. Selena Gomez, Ozuna, Cardi B
You Should See Me In A Crown—Billie Eilish
Indestructible—Welshly Arms
Same Ol' Mistakes—Rihanna
Apartment—BOBI ANDONOV
Play With Fire—Sam Tinnesz, Yacht Money
Middle Finger—Bohnes
Head Above Water—Avril Lavigne
Power Over Me—Dermot Kennedy
Won't Go Down Easy—JAXSON GAMBLE
wRoNg—ZAYN, Kehlani
Too Good To Be True—Danny Avila, The Vamps, Machine Gun Kelly
Without Me—Halsey
Blood // Water—grandson
I'm A Mess—Bebe Rexha
Dangerous—Royal Deluxe
Day Dreaming—Jack & Jack
Nightmare—Halsey
Horns—Bryce Fox
Let You Love Me—Rita Ora

For the ones who laugh through the pain
simply because there is no other choice.

Detour: taking a roundabout route or alternate route; whether by choice, out of necessity, or possibly even unknowingly at times

CHAPTER 1

Angela

"YOU RUINED MY LIFE!" MY MOTHER SHRIEKS IN MY ear as I crane my neck away.

Tell me something I don't know, I think to myself, clutching this crappy railing with both hands, hoping it'll hold firm to the wall until she's through with her violent fit. Thankfully, at eighteen, I'm stronger than she is. Finally. It wasn't always that way, what with my mother only being in her late thirties. She started having kids early, very early, too frickin' early. But now that I can hold my own, she's resorting to more drastic means. I must say this one tops the dysfunction cake, too, even for her.

I only have to hold on a little bit longer.

Arms wrapped tightly around mine, she holds my body to hers, trying to shove me down the flight of stairs in our small townhouse. With my heels dug into the worn Berber carpet and the banister held in a death grip, I'm able to wait her out, letting her tire herself out until she gives up—hopefully.

She's telling me what a mistake it was to have me, to give a child of her own flesh and blood a chance at life, and I can't stop the eye roll begging to be released. Like that's when her life took a turn. *Right.*

Her fourth marriage just imploded, much like the first three, and she's looking for someone, anyone, to blame. Since she's pushed almost everyone else in her life away, the blame falls solely on my shoulders. Again.

Unfortunately, this same song and dance happens about every month or so depending on how her romantic life is going. The problem is always different but the reason remains the same: me.

Just a little longer though.

Soon I'll be out of this house, too. Then who will she blame all her misery on? My older sister, Kelsie, got off easy by choosing, from a young age, to live with her dad after the divorce. According to my mom, he's the one that got away. Personally, I think she got pregnant at sixteen to trap him into marrying her in the first place. Alas, the marriage didn't stick through thick and thin like she had hoped, but that hasn't stopped her from pining after the delusion she sells herself.

I never had a choice though. In any of it. I didn't choose to be born, especially not to a life like this, and living with my father was never an option. No, my mom got pregnant with me during a rebound one-night stand shortly after losing Kelsie and her dad. She's resented me and the regrettable memories attached to that dark time everybody, including dear ol' Daddy, would prefer to forget. Well, I can only assume since he's been paying child support each and every month like a woman's trusty menstruation cycle yet hasn't bothered with contacting me even once over the years.

I swear that monthly check taunts me, too. Some days—like today—more than others. I mean his address is *right there*. Colorado. I've never reached out to him though. All too familiar with being unwanted, I don't need one more reminder what a mistake I was.

The bite of nails on my wrist brings me back to the moment, and I clench my jaw. Things are getting worse. *She's* getting worse. Last time, she threw a plate of food—delivery, of course, since my mom doesn't cook—at me when her soon-to-be ex-husband didn't come home for dinner. Before that it was a bottle of hair product lobbed at my head—which I dodged just in time, luckily, only to watch as it splattered against the wall, inches from my face.

Her grip loosens, arms crumpling like wet pieces of paper, allowing me to relax my grip a fraction. The cheap-ass wood from the banister has begun flaking off into my hands as she approaches the wind-down portion of today's tantrum.

She's sobbing uncontrollably now, and even though the angry streaks staining my hands give me pause, I don't dare let go yet. She's like a wild animal—one wrong move could spook her causing my ass to go tumbling down the stairwell.

These clothes, along with my body, will need to be thoroughly washed after this shit show is over. My mom's perfume is incredibly strong from a healthy distance, like a football field, but with this close proximity I'm afraid the fragrance will seep in forever if I don't scrub it off immediately. I shouldn't say I hate anything about my own mother, but, on a list a mile long of things I strongly dislike about the woman, her overpowering floral perfume is high at the top. It almost makes me despise all flowers on principle alone. It's like she uses it to mask the stench of desperation she's constantly oozing. If only it worked that way.

Tiny droplets of sweat fall from her short wavy hair landing on my tense forearm as my feet work to stay rooted to the landing. Her waning exertion is finally taking its toll, and I count down the minutes until this is all over. And not just this, today—I mean all of it: the put downs, the physical attacks, the all-out psychological warfare my mother has become proficient in. How much is enough? When will it all end? And at what cost? Because with Rianne, there's *always* a price.

Just a little longer.

Now she's leaning her full weight on me in a childlike manner, leaving no doubt in my mind that the perfume has spread to my person from the heavy contact. *Damn it.* Slowly releasing the rail, I spin toward her—keeping my back to the wall rather than the empty stairwell—and wrap my arms around her thin, trembling frame.

The few steps to her bedroom feel like miles as I guide her inside. Her body shaking with sobs, she shuffles into bed before I tuck the blankets loosely around her. I can't console her like she wants. Like she expects. That stopped a long time ago. All I can do now is weather the storm that's sure to pass just as quickly as it blew in. I'm not the villain here and I refuse to be her victim. I'm just surviving until I can get the hell out of here.

With that thought, I grab the tweezers from the bathroom to remove the slivers that have embedded themselves in my palms knowing it'll be easier than extracting myself from this hell hole when the time comes.

Just a little longer.

CHAPTER 2

Angela
2 Months Later

I SIGH, TAKING IN MY SMALL APARTMENT. SMALL IS ACTUALLY an understatement. More like tiny. Minuscule. What word did the landlady use again? *Micro.*

A micro studio apartment, but it's mine and it's absolutely perfect.

My mom and I never lived anywhere big or fancy save for that short stint with husband number three when we actually lived in a house. Not a shitty house either like the marriage before that, but a decent one with a bedroom just for me that I got to paint whatever color I wanted. I mean I didn't, knowing we'd be out of there before the paint could even dry, but having the option mattered more than painting the room itself.

Between husbands, and live-in boyfriends, and whatever the hell else title my mom would use to describe her many suitors over the years, we would bounce around from dumpy apartment to dumpy apartment, each one crappier than the last, until my mom's crazy would show, getting us evicted. That or the unpaid rent would finally catch up to her, forcing us to flee during the night in order to escape criminal charges for essentially squatting for months at a time.

Not anymore though. History will not be repeating itself. What the local car wash I work for lacks in hourly wages more than makes up for with tips affording me a chance to live on my own before high school is even over. That paired with the measly savings I was able to stash away are what got me into this micro studio a month before I graduate. With my mom's freak-outs getting increasingly worse, I couldn't wait until graduation. So, when the apartments next to my school posted a vacancy within my meager budget, I ran over during lunch break to fill out the application. Upon paying the deposit, I was handed the keys to not only my first place but my long-awaited shot at freedom. Freedom I'd been holding out hope for since I was too young to understand just how much it would actually cost. More than money, more than wishful thinking, more than anything I could've anticipated. But after years of tireless work, both mentally and physically, I'm finally here; move-in day, but more importantly, move-out day.

Today begins my chance to break from the dilapidated mold my mother haphazardly cast for me years ago—eighteen to be exact.

Drew, my ex-stepbrother, shuffles through the door carrying an overstuffed box, asking where he can set it. With a jerk of my chin, he takes the couple steps to find the bedroom portion of my studio, it really is small in here, then drops the box full of shoes next to the bare bed.

Drew's father was the one with the big house matched with even bigger expectations of a blended family involving the Great and Formidable Rianne and her munchkin. It's safe to say he did not find his happily ever after following that yellow brick road.

Drew, having the same sixth sense all kids and animals have, wisely chose not to visit his father all that often during the short marriage to my mom, but when he did, we were inseparable. A couple years older than me, Drew had no trouble slipping into the role of protective big brother once he witnessed my mother's harsh treatment. Fortunately, instead of going our separate ways after the divorce, our relationship changed from part-time siblings to full-time best friends. Due to the constant upheaval, in both the physical and emotional sense, I was never able to make any long-lasting friendships, so Drew's been the one constant in the last several years. Now that we're older, we don't get to see each other as much, particularly with his new girlfriend in the picture, but we still make it work when we can. His girlfriend, who lives in Portland, isn't the biggest fan of our close bond which I can understand. I get how it may look on the outside, especially given my mother's track record with men—she only keeps guys around long enough to get into their wallets with hopes of reaching their bank accounts soon after—however, even considering I'm nothing like my mother, I've only ever seen Drew as a brotherly figure. A relationship I fully cherish.

"Want me to help you unpack?"

"And have you put things where they don't belong? No thanks," I snicker.

"What do you mean?" Arms out, he gestures to the cramped space. "There's only one room."

Waving him off, Drew follows me to the door, glancing around on our way out.

We find one small box left in my Jeep that I reach for before he stops me with a hand on mine.

"Are you sure you don't want me to stay the night?"

With a shake of my head, I tell him, "Not tonight. I need to do this by myself." It'll be my first official night in my first official apartment and I want to face it alone. A test of sorts to prove I not only can, but will, make this dream a reality. "Plus, I need to get used to the noises and smells of my new neighbors."

Drew's mouth dips. "Smells?"

"Yes, smells." I roll my eyes playfully. "With my windows open, I'll be able to smell all kinds of things from the people living around me." He knocks my hand away when I try to ruffle his auburn hair, not that I could what with all the gel he uses to keep it in place. "Oh, that's right. You're not used to living in apartments, are you, rich boy?"

Now he's the one rolling his eyes.

"I don't like the idea of your windows always being open. You're a young, pretty girl living all by herself. People might notice and try to take advantage of that."

Hands in the pockets of my shredded shorts, my oversized cardigan falls off one shoulder from the steady breeze making this otherwise hot day bearable. The loose white tank peeking through conceals the nerves in my stomach leaping about just beneath.

"They won't be all the time. Just at night when the temperature drops."

Drew's already shaking his head. "It's like eighty degrees at night still. What the hell is opening your windows going to do besides invite perverts in?"

Is he serious? "Save money." *Duh.* The truth is he doesn't get it. Drew's never had to skimp and save for everything he has. He's never had to go to the store, paying with lost change he scrounged for. "Also, I'm on the second floor so it'd be pretty hard for someone to get through my window."

Drew just shakes his head again, refusing to argue, instead leaning in to envelop me in a hug. He knows he's in uncharted territory when I bring up money, or more accurately the lack thereof, and he's smart enough not to push me on the issue.

Minutes pass as we breathe each other in before he speaks. "I'm so proud of you."

"Please don't go soft on me now. I moved out. People do it every day. I survived a crappy childhood. People do that every day, too." Stepping back, he releases me but holds me at arm's length, neither of us ready to let go quite yet. "I just...I want to be free. You know?" I don't want to lug my mom, or the baggage she's saddled me with, around with me for the rest of my life.

Eyes penetrating mine, he says, "I know. But that's exactly why I'm proud of you. You're breaking the cycle. You'll do better. You. Are. Better." The way Drew grits out each word makes them that much more believable. Kind of. "I just hope she lets you go. I don't want her popping back up, trying to drag you down to her level."

With a sigh, I sidestep him, glancing at the lone box labeled KITCHEN. I filled it with supplies I bought from the local discount store. Not that I know how to use any of them or anything;

I just felt like it was the adult thing to do. Baking sheets? A spatula? Not sure what those would ever be used for, but one day I'd like to learn how to cook and those seem like important pieces in helping with that.

"Me, too. She doesn't know which apartments I moved to though, just that I'm still in the area." I thought that was close enough. "And since she despises the idea of earning an honest living, I doubt she'll bother me at work. Those checks should do a good job holding her off, at least for a little while."

When I first broke the news I was moving out, my mom went into full panic mode, scrambling for any excuse to keep me under her roof. For a woman who hates the very idea of me, I thought she'd be thrilled to finally see me off. Instead, she freaked, which I figured had less to with losing her youngest and more to do with the loss of the child support she receives while "caring" for said daughter. I offered her the two remaining checks as a sort of peace treaty to which she jumped on faster than a party of sugar-crazed toddlers at a trampoline park. How long it'll last is anybody's guess but I just needed out from under her cruel thumb and money was the quickest way of accomplishing that. I kept the exact location of my new place a secret in hopes of buying myself more time without her.

"That's what I'm afraid of. What happens when those payments stop? Who will she take her misery out on? I think she'll come looking for her favorite plaything sooner than you think." He gives me a pointed look that I promptly ignore.

He's right. I know it. He knows it. We all know it, but I've lived in fear for too damn long. I can't let it, or her, squash my happiness any longer. Today marks the beginning in a long, hard journey but if I don't take the shaky first step then how will I ever reach the highly anticipated destination?

"Thank you," I say, poking his side. "Thank you for saving my sanity more times than I can count."

"Well, we both know you can't count that high so…"

I can't help but laugh at his horrible joke. *Jerk.* Well accustomed to using humor to diffuse uncomfortable situations—hey, if you don't laugh, you cry, right?—I recognize what he's trying to do here. Drew likes to downplay his role in my life but there's no denying he's played a very large part in keeping me from falling into hopeless oblivion. He didn't have to stick around after our parents turned into bitter rivals but he did—thankfully.

Drew plants a kiss on the top of my head while I crush myself against his chest, his usual tangy, berry-like scent as calming as his very presence. With one last squeeze before he walks over to his dad's borrowed truck, he hops onto the shiny running board, pinning me with his tawny eyes, saying, "Call me if you need anything and I'll be right over. I mean it."

"I will." In my own attempt to lighten the mood, I call out, "You're my boy, Drew."

Barely earning a smirk from my former step-sibling, he ducks inside while I swallow the stubborn lump in my throat.

Three motorcycles, with almost obnoxiously revving engines, pull into Creekwood Apartments just as Drew reaches the entrance. His brake lights hesitating tell me exactly what he's thinking without even needing to see his face, but who says they live here? They could be visiting someone, anyone really. I haven't met any neighbors yet so Drew's guess is as good as mine.

As the noisy machines approach, three heads snap my way just before finding parking spaces across from my Jeep.

The winding engines cut off, filling the lot with complete silence save for Drew's awkward idling. Why do big brothers, even ones not born to the position, lack any sense of subtlety?

With a flick of my hand to the truck, I grab the last box and make for the stairs but not before darting a glance over to the guys still sitting atop the street bikes. Motorcycles aren't my area of expertise but these ones look nice. The car wash I work at doesn't cater to bikes, which is a serious drawback in my opinion. Due to the relatively mild climate, this entire region is known for housing toys of all shapes, sizes, and speeds. Whether they're for land, air, or water, they all get dirty just like cars do and would benefit from a place that could accommodate them accordingly.

None of the guys have removed their helmets yet and I almost don't want them to. What if they do live around here? And they're complete assholes?

What if they're picking up a friend and I'm worrying for nothing?

I can't help but admire their rides though. One is red with some numbers near the handlebar. The neon green one in the middle has the word Ninja splashed across the side while the last one is flat black with no distinguishable markings whatsoever.

The first two reaching for their helmets have me quickening my steps but the last one, the guy on the black bike, holds my gaze hostage. Even though I can't make out his eyes hidden in his helmet's shadow, it's like I can feel them on me. Phantom gawking. It's a thing, right? A chill runs up my spine despite the sporadic breeze dying down moments ago, leaving the sultry air to almost crackle against my skin. I tear my eyes away as I climb the rest of the stairs leading to my apartment.

Safely back inside, I turn on "Young, Dumb & Broke" by Khalid before taking stock of my limited belongings. I stay busy the rest of the night unpacking and decorating, dancing and singing, genuinely having a good time in my new place.

My place.

I like the sound of that.

CHAPTER 3

Angela

"Y ou've got to be kidding me," I grumble from my bed.

It's been a quiet couple of days, but here it is Friday night and the neighbors are having a party. Oh, excuse me, it's now Saturday morning. Hours into the shindig and it seems to be growing in both volume and size—if the amount of door slams are anything to go by. My shift starts in exactly six hours and I've got shit for sleep so far. With the party only gaining momentum, I doubt that'll change anytime soon. Saturday is the wash's busiest day, but more importantly it's the day I open. Vacuum canisters need emptied, towels need folded, spray guns need tested, along with many, many other tasks that can only be done once the sleep has been slept.

Damn it.

Checking my phone for what feels like the hundredth time, I groan seeing those minutes ticking painfully by—with me still awake. My finger hovering over the keypad, I contemplate calling the cops but the fact that nobody else from the other apartments has so much as banged on the wall or yelled outside for the partiers to shut the hell up makes me reconsider.

A door, that sounds suspiciously close, crashes against the wall making me flinch. Raucous voices filter through my wall, directly into my bedroom feeling particularly invasive. Yes, my bedroom is also my living room which is also part of my kitchen but still, hearing slurred partygoers only feet from your bed is disturbing on a good day. And today is not that day. Today is the day I meet my neighbors.

Groaning, I pull a loose cardigan over my sleep set, trudging the few steps to my front door. Upon opening it, I find that the party is directly across the hall, like I suspected. People in all states of inebriation fill the hallway between the two doors. My feet freeze in the doorway while my hand jiggles the phone. It's not too late. I could still call the police. Or maybe just the manager since I don't want to add snitch to my resume for such a pitiful excuse of a party. Not that I know what makes a great party but if this hallway is their most desired location it makes me wonder who the hell is hosting it to begin with.

A glance down at my outfit, or lack thereof, has me second-guessing this plan altogether until a shirtless guy halfway down the stairs lets out an obnoxious howl.

People take calm for granted. When silence is used as a weapon your whole life, you learn to appreciate how valuable the quiet can actually be and these assholes are screwing with the peace I've finally found in living here.

My fist rapping against the metal goes unnoticed, unless you count the kissing couple perched next to it shooting a glare my way at the interruption. *Whatever.* The warm hallway feels sticky, muggy, as if the alcohol's seeping from its occupants' pores into the narrow gap, intoxicating everybody present.

Another crack of my knuckles proves useless, so I do it again, this time much, much harder. Some call it pounding, I call it making a point. Either way, it's time to introduce myself.

When the door finally swings open, I'm met with a black shirt that reads *Save A Horse, Ride A Biker* stretched across a toned chest in bold white letters effectively solving the mystery of who owns one of the motorcycles from the other day. Except this torso appears to have no end in sight as I search for the face of my neighbor. I've always been fairly tall at 5'8" but this guy must be well over six feet as my neck cranked almost all the way back is the only way I can even make out his chin. The striking blue eyes peering down at me hold so much mischief I swear they actually twinkle.

I mean, how? He's sporting the most playful smile I've ever seen along with some light facial hair to round out an incredibly handsome face. A tilted baseball hat with blond bits of hair peeking out, and the guy is hot. As hell.

Losing myself in the easy tilt of his lips, I almost forget why I came over to begin with. Nobody's ever been that carefree around me. That uninhibited. Without warning, my body sways forward as if the cheery virus might be airborne and his happy vibes will infect me.

Just then I realize he's talking, snapping me back to reality with a huff as I step backward.

"What was that?"

"I said you must be our new neighbor girl."

Our?

"Oh, uh, yeah. I just moved in across the hall. Your party is keeping me up. It's really loud." I tap my ear, demonstrating my point. *Smooth. Real smooth.*

Instead of an apology, blondie opens the door wider beckoning me inside. Did he even hear me? At that exact moment a new song comes out of the expensive looking sound system in the corner, blaring loud and clear, right into my very awake and soon to be pissed off ears. No one, including my ridiculously tall neighbor, so much as offers to lower the volume, making me question my decision to barge over here at all.

"I'm Beckett," he says, then splashes random types of alcohol into a tall glass before eyeballing the mixture suspiciously. "I live here with my roommates." With a thumb over his shoulder, he gestures to a guy on the balcony with a girl tapping on his chest to get his attention. It's futile though because the only thing he sees is the fresh meat dangling in his doorway. Instinctively, I take another step back, taking me further into the hall. This move does nothing to break the intense staring contest though, so I browse my neighbor while he sizes me up. "That's Marc." Where Beckett is light and bubbly, Marc is dark and severe. Dark hair cut close to the scalp, dark eyes that penetrate anything, or anyone, they land on, dark skin hinting at a Hispanic heritage. Flame tattoos licking up his forearms match the lit cigarette dangling precariously from his mouth. The guy is fire and ice personified. Hot, just like his roommate, but in a completely different way. The way dry ice entices you to touch it even though you know damn well it's dangerous. "And that one over there is Coty." Beckett finally looks up from his shoddy cocktail, meeting my eye as he turns to point out his other roommate.

Unsure who he's talking about, I glance around the crowded dining table—a table that couldn't even fit in my apartment—until a chill starting at the base of my spine spreads the rest of the way up my backbone ending at my hairline when my gaze collides with his. *Coty.* Or that's who I'm guessing is Coty since the guy makes no move to introduce himself other than pinning me to the spot with his mocha swirl eyes alone. Yes, mocha fucking swirl. The swirl is important. Not to be confused with just regular mocha eyes, Coty's are a deep chocolate color with a distinct swirl of mocha right through the middle making me crave a coffee creation containing both immensely, even though I'm pretty sure mocha already has chocolate in it. The longer his gaze stays on mine, the more everyone else fades away, including his talkative friend. Movement steals my attention as I watch his lips tilt into a devilish smirk. Even though I'm not very religious, I send up a *forgive me Father for I'm about to sin* so I'm covered. You know, just in case.

With unkempt brown hair and a wicked curve of his mouth, this guy is the perfect mixture of his counterparts. He runs his gaze the length of my body, leaving behind that same pesky chill I've felt twice in his presence now, so I return the favor. Immediately tucking my cardigan tighter, my eyes take the long route roaming along my new neighbor, exploring every visible inch. He's tall, not as tall as his boy, he's dark, not as dark as his other boy, but damn if he's not just as wildly attractive as both. Relaxed jeans hanging low on his hips, a shoulder thrown over the back of a chair next to him, making his shirt stretch tight against his well-built chest, I can honestly say I've never wanted to be a garment more in my life than I do admiring Coty's gray V-neck. Who did I move in next to? A pack of male models?

Beckett still talking next to me, raucous laughter around the table, hell, a nuclear bomb just outside couldn't break the intense stare down Coty and I are having, but the word boyfriend tossed through the air goes off like a grenade silencing what feels like the entire complex.

I tilt my head to Beckett, eyes narrowed.

He lets out a small chuckle. "We should celebrate. Do you need to get your boyfriend? Or girlfriend maybe?" His wriggling eyebrows jostle his already slanted hat making me smile even as I'm reminded of Drew's words. *'You're a young, pretty girl living all by herself. People might notice and try to take advantage of that.'*

The question, although presented as innocent, feels more like a probe. A probe for information I'm not ready to reveal. Not now. Maybe not ever. Before I can answer, the music drops in volume dramatically causing the party to erupt in protests. Coty stands at the system with his finger pressed to a button and his eyes locked on mine.

A glimpse around the room proves all three painfully beautiful roommates are watching, listening, for my answer. I shake my head, looking back to Beckett. "I need to be up early for work. I'd appreciate it if you could keep it down."

"It's Friday. When the fuck are we supposed to party?"

Coty glances over to Marc but Marc doesn't notice. His sharp gaze follows my throat as I try to swallow inconspicuously. Try and fail, as I half choke on the worthless saliva.

Somehow during the stare off with Coty, I managed to step further into the apartment, bringing me into the heart of the lion's den. If I show fear for even a second these animals could pounce, but I've got plenty of practice battling a beast.

Steeling my spine, I cock an eyebrow at Marc mockingly. "Party whenever you want. I'm just asking you to turn the music down." I nod my head outside. "Maybe keep the dogs on a tighter leash instead of out on the stairs where your *neighbors* can hear their sloppy ass mating calls all night."

I ignore Coty's narrowed eyes as they shoot back my way. It's not like I'm asking for much. I need this job and the opportunity it's provided me so far—a chance to escape the mental prison of living under my mother's roof. I'm not risking that over a stupid party. If they can't shut up, I'll shut them out, but I have to try. This isn't some paranormal romance novel where buff guys howling at the moon is hot, this is real life and that shit's plain annoying.

I meet all three sets of eyes. Marc scoffs, going back to his entertainment still vying for his affection. Beckett's grinning as if this *is* his entertainment for the night. And Coty...Coty hasn't so much as blinked, watching me like the predator he must think he is. As much as I've been led to believe, I'm no prey, so I spin on my heel to leave then come to a stop when a dripping hand is thrust in my path.

"What'd you say your name was again?"

Beckett's glossy gaze is about as syrupy sweet as his drink concoction. For someone as big as Beckett, he sure is a slippery little sucker. One I'll have to keep my eye on. Hell, maybe both eyes.

Coty still hasn't restored the music to full volume as he takes in the scene from across the room. Next to a big brown leather couch, he rests against the edge like he's got nowhere better to be. Nothing else to do besides wait for something as insignificant as my name. When he winks, it takes everything in my power to keep my feet from moving forward. From going straight to him. That little tug at my restraint shows me exactly how I got inside in the first place. I may not be an easy target, but Coty's showing part of his arsenal whether he knows it or not. I can only hope that stupid wink is the only flex he's got. But I have one of my own, so dropping my eyes down his casual stance, I bring them back up making sure to meet his gaze before smirking and looking away altogether. The clench of his fists doesn't go unnoticed. By anyone.

With a step around Beckett's proffered hand, I say, "I didn't," before returning to my apartment without so much as a backward glance.

Just as my door's closing, I hear an amused laugh as Beckett calls out, "Oh, this is gonna be fun, boys."

Once in bed, I roll to my side, watching lights dance through the open windows then grimace as the music jumps back up to full volume.

Damn it.

The howls also start up with a gusto causing me to cover my ear with a pillow.

Too bad it can't hide the smile splitting my face, too.

◆ ◆ ◆

The next day I'm exiting my Jeep when I hear a car door slam behind me. Peeking over, I notice Beckett walking from a hunter green Tahoe with tinted ass windows and bigger than life rims. He's wearing a holey tank that says *Ride Hard Or Go Home* with a grin stretched from ear to ear. He's dirty and sweaty in what look like mechanic's pants, but still just as adorable. His dirty blond hair is sticking out like a frenzied free for all like he just took his hat off and the strands don't know how to behave.

Just like Beckett, I smirk to myself.

"Hey, neighbor girl."

I flip my hand in greeting before gingerly tossing my backpack over a shoulder. The sun was brutal today even with the copious amount of sunscreen I slathered on my skin. Hot Spots gives t-shirts to all their employees but there's just no way a shirt with sleeves will cut it when you're using your arms all day in the scorching heat. Most of the employees take advantage of the laidback management by altering their uniform to reveal more skin. Tighter, shorter, you name it, they've done it. I only cut the sleeves along with the arm pits out of mine so I can work without getting a rash in the process. We all have our own personalities, theirs are just a little more revealing than mine.

A sleek black Camaro pulls into the space next to Beckett's Tahoe. Marc emerges from the passenger seat the next instant with "Heathens" by one of my favorite bands following close on his heels before closing the door behind him and cutting the song short. His black tank, showing off his tattoo sleeves and chest, paired with dark green shorts are a little cleaner than Beckett's but still show a hard day's work with random stains. With a New York baseball hat perched gingerly atop his buzzed haircut and his caramel complexion, he looks like the kind of guy you'd let run over your foot as long as he'll talk to you while you bleed out. Unfortunately, his pissed off expression suggests he'd let you.

The takeout bags in his hands mock my already growling stomach. I didn't have time to grab a bite before work and the tiny lunch I had hours ago isn't holding me over until I can tear into my frozen dinner awaiting me upstairs like I'd hoped.

Coty gets out of the driver's side next making me hungry in an entirely different, but just as pertinent, way. The growling intensifies much to my horror. At least it's just my stomach though. I mean, I think it is. Coty's black tee sculpted to his torso like a damn second skin has made some deep-seated animalistic yearning spring to life, making it hard to focus on anything other than what my body wants. Now.

His eyes immediately fly to mine with a dimple on his left cheek suddenly announcing its delectable existence as he smirks wickedly.

My shoe catches on a stair and I send my hands out in front of me before I can fill up on concrete for dinner.

Shit.

I right myself as quickly as possible, then take the rest of the stairs two at a time. I thought these guys might be dangerous but I had no idea just how much.

CHAPTER 4

Angela

I<small>T'S FINALLY EARLY ENOUGH FOR ME TO GET SOMETHING</small> done other than work and school and school and work—like laundry. I've been doing my own laundry for years, but now I have to use shared machines with the rest of the building so I'm at the mercy of other people's schedules, another thing I didn't anticipate moving in here, but luckily, after finding a washer open today after work, I chose to go for a swim in the pool at the back of the property while my other clothes were out of commission.

The cool water skims across my skin as I make my way from end to end. Even with it being nearly dark, it's still ninety degrees out and stifling hot. My half a sandwich I brought down sits untouched at the table next to my things. My mom never taught me how to cook. Or sew. Or budget. Or prosper as a regular functioning adult. The latter I'm working on figuring out through trial and error alone. The rest will follow in time. Hopefully. Probably.

Although she didn't technically teach me how to clean either, I picked up that useful habit by actually giving a shit about my few possessions. Take my old as dirt 1986 Jeep for example. It offered me the first taste of independence and for that reason alone I love it. Hence why I clean it more than most people with luxury cars would. My studio hasn't so much as had a single dust mite before I readily wipe it away with enough force to scare all its friends back to whatever filth pit they hail from.

As I float around on my back, soaking up the last few rays for the day, voices drift down causing me to glance up at the balcony overlooking the pool area. The boys' apartment is so big it has two balconies. One in the front, like mine, overseeing the less than glamorous yet still overstated parking lot, then this one with a full view of the pool and surrounding yard. Marc, Beckett, and Coty all step through their sliding glass door laughing together. I take the moment to watch them unguarded, unfiltered, as they joke light-heartedly with each other. I never would've guessed Marc knew how to smile yet there he is openly laughing at something Beckett is saying. I find myself smiling along with the group even though I can't make out a single word of the tallest one's animated story. Whatever he's sharing has them all in stitches and my moves slow in effort to share in the casual moment, even if only as an outsider. Outsider being a role I've grown accustomed to, I take comfort in my place on the cusp, secure in the anonymity being disregarded provides. My entire life has been spent meandering within the unknown and unwanted. I don't even know any other place to wander.

My smile drops however as soon as Coty's gaze collides with mine. There's something in his stare that threatens ruination. Damnation. It may start at the base of my spine but it could spread to the rest of me, the rest of everything, if I let it. Total domination by a pair of mocha swirl eyes.

I dip my head under the water effectively severing the connection, the influence that devil dressed as my neighbor has. A huge disruption has me surfacing well before I'm ready to, only to be met by a grinning Beckett. With his clothes still on. In the pool. I can't help but laugh even as I back up, eyeing him while I make my way over to the edge. The easy way he has about him, it's infectious.

I hop up onto the ledge, wringing my hair out as he treads closer, studying me carefully. When his arms make circles out to the sides, I'm reminded of this video we watched in health class once on water buffaloes. His shoulders taking up most of the shallow end have me wondering how I even managed to stay in the pool when he jumped in. Or how he got down here so fast. I peek over my shoulder, noticing his roommates are exactly where I saw them last. Coty's eyes are glued to mine, not missing a second. Marc is taking in the scene with vague curiosity.

It's been a few days since I crashed their party—more like they crashed my sleep—and they are...a lot to take in. Especially dressed like they are. Like they just got done causing trouble. Judging from the wide smile on Coty's face, they're ready for some more.

"So, neighbor girl, where do you sneak off to all the time?"

His question catches me off guard but I recover quickly, throwing out, "School's a bitch like that. Can't live with it, can't live without it." Well, I can't. I have a point to prove. A point that I am more. More than what my mom thinks of me. More than what she's said about me. More than her, period. My mom never finished high school after becoming a teen mom. Back when teen moms weren't cast as dysfunctional reality stars for public consumption, rather they were hid away from judgmental eyes to disintegrate in private. *And crumble she did.* Completing high school is only one of many steps to get there, but I will, damn it. I have to.

"What year are you?"

Beckett's words pull me out of my own head. Pointing across the street, I say, "Almost done. Graduating in a couple weeks actually."

My high school is just across the street making for an easy—and green!—commute.

His eyebrows jolt. "You're still in high school?" Accepting my easy nod, he continues, "Why the hell do you live on your own then? Did some needy as fuck douche convince you to move out so he could stop sneaking into your parents' house every night or something?"

Using my toe to kick water at his face, I mock frown. "Are you talking from personal experience?"

The wall of water thrown back at me almost knocks me backward and I have to fight to stay upright, breaking into watery laughter. *Water buffalo indeed.*

Finally, through the tsunami Beckett flung my way, I hear him ask, "Seriously, what's the deal? Why wouldn't you wait until after you graduate like everyone else?"

Running my fingers through my dripping hair, I consider his question. There's no way I'm telling him the truth. Even if I was the sharing type, Beckett's too carefree, too light to be dragged down by my gloom. He wouldn't know what to do with the bleak answers that question produces. You can't touch tar without getting dirty and the last thing I want is to infect his sunny disposition with my grime. So, I settle for a portion, a very small portion, of the truth by shrugging my shoulders and saying, "I just couldn't."

His eyes narrow before jumping over my shoulder. My gaze follows to see Coty watching from his elevated spot. He looks at his roommate, unease marring his beautiful features, then as I begin to turn away, he calls down, "hey, neighbor girl," bringing my attention back to him.

Where Beckett uses the term in a playful, borderline endearing manner, Coty says the nickname like a caress. A tender stroke straight to my core. One that robs my ability to think clearly, breathe regularly, or behave properly as I sit here frozen in place. This is the first time I've heard him speak and it was to me. Not about me. Not around me. But *to* me. A single look eclipsed an entire party. A simple smirk short-circuited my motor skills. And now a friendly greeting threatens to send me hurtling through space without so much as a parachute. *Danger.* Pure, unadulterated danger. That's what Coty's interest suggests. What his attention warns. What my persistent survival instinct is screaming at me to realize.

My fingers snag on a tangle sending me spiraling back to Earth. Several strands become collateral damage as I rip my hand from the hair snare, standing so suddenly Beckett frowns beside me. With weightless limbs, I gather my small pile of things before scurrying past the gate, under the boys' balcony to the stairs. A quick peek reveals Coty flashing that sinful smile that's sure to keep me up later than their obnoxious parties ever could. I try to stifle my own, I really do, but my mouth betrays me and lets it slip anyway.

◆ ◆ ◆

I throw on some active shorts, a loose short sleeve shirt that hangs off one sunburnt shoulder and my Adidas slides. As soon as I enter the downstairs laundry room, I spot Coty pulling clothes from a dryer into a basket and stop. He finds me frozen in the doorway before I can retreat and smiles warmly. I eye the empty walkway, considering waiting outside until he's done but his voice lures me inside much like his eyes did the other night. Propping the door open with a nearby rock, I walk in slowly, methodically, keeping him in my peripheral.

"Hello," I croak out, immediately regretting my need to wash my clothes. Who needs them anyway? A swimsuit and some strategically placed leaves could suffice, right?

Coty returns to his task while I stand here, not knowing what to do with my hands. He's at an advantage having something to keep his busy.

I open the washing machine my clothes are in and push them around sluggishly, waiting for this to be over already. My shirt falls further down my shoulder but I don't bother fixing it. The heat from the dryers mixed with the warm air wafting into the room is making me downright feverish. Maybe it's just being in the same room as Coty. I glance over, noticing his movements have stopped altogether. *Yes, it's definitely him.* Finding his gaze zoned in on me like a starved animal stalking its next meal, I clear my throat still randomly poking at the sopping pile. When he makes no move to continue with his own load, I surreptitiously glance around the floor checking for anything embarrassing that might've fallen out. If there's a pair of period panties lying out, I will die right here, right now. Just climb into the machine and hope for a death less tumultuous than the life I've lived so far. Luckily, there's nothing— unless you count the few hundred lint clusters littering the scuffed linoleum.

Frowning, I ask, "Are you done with that?"

My voice seems to snap him out of whatever trance he was in and he looks down to his hands gripping the top of the machine. "Uh…" His white knuckles regain color once he releases his tight hold. "Yup. It's all yours."

He strolls toward the door, leaving me plenty of room to switch my load over, so I work quickly but efficiently getting all my clothes into the vacant dryer without leaving anything behind. With his basket overflowing, I expect him to leave straightaway. He doesn't. His black cut-off muscle shirt is doing a hell of a job showing off his muscles which I take great satisfaction in surveying. Coty's the one to clear his throat this time making my already flushed cheeks bloom a deeper shade.

The final handful of wet clothes nestled in the still warm dryer, I hear coins tinkling beside me so I shoot my hand out to cover the slots before Coty can get any in.

"I can pay the dollar to dry my own clothes." Which today is actually true. I almost never carry change but one of the last customers of the day tipped me in quarters which made doing laundry that much easier. Well, before this whole fiasco.

A multitude of thoughts cross his face—questions, assumptions, fears. All silenced as he drops his hand along with the issue.

"Hey, I never got your name. I'm Coty, in case you don't remember."

"I remember." I shut the lid with a bang, insert my own quarters, then press start. My eyes find his. "I was tired, not drunk."

Ignoring my jab, he presses, "And your name is?"

His arched eyebrow dares me. To answer? To run?

I decide to throw him a bone if not to get out of here that much faster. That's what I tell myself anyway as I say, "Angela."

I stick out my hand to shake his but he ends up enveloping mine with a soft palm accentuated with long, tender fingers. There's no quick shake. There's no movement at all save for the thrum of the metal against my thighs as the load inside picks up speed. His eyes bounce between mine as my heart begins whirring to the rhythm of the machine. The moment stretches, expanding, folding in on itself until I feel like maybe I'm in the dryer as well.

I yank my hand out of his grasp, mumbling out, "It's nice to meet you."

I grab my own basket when he presses, "Have I seen you somewhere? Maybe at your work?"

Again with the probe disguised as an innocent question. These guys are relentless. "Maybe," I say carefully.

Walking backward, he surprises me by saying, "At Hot Spots Car Wash maybe?"

Damn. So, he was checking my clothes out. Hopefully he didn't see *everything*. Never have I wished I could afford to shop at Victoria's Secret more than I do right now. I'm adding that to the top of my adult list as soon as I'm back upstairs.

I shake my head lightly. "I'd remember if I saw you before." Instantly, my lips clamp shut as I eye the empty washing machine, gauging if my body will fit in there after all. A chill like the one Coty's mere presence evokes is not something I'd ever forget but he doesn't need to know that. Or that his face has been burned into my memory with no chance of rehabilitation. Fourth-degree. Straight through, zero interference. When I donate my body to science after I die, they'll find an exact replica of Coty's face right there on my hippocampus.

Planning to get the hell out of here before anything else slips out of my mouth without my brain's consent, I attempt to step around Coty when he shifts to block me. Not in an aggressive way. More like a last-ditch effort to get my attention. *Little does he know, he already has it.*

And there it is. That alarm blaring as loud and persistent as someone else's dryer buzzing from across the small room. The one telling me to avoid the looming threat by way of either fight or flight. My stupid body, not consulting with my brain yet again, chooses the lesser known option—to freeze, like a mannequin modeling last year's newest laundry basket. Mid-air. I'll never be able to look at this stupid thing again without remembering this day. The day my neighbor realized he was living next to a woman with the equivalent of blow-up doll arms—utterly fucking useless.

Coty regards me another moment so I take the opportunity to do the same. His shirt's open arm pits are cut so wide I can just make out tattoos under his collarbone on each side. Something intricate. Something with wings.

Shuffling the basket into one hand, I push back some hair that fell forward over my shoulder and fan my face.

"That wasn't a lot of clothes over there. Is it just you upstairs?" His eyes hold mine with something that looks an awful lot like hope but might actually be a reflection of my own futile desire. "Or maybe you have a roommate you've been hiding who's opposed to wearing clothing?"

My previous idea of becoming a nudist returns, making me smile. "Hence the need to keep them hidden."

We both breathe out somewhat strangled laughs.

"Right," he drawls.

"You caught me," I joke, leaving the truth suspended somewhere above us to join the hot air creeping along the ceiling before it can all float out together where I left the door cracked open.

So quiet I almost miss it, Coty utters, "Not yet." Then louder, he says, "I'll see you around, Angela. Let me know if you ever need a cup of sugar or something."

I bite my lips between my teeth to keep from laughing. *Sugar, huh?*

With that, he takes off out the door and out of my head.

Hopefully.

Probably.

CHAPTER 5

Coty

SUGAR? REALLY? THAT'S THE BEST YOU COULD COME UP
with?

Neighbors do that kind of thing. *Right?*

Fuck it, they do now. I'll get her the whole damn baking aisle if I have to.

I pound up the stairs a little too hard thinking about our new neighbor. Our frustratingly cryptic, sarcastic, takes no shit, drop-dead gorgeous neighbor.

Angela.

With her tan skin layered with a slight sheen of sweat from the balmy day. That bare shoulder taunting me. Testing me and my thin-as-thread patience from being cooped up in that heat swamp of a laundry room before she walked in bringing that much needed breeze I didn't realize I'd been hoping for.

Her straight, sun-tinted hair, reminding me of the Californian surfers we saw on one of the many trips Marc let us tag along on, reaching just above her perfectly toned ass. It would look better splayed across my bed than stuffed under those hats she's always rocking but we'll get to that. One day. She may be on the skinnier side but her body holds a layer of muscle at every angle that proves she's a hard worker. If what she told Beck is true about her still being in high school, then she must work hard to live on her own. *If* she lives alone.

Those hazel eyes beg me to take a closer look, even if her mouth says otherwise—chameleons in their own right, much like Angela with her vague responses and non-answers. She's one of the most interesting people I've ever met and I know nothing about her. *Yet.* She takes in everything around her without revealing anything in the process. She's holding back, that much is obvious. She knows what's going on but doesn't use that knowledge until necessary, and not a moment sooner. She demands attention without even trying. It's almost like she's trying to hide herself from anyone and everyone, which is the opposite of what happens. All eyes land on her. And stay.

Once I caught sight of her today in the pool, I couldn't focus on the shit coming from Beck's mouth any longer. Hell, I couldn't remember where I even was let alone the details of his story about some turtle he saved from crossing the road. His words were muted the second my gaze fell on her in that temptation she thinks passes as a bikini. That little number had me wound up. Tight. I even managed to miss Beck climbing down the balcony to join her.

Bastard.

I head straight for my room to drop off my clean clothes on my way for another cold shower. I've needed a lot of those lately. Too many. Ever since a certain dark-haired beauty moved in next door actually. And I'm not talking about Gary. I mean the dude is cool but he's just not my type. First, and this is a big one, I'm into girls. Second, I'm pretty sure Gary hasn't come out of his apartment for over a year other than to do the occasional load of laundry. The guy orders online like a champ though. His door step is always chock-full of packages. Of…things that further prove why he just isn't for me. In any manner.

Beck's annoying laughter follows me down the hall as I pass Marc's open door. It's usually closed and locked so he must be inside but forgot to close it all the way. I decide against saying anything. Dude is private but will open up bits at a time when the mood strikes. Not that it strikes often, but once in a while he'll let us in. He used to disappear for a week at a time without a word until Beck had the brilliant idea to follow him one day. When we confronted him at the airport, his response was a simple shrug along with an invite to Key West. Hell yeah, we went. With just the clothes on our backs and the cash in our pockets and it was one of the best trips I've ever been on. Dude does that shit on the regular. He'll blindly pick a destination and go. Just go. The guy is crazy but we love him.

"What happened to you, bro? You're gone for a while, then come storming in. You run into our fine ass neighbor girl out there?"

Ignoring him, I move for the bathroom which only spurs him on further.

"*Another* shower?"

Yeah, okay. Everyone is aware of my increased showering lately. Can you blame me though? I got two doors separating me from a girl I can't get out of my head, or line of vision. A girl with a name—finally. An extra shower, or two, is the least of my worries right now.

"Her name's Angela," I say just to be a dick, slamming the door shut.

"What?" I hear Beck roar seconds before something hits the door from the other side making me grin as I start the water.

He'd really lose his shit if he knew I found out where she works, too, although I think I'll keep that little tidbit to myself for a while longer. I might have some fun with that knowledge. I still can't believe we never noticed her work shirts before now. It just goes to show that with the girl next door, there's so much more than just checking out her tits. I'm no saint, I looked, but that's not what I'm about. I could name five characteristics of Angela's that have nothing to do with her looks and I've only had one, albeit difficult, semi-conversation with the girl.

And even though Beck may think Angela looks good, he doesn't feel it like I do. I saw something in her that first day even through my helmet visor. Something bigger than even Beck's gigantic ass was at play and has been every day since. I had an overwhelming urge, this need to go to her. To help her, to be there for her, in any way possible.

The way she held herself so strong and determined, yet still looked about like pain was lurking around every corner. I want to know why. How. I want to know who could hurt someone that much to leave a person suspicious of their own shadow. I want to be the one to show her she doesn't have to be. That there are people worth letting in. People worth trusting. The problem is getting there. Angela isn't having it. At. All. Her and her slippery evasion tactics are proving more challenging than I'd anticipated. Whatever has her constantly checking over her shoulder is keeping her from seeing what's right in front of her. And that just won't work. Not when I'm the one standing there, waiting to be taken seriously.

The spicy body wash fills my palm and my nostrils as I think over the few words Angela spoke downstairs. She did say she'd remember me if she saw me before. Maybe that means she sees me now. And maybe, just maybe, she likes what she sees. That idea has me cranking the water to cold real quick.

I am so fucked.

◆ ◆ ◆

A couple days later a call comes in on my way home from work. Noticing it's my mom, I pull off into a near-dead shopping center to answer. New businesses have a hard time staying open long-term around the area. People love the novelty in green stores making them an instant success, then move onto the next fresh idea leaving the juvenile companies to crumble. Quickly. Sadly, this entire plaza was no exception.

"Hey, Mom. What's going on?"

"Did I catch you at a bad time?"

I'm just sitting in a pan of hot asphalt frying like a piece of bacon from this insane early summer heat without so much as a puff of wind in sight.

"Perfect timing. What's up?"

I spend the next few minutes listening to her ramble on about the exciting events in her life such as the local grocery store now carrying both types of cherries instead of just the early batches of Rainiers, and which neighbor got their mailbox knocked down by some wily teenagers this week.

"That's unbelievable," I finally chime in, unable to hold back my cynicism any longer.

"Well, Janice two blocks over, the one that has that gaudy flag pole in her yard, swears she saw a car full of teeny-boppers speeding off while she was letting her dog out. I'm just glad it wasn't ours."

"No, I can't believe kids are still doing that. Don't they have Netflix or something?" Social media? Anything? I'm glad I found something early on that kept me out of trouble. Mostly. Riding dirt bikes may not be the safest sport but it occupied me enough that I never did stupid shit like terrorize unsuspecting mailboxes. That's pretty damn lame, even for this boring town.

Acting like I didn't even speak, she says, "Anyway, what's new with you?"

I try to fill her in on the bits of my life that have changed but nothing really surfaces as interesting making her cheerful enthusiasm seem that much more newsworthy. Maybe I'll check our neighborhood store after this to see if everyone else got the highly coveted fruit yet. If I really wanted to, I could ask Marc to pick some up from his family's farm but that's always a risky chance to take. I don't wish that stress on anybody.

"We got a new neighbor."

"Did Gary finally pass?"

"What? No." I sit up straighter, stretching my back. "He's not that old." *I don't think.* "Directly across the hall from us."

"In that tiny little box they try to pass off as an apartment?"

I nod even though she can't see. "That's the one."

"I can only imagine what kind of person would willingly pay to live in that crack in the wall."

Oh, I can imagine her just fine. It's actually one of my new favorite hobbies. Picturing Angela walking around, possibly barefoot, hot from the windows we've noticed she keeps open, snacking while watching her favorite series, laughing. I'd give anything to hear her real laugh. So far, the only noises we've heard from next door have been the songs she listens to on repeat. Loudly. It's downright comical considering the first time we met was because she was upset about our music. I'll crank that shit every night if it gets her to come over again. Wearing her sleep clothes. Ready to hand me my own ass.

My smile spreads. Tonight can't come soon enough.

"She's actually nice." *Nice?* Is she nice? Okay, so that's yet to be determined but a little hopeful thinking never hurt anyone.

"She? Well, she must be young then. Is she a student? Maybe your father knows her."

All the good energy swirling around, warming my insides to match my overheated outsides, stops. Dead cold. Twisting into a tight knot stationed at the bottom of my stomach.

"He doesn't," I snarl more aggressively than I'd intended. Beck said she went next door which is a high school. Not a university. With professors that...

"Coty, really," she huffs. "I didn't mean anything by it. I just know a lot of his students are struggling artists and that pit is just the place a broke writer could find some inspiration in. Poets need to suffer and all that." I can hear her eye roll.

"Is that what he tells them?"

"What's that supposed to mean?"

I scoff, folding one arm under the other. "You know exactly what I mean. Dad is a-"

"He's a wonderful teacher that is held in high regard. Now that's enough. I wouldn't want anything to tarnish the reputation he's worked so hard to achieve."

What a joke. His reputation's been formed by his own hands all right. And then some.

"Whatever." Same conversation, different day. Same denial,

different approach. Usually she leaves her head in the sand a little longer. Lets the truth circle her like the starving vulture she knows it is. Once it finally reaches her, it'll only find an empty shell of deprivation though. She knows. She's always known. It's just a ruse she uses to keep her life together. Precariously, but together nonetheless. I've never been married so I can't begin to understand what goes through her mind but I am a man. A decent man with a moral compass that points straighter than my father's, if he even has one at all anymore. Maybe he never did.

In neutral, I give a couple quick wrist flicks, filling the strained silence with a sound that always soothes my nerves. "I gotta go, Mom."

"Wait, I want to hear more about this girl that's got you in a tizzy."

I almost laugh. I wish Angela had me in a tizzy. Then I might be able to get something done other than constantly wonder what the girl only steps away from my front door is doing.

"There's not much to tell." *Yet.* "She's...just our neighbor girl." Although true, the words still taste like a shot of Jägermeister at the end of a long night—a fusion of remorse and sorrow followed by a repulsion so strong you want to claw your own tongue out. "I'll talk to you later. Watch out for those crazy kids. Let me know if they do anything to your house. I'd be happy to deal with them." I bet I could even enlist the guys to help. It's been too long since we've had to put someone back in line and fucking with a group of young delinquents sounds fun.

We hang up with a promise to talk again soon, sooner if those little shits strike again, then I leave the deserted parking lot, ready to be home already. My parents' house was always that: a house. A house full of tension and misery. Confusion and rejection. Deception. Not in the typical upfront way other dysfunctional families might showcase their troubles, but in the unnerving silence where reality hid its ugly face. My parents chose their life, together; I chose mine, separately.

Living with my boys, that's home. That's where I can be who I know I was meant to be. Not the inconspicuous bystander my parents treated me as, but the driver of my own journey. The person navigating what routes to take, or better yet the ones to avoid, through life. I may not know where I'll ultimately end up yet, but I do know my path will never lead back there. Back to that stifling environment where you grin and nod while turning the other cheek.

No, I prefer sharing a three-bedroom apartment with my best friends. For now, at least. Although the prospect of staying there that much longer just got a whole lot more appealing with the addition of a certain stunningly stubborn girl next door.

With that thought, I race toward Creekwood. Halfway there, I decide against stopping off for cherries. A confrontation with Angela will be more rewarding and a hell of a lot cheaper. Seriously, why the fuck are cherries so expensive all of a sudden? If you grow up in the Northwest, you eat cherries. But lately, they're making it harder and harder. Winning over the girl next door, however, harder, will only make the reward that much sweeter.

CHAPTER 6

Angela

J UST A LITTLE LONGER.

With only a few weeks left of school, the teachers are cramming in as many big projects as possible right up until the final grades are collected. That's cutting things awfully close in my opinion. At least I know I'll graduate on time with honor roll but what about all those stragglers? The kids on the verge of failing? When will they find out if they can graduate or not? After the caterers have set up? When they're the only ones still waiting for their names to be called onto the stage?

My English paper needs to be typed before I can turn it in which means I'll need to go back to the library this weekend. I've already written most of it on my notes app on my phone but I still need to finish it, then print the stupid thing. All my other teachers let us email our assignments—*save the trees!*—but for whatever reason my English teacher insists we physically hand our reports in. Typed, printed, leather bound, sealed with wax, covered in blood and whatever else medieval shit she can think of.

I don't have the time, or patience, for any of it though. I have to open the wash both Saturday and Sunday which could end up being two full days of work. Hopefully anyway, since I need the extra tips right now while my schedule is still limited with school.

Tonight though, tonight I'm taking a bubble bath while simultaneously shoveling handfuls of popcorn in my mouth, careful not to drop any in the water. Popcorn is cheap yet filling, making it the best of all snacks, especially right before payday.

It's Friday night so I'll need to be up early again tomorrow. The guys across the hall have been somewhat quiet except for the other night when someone over there played music like they were trying out for America's Next Top DJ. I ended up actually liking their song choices, so it didn't bother me in the slightest. In fact, they did me a favor by saving me from playing my own before bed. A trick I picked up to drown out the incessant arguments between my mom and whoever her nightly opponent was. I can sleep without music playing, I just prefer not to. Music is the one thing that can make you feel while making you forget all at once. It can take you away or bring you back, depending on the song.

All three motorcycles were missing from the lot earlier, not that I'm keeping track, so I'm hoping they won't be entertaining again tonight. Maybe they'll be gone all night, leaving me to sleep in peace. Although the images that scenario conjures aren't all that relaxing either. Thoughts of nighttime activities they might partake in ruin my good mood, so I dry off just as my skin begins to prune.

In a sports bra and matching shorts, I open the windows noticing the bikes are still gone then crawl into bed. The last couple weeks play through my head but my mind keeps stopping on Coty. There's no arguing the man is attractive but it's his eyes that tell me there's something deeper, something warmer, something I've never experienced but could easily covet with greedy hands. Those mocha eyes hold a mischievous glint like Beckett yet a seriousness to rival Marc's. The few interactions I've had with him somehow leave me yearning for more. More from him. More of him. Just more.

That's the sole purpose of that deafening alarm that sounded the second he threatened my resolution. To protect against that little pang of want his company creates. More is a luxury, an extravagance I can't afford.

"Issues" by Julia Michaels fills the small space of my studio. I hit repeat, hoping the melody will lull me into an effortless sleep.

◆ ◆ ◆

A few hours later, the steady purr of motorcycles cutting off startles me awake. Through squinted eyelids, I watch headlights bounce across my ceiling as other cars pull in. Voices rise in unison while car doors slam shut making me groan.

What sounds like a stampede stomps up the stairs outside, reverberating through my tiny home. How many people did they bring back with them? Judging from the high-pitched giggles that keep erupting it's too many. *Great.* Just fucking great.

My eyes land on my open windows. Just as I move to close them my name, or nickname anyway, has me freezing in place when I hear what must be Marc sneering, "Quiet, guys. We wouldn't want to wake up the neighbor girl."

With his callous tone and who knows what gesture, the crowd does not quiet. At all. If anything, they grow louder. And louder. How many more steps are there?

"Nah, she's too busy getting hers to be sleeping. Don't you hear the music? That's making love music right there." There's a short pause before Beckett adds rather distastefully, "Don't come a knockin' when the neighbor girl goes a rockin.'"

"Shut the fuck up, B."

Huh. I guess Coty didn't like his buddy saying that. Well, join the club, because I don't like any of what they're saying. What I do, or don't do, is none of their business. I just want to finish high school, make enough money to stay in this place, and never, ever, go back to my mom's. Where digging for gold was my mother's game, digging for answers is the sport of choice for the boys next door but I'm already bored with their shit. Flirty looks paired with constant questioning doesn't work on me. I don't want them, or anyone, to know what I've gone through. I don't want my past to define me and until I can rectify the damage it's done, that's all they'll see. Those things happened to me but they didn't make me. I make myself and I'm just getting started. You don't put a bare seed on display at the grocery store and expect people to see the mature fruit it'll bloom into one day. You hide the growth away for safe keeping until the time is right. Until they're ready to handle the responsibility of such delicate goods. And I can tell right now those party boys across the hall aren't ready for fragility. Pushing my limits for kicks doesn't wear me down, it only pisses me off.

Thankfully, all goes quiet after a door closes until a few minutes later when a series of four quick knocks on my door jolt me out of bed. I'm across the room in the next instant, yanking the door open before I can even think it through.

Coty, with the ease of a house cat relaxing in a warm window, lounges against the doorframe. My doorframe. I plant my foot behind the bottom of the door, keeping it firmly in place. Unabashedly, his gaze runs the length of my body reminding me I'm only wearing a sports bra and tiny shorts.

My fingers clench around the cold handle.

"Yes?"

His eyes meet mine, holding for a beat before moving past me to scan my apartment. I resist the urge to turn and check what he might see. If a box of pantyliners, or worse, is on the counter, I will die a quiet, yet agonizing, death of embarrassment after he leaves. But not a moment sooner. Coty might try to beat mortification to the death punch by killing me himself and I can't have that. No overzealous neighbor of mine is going to kill me before I can ensure my feminine products are properly hidden away first. I refuse to show up to my afterlife with unfinished business on the other side. It'd be just my luck to get stuck haunting this shithole for the rest of eternity.

While he searches my humble abode, I give him a once-over. Hair adorably ruffled from his helmet, alert eyes taking in more than his casual posture suggests, with a clean white shirt and low hanging jeans on, he looks like the kind of guy any girl would be lucky to move next to. *Any girl, but me.*

Coty nibbles the corner of his mouth as I pick up the distinct smell of beer. It's faint but it's there. Corona. *With lime.* My hold on the doorknob tightens. The hint of citrus on his breath tempts me more than if he were to have shown up naked. Him showing up naked would be weird. And awkward. For both of us. But the promise of tasting lime, my all-time favorite garnish/fruit/snack/side dish/whatever, directly from those restless lips, nearly overrules all the guidelines I've previously written. The citrus mixes with his usual coconut fragrance making my mouth fill with enough water to put Hot Spots out of business. Well, for at least an hour. Coty's chocolate eyes make their way back to mine. *Maybe two.*

Finally, he releases me from my tropical haze, stepping back. All the way to his door, in fact, without so much as blinking. I wonder briefly if he knows how hot men multitasking is. It shouldn't be. It should be commonplace, yet somehow, we're always amazed when someone from the male species is able to pull off more than one task at a time.

"Goodnight."

Coming to, I shake my head, asking, "That's it? You woke me up to say goodnight?"

He stops in front of his apartment, peering across the hall at me. "So, you were just sleeping?"

My eyes search his. The few feet between us seems minor, insignificant. The wall erected directly in the middle of it though, the one Coty has yet to learn about, that's fucking insurmountable. The stairwell chatter from before springs to mind. "Goodnight, Coty."

I close the door softly, leaning against the scuffed metal, blowing out the breath I so desperately needed a few seconds ago. A glance at the clock has me groaning. Thanks to Coty, I'm now horngry—horny and hungry—with little to no chance of sleep without solving at least one of those issues first.

Tossing a frozen waffle into the toaster, I settle on the easiest of the problems, shelving the other for a more…convenient time. As I wait for my snack to pop up, I glance around my countertop thankful when I don't find any rogue tampons. Sighing, I scoop up my tips from earlier still scattered across the worn laminate and stuff them next to the new jar containing coins for laundry.

What was he looking for?

Coty's wakeup call was odd for sure. He said six words. Six. And not one of them was important enough to warrant knocking on a neighbor's door at one o'clock in the morning. I mean it was nice he wished me a good night and all, but wouldn't the night have been better without needing to be dragged out of bed in the first place? One could argue that hearing the sentiment straight from Coty's citrus-spiced lips made the slight inconvenience worthwhile.

One would be right.

CHAPTER 7

Angela

I SLIP ON MY WHITE WITH BLACK STRIPES SHELL-TOE Adidas then take a quick glance in the mirror to throw my wet hair into a ponytail, pulling it through the back of my black sports hat knowing it'll dry on the drive over. Luckily, my hair is easy to maintain even though it's long. Thanks to a life of limited funds, I rarely get it cut, allowing my locks to grow unchecked. Even making my own money now, my hair isn't a top priority. Call me crazy, but I'd rather buy a new pair of shoes any day over getting a trim. It's a dark brown naturally but the sun has played master color specialist by bleaching blonde streaks throughout. It's why I choose to wear hats to work over the visors Hot Spots provides. Now. I learned that lesson a little too late and after months of working at the wash, my hair currently showcases more colors than a paint store display.

Parking in the back lot, I grab my small bag and climb out, smoothing a hand over my altered work shirt before noticing my sunscreen slipped out onto the passenger seat. Unlike the ugly visors, sunscreen isn't optional. Working in the sun is downright dangerous, just look at my hair to see the damage it can cause, and I never want to get caught unprepared even if skin care isn't as important to Hot Spots as logo-splashed merch. If I had my own car wash, it'd provide sunscreen by the bucketloads. Non-negotiable bucketloads.

As I reach back in to grab the tube, I get that feeling. The feeling every woman knows by heart. The one that says someone is watching. Someone that makes your skin tingle in an unwelcome, unflattering way. With a peek over my shoulder, I see the outline of my boss, Joe, through the office window. My mouth scrunches into what I hope passes as a friendly smile but feels more like I ate something incredibly bitter. Meekness. It tastes like oppression going down, so I keep it floating around my mouth until he looks away then blow it out on a fortifying breath.

When I first started here, Joe was nice but distant. The way a manager should be. Lately though, he's been different toward me. Lingering looks that seem more intrusive than curious. Comments that sound more flirtatious than friendly. My hours were something we both agreed on when he hired me. I needed the money, he needed the help. With a long line of irresponsible teens as my predecessors, my reliable work ethic came at the perfect time, making my employment a fortunate arrangement for both sides. Or so I thought.

I've heard rumors whenever someone at school finds out I work here. He's known for dipping in the staff pool. A very young, very feminine pool. A pool that should not only be off limits to him for ethical reasons but also because he's married. Like with kids and a dog and probably a white picket fence that's in desperate need of touch-ups.

I haven't seen any of his supposed affairs for myself, thankfully, so I try not to buy into the gossip but his behavior has become a cause for concern lately, where before it was something I didn't have to think about. Just yesterday I caught him standing next to the towel spinner just inside the door leading out to the drying station but when I went to grab new towels, there were no clean ones to be found. If he saw the pile of dirty towels sitting there, why wouldn't he put them in the washer himself? Why else would he be standing there?

It's a small car wash, so the owner won't hire that many employees, but we make do by helping wherever we can. I usually work in the front where the cars roll out of the bay after going through the wash cycle. I like the front for two reasons: solitude and tips. Technically we all get tips since we split them up equally at the end of every shift but I like knowing I got the tip when there was a tip to be had. I've seen so many girls botch the opportunity by mindlessly drying and walking away. I, however, have a foolproof system for getting a tip every time, provided the customer was going to give one to begin with. The trick is to always end at the driver's door so that when you open their door to wipe the doorjamb, they can easily hand you the tip before driving away happier, cleaner, and a few bucks lighter than when they drove up.

I get hit with the most sun upfront since there's no overhang like the back but it's worth it to me. The back is where the payments are taken and the cars are hosed down before entering the mechanical portion of the wash so there's at least two people working back there at all times. Nobody usually bothers me unless to help with the towels, which is never-ending since the ancient machines we use to clean and semi-dry them are slow and sometimes even ineffective causing the laundry to pile up quickly on busy days. There must be better machines out there but, in the months that I've worked at Hot Spots, I have yet to lay eyes on the owner, so it shows how much he cares.

Occasional sunburns aside, I still prefer working away from the others, Joe included—since he has to stay by the cash register. Luckily, there's a container by my station I put all the tips in so I don't have to go to the back very often. The camera directly above it helps keep everybody honest even while I'm busy drying. I've never worried about management recording the thing though, because I only accept what I deserve. If I didn't earn it myself, I don't want it, and stealing from the community tip jar defeats that purpose entirely.

There's another side of the building where additional detailing is offered but the two sides don't mix often. For one, they're all males. Males that think they're God's gift to cars just because they get to vacuum and shampoo the insides while we're only allowed to rinse and dry the outsides. They wield their shrinking hoses in true macho bullshit fashion which I find both comical and pitiful at the same time, mostly pitiful if I'm being honest, so I just ignore them altogether which isn't all that difficult since they're steadily busy on a daily basis whereas the wash's rushes vary from day to day. You would think that with one side being comprised of teen girls and the other side full of arrogant guys that the two would come together as a muddled mating ground of sorts but it's not. It's weird, but true.

No matter who's around though I try to always be aware of my work outfit and the hints of skin it can reveal if I'm not careful. Although shorts are a must in three-digit weather, I make sure they don't show my ass cheeks as I bend over the cars I'm working on. The armpits in all my uniforms may be cut out but I double up on the sports bras underneath just to further prevent accidental nip-slips.

Even though the early morning has a delicious bite to it, it'll start to feel like a damn convection oven out here in no time. Later when I take a bathroom break, I'm sure I'll resemble something akin to Ross trying to get his leather pants back on from one of my all-time favorite episodes of *Friends*.

Contrary to popular belief women get overheated just like men, even though we're expected to cover up while men are free to walk around shirtless in public without repercussions. I have to wring out my bras after every shift but if I wear anything less, I risk someone catching a peek at what is most definitely mine to show when I want to. Key word here is *want*. I don't cover up for them though. I cover up for myself. I was raised by a hustler, so I've seen firsthand how a woman's body can be used as a tool. Both by her and against her. I've watched the damage it's caused treating something so sacred like a game piece in a seriously fucked round of Chess. I've always been more of a Checkers girl myself, plus I like knowing my tips were earned without stooping to my mother's level of scamming. She wove a thread of fraud so tangled that I've never even toed the line for fear of becoming ensnared forever. Yet another reason she's never liked me.

"Good morning," I say as I enter the confined office.

Ignoring the pit in my stomach, I squeeze past Joe who's positioned himself beside the outdated time clock to punch in my code, careful not to touch him on my way back outside. Outside. Air. Space. Witnesses. All very good things.

I work independently the rest of the morning, getting the wash ready for the day, only losing focus each time I turn to find Joe's beady eyes scanning me. There's a difference between a sexy gaze and a disgusting leer. News flash: if a girl isn't eye-fucking you back, she's just not that into you.

Finished with the opening duties, I bypass Joe as he continues counting out the till and head down the hall to fold any towels that were cleaned overnight. I halt when I hear my name.

"Come in at 11 tomorrow."

What? Two crappy Sunday shifts in a row? Last weekend was bad enough getting off earlier than usual and now he's taking away extra hours of easy work before the real day even begins. Joe knows I need full shifts on weekends. It's always been that way but why is he changing it up all of a sudden?

"Are you sure? I don't mind opening."

He peers at me over the top of his reading glasses before murmuring something like, "I doubt that." I take a step closer to hear better but he waves me off saying, "I'm sure. You're not needed."

Grudgingly nodding, I turn for the machines but swear I hear him add on, "yet," as I leave.

The towels end up getting folded with more force than necessary after that.

I manage to avoid Joe the remainder of my shift, staying busy without any further distractions. It's the best method at pushing my own issues out of mind. Busy work has always kept my troubles from consuming me whole and working at a car wash leaves no room to dwell on anything other than the four thousand pound car rolling directly at you. If you get sidetracked for even a second, you could lose your toes in the blink of an eye. Well, the roll of a tire to be more precise but still, this job's been the perfect fit for me so far and I want it, no I *need* it to stay that way.

◆ ◆ ◆

That evening, after confirming the library was closed for the night, I grab a bite to eat at my favorite Italian restaurant on my way home as a treat for such a long day. There were barely any lulls in customers, giving me more than enough for a dinner out in lieu of the rubbery chicken I still have in the freezer.

Pulling into Creekwood, I notice the boys' cars are gone which leaves their motorcycles open for the ogling. I take my time admiring the beautiful bikes, wondering how fast they can go, if you fall over speeding around a corner, and what happens if there's one of those humps on the highway that warrants a huge sign that says BUMP but it's never placed correctly so you hit it as you read it sending you—what feels like—airborne for a split second. Those seem like legitimate concerns. I mean does the rider fall off? My Jeep doesn't have any doors or windows, save for the front windshield, so I know all about the wind battering you while driving, but I can't help imagining how it feels slapping against your body without any barriers as you charge down the road. I picture Coty, with his impressive physique, not having any issues handling such a powerful machine. His forearms contracting each time he lays on the gas, his thighs flexed around the seat, his back rigid as he leans down.

And just like that now Coty's body is all I can think about, the bikes easily forgotten. Right when I was starting to cool down, too.

With the sun just starting to set, I decide to go for a swim. It's that beautiful time before it gets dark when the entire sky is on its best behavior just long enough to give you hope that tomorrow will bring a better day.

Back in my color-block swimsuit, I descend the stairs in time to see Marc approaching the back set of stairs. I hadn't even noticed him arrive and his fierce red BMW is hard to miss. I've caught glimpses of the red with black accented leather interior—it screams custom. Sometimes the detailing guys will send over a car they're working on to run through the wash. They won't bother driving it themselves, so one of us—usually the dryer on duty—has to ride it through the wash then drive it over for them to finish. I've done it enough times to know what kind of cars pay extra for extensive detailing. And Marc's beauty qualifies. Without question. No simple car washes for him. No simple anything probably.

He must've pulled in while I was changing or he parked somewhere else entirely. He hasn't noticed me yet, obviously lost in thought, so I glance over his shoulder, not finding anyone behind him. No open doors beckoning him in, no women drooling after the broody hunk, no angry husbands yelling about their wives being stolen out from under their noses. Yes, he's that good looking. The gray joggers he's wearing alone are enough female kryptonite to take down this entire complex. Never mind the all black hat with a white upside-down symbol giving him the perfect amount of careless vibe to attract you anyway, or the deep V-neck tee that fits all the right places urging you closer for a better look, or the ridiculously hot red sneakers unlaced to ensure you fall at his feet accordingly. Seriously, where did he come from?

He finally notices me as I hit the bottom step but instead of frowning or ignoring me altogether like usual, his face morphs into fear—or something like fear—before he swings his gaze behind him frantically. I can't figure out where he's looking or why he'd be afraid, so I smile politely, sidestepping him for the pool area, saying "hey" as I pass.

When he realizes I'm not as nosey as his roommates, he grunts out a greeting of his own. Unfortunately, it's completely incoherent but I take it as a good sign nonetheless. It may be his first official word—or two, I'm not sure—to me and I'm not about to ruin the moment by badgering him into repeating it.

I swim for what feels like hours before the cold sets in. By the time I leave, it's dark and several degrees cooler than it was when I got here. My plan to keep my windows open at night hasn't exactly worked like I'd hoped, considering said windows are not in the optimum wind catching position which leaves me a hot, sweaty mess most nights with the oven-like air settling around my bed instead of flowing in or out whatsoever. With my hours being tweaked lately, I can't risk any unnecessary costs like air conditioning at night so a cold shower, or tonight's swim, before bed is my best bet for combatting the cocoon of heat my apartment truly is.

As I wrap the towel around my torso, I look up as if being summoned and there at the sliding glass door of the boys' balcony is Coty. Staring right at me. Completely unashamed. Not even pretending he's not looking. He's inside but has both arms resting against the glass framing his body making me wonder how long he's been there for. He boldly cracks a smile which I almost return until I realize he's been creeping on me—not unlike my boss from earlier today. Although, my body doesn't respond to Coty's gaze the same way it does to Joe's. Not at all. My body detects Joe like a rabbit knows a fox is near whereas Coty is more like a bear. He could be a threat if he really wanted to but my body doesn't sense a predator when he's near, even if his presence would still do a hell of a job scaring off the shifty fox.

I still don't like feeling trailed though, so I return my eyes to the ground without acknowledging him.

Coty, however, meets me at the top of the staircase smiling even more unabashedly, if possible. *How do they get around so quickly?* I watch my neighbor, who closely resembles sex on a stick, while slowly climbing the stairs and inconspicuously squeezing out half the pool from my padded bathing suit top. I laugh because really, what else am I supposed to do? His athletic shorts rustle from a light gust as does his muscle shirt with the arm pits ripped out—like much of my own wardrobe—and his feet are bare. For some reason, him dressed like this, so laidback and unassuming, it's refreshing. He didn't hose himself down in awful cologne. His hair is flattened on one side like he just got up from watching TV. I mean he didn't even bother with shoes. He's completely relaxed and comfortable and...at home.

My chest fills with my first real tinge of jealousy I've felt in a long, long time. I thought that urge was banned for good but here it is, rearing its ugly head, reminding me what I've never had, as if I didn't already know. As if I don't see it when I look in the mirror every single day.

He's so beautiful, it almost hurts which is totally unfair considering I look like an agitated cat straight from an involuntary bath. My hair is flat down my back, making a puddle at my water-wrinkled toes, my skin is practically flaking off in chunks from the harsh chlorine, and I'm pretty sure my lips are purple and trembling. Coty's eyes narrow at them in concern confirming they are, in fact, one step away from frostbite.

The towel is doing little to keep me warm but I wrap it tighter across my middle in any case. At least my hands have something to do unlike the rest of me. I'm practically naked with only a damp, holey towel plastered to the skin that isn't covered by my bathing suit. He's crazy if he thinks I'm going anywhere with him.

"Neighbor girl," he says with a tip to his lip.

One eyebrow arched, I return, "Coty." His breath leaves in a silent laugh I wish he would've let me hear. "What brings you out to my neck of the woods?"

"I noticed you were walking home alone," I pin him in place with skepticism, making him finally release an audible laugh, "and I thought I'd see you to your door." He tacks on, "it's the neighborly thing to do," to which I shake my head at.

I motion for him to go first while keeping an eye on his back. And ass. And calves. And ass. Okay, but it's a good one. Like really good.

I'm so busy appreciating Coty's finer points, I forget to draw out the guidelines regarding my vulnerable state of undress and his proximity. And my door. And why none of that can mix. Ever. But he surprises me by making a beeline for his own instead.

His back against his door, I mimic his pose by resting against mine, watching Coty in earnest. Most guys would have tried. They would have flirted. They would have teased or coaxed or sweet talked. Not Coty. He did exactly what I would've asked of him without me even saying a word.

"Well, thanks for getting me home safe and sound."

He tilts his head back, gazing down at me through hooded eyes. "My pleasure. You never know who might be lurking, waiting to pounce on a beautiful girl."

"Like you?"

My previously frozen skin is now fully thawed as Coty's warm eyes blaze a fiery trail starting from my toes, past my cheap ass towel, up to my hair, then coming to rest on my face.

Holding my gaze, he says slowly, deliberately, "I wouldn't pounce, Angela." My name, my real name, on his lips makes me bite the inside of my cheek to keep from begging him to repeat it. "That's not my style. I'd like to think I have more control than that." His eyes drop briefly making me feel more naked, more *seen*, than I am. "Although that bikini is chipping away at that restraint every time you wear it."

Somehow finding my voice, I squeak out, "You could get curtains."

Before he can agree, or disagree, someone behind him yells out, "hey, neighbor girl!" causing us to laugh at the tension being cut by a huge, but cute, knife named Beckett.

Coty tilts his head to the side, shouting back, "Go away!"

I take the opportunity to open my door, eyes still trained across the hall but my phone ringing halts my movements. Seeing it's Drew, I answer instantly. His girlfriend was just in town recently, so we haven't spoken in a while.

"Hey, you. Calling to square up?" I joke into the mouthpiece.

Drew thought he'd be the only one visiting Jamie once she

moved to another state but I bet him she'd make the effort to see him just as much. The two of them are crazy about each other and I knew she wouldn't stay away for long. She's already endured the boring six-hour roundtrip drive twice this month. Twice! In one month. I hate to think of Drew in anything other than a brotherly way—*yuck*—but I can't help but wonder how you can miss someone that much? Isn't FaceTime enough? They talk enough times a day to make anyone sick. I can attest to that.

When I'm met with silence, I look down at the phone, noticing the call hasn't dropped. "Drew, are you there?"

Just as his voice comes through, the door across the hall shuts heavily, leaving me alone to question what the hell just happened. Coty made the effort to walk me to the door, then slams his in my face? It wasn't exactly *in* my face but close enough. The intention was clear: Coty's pissed. About what though? That I don't have an answer to, nor do I want one if that wall dividing our hallway has any chance at staying intact. Shaking my head, I tune back into Drew as I slide the lock across my door, hoping it works both ways.

CHAPTER 8

Angela

AFTER STAYING UP LATE LAST NIGHT TO CATCH UP WITH Drew, I let myself sleep in. A rarity, for multiple reasons. Before I had a job to occupy my time on the weekends, I would sometimes find my mom hovering over my bed. With me still in it. Sleeping. And it wasn't in a concerned motherly type of way either. It was like she was scrutinizing me, sizing me up during my most vulnerable state. Like she was looking for weaknesses to capitalize on later.

I started waking up earlier to leave the house before she was up. I would walk to different spots. Places I knew Rianne would never venture for fear of appearing as common as everyone else. Parks where I could exercise. Bakeries to do homework. Maybe those were places she went to when she was still playing at being a good mom. Long before I ever came along. Back when she was just a kid herself. A kid raising a kid, she didn't know any better. Now though, now she does but just doesn't give a shit.

Sometimes Drew would pick me up and we'd go for a drive. The kind of drives where no talking is required. Only music, the road, and a mutual understanding. Those were the best. We would drive for hours, taking turns picking songs. He would play his favorites. I would play ones that were actually good. It was so…simple. I've never had to question Drew's intentions. I've never had to shield who I am with him. He's the only person I've ever felt truly comfortable with.

Until last night that is.

I didn't tell Drew about the boys across the hall. I didn't tell him how Beckett's jovial antics remind me of the ease Drew and

I share with each other. I didn't tell him how Coty has this crazy way of making me feel safe and threatened at the same time. I didn't tell him about Marc's penetrating personality that I can't help but want to learn about. Last night was the first time I kept things from Drew. Even though my new neighbors are just that—neighbors—their presence is something I don't want to share just yet.

Padding over to the fridge, I take out some eggs and a slice of cheese. Eggs I can do. Mostly. Scrambled eggs are my safe zone. Over easy, hard boiled, poached, those are far, far outside of my wheelhouse. My mom was usually too high strung to form an appetite, apparently assuming her child worked the same way. I didn't. I went hungry more often than not since I didn't know how to cook. The only time I've ever eaten regularly was at my last job where the restaurant provided one free meal per shift. Now I'm back on my own though and forced to figure it out, just like I always did, but with more food available to work with, so that helps.

A plate packed with cheesy eggs and toast in hand, I go out to the balcony to enjoy my late breakfast. The slow-to-warm weather is calling my name, so juggling the glass of orange juice along with my slippery plate, I somehow get the sliding glass door open only to find the balcony completely empty. Oh, yeah, I haven't bought a patio chair yet. *Shit.* I mentally add it to my growing list, then sit on the gritty artificial turf-covered ground, trying not to look too hard at what I'm sitting on. I will sit out here. I will eat my breakfast al fresco. And I will enjoy it, damn it.

Mouth full of soggy eggs, I take in the crowded parking lot below noticing Coty's Camaro and bike both parked in their usual spots. A lazy Sunday morning for both of us.

Just then the sliding glass door to my left opens revealing Coty as he steps out onto his balcony. Shirtless.

Jeee-sus.

He catches me gawking and raises his bowl of what I'm guessing is cereal in greeting.

My mouth still stuffed with food and my throat suddenly dry, there's no way for me to swallow without needing the Heimlich maneuver so I flop my hand up haphazardly before letting it fall back to my side.

Coty smiles tightly, saving me from total humiliation, and continues scooping spoonfuls in silence. I, however, can't take my eyes off him even if I tried and without a shirt covering his tattoos I obviously don't want to, so I peruse his skin like the dermatologist I'm not. A small bird on each side just below his collarbone with roses underneath. Intricately feminine pictures, yet they fit him perfectly. Very interesting choices that I'd love to know the reasons behind. I drink in the rest of him as if he were the juice neglected at my feet. He's once again barefoot which I'm starting to think might be his norm. His oversized athletic shorts reach just below his knees and just shy of his boxers' waistband. Although boxer briefs might look good on him, too, I'm glad he's sporting boxers. They've always been my favorite. Honestly, the guy would look good in a ripped paper sack. He's so sexy without even trying. He just rolls over, throws on shorts, pours some cereal and BAM!—hottest guy alive nominee. It's so unfair. He knows it, too. How could he not? It'd be like a bird not knowing it flies. Neither of them have to work at it, but they don't flaunt it unnecessarily either. Coty probably thinks he's just enjoying his breakfast outside, not even realizing he's driving me insane with want like I've never experienced before. Last night ended abruptly but more than that it ended with a pit formed in my stomach. A pit called *confusion*. Why he slammed the door so suddenly after being so kind was strange, to say the least.

Unsure what to say, I remain quiet as I finish my food. The peaceful silence is only interrupted by a family of church-goers as they load into their van.

"Are you off today?" Coty's voice wraps around me, settling like a cozy blanket on my arms. Even though it seems off, not as thoughtful, I still snuggle into it.

"No, I go in later." My eyes stay on the van as it pulls away but finally give in to look over at Coty finding him watching me intently. "You?"

After a moment, he nods. "We all work together and try to keep similar schedules but our days off don't always match up. Today I'm the only one home but it's too quiet in there. You should come over and keep me company." He lets that thought land between us, perched and ready to take flight before adding, "Unless, your boyfriend would care."

Boyfriend?

My mind filters back to last night when I took Drew's call. It was only after I answered the phone that Coty left without so much as a wave goodbye. Maybe he heard Drew's voice and assumed that was my boyfriend. Maybe he had a bad case of diarrhea and couldn't wait for me to get off the phone. Either seems plausible but with his guarded demeanor today and his near-accusation, it's safe to say Coty's stomach wasn't the issue. I stop myself from blanching at the idea of Drew being my boyfriend. The mere mention of it is laughable but something has me staying quiet. Self-preservation or self-destruction, whatever you want to call it, they typically go hand-in-hand in my experience and this is no exception. It would be too easy to clear things up, but it would also remove a brick from the metaphorical wall separating us. The one that needs to stay in place. For everybody's sake.

"Actually, I need to hit the library before my shift. I've got a paper I need to finish and print off before class tomorrow."

Oddly, Coty's face reveals as much relief as it does disappointment. Did he even want me to come over? Was he testing me? Another one of his tricky tactics in trying to figure me out.

He masks it by asking, "What kind of paper?"

Getting to my feet, I answer easily, "The bullshit kind. My English teacher didn't get the memo that school is almost out and insists on assigning ridiculous projects up until the last minute." Literally.

"Don't you have a computer that you could type it up on? I could print it at my shop for you. It'd save you the extra trip."

I'm already shaking my head as I gather my dirty dishes, blowing a strand of hair out of my face when I stand again.

"Well, shit, you should come over here then. We have every kind of device you could dream of, including three laptops. Our entire apartment is basically saturated with Wi-Fi." Coty uses his hands, one still holding the bowl, to emphasize his point. "I can email your paper to Marc and have him print it there before he leaves for the day."

"That's okay. I, uh," I stumble over my words, over my reasoning. "I was just getting ready to leave."

His raised eyebrows mock me but he lets me off the hook by changing the subject. "You can always DM me if you change your mind." I drop my gaze to the lot below, biting my bottom lip into my mouth. "You do have Instagram, don't you?" My eyes meet his. The lines in his forehead crease. "No social media at all?"

"I don't see the need." While everyone else is celebrating their lives, I'm just trying to survive mine. No amount of filters in the world can disguise that particular struggle.

Quietly, he asks, "Are you running from something?"

Smothering my scoff is useless. He isn't far off. I'm not running from something; I'm running from *someone*. Always have been, perhaps always will be. The characteristics our parents pass down to us don't even have to be handed off at close range for them to still cause damage. Who knows what kind of features I carry from my father? And my mother…I'll be working the rest of my life to stop traits I've inherited from her from coming to life and taking over. But still. Coty doesn't get to make assumptions just because I'm not like everybody else. I've never needed validation from strangers because I know what I bring to the table and I'm okay sitting there alone. Especially without the selfies to prove it.

I run my eyes over my Jeep when Coty speaks again. "Hey, I didn't mean to offend you."

"You didn't."

"I'm impressed you're able to live on your own, that's all. Most people our age brag about every aspect of their life and an apartment to themselves would make anybody's feed. You won't tell me anything about yourself and all anyone does anymore is overshare. I like that you're different. I like-" He stops suddenly, shrugging his shoulders. The move draws my attention back to his tattoos and away from whatever he was about to say. While I try, and fail, to stop staring at the only flowers I'm not opposed to he says, "I just want to help out, if you need it."

I'm jolted back to the conversation. *Typical.* Men thinking all women need help. And from them of course. What about all the times we need help *because* of them? What about the idea that we should be able to live out a successful existence without their interference at all? Such a foreign concept, I know.

Bonding time is over.

"Enjoy your day off, Coty."

His eyebrows pinch together. "Alright, I can take a hint. Just remember we're here if you need anything. And if your teacher gives you another assignment, feel free to stop by anytime. Nobody will even bother you." My lips purse together on their own accord making him laugh lightly. "Yeah, okay, Beck will most definitely bother you but that's just his personality. He's got a great heart, bigger than people think."

I don't correct him that people probably imagine everything about Beckett is big. Instead I nod, giving a thin smile. With a wave, I leave Coty outside, returning to the refuge of my studio.

Dishes clean, I jump in the shower using extra shampoo to wash away the chlorine from last night. It may be the cheapest shampoo sold in stores but it still smells better than the more expensive brands. To me anyway. I'll take the strong strawberry scent over the faintest of floral notes any day.

The memory of my mother's overwhelming perfume alone makes me shudder. Luckily, I still haven't heard from her which means one of two things: she's plotting, waiting for the perfect moment to spring her bullshit on me, or she's found someone new to pour her frenetic energy into. For now, at least. She'll come around. She has no one else to blame, never herself certainly, so she'll come looking for her favorite toy. Just like Drew predicted. When she does, she'll try to tear down anything she can. My job, my hair, my new place, my new-

No.

I shake the thought away. I didn't tell Drew about the nosey neighbors because it'd make them real. Tangible. And Rianne can't reach what she doesn't know about. What isn't there. What will *never* be there.

My tiny studio doesn't have a closet so I use an industrial-style clothing rack off to the side of my bed to hold the little bit of clothes I do have. It also adds a pop of color to the monochromatic scheme I've got going in the rest of the apartment.

Never wanting to wear my poorness on my threadbare sleeve, I hid it away beneath secondhand athletic clothes. People expect workout clothes to be worn, frayed, beat to shit. Yoga pants look like yoga pants, no matter how much money you spend on them. I think that's why moms always wear them. They give the illusion you've got your shit together when really, it's anybody's guess what someone's actually going through. Clothes should highlight a person's interests, not define where they came from or where they're trying to go.

Dressed for work in capris and a logo tee, with two French braids framing the sides of my head, I stroll downstairs, casually checking the boys' balcony. Unsurprisingly, Coty's still standing there like some kind of loyal watchdog. His arms rest against the railing and he's still very much shirtless. And hot. Honestly, he's just too tempting which most, if not all, females would agree on should I care to ask. A guy like Coty could, and probably does, get any girl he wants, yet he's been pestering me since we met. Okay, I wouldn't exactly call it pestering, but he's working hard for the

non-details I've been giving him. Indifference has been my approach but maybe that's his thing. Maybe he likes the chase. The challenge.

The headfuck route is my mom's game though, not mine. That's how she managed to land four husbands and countless boyfriends before she'd let the façade slip away revealing who she really is—a cold, cruel woman looking to fill an insatiable hole ripped open when she was just a teenager. She's never recovered from that first love with my sister's dad and I doubt she ever will. She tried anything to get him, then everything to keep him. Unfortunately, it wasn't enough and he left her anyway. She gave up the perfect mom act but not the perfect wife role. It became her addiction, to hook a man, then reel him in, only to end up being the one to eventually be released all over again. The vicious cycle is bad enough to put yourself through, but Rianne added a child to the process, one that got a front row seat to watch it play out like a bad movie repeatedly throughout a childhood that should've had stability and protection, rather than turmoil and neglect.

I may not fuck with guys' heads but I'm not completely inexperienced in the dating realm. I've hooked up with a couple boys over the last year but none with anything extra attached. No stupid games, no irrelevant labels, no unnecessary expectations, no lovesick declarations, and certainly no introductions to family. Boys make better distant friends than girls. They don't judge, they don't pry, they don't read between the lines, they don't look below the surface if you don't let them. It's just…easier.

I've never wanted to keep anyone, friends or otherwise, around long enough to witness the shit show that is my life.

No, that *was* my life.

I'm not a part of that anymore.

I'll never be a part of that.

I can't.

I honk the horn twice at Coty, reversing from the curb and catch a glimpse of him just before speeding away. That sinful smirk plastered to his face should be illegal especially as he's technically only a short distance from my bed. That image has me pressing on the gas a little harder than appropriate driving through a parking lot.

Once I'm settled back into my Jeep after picking up an iced tea from a nearby café, my phone rings. However, seeing the caller I.D. read UNKNOWN, I let it go to voice mail and mentally scroll through the people it could be. There's only one real possibility. Only one person that would go through the trouble of blocking their number. My heart starts racing, so I gulp down as much tea as I can without causing a brain freeze. A couple squeezes of the steering wheel later, I'm as cooled down as I'm going to get.

Maybe it was a wrong number. Maybe she's moved on with her life. Maybe she's forgotten all about me already.

Maybe I'm lying through my cold-sensitive teeth.

CHAPTER 9

Angela

I JERK AN APPREHENSIVE NOD AT AMITY, A GIRL WHO usually only works weekday mornings, as I pass through to the office. Amity used to be a cheerleader and it shows. Her practiced movements, her overenthusiastic smile, her never-ending pep, all of it practically oozes from her nearly perfect pores. She's everything I'm not—blonde, bubbly, and beautiful. We rarely work together so I'm confused to see her here on a Sunday. A Sunday I was supposed to open.

"How's it going?" I ask, swirling my thumb across the top of my to-go cup.

"Great!" She follows me inside after sending the soaked Ram down the conveyor. "It's been surprisingly steady all morning. Lots of *Ultimates* today."

Amity's effervescent attitude helps push customers toward the more expensive package options. People are so caught up in her animation, they don't even realize, or care, they're being suckered into spending more money. She works exclusively in the back at the register because of this and she rocks it.

"Did you open today?"

Almost absently, she says, "Joe begged me last night to help out."

My eyebrows snap together before I can school my features. Looking over, she notices and rushes to add, "He wanted to make sure he was covered." Her near violet eyes—those can't be real, right?—shift past my shoulder. "I mean the wash, he wanted to make sure the wash was covered." A chipper smile stretches her mouth as she regards me fully again. "In case it got busy."

A mini-van filled with a rambunctious family approaches, stealing Amity's focus. She leaves me to my thoughts to tend to the anxious parents, no doubt turning up the charm.

Why would Joe tell me to come in later when the opening shift wasn't even covered yet? And why call in Amity of all people who never even works on the weekends? I was available and willing, so it makes no sense.

Behind me a throat clears making my shoulders jump to my ears. Spinning around, I find Joe leaning against the wall. His gaze penetrates mine until I mutter a quick greeting and clock in.

"You didn't try calling me, did you?"

He shakes his head. "Must've been some other guy."

I hum lightly, murmuring, "Not likely."

Feet planted in front of him, I wait for Joe to move so I can put my things in my locker. After an uncomfortable amount of time, he finally stands to his full height to let me pass. He still manages to brush against my arm even as I twist away from his bulky form, almost flattening myself against the opposite wall.

Every employee gets an assigned locker to store their stuff but they're all missing doors, making them more cubbies than anything. I never carry anything worth stealing so it's never bothered me before. Seeing Amity's boho chic purse stuffed in the space above mine, I notice her lip gloss on the verge of falling off the edge. I grab the tube and tuck it down into her purse with just the lid sticking out, then roll my eyes. *Lip gloss.* Our differences continue.

An hour later the sun breaks from the morning haze, so I run back to my locker to grab my visor but as my hand grasps the strap, I see a folded up ten-dollar bill that wasn't there before jammed next to Amity's lip gloss. The dryers come on upfront and pushing it from my mind, I hustle back outside to dry the next car.

By midafternoon the steady flow finally dies down to a trickle of sporadic customers. Joe finds me folding towels to tell me I can take off and I don't argue. The library closes early on Sundays so I'm relieved to get out of work early. This time.

Back at the lockers, there's a handful of various bills stashed on top of Amity's purse covering her lip gloss completely. We haven't split the tips from our shared shift yet and something feels off about the loose cash's sudden appearance.

Suspicion sitting heavy in my stomach, I round the corner only to stop short at witnessing Joe's hand on Amity's ass. She's busy running a card at the register but there's no way she doesn't feel it. It's not an accidental graze, or an oversight, or a misunderstanding. It's a familiar caress on a body that Joe knows—well.

What in the actual fuck?

My keys fall to the floor giving me away but instead of Joe retracting his hand, he gives her cheek a squeeze before directing a raised eyebrow at me. His eyes are ablaze in something that looks like lust which I can only hope is aimed at Amity and Amity alone. Even with the rumors about Joe running rampant, I'm still shocked seeing it in person. It's one thing to hear some gossip, it's another to watch it happen in disgusting detail.

I still need to get my cut of the tips so, bile lodged in my throat, I scoop up my keys and amble over to the desk indicating to what should be a full bucket.

"Want me to grab this car while you divvy up the tips?" Anything to get out of this office right now.

Amity speaks up, completely unfazed, "I'll get it. Enjoy the rest of your day."

She disappears into the bay finishing up with the customer while I'm left staring after her. Her words were spoken with her usual chipper tone but the way she delivered them was like she's the one giving me the okay to leave. Like she's in charge. I swing my gaze back to Joe realizing he's keenly watching the interaction.

Despite Amity being absent from the room there's still very much a third presence otherwise known as the rising bulge in Joe's jeans. I avert my eyes as quickly as possible, but the damage is done. I'm forced to swallow the chunks down repeatedly as this morning's eggs try their hardest to make a grand reappearance.

Just a little longer.

Moisture builds in the corners of my eyes while Joe leisurely dumps the pile of tips onto the desk like I've seen him do a hundred times. This time though he looks up at me, scoffing. "Losing your touch?"

Confused, I look down to find a lot less cash than I put in there. What I *know* I put in there.

"I could've sworn there was more…" The mysterious bills in Amity's purse come to mind. "Did you already split them earlier?" Sometimes, if someone needs money for lunch, Joe will divvy up the tips before a shift change, making sure everyone gets their cut at that time, it wouldn't be fair otherwise, but I haven't received shit today so something isn't adding up.

Swaying in his beat-up office chair, Joe's knee bumps my leg as he says, "No reason to. Guess you're just slacking on your skills."

Bullshit.

Bullshit on this pathetic pile of tips being my fault. Bullshit on any part of his body touching mine for any reason other than a professional handshake at best. I have yet to see an ounce of professionalism from either him or this dive of a wash so that idea is scratched off entirely leaving zero acceptable reasons for his person to come into contact with mine. Fuck. That.

I pocket my half and turn to leave, stopping when Joe says, "You need to update your address on the payroll before you go."

"It's on there. Besides I get direct deposit."

I'm almost out the door when he insists, "You put down the apartment's name but not the number. Boss is cracking down since you don't live with a responsible adult anymore." I mash my lips together, halting in the doorway. "Right? You live alone now, don't you?"

A whoosh of air leaves my lungs as I spin to write out my address on the form. Without another word, I practically sprint from the office. Joe calls out to my back but in my haste, I can't make out his words. It's only when I'm safely in my Jeep that I realize what he said. *"See you later, Angela."*

♦ ♦ ♦

The library is closed. It's the middle of the afternoon on a weekend and it's closed. Because what else could go wrong today?

A sign on the door says it's closed for a private event so cupping my hands around my face, I peer through the window to see what kind of occasion requires a library as its venue. All I see are books on books on books.

Then I see her. A bride swathed in a white form-fitting dress makes her way down the aisle between rows of overflowing bookshelves. A thin veil covers her face but does nothing to conceal how happy she is. She's glowing.

Guests are interspersed amid stacks of books as if the fictional characters within the pages are witnesses themselves. Strands of white twinkling lights hang overhead as well as glowing paper lanterns. An old oak card catalog sits off to the side with greenery spilling out of open drawers. Flickering fake candles dot the top along with handmade signs displaying names written in calligraphy.

Slowly making her way to the groom, the bride passes flower arrangements made of pages that look like perfectly shaped literary blooms. Her petite train floats over what appears to be different colored date-stamped heart cut-outs dusting the aisle. There are so many small details highlighting the true beauty of books, I realize I've spent years overlooking just how magical libraries are. A place I've always taken for granted, this couple is making the focal point on one of the most important days of their lives. I make a vow of my own to come back another time when I don't have an assignment due. A day to explore what this literary haven holds.

Having been in a few weddings myself, I can honestly say I've never seen such pure adoration as I do now when the couple faces each other at the altar. An energy that I swear I can feel from outside sizzles between them, one that was absent from all of my mom's weddings. The groom wipes errant tears on his cheeks as discreetly as possible but I see it, as does his soon-to-be wife. She breaks into watery laughter herself reaching to dab them away with her sleeve pulled over her palm. The sweet gesture leaves me breathless. She adores him. It's clear in the way she looks at him. Like he's the one that taught her how to love to begin with. But he fucking worships her. Every move she makes, he counters it with one that puts him directly in her path. There's nowhere she'll go in this life without his full support.

A secret smile passes between them. An inside joke maybe. A silent promise perhaps. Either way, it's private, too private for an interloper, and makes me drop my gaze. I'm filled with a jealousy so suppressing I almost drop to my knees.

The relationships I've watched over the years never held that. That deep understanding of one another. The kind where words aren't even needed. The type of connection that splits one being in half right down the middle, allowing two separate individuals to take on life as partners in every sense of the word.

Glancing back up, they're now hand-in-hand, clutching each other's fingers like the last few minutes apart were torturous on them both. My face splits into a smile despite my melancholic state. Love is infectious. That love is transcendent. I can't help but wonder if I'll ever be fortunate enough to find someone like that. If I were to believe what my mother told me my entire life, then I'd say no.

Good thing I don't listen to her anymore.

CHAPTER 10

Angela

J UST KNOCK.

All I have to do is knock. That's it. Two little taps on a door that if I squint real hard, I can pretend is mine. But really, it's less about the knock and more about what comes after the knock that has my hand limp at my side, refusing to participate in such a barbaric ritual like knocking on someone else's door. It's so aggressive when you think about it. Why don't our apartments have doorbells anyway? Someone should complain. Like right now. I shouldn't be here waffling in the hallway like a moron. I should be out fighting for doorbell equality. Those annoying chimes deserve a chance-

"Library closed?"

Coty holds his door open with one hand while the other rests against the doorjamb, a self-satisfied smile lining his face. He's as flawless as he was this morning but he's shed the hesitancy and in its place is triumph.

Hands twisting behind my back, I say, "Actually I was hoping I could get that cup of sugar from you now."

I smother a laugh as his face falls.

"I don't know if we even have any sugar. Shit." He looks over his shoulder, debating, then back to me. "I'll go get some."

He reaches for a set of keys from their bar and I can't hold back anymore. Laughter spills from my lips.

"I'm kidding." His eyes snap to mine, confused. "If I needed sugar, I'd get it myself." I watch amused as his face relaxes. "You were right though, the library's closed today. Do you think I could, um," the foreign words clog my throat. "I was wondering if-" I drop my eyes to my toes, watching them squirm in a similar rhythm as my insides.

"Come on in." Coty widens the door with a knowing smile. "You can use my laptop. It's charging right now so you'll just have to sit at my desk, if that's okay. Don't worry, my room is clean for once. One of the benefits of having the place to myself for the day." He winks as I duck past, careful not to touch him. Unfortunately, this causes me to slam my shoulder into the doorjamb on my way through giving me a massive Charlie horse. Hand clamped to the soon-to-be bruise, I turn to watch him close the door and head toward a hallway. He gestures for me to follow, which I do at a much slower pace while taking in the living room along the way. Coty continues talking while I look around the warm space. Warm as in homey. The whole apartment is actually freezing. I bring my other arm up to hug the one already wrapped across my chest trying to trap some body heat before it all leaks out. *Holy shit.* They must keep their air conditioning cranked around the clock. "I bet I can find one around here somewhere if you'd prefer the bed."

Halting, I pin Coty with a glare, my arms falling stiffly to my sides. Coty, at his bedroom threshold, notices I'm not following and turns to face me. Realization dawns, making him double back. For every step he takes forward though, I take two back until he finally stops, sensing my retreat.

"I didn't mean it like that. I swear. I just want you to be comfortable." His eyes land on the kitchen and he points a finger at a drawer that doesn't quite close all the way. "See? I'm almost positive there's one in here."

While he searches what must be their junk drawer, I slowly tread closer to the front door, palms sweaty despite the cold.

A zero on one assignment won't sink my grade. I'll still graduate with honors, easy. I repeat that mantra as I reach for the door handle.

"Found it." Coty brandishes an extension cord proudly. My eyes widen before lifting to the ceiling. An extension cord. So I don't have to sit at his desk while his laptop charges. I close my eyes briefly, filling my lungs on an inhale. As I open them again, ready to apologize, Coty says, "You know what? You can use the couch." He gestures to the brown leather couch. Somewhat softer, he adds, "Make yourself at home and I'll go grab it."

He's gone the next instant, leaving me to shuffle awkwardly on my feet. With his captivating presence absent, I look around properly. The oversized couch is accented with soft tan pillows at both ends with a matching chair sitting caddy corner. A large cherry coffee table decorated only with a fancy glass bowl on top takes up the middle of the welcoming space. Walking closer, I smirk noticing it's full of beer caps. *A little classy, a little trashy.* In the corner is the badass sound system that's kept me up with its thumping bass. I glare at it on principle as I plop down on the opposite end of the couch. An end table off to the side is piled high with electronic devices reminding me of Coty's admission about their gadgets.

Coty returns with his laptop and extension cord, and after setting everything up, he stands, wiping his hands down his thighs. "I'll leave you to it then. Beckett and I share a bathroom and we rotate who cleans it. Today's my lucky day." The extreme dip of his lips says otherwise.

"Thank you." I finally manage to get some words out since entering his apartment. The next ones are as foreign on my tongue as escargot. "I appreciate your help."

He smiles down at me kindly. "My pleasure." He winks as a departing gift that might be more for my pleasure than his.

Trouble.

That wink is trouble.

My fingers, flying across the keys, halt every time I hear Coty dramatically gag from somewhere down the hall. Pressing my lips together, I type furiously until I finish with the last sentence. I send it off in the email he'd already opened for me, then sit here unsure. The shower started several minutes ago but Coty didn't mention how much longer he'd be. Do I stay here until he's done? Do I knock on the door to tell him I'm leaving? The thought of being just outside the door while Coty's naked body lathers up inside has the temperature of the chilled room ratcheting up a few degrees.

I listen as the water runs, pulling my shirt away from my skin, wondering if the heat really did just kick on.

My imagination refuses to stay where I want it, traveling down the hall, past the bathroom door, right into the shower with Coty. Images filter in before I can stop them until suddenly, I'm burning up, with no release in sight. Not with Coty and me in opposite rooms anyway. *Shit.* That train of thought will only lead me, and Coty, to a dead end, so deciding to leave a note while he's clearly indisposed, I stand from the couch, holding his laptop.

Somewhat reluctantly, I venture further into the hub of his home looking for the room Coty gestured to earlier. However, halfway down the hall a door opens, making me freeze in place. I was so caught up trying to ignore the shower being only a few steps away, I missed hearing the water turn off entirely. I'm about to apologize when Coty steps out wearing only a towel wrapped around his trim waist causing all coherent thoughts to flee on their own volition. My eyes, greedier than they've ever been, take in every small, and not so small, detail while Coty's distracted. Momentarily busy brushing water from his beautifully jumbled hair, I take the scenic route by starting at his unguarded face and making my way down lower. Much lower.

Drops of water lazily roll down Coty's perfectly sculpted abs and I don't blame them one bit for their leisurely pace. I'd spend days lost in those valleys before even considering sending for a search party. I do feel sorry for the poor towel straining to cover the impressive package barely hidden just beneath though. And by feel sorry, I mean I vehemently wish the worthless barrier would fall to the floor. It's called compassion. Or personal gain. Either way, it should be relieved of its duties immediately.

Coty finally notices me in all my awkward glory but doesn't make a move other than planting his feet just outside the bathroom and pinning me with murky eyes. In this light they look darker. Less like mouthwatering sweet treats and more like bottomless pits I'm on the precipice of falling into—hard.

The laptop in my grasp becomes deadweight as I jiggle the device futilely. Coty watches me squirm, not offering to help me out of the precarious position I've put us in. Tense silence creeps across the confined space, reaching its unwanted hands up my jittery legs before settling on my overheated stomach.

I thrust it toward him, hoping he'll take the hint but still, he doesn't oblige, leaving my boneless arms to struggle with uncertainty. Coty's gaze too intense, I drop mine to the floor, wondering if I could abandon the heavy machine there, but with a voice too hoarse for just coming from a steamy shower, he rasps, "Finished?"

My eyes collide with his. Finished? Whatever game we've got going on—the one filled with flirty looks and coy conversations—is more obvious the longer I stay suspended in this hall, unable to walk away as easily as I should, which is why I'm guessing we've only just begun. And watching Coty's Adam's apple bob as he swallows thickly, I can tell he's thinking the same thing.

I need to leave. Now.

"I'm going." I cringe, ready to slap my own forehead when Coty springs into action to finally take the laptop from my grasp, scowling like I've offended him.

"Did something happen? I didn't think I took that long." Now he swings his accusatory stare back toward the bathroom.

He wants answers that I can't give him. I don't even know what the hell I'm doing, let alone how to explain it. One minute I want to hide inside my apartment with the door locked to everyone, the next I'm staring Coty down like he's my next great adventure. It's fucked. I'm fucked. The only thing I do know is I can't stay here with his towel looking more and more like my own personal invitation to explore.

Focusing my eyes on his tattoos, I open my mouth to speak but am cut off by the front door opening. Beckett and Marc file through, no doubt catching the tension lining their home.

"Oh, shit!" Beckett exclaims, not bothering with formalities. "What's up, neighbor girl? I didn't think you'd still be here." Behind him, Marc holds up a thin stack of papers before placing them on the counter. "Did we interrupt something?" Beckett's beaming smile doesn't hold an ounce of remorse. Marc, however, pins Coty with an unreadable look.

Glancing over my shoulder, I realize Coty is closer than a moment ago, but he's oblivious to his roommates. His eyes are glued to mine, frown still firmly in place.

"I, uh, need dinner. So, I'm going to leave. And go home. To eat." *Shit.* I pick up my report on my way past, then throw out a vague thanks to the trio. Coty, for letting me crash his day off, Marc, for printing out my assignment, and Beckett, for unknowingly creating the diversion I desperately needed for an escape.

"Whoa, whoa, whoa. Where are you going? We just got here."

Ignoring the big guy, I skirt around him in his dirty mechanic type outfit, heading straight for the door when Coty asks, "What are your plans for dinner?"

I spin, placing my back to the front door and narrow my eyes. My stuttering slew of verbal nonsense must've tipped him. His knowing grin confirms it.

"You got a hot date?" Beckett guffaws as Coty reels back like he's been hit. "Coty, man, you did a shit job if she's running off to someone else."

Recovering quickly, Coty takes a menacing step toward a still chuckling Beckett, gritting out, "Fuck you."

I take in the whole scene, my gaze landing on each of the roommates. Beckett inferring Coty couldn't keep my attention, Coty threatening his absurdly tall best friend in nothing but a towel, Marc watching it play out like this is a normal occurrence. The strained moment is broken by my unexpected laughter. All eyes swing to me, surprised, which only makes me laugh harder. Everyone seems to realize what I'm seeing because they visibly relax, joining in my amusement.

Beckett gets ahold of himself first, asking, "Seriously, what are you doing tonight? We're making fajitas using fresh tortillas Marc's mom makes us. You gotta try 'em."

The others have sobered as well and are watching for my reaction.

Somewhat regretfully, I shake my head, trying one last time. "I have home-"

Coty interjects, "You just did homework. Say you'll stay. We'll behave, I promise."

"I don't," Beckett disagrees playfully, making a smile tug at my lips.

Marc speaks up for what feels like the first time ever. "Coty, throw some clothes on already. You're not fooling anyone with your good guy act with a fucking cloth covering your shit." Without meaning to, my eyes drop to said cloth. Coty catches the movement and smiles proudly. Busted, I throw my hands over my face, rubbing them down the heated surface. "I'll watch neighbor girl for you. She can cut tomatoes. I hate that part."

Not waiting for my response, he turns for the fridge, grabbing out a plethora of ingredients. Beckett disappears into another door I'm assuming is his bedroom while Coty pins me with a vulnerable stare. One that says so much more than he ever could in front of his boys. One that begs me to stay. One that I can't answer without lying through my teeth so I look away, snatching up a tomato before Marc bats it away claiming it's an apple. *How was I supposed to know?*

◆ ◆ ◆

Dinner next door ends up being one of the top meals I've ever had in my life. The homemade tortillas made the fajitas far superior and I'm glad they insisted I stay.

After getting changed, both Beckett and Coty joined Marc in the kitchen. One look at my "cooking" skills, and Marc banished me to a stool for the bullshit role of supervising. It turned out to be quite the show though, so I didn't complain. Watching all three friends work together to cook one delicious meal was something I didn't know I needed in my life. I found myself laughing along with inside jokes that had nothing to do with me but were funny just the same. They moved around each other with such ease and respect, it was a sight to behold, one I'll never forget.

Full—fuller than I've been in a long time—I'm sitting at their round patio table looking out over the pool, chatting with Coty as he tells me more about himself. So far I've learned he's an only child. He met Beckett, who they call Beck for short, and Marc, short for Marcos, from riding dirt bikes as kids. They work together at an auto body shop. Beckett's a mechanic, able to work on anything with an engine, while Marc and Coty share managerial duties. You can tell Marc prefers to work under the hood but I get the feeling his leadership skills call him into action more often than he'd like. There's more to that story, his tight jaw while on the subject told me that, but none of the guys divulged anything more than surface level details. Marc, at twenty-one, is older than the other two by one year even though they all finished high school at the same time. After graduating, with honors like me, Coty bought himself a street bike while Marc and Beckett followed soon after with purchasing theirs. They've been living together ever since. Oh, and he hates spinach. Got it.

Bringing my gaze back to him, I watch his eyes light up talking about his friends. The other two went back inside as soon as we finished eating on the boys' back balcony. Now, he's telling me about a time the three friends threw an epic party out in the boonies with dirt bikes and bonfires before the cops showed up to bust them. Luckily, everyone got away but not without incident. Apparently, Beckett had to run carrying his dirt bike instead of it carrying him away from the melee.

They're extremely close and it shows. Not just by the entertaining cooking show they put on for me either, but by the way they have each other's backs. No matter what. Story after story, it's clear how much they love one another. The three of them have been inseparable for years. Like brothers but stronger because they don't have to be, they choose to be. They truly want to be there for each other, it wasn't ingrained in them from birth. Which might be one of those beautiful, yet heartbreaking, exceptions in life. What does someone have to go through to choose a person that isn't related to them over anyone in their actual biological family? Drew pops into my head and I tuck my hands under my thighs.

Coty notices my change in demeanor and drops the subject. He's been doing that since I showed up. It reminds me of a mood ring one of my mom's many boyfriends gave me, blending to adjust based on my moods. He doesn't force me to stay where I'm uncomfortable, he just rolls with the changes once he senses the shift. It's unnerving and charming, just like him.

"I never got to show you around earlier. Want a tour?"

My feet peddle back and forth, waking them from their sleepy state. "I should probably head out. Surely, you must be sick of me by now."

"First of all, that'll never happen." I look over at him, eyebrow raised. "Second, don't call me Shirley. I had a great aunt named Shirley. She liked plain oatmeal and let her poodles eat straight from her bowl." He fakes a shudder. "It's a touchy subject." I roll my eyes before he finally cracks. "Okay, fine, her name wasn't Shirley but she did do that and it always freaked me out."

"You don't like dogs?"

Eyes latched to mine, he says, "I love dogs, but plain oatmeal is fucking disgusting."

After a beat of silence, we both break into a round of laughter. *Fair enough.*

The tour starts out in the dining room which my studio doesn't even have so I take my time letting my gaze soak up the large table filling the space. A delicate looking chandelier lights the room, giving it a soft glow that overhead lights usually wash out.

The kitchen is next which I already got my fill of while watching dinner prep. I run my fingers over the shiny granite countertop I sat at earlier as the two boys finish loading the dishwasher, another luxury my micro didn't come with, before we move down the hall. Pointing out the first closed door as Marc's, he explains how Marc got the master to begin with. Something about a race and a near death experience.

Further on, he shows me Beckett's door which is wide open without a care in the world. The idea makes me smile thinking that's exactly how Beckett comes off. That is until I step into his room finding it meticulously clean, something I would've never thought possible. His carefree vibe does not carry over into his possessions. Not by a long shot. Posters of hot cars and even hotter women line the walls but in perfect uniformity. Almost like the guy measured each one out before attaching them. The attention to detail is astounding.

Before I can ask any questions about the blaring contrast, Coty maneuvers me across the hall to his room. He walks into the cozy space while I hover in the doorway.

He sees my indecision. "You can come in. I don't bite."

I swear I hear a muttered "hard" as he leans against his desk off to the side waiting me out. The thought of Coty's teeth sinking into my flesh, even softly, sends a shiver up my neck. He threw a baseball hat on his wild hair after his shower and with his white tank just barely revealing those mysterious tattoos and soft shorts sitting low on his waist, I find myself struggling with want and need yet again. The need for self-preservation that's ingrained in my every fiber. The want to buck that instinct to see what destruction Coty may be capable of. The two impulses war with each other until I can't tell which one is which anymore.

Coty's scent is stronger the further in I venture. Almost like a spicy coconut—it sounds weird but totally works—the smell is

borderline overwhelming when I reach the foot of his large uphol-
stered bed. His gray comforter adorned with a few matching pillows and a white throw blanket draped across the bottom corner is
both inviting and foreboding. Focusing on the cushiony headboard,
I notice a huge mural just above acting as the focal point of the entire room. It's a mural of the desert with a quote scrawled across the
sky that reads *In The End, We Only Regret The Chances We Don't
Take.* The landscape is striking all on its own. The heightened colors of the sunset give it a mesmerizing effect. But the significant
saying is what makes it such a poignant piece though instead of
just a pretty picture hung over someone's bed. It means something.

I glance over to find Coty watching me closely. I drag my fingers across the blanket, leaving streaks against the grain of fabric
that resemble claw marks. *Just like I'd do to him.*

Quickly turning away from his bed, I give his desk a once-over
noting its contents without fully snooping. Car magazines and
random papers. Nothing too exciting. The picture hanging on the
wall above the desk however more than makes up for the boring
workspace. It's an abstract black and white painting with the words
Strength, Love, and *Honor* scattered amongst the frenzied lines. I
stare at the piece for longer than necessary as if the meaning behind the picture will reveal itself if I look hard enough.

Coty clears his throat at my side, reminding me how close we
are. In his bedroom. Alone.

Dropping my gaze, I create some space between us, pacing to
the other side of the room.

"It's beautiful." I gesture to the artwork but really, the whole
room caught me by surprise. The entire apartment if I'm being
honest. The immaculate state, despite his proclaimed day of cleaning, have me doubting he had as much to do as he let on. These
guys aren't what I expected. At all. They're tidy, and intelligent, and
caring, and responsible—I glance at the different mottos—and
deep. They're not the shallow party animals I first thought they
were.

Coty interrupts my reverie. "They mean a lot. Those words." He points at the messy painting, then to the mural. "They all do actually."

I nod slowly. "This place is spotless. Are you sure you even had to clean anything? I feel like you guys aren't the typical male slobs."

My joke falls flat as Coty's eyes bore into mine. "I take care of what's mine."

The intensity of his gaze, the promise of his words, the sudden heat that's been missing since I stepped through his front door, the delicious coconut scented atmosphere—everything smashes together in an unescapable combination. Coty sees it in my wavering determination. I feel it in the invisible pull of his mere existence.

The moment stretches, neither of us moving other than the labored rising and falling of our chests until Beckett bellows, "Let's go!"

Eyes wide, I recoil.

Coty, unaffected, says, "Come with us."

A nervous laugh bubbles up outside of me. "Where?"

"We're going for our Sunday night ride. You should come."

"What? Like on a motorcycle?" I don't even remember riding a regular bicycle, let alone adding in a high-speed motor.

"No. On *my* motorcycle, with me."

Oh.

That scenario worries me for a whole different reason. There's danger, and then there's *danger*.

"Say you'll come. You won't regret it."

Referencing the motto above his bed is a cheap shot but I understand. Coty's a risk taker. He lives his life doing what he loves. You can see it in the way he describes his life. His friends, his job, his hobbies—he's truly fulfilled. I want that, instead of always doing what I have to. What I need to do to survive. I wish I had the freedom he does. And maybe I will one day. Maybe today's another step toward a place where I can do things that not only make me feel alive but hopefully as carefree as Coty appears. But, does that step really need to be from the back of a two-wheeled death trap?

Coty's triumphant smile gives me my answer.

CHAPTER 11

Angela

I AGREE TO MEET EVERYONE DOWNSTAIRS AFTER CHANGING my outfit. Coty suggested dressing warmly despite the early summer heat raging well into the evening hours. My skinny black jeans with the knees ripped out, my pink and beige Adidas running shoes—far more flexible than my shell toes—and a gray hoodie thrown over my plain tee are a welcome relief after spending the afternoon in that ice chest the boys live in.

Wobbly legs carry me across the lot, putting me directly in front of Coty's black stallion of a bike as I take in my neighbors with new eyes. Gone are the casual outfits from earlier. All three are wearing thick motorcycle jackets, formfitting jeans, and seriously heavy-duty boots. Suddenly, I'm brought back to move-in day, the first time I saw the trio. Their faces masked by their helmets, I assumed the worst. I judged them before I even knew them. Guilt claws at my chest while I twist the strings at my neck between my fingers.

Coty cocks his head to the side watching me with an unreadable expression.

"Neighbor girl, we didn't know you owned so many clothes. We only see you rocking your bikini and tiny outfits."

Beckett's unzipped jacket reveals a crisp white shirt underneath that says *Get On Your Knees Every Sunday*.

"What do you think I wear to school?"

His face clouds over. "I don't know. We only do our spying at the end of the day."

Both friends snap their heads to him, causing me to laugh clumsily. *Creep much?* Marc shakes his head, mounting his red motorcycle while pulling his helmet on simultaneously. Beckett shrugs unapologetically before following suit and lifting his visor.

Coty whacks the back of it making Beckett flip him the bird, muttering, "It's true."

I take a step backward. "Maybe I should sit this one out and go for a swim. You know, now that my audience is leaving."

Coty lurches forward, grabbing my front pocket, making me yelp. "Not a chance. You're comin'."

"That's what she said!"

Now Coty's the one flipping Beckett off. They're more like brothers with their easy-going, comfortable bond. Even Marc, with his severe stare and aloof demeanor. He let loose a little during dinner but he's back to his reserved side now, watching everything in earnest.

Coty tugs one of my braids. "These are perfect. It'll save you from getting helmet hair."

My eyebrows dip. "Helmet hair?" Normally I'd be embarrassed by my lack of knowledge on a topic and fake my way through until I figured it out on my own. With Coty though, his composed approach puts me at ease even as he lowers a black and white helmet over my head, careful not to catch my cartilage piercing in the process. Deft fingers fasten the chin strap before I even have to ask.

"For guys, it's similar to bed head, but for girls, it's more like sex hair," Beckett explains, using his hands flinging wildly around his head to demonstrate.

All at once Coty stops his hands, meeting my eyes. The fire I see there matches the one stirring in my belly. He lightly brushes the side of my neck and I, unfortunately, gasp. The feather light stroke feels different than a simple touch. More significant. A reunion between two old friends desperate to meet again.

"A few things." Coty clears his throat, giving me some space. "I'll get on first, then you get on after me wrapping your arms around my chest or stomach. You don't want to let go at any time. If you have an itch or something, feel free to scratch it quickly, otherwise keep ahold of me." He slips his own helmet on, lifting the visor to continue. "Every move you make, I feel and vice versa. We'll be connected so just be mindful of your movements. Don't lean. I'll do all the leaning but where I go, you go, yeah?" I nod stiffly. "I've been riding for years and aside from a few minor wipe-outs on my dirt bike when I was younger, I've never had an accident. I won't let anything happen to you. I promise."

I fill my lungs watching Coty situate himself on his bike before he reaches a hand out to me. He helps me aboard then shows me the pegs to place my feet. Once secure, I wrap my arms around his torso like a monkey clinging to a tree making him chuckle.

"Don't worry about gripping me too tight. I can take it, plus it makes things easier if we're close." He doesn't bother loosening my hold but he does readjust my arms to rest lower on his stomach as he sticks the key in the ignition. "If at any time you feel uncomfortable, squeeze my thigh and I'll pull over."

A thigh squeeze? That's my exit strategy?

"Are you sure you'll feel it?"

Head cranked over his shoulder, he says, "Trust me, I'll notice." Still sensing my reluctance, he grabs my helmet with his now gloved hand. "If you want to stop, I'll stop. Simple. I'm not going to force you into anything you don't want to do. I promised to keep you safe and I will. Okay?"

The sincerity in his eyes pulls the assent straight from my mouth. "Okay."

He closes our visors then twists back around. As he does, I notice a small device attached to the side of his helmet. Reaching up, I feel mine has one, too.

Beckett sees, saying, "Bluetooth speakers."

Coty grabs my hand, putting it back where it was then leans forward starting the bike up. The 45-degree angle makes my stomach lurch. With nothing other than another person to rely on, I shoot my hands out, bracing them on the gas tank in front of Coty's seat. My arms still fully around Coty on each side, just holding my weight independently rather than fixed on him, I immediately feel better.

Coty's head rotates to the side again. "What's wrong?"

I give a humorless laugh. *Where do I start?* "I can't do it. I just can't sit that way." Not only is the unnatural angle discombobulating, it feels like I'm literally handing Coty my mind, body, and soul to maneuver as he sees fit. I'm keeping some semblance of control whether he likes it or not. Either we go like this, or I don't go at all.

"Are you gonna fight me on everything?"

I pop a shoulder. *Probably.*

"Alright. We'll try it your way but your arms will burn out fast like that." I let that comment slide since he's never seen me work a busy Saturday shift. "If you get tired, just grab onto me. I got you."

I see Beckett shake his head out of the corner of my eye. "Dude, you got a live one there."

I bristle at the insinuation as Marc barks out, "We ridin' or what?"

All at once the motorcycles start up creating a whining buzz I've become accustomed to. From upstairs. Indoors. Out here though, it's a whole different experience. The roaring hum isn't just audible, I can feel it—everywhere. The vibration penetrates my skin, sinking its pulse into mine, until I can barely register it over my own shudders.

Coty revs his engine a few times then reaches back to squeeze my thigh. Given his earlier instructions on a quick exit, I assume this is his way of telling me my time is up—that I'm now free to curl up in a ball at home and count carpet fibers while him and his friends have a terrifying night of fun—so I move to disembark when Coty, chuckling, brings both hands back to stop me. Shaking with laughter he points toward the street, indicating where we're going. I drop my head against his shoulder blade as it continues to bob.

Coty's hands still on my thighs, he reaches under to grip the bottoms of both then drags me forward until water couldn't slide between us. Plastered to him, my legs are forced to spread wider to accommodate our intimate position. I squeeze tight, tighter than before, scared my grip was lost along with my sanity the second my crotch touched him. I mean the man's wearing jeans but she doesn't care about an insignificant detail such as clothing. Blood pumps to the rhythm of the pulsating machine below, heading straight for where our bodies meet, making the connection that much more pronounced.

Shit.

Through muffled ears, I hear a collective shout of "Ride it!" I'm not exactly sure what 'it' is but before I can volunteer as tribute, we're already moving, every part of my body closing around every part of Coty's like a Venus fly trap. Coty tenses beneath my touch but doesn't complain, letting me get comfortable. As comfortable as one can be riding on a hunk of metal with no seat belts, or general safety precautions, anyway. Fused together as one, we trail after Marc's bike with Beckett's vivid green monster bringing up the rear.

Stopped at the first light, Coty flips his visor, turning his head slightly. "All good?"

Nervous he won't hear me, I nod. With a smack, his visor is back in place and we're off again, flying down the crowded street causing me to squeal like the girl I am. Coty's body rumbles between my arms.

All at once music fills my helmet. Slowly peering over my shoulder, I see Beckett jerk his chin in my direction before speeding up next to us, then slowing back down into their zig-zag formation. Even through our helmets I can see the twinkle in his eye. He's singing, laughing, teasing. All while blowing past the legal speed limit with little regard for his own safety, just like the others. This is downright crazy. But incredible, too. The three of them keep the same speed, same distance between bikes, same route, everything, all without uttering a single word. They just know what the other will do before they even do it, like a sixth sense.

Watching them like this, their bond is undeniable. They're in their element and it shows. Confident in their individual skills, they come together as a daunting team. They're lucky to have found each other and I'm finally able to witness their unshakeable connection firsthand, not just from behind a cloudy peephole.

Okay, so the boys might not be the only ones at Creekwood with stalker-like tendencies.

We turn away from town until buildings disappear replaced by rolling hills covered in dirt and sagebrush. Miles and miles of sagebrush. Most people picture Washington as a green, rain-soaked forest. While that may be true for the northern half of the state, the southeastern section is much like the only batch of brownies my mother ever tried to make—lumpy in spots, cracked in others, under-baked brown, and dry as all hell. Unpalatable. To some. To the rest of us, it's relaxing. Gazing out at the horizon, seeing everything around you. No skyscrapers blocking the view. No trees caging you in. No people drowning out the silence. Nothing to distract you from the natural beauty that is Washington State.

After a while, my arms begin to tingle with numbness. I take turns rolling each wrist out, replacing them on the tank when I'm done. Coty looks down briefly before returning his attention to the road. I chance a peek over his shoulder at the speedometer then cringe at the number shown. Coty's been handling the bike with poise and precision, giving me complete confidence in his skills, but I don't think I'll ever be used to going that fast. I'm definitely calmer than when we started but I wouldn't say I feel safe, regardless of his expert driving thus far.

Just then his left hand reaches back, grabbing the bike under my seat. His forearm resting against my hip becomes much more notable than our speed. The instinct to squirm, and not being able to, almost drowns out all other thought, even the small nips on my back from my hoodie's drawstring—the powerful wind creates a cyclone of strings causing the eyelets to repeatedly pelt against my shoulders. Actually, no, that's pretty painful. It's been happening the entire ride but I'm not about to tap out, even if it does remind me of Chinese water torture. I'm already in the fast lane to Crazytown, might as well show up wearing a few—*hundred*—tiny bruises. Nonetheless, I ignore the pain, concentrating on keeping my breaths steady.

Coty removes his hand and the momentary respite his touch created. The trio veers toward a convenient store, pulling in and killing their engines once parked.

We all dismount, Coty helping me again.

"So, how was it? As bad as you thought?"

I answer, "yes," instantly making the group laugh. "But it was nice, too." Our helmets now attached to hidden hooks under the back seat, Coty's gaze flashes to mine making me swallow thickly. "I don't know. It was freeing." I drop my eyes.

His hands wrapping around my wrists steal my attention away from the oil stain next to my foot. "How are your wrists?" Gently, he pulls, bringing me closer. Sweaty strands stick up all over his head reminding me of Beckett's earlier description. Pretty sure bed-head is my favorite now.

His fingers are rubbing small, mind-altering circles on the sensitive skin just over my throbbing veins. Somehow past a lump, I manage to say, "Good."

Coty quirks an eyebrow but doesn't push the issue.

"What do you think, neighbor girl? Addicted yet?"

I try to pull my hands away but Coty keeps his hold on my wrists, gentle yet firm. He's keeping them. I allow him to, for now, by looking to Beckett. "It's cool. Scary, but cool. I'm just glad we didn't have to do any crazy turns or anything."

They share a cryptic look. My eyes narrow to slits but they're on the move in the next instant giving me an excuse to extract my hands from Coty's. The guys head to the back of the store but I linger near the front door, rubbing my shoulders.

Marc's the first to the register. The surprise on his face matches his tone. "Aren't you getting anything?"

I shake my head softly. "I'm still full from dinner."

His gaze drops, taking me in as an unreadable expression crosses his face but he doesn't say anything more. Thankfully. The truth is I didn't bring my wallet. My front pocket already packed with my phone and keys, I didn't have room for it. Plus, I didn't think I'd need it. I really am full, even if the pop and candy bar Marc's holding look appealing now that they're dangled in front of my face.

Over his shoulder, he catches Coty's eye and I watch as another unspoken conversation passes between the friends. One I'm not privy to. One I don't even want to hear anyway, so I walk to the bathroom leaving them to their eye-talking while I check on my own 'sex hair'.

Back outside, I meet everyone lounging on the curb. Luckily, they're just finishing up with their treats as I rejoin them.

Noticing my approach first, Beckett stands, handing me a wrapped chocolate covered peanut butter bar. *One of my favorites.*

I dodge the goody. "Thanks, but I'm not hungry."

Determined, he pushes it into my hand. "It's tradition. You have to eat something."

The looks around the circle range from amused to hopeful to doubtful. I peel back the wrapper and break it in half. Giving Beckett the bigger portion, I bite from the smaller piece while trying not to moan. I'll have to figure out a way to repay him later.

"Thank you."

I watch in horrified amazement as Beckett devours the whole thing in one bite.

"How tall are you by the way?"

Cheeky grin in place, he answers, "6'6" and still growing."

"The fuck you are, man." Marc makes a show of squinting up at his towering roommate.

Mock innocence for days, Beckett says, "What? I didn't say where I was growing." The hands in front of his crotch say otherwise.

I put my hands over my face to cover the blush threatening to spread, only to peek back out between my fingers. The guys throw their heads back in amusement.

"Who did I move in next to?" I muse.

Remembering my punishing hoodie strings, I tuck them inside the collar of my sweatshirt. Coty notices, arching a brow, so I explain what happened.

"Shit. I didn't even think about that. Want this instead?"

He begins removing his thick jacket.

"No, no, it's fine." I wave him off, not wanting to steal the only source of warmth, and probably protection, he has.

"Sorry. I haven't had passengers on my bike for a while." He holds up my helmet from before. "This is Beck's spare."

"He only lets his *girlfriends* ride with him is what he means," Beckett teases as Coty helps me with the helmet, avoiding my gaze in the process.

Girlfriends? As in plural? Of course girlfriends because look at Coty. I mean why wouldn't he have girlfriends? Lots of them. Boatloads even, according to Beckett. It's nothing that should make me jealous, that's for sure. Picturing another woman, or women if his best friend is to be trusted, wrapped intimately around Coty should do nothing to me. Certainly not make me want to power walk my ass to the back of the gas station and scream until my lungs give out. It shouldn't. And yet, the urge to do exactly that has me bouncing on the balls of my feet anyway.

Proficient in emotionally detaching, I bat down the nasty bout of heartburn plaguing my insides, and throw my hands up in surrender. "No worries here. I'm not looking for a relationship." It isn't until I pull away that Coty meets my eyes. Another step backward puts me in front of Beckett. "Just looking to get home." Coty's eyes narrow but I ignore them and the ache in my chest facing Beckett fully. I jut my chin out soliciting a little help with the straps but Beckett doesn't bite, instead his head whips over to Coty. I will Beckett's eyes to return to mine only for him to feign ignorance to my very existence. The guy is more than devoted to the mantra 'bros before hoes' and having me ride on the back of his bike rather than Coty's apparently falls directly under that misogynistic umbrage. I don't even waste my time looking at Marc. A girl always knows when she's unwanted. Well, this girl does.

A hand suddenly wraps around the mouthpiece of my helmet and I'm pulled back to Coty with a tender but demanding guide. Helpless to stop it, my feet follow their newfound leader, but before I can tuck away all the emotions bubbling too close to the surface, Coty is there. Observing. Taking in everything I don't want him to see, forcing me to be the one to drop my eyes.

"I'm picky with who I let on my bike. It's not about who I'm sleeping with." I can feel the glare he shoots Beckett. "It's about trust. I lean, you lean, right?" He lowers his head, catching my eye. "But it's more than that. It's-" he starts only to stop, frustrated. "Remember how I told you that every move you make I'll feel?" I nod. "Well, I have to trust that you feel our connection when we're together on there. And that you respect that connection as much as I do. I have to trust you won't make careless moves that'll affect either of us. Moves that could hurt both of us. Moves we can't come back from."

His eyes tell me his words carry more weight than he's letting on. They also tell me he's waiting for my reply with an equally profound sentiment but what am I supposed to say? *"I swear not to crash us?"* I mean I would if I could but I can't, so I don't. What if I career us into the first ditch as soon as we're safely off the bike? I can't promise a smooth ride to anybody because I've never traveled one myself.

Marc interrupts the strained moment. "It'll be getting dark soon. Should we go home or stay out a little longer?"

They look to me for my response. The fact that jealousy reared its ugly head on our first official time hanging out together scares me. Coty's deep proclamation scares me. The look he's now pinning me with scares me. But the thought of not being wrapped securely around Coty at least one more time, breathing in everything he is, fucking terrifies me. Admitting that, even if only to myself, is out of the question which is why I pick at a random cuticle when I mutter, "longer."

"What was that?"

The circle constricts with strained ears.

With a huff, I look up. "Let's ride longer."

The boys whoop loudly, shouting another round of "ride it" before everyone busies themselves on their own bikes.

Take off is much the same as before except for the different route back. Once clear of the store's light traffic, Coty pulls one of my hands off the gas tank, placing it on his chest while keeping it there momentarily. It's such a relaxed gesture, almost like a reflex, I don't dare pull away. The slack allows me to sit back, creating a small gap between us so I glance out over the landscape. The sun is slowly sinking toward the horizon, painting the sky pink and light blue in its wake. Cotton candy colors. The stunning backdrop reminds me of the mural in Coty's room and the accompanying quote. As I take in the triangle composed of motorcycles, I wonder who will be left with regrets when all's said and done—me or them?

My musings are cut short when Coty returns my hand to the tank, my body conforming to his only seconds before he lays on the gas, all three bikes collectively picking up speed toward an on-ramp with no signs of slowing.

Oh. Shit.

A quick thigh squeeze the only warning I get, then we're barreling around the curve going way faster than I would attempt even in my own ride. "Taki Taki "by DJ Snake and what sounds like Cardi B fills my helmet as Coty leans his body down and to the right. *Far* to the right, directly into the fucking turn, leaving me no choice but to go with him. Careful not to anticipate where he's going before he goes there, I feel his body as it's moving and follow blindly even though everything in mine begs to go left, away from where the motion is pulling us. Sensing my compliance, Coty's back relaxes a fraction and soon we're like magnets but better. There's no pull from him or push from me because we're already there, together, no hesitancy whatsoever, only total harmony between us. The fear of falling off the crotch rocket is quickly replaced by the fear of falling somewhere else. Somewhere completely foreign to someone like me. Somewhere even a leather jacket can't cushion the blow. The ground at love's feet isn't as forgiving as the asphalt whirring beneath ours. Road burn heals. It can leave nasty scars, yeah, but over time it does heal. Heartbreak leaves no trace other than the unfathomable pain nobody else can see. The kind I've endured for years and refuse to add to after one Sunday night ride.

Out of the bend, Coty rights us, forcing our melded bodies to shift as one then we're zipping onto the highway toward town. Marc and Beckett take turns cutting across the open lanes ahead. What starts out as lighthearted fun though quickly turns into cutthroat competition when they lower their bodies almost flush with their bikes then shoot off into an all-out race. Anxiously watching, I let out a squeal when their taillights disappear in the growing darkness. Coty's back shakes with another silent laugh. Suddenly hungry for his calm, I rest my head between his shoulders, praying it transfers by osmosis. He does the thing again where he grips the seat under my ass, and I do the thing where I pretend not to notice.

Back at Creekwood, a white extended cab pickup is pulling out as we near the entrance. The resemblance registers a moment too late and by the time I chance a second look, it's already gone. Facing forward, I notice Coty honed in on the truck as well. Maybe he knows the driver and that's why it looked familiar. It couldn't be... No, it's just a coincidence.

"Well, as promised I got you home all in one piece. I think anyway. You may have left a vocal cord or two back there with all the screaming you did," Coty teases once we're all dismounted, approaching the stairwell. He doesn't mention the truck and neither do I.

I smack his arm playfully. "I wasn't that bad."

"Neighbor girl, you're gonna have to start closing your windows at night if that's even close to how loud you are when you-"

"Dude!"

Everyone laughs. Except for Coty. He just looks pissed.

Rolling my eyes, I say, "I don't think so. I'll be sure to send over some good earplugs when that happens." I waggle my eyebrows at Beckett earning another round of laughter. Coty still isn't amused. I thought it was funny. "Anyway, thanks for letting me tag along tonight."

"You're welcome anytime."

Upstairs, Marc and Beckett bid me goodnight then disappear inside. Coty hangs back, quietly watching me. His gaze locks onto mine and that pesky chill returns, making me want to wrap my arms around my middle. Instead I turn to unlock my door.

"Did you like riding with me?"

Absently, I throw over my shoulder, "Yeah, it was fun."

"No." Coty's chunky boots drag across the concrete, sending echoes down the hall. I spin to find him less than a foot away. "Did you like riding with *me*?" He doesn't stop until there are only inches between us.

Firmly pressed against the door, I work to get the key out of the lock behind my back. A light sweat breaks out on my forehead despite the subsiding temperature. Swallowing, I say, "It was…an experience."

Leaning forward, Coty reaches behind me leaving only a breath of space between our faces and twists the key out of the deadbolt. My eyes never leave his even as he pulls back brandishing the key like a gift. When I grab for it though, he keeps it just out of reach, toying with me. Little does he know, I'm broken and can't be played with, so rocking onto my tiptoes I pluck the metal from his grasp.

"That guy from the other night isn't going to get mad, is he?"

"What guy?"

"Drew, was it?"

Realization dawns and a laugh slips past my lips before I can stop it. Coty's eyebrows plunge downward. Drew is protective of me, even bordering on overprotective at times, but confronting my neighbors over a friendly motorcycle ride isn't really his style. If I were to admit to riding on a street bike, the worst he'd do is give me a lecture I'd roll my eyes through. I know for a fact he's raced his pretty Acura plenty of times so his hypocritical speech would fall on deaf ears.

"You started your day eating breakfast with me while I was half naked." Recovering, my eyes harden, my tongue pressing into my cheek. "Then you ended it with your legs wrapped around me. I just want to be prepared if some dude shows up at my door pissed off. I know I would be."

I can't stop the sting of his words before they land as carelessly as they were delivered. How dare he turn this into something he knows it's not. Yes, I enjoyed spending time with him today—more than I should've—but for him to twist that into something perverse is insulting. Insinuating Drew, or any man, has a say in what I do is even worse.

Too many emotions fight for purchase in me but I've had years to perfect covering them up, so I just paste on a mocking smile, saying, "Who says I'm ending my day with *you* between my legs?" I push my door open, slipping past the threshold. "Excuse me while I make sure all my windows are closed. Wouldn't want to wake the neighbors." I add a wink for good measure then slam the door shut.

Fuck.

Him.

CHAPTER 12

Angela

"GET OUT."

Ignoring me, Beckett makes himself at home in the front seat of my Jeep, a downside to not having doors attached for the summer, but I don't have the time, or patience, for his antics right now. Today's the last day to pick up my cap and gown for graduation and I'm already running late from swinging by my apartment after work to grab the rest of the payment.

This week's gone by agonizingly slow with only school, work, home, repeat. I haven't seen the neighbors much except for the occasional greeting in passing. It's been a little awkward but necessary—for everyone—so, I'm surprised to see Beckett now. His blond hair is wet like he just got out of a shower and he's wearing a dark blue shirt that says *You Lost Me At "I Don't Ride"* with long cargo shorts. A tattoo I hadn't noticed peeks out from under a sleeve. It looks like a line around his bicep but random spacing keeps it from being totally solid.

"Why are you ignoring us, neighbor girl? I thought you liked us." He actually has the nerve to look put out, too. The couple times I was able to make it down to the pool, he would wave morosely from the balcony but otherwise remain silent. I hated it. And I hated that I hated it. I should welcome his silence, considering who his alliance is with, but Beckett's like an innocent puppy wagging his tail in excitement over every little thing. You can't help but get caught up in his good mood. Okay, he's not that innocent, but still, his enthusiasm is infectious. Mostly. Just not today.

I sigh. "You guys are okay. I mean from what I know about you guys so far you seem nice enough. I had fun on Sunday and dinner was great." His chest puffs up at the compliment. "But I'm really busy. Like right now, I need to leave, damn it," I growl.

"Have you talked to Coty?" He continues when I only drop my eyes, saying, "He's been off all week."

"Like from work?"

"No, not from work, smartass. Just his attitude. He's been... moody." He raises his eyebrows like that surprises even him.

I can't help but laugh. "Oh, yeah? Are your cycles not synced up anymore?" I can tell the period joke went over his head by the blank look on his face. Pressing my head into the headrest, I peer over at him. "I don't know what you want from me. I have no idea what his problem is. We haven't spoken since after the ride and that conversation didn't end well. So, whatever is going on with your friend, it has nothing to do with me." And it's true. Last weekend Coty was accommodating and generous. He knew what I wanted, what I needed, without me even having to say a single word. He was flirtatious and downright sweet. But then he turned, flipped an accusatory switch, and grew outright angry. Around the same time I took that call from Drew. "Now, will you please get out, so I have something to wear to my graduation?"

Instead of listening, he buckles his seat belt, the click emphasizing his intention.

I throw my hands up from the steering wheel. "No."

"Yes. I'm bored and we haven't spent any time together. Let's go."

Groaning, I start my Jeep and throw it in reverse, knowing I'm already cutting it close.

"Why would we spend any time together? We're neighbors, Beckett. We're supposed to pretend we don't notice when the other one waves and forget to water each other's plants if one goes out of town. That's it. Not this friendly crap you're pushing."

He pins me with an incredulous look. "The fuck kind of neighbors have you had?"

"The best kind?"

"Not yet, you haven't." He laughs. "You'll see. We're awesome."

Beckett keeps the conversation flowing, basically unprovoked, as we make the short drive but quiets once we're inside the uniform shop. Almost eerily so. Even as I spin slow circles in front of the mirror to admire the unflattering gown and ill-fitting cap, he keeps his opinions to himself, lost in his own head. An unreadable expression crosses his face when the cashier mentions the lack of parent involvement regarding my bill. Assuming his interest is solely about the money, I pay as quickly as possible then feel Beckett's disconcerting stare bore into the side of my face when I hand over the cash. Some sort of heat rash immediately creeps up my neck and I scratch the skin raw until I feel his hand swat mine away. Still, he says nothing.

Beckett's gloomy mood doesn't hinder my elation though. I'm beaming from ear to ear by the time we're back on the road. I'm actually doing it. I'm graduating. And I was able to pay for all of my graduation outfit myself—thanks for nothing, Mom—even the special medal showing I made honors. It's cheesy and I looked ridiculous in the ensemble but I love it. Another step in my road to independence, albeit in an ugly gown, but a step nonetheless.

Finally breaking the tense silence, Beckett offers to buy me dinner but I manage to talk him into splitting the bill at a fast food joint on the way home instead.

With a fry that's more ketchup than potato, Beckett points at the medal currently dangling from my rearview mirror, asking, "Why didn't your parents help with any of this stuff?"

I take a giant bite of my burger before the question is fully out of his mouth, shrugging noncommittally in answer.

He nods pensively but drops the subject.

We chat easily the rest of our meal then laugh at each other's horrible singing the whole way home. He's actually incredibly smart and kind when you get to know him. He just lets his horny side take the lead normally, hiding what's underneath. It makes me wonder what else is hidden in his secret depths. Someday some brave woman will find out, and I can only hope she's strong enough to take on whatever Beckett works so hard at burying.

I'm parking just as Coty gets out of his Camaro. Instead of going upstairs, he heads straight for my car though.

Beckett turns to me and says, "uh oh," before climbing out. "See ya later."

He goes to fist bump Coty but Coty glares at him, ignoring his extended hand. In the next minute, he's draping both arms casually on the roll bar of my Jeep while Beckett glances back, remaining shamelessly nosey.

I quirk an eyebrow, fully prepared to wait him out.

He finally breaks with a thick, "Neighbor girl." It's the most he's said since I slammed the door in his face and it's not enough. Not by a long shot.

"That's what you lead with?"

"What?" He genuinely looks confused. Men are such idiots.

With an eye roll, I busy myself grabbing my garment bag but stop when he leans in further.

His tone a little too calm, he asks, "What were you two doing?"

"Go ask him."

"I'm asking you."

"So it seems."

"How have you been?"

"Fine." *Not fine.*

"You've been avoiding me."

"You guys are so clueless. First him," I gesture wildly at the hulking figure posted on the stairs, "and now you. I haven't been avoiding you, I've been busy. But you *were* an ass and you know it. I don't have any time for drama especially not at the one place I feel comfortable." I stop myself when my throat gets thick with emotion I refuse to show.

"You're right." Coty drops his head, then lifts it again meeting my eyes. "I was irritated and I took it out on you. I'm sorry."

I buy some time glancing around at the various windows all draped in different coverings.

"You should be. You were completely out of line." I pull a long breath. "But, going forward I think we should keep things cordial. We're neighbors and I don't want things to get messy."

He tilts his head slightly, practically whispering, "What if I want messy?"

"Haven't you ever heard the expression 'don't shit where you eat'?"

I expect him to laugh, instead he leans in even closer and says in a husky voice, "Yes, but I've got a big appetite."

My face heats as I run my gaze down his body remembering what it felt like to be wrapped snugly around it. His dark hair is slightly wavy and looks like he just ran his hands through it. He's wearing a plain white tee giving him a casual look. It's slightly baggy but still clings to his lean muscles in all the right places. His slim waist tapers down to gray athletic pants with a hint of his boxers peeking out of the top. How he makes a simple outfit look so sexy, I don't know.

Wetting my top lip, I say, "I bet you do, but some things aren't on the menu."

I climb out with my arms full, walking toward the stairs, noticing Beckett's no longer lingering. Coty matches my every step, not ready to let me off the hook quite so easily.

"Why are you always running, Angela?"

I scoff. "I live next door. I couldn't run if I wanted to."

At the first stair Coty grips my elbow, begging me to look at him. His big brown eyes hold mine for a beat. Softer, he asks, "What were you doing with Beckett?"

"The jerk jumped in my car when I was leaving. We grabbed a bite to eat."

"Like a date?"

The thought of Beckett on a date makes me smile. "If you consider drive-thru a date." I shrug his hand off.

"Go out with me. Let me apologize for Sunday."

"You just did. And I…can't."

"Why?"

My phone pings with a text just as Drew pulls in, honking. With Beckett's earlier distraction, I forgot Drew was taking me to the movies tonight. Jamie returned to Portland and he wanted to catch up. He's even letting me pick the movie.

I toss him a wave, breaking the intense moment with Coty.

"I told you, let's just keep it cordial, okay? It's better."

Walking to greet Drew, I hear Coty murmur something else but ignore it and rush over to the only person I've ever truly trusted. He pulls me into a big bear hug, kissing my cheek before setting me down.

I'm not surprised when I find the stairwell empty.

◆ ◆ ◆

"Is it always like this?" Drew asks as he searches for a parking space.

One look at the boys' balcony full of people and I grimace.

"They've had a couple parties, but this…I've never seen it like this." The parties were getting better, or so I thought.

"Do you want to stay with me tonight?"

I shake my head, keeping an eye on the party-goers spilling out onto the sidewalk. "I'll be fine."

Just then someone lets out a high-pitched squeal making Drew whip his head over to me wide-eyed.

"Are you sure?"

"Maybe? Come on, let's go upstairs so you can see the three decorations I put up since the last time you were here."

At the top of the stairs, the boys' door flies open with Beckett all but stumbling out with a girl glued to his front. He's so tall that it's all kinds of awkward.

"Hey, neighbor girl. Want to come in for a drink?" He's late to notice Drew standing close behind me. He must be feeling his poorly mixed drinks.

"Ah, no thanks. I've got an early morning tomorrow like every other weekend I've lived here," I say with more snark than necessary but I want to make sure it penetrates his buzz field.

Drew looks between us with confusion. I may have left the knuckleheads next door out of tonight's conversation, too. I didn't want him to worry. I have to take care of myself without a backup plan. He's been mine for too long.

"Indestructible" by Welshly Arms blasts through the open door while the girl hanging on Beckett whines about wanting to dance.

"We'll leave you to it then."

I grab Drew's hand so we can squeeze by the sloppy couple but Beckett steps forward severing our connection. Swinging my head back, I see Coty on the couch with a girl dancing in front of him. It's not exactly a lap dance but she's working every angle to get him to notice her. Unfortunately, for her, it's still not enough. We hold each other's eyes before his move to Beckett. His entire face hardens until I expect it to crack wide open.

Marc is suddenly there, moving between us as he approaches the door.

As I try to side-step Beckett, Marc grabs my elbow and pulls me backward. It's gentle but jarring nonetheless. I spin, shoving him in the chest but he doesn't release me.

"Get the hell off me."

"Chill the fuck out. He's out of his fucking mind right now." He nods his chin at Drew and Beckett still frozen in a wordless stare off. "You don't need to get caught in the middle of that."

Beckett glares down, like really far down, at Drew, not letting up for even a second. Drew looks to me, concern lining his amber eyes until he zeros in on Marc still grasping my elbow, the concern quickly replaced by something more sinister.

I rush forward to calm the situation that's gone off the rails somehow and, luckily, Marc lets me.

"I'm fine. I'm okay," I say to Drew, then look to Beckett,

gripping his taut forearm. "What the hell? We're just passing through. Go back to your party and we'll all forget this even happened. Deal?"

He seems to relax slightly, dropping his gaze to mine. It's cloudy but Beckett's still in there.

"I wonder if the windows will be open or closed tonight." Coty muses as he fills their doorway. There isn't a trace of humor in his words but Beckett barks out a laugh anyway. *Idiot.* There's the Beckett I know and love.

No.

Marc guides Beckett away but when his arm brushes my flowy shirt, Drew surges forward, placing himself between me and my neighbors. Marc levels Drew with a glare and I swear a menacing growl rumbles from the guy's chest. I'm not sure why but my eyes fly to Coty. He takes in the chaotic scene, his eyes tightening on Drew's protective stance. There's so much testosterone, I'm nearly choking on it.

"I guess we'll see soon, huh?" I grab Drew's shirt, turning to unlock my door at the same time. Hand on the knob, I hear Coty speak again.

"Why don't you introduce us to your *friend?*"

Lips pursed, I look over at him. "Guys, this is Drew. Drew, these are my neighbors. They're like stray cats, always multiplying and sniffing around where they don't belong." Someone clears their throat. "It's better if you just ignore them though, otherwise they'll never leave you alone. Now if you don't mind, I have to get to bed."

"Angela, you can't be serious," Drew pipes up. "You're staying?"

"Angela *lives* here. Where would you prefer her to go?" Coty grips the doorframe and I'm pretty sure I hear a crack.

Enough already.

I shove Drew through my door before throwing an exasperated look over my shoulder to the terrible trio. Coty steps aside to let the others by. Beckett is full out leaning on Marc at this point. His female companion ditched him as soon as he turned into the

Inaudible Hulk. Cheers ring out from their apartment, the party still going strong even with the hosts preoccupied.

Coty yells out, "I'm hungry," while meeting my eyes. Laced with more heat than I thought possible in that ice-cold apartment, his declaration reminds me of our earlier discussion. The door slamming shut tells me I won't be the one to extinguish it though.

"Don't even start. It's late and I'm tired," I tell Drew, walking to the bathroom with a change of clothes.

"Fine. But I'm staying the night."

Too many things are running through my mind to argue. Like what the hell that crap with Beckett was. His behavior was nothing like our time together earlier. His size alone is intimidating without throwing a silent death stare in the mix. And Coty, well, Coty was just an ass. Again. His problem with Drew was entertaining at first, now it's just irritating.

Ready for bed, I crawl under the covers, watching as Drew pulls his shirt off. He's beyond handsome—there's no denying it. He has short auburn hair that he styles slightly to the side. His eyes are like the brightest part of a sunset. He almost always has a five o'clock shadow that I've been teasing him about since he first shaved. He wears polos, khakis, and loafers. Always. It's not my style at all but I'd be stupid not to appreciate how attractive the man is. I've just never seen him as anything other than a brother though. Even sleeping next to him shirtless, the thought has never crossed my mind to blur those lines. I know the feeling is mutual so we've never had to worry about it. He's had girlfriends over the years and I've had the occasional friend with benefits, neither of us once showing a single sign of jealousy.

Sometimes I wonder if him putting me first has made his relationships end quicker than they should've though. He's never said anything to that effect, but I don't know if Drew has a limit when it comes to me either. Would he ever find a girl worth walking away from me for?

That thought would've sent me into a panic a few weeks ago

but now that my independence is strengthening, the idea makes me more hopeful than anything. I don't want to hold him back. We're not kids anymore. We both have bigger and better lives to go after. I can't be selfish by constantly keeping him tangled in my troubles. It's not fair to either of us.

"Thank you for being you, Drew. I love you," I whisper, facing him as he climbs in next to me.

He flops onto his stomach—his signature sleeping position. Teasing with my own words, he cracks one eye and whispers, "Don't get soft on me now." Then, softer, "I love you, too."

I leave him sleeping the next morning with a note on the counter about locking up when he leaves. The apartment across the hall is quiet as I make my way downstairs. Pulling my long ponytail through my hat halfway down, the voices on the boys' balcony have me pausing my steps.

"Last night was..."

"You fucking puked in the tub, dude. Coty had to clean that shit up."

"I almost puked just looking at it. What the fuck did you eat anyway?"

"Ugh, it must've been from yesterday with neighbor girl. Double cheeseburger."

Three groans erupt.

"Dude's car is still here. And she kept her windows shut for once. Think she got some?"

I stomp on the last two stairs announcing my presence.

"Oh, shit. I love a good walk of shame."

"Morning, boys," I greet, using a chipper voice I don't feel in the slightest.

"Morning."

"Good morning."

I think Marc grunts out some form of greeting but I can't be sure.

"Ready to apologize yet?"

All three are looking a little rough and it makes me feel slightly better that they're paying for last night.

"For what?" someone asks.

"Being assholes," I deadpan. *Isn't it obvious?* "You treated my guest like shit. I live here, too, you know? If you guys can't be civil, then you're going to have to stay the hell away from me."

"Oooh, neighbor girl's still feisty. What's wrong? Your *guest* didn't wear you out enough last night?"

Shaking my head at Beckett's stupidity, I climb in the driver's seat, calling up, "He's the one still sleeping. What do you think?"

He throws his head back in a hearty laugh while Marc whistles. Coty refuses to meet my eyes.

Yeah, I'm continuing this nonsense about Drew being my boyfriend, or whatever, but they make it too easy.

With a wave goodbye, I leave them to their commiserating, hoping they'll take me serious about leaving me out of their drama from now on.

CHAPTER 13

Angela

GETTING OFF WORK LATER THAT NIGHT IS BITTERSWEET. The sweltering weather brought lots of customers, keeping me pleasantly occupied my entire shift. But it's left me overheated and drained as I pull up to Creekwood. The tips stuffed in my bag help perk me up though, as does the smoothie—with spinach, lots of it—I stopped off for on my way home.

It's been calm at the wash since Joe's off for vacation. Luckily, I haven't shared another shift with Amity since that dreadful day. I have a pretty good guess as to where those missing tips went but I don't know what to do about it. Joe was Team Amity last I saw him and I doubt one flimsy accusation will change that.

Bag in one hand, smoothie in the other, my phone rings. When I peer down, it's another UNKNOWN caller. This has been happening all week. I still haven't answered any and they've yet to leave a message. Next door is silent and my door is locked just as Drew promised via text this afternoon. He was peppering me with questions during my break. I gave him enough information to pacify him while not exactly revealing anything either. If I want to prove how strong I am on my own then I can start with handling the three guys next door.

Walking into my apartment feels like walking over hot coals on a summer day. The stifling air hits me square in the face making me groan. I forgot to tell Drew to turn on the air conditioner before leaving. *Damn it.*

I rush over to the A/C, cranking it full blast then quickly change into my bikini. A towel over my shoulders, hair in a messy bun, and I'm off to the pool a few minutes later.

The water feels heavenly as I jump in. The sun now behind the building, gives my sunburn a necessary reprieve with the delicious shade.

I take my time swimming under the cool water trying to lower my body temp that feels dangerously high. Popping my head up after a lap, I catch sight of some people decked out in swimsuits entering through the gate. My meddlesome neighbors bring up the rear of the motley group and as soon as I see them I consider leaving. My earlier vow to be strong even when it comes to them springs to mind and I decide I'm not done yet. They can swim, or splash from the looks of some of their more dolled-up friends, around me.

One of their guests—one of their cute male guests—greets me from the ledge, so I make my way over to him. He introduces himself but before he can ask my name Beckett yells from across the pool, "Hey, neighbor girl! Working out some pent-up energy?"

The guy, Tony, looks at me with confusion so I ignore my tall neighbor to explain how we know each other. When he remarks how convenient that must be, it's my turn to look confused.

"You're beautiful. If you lived next to me, I'd find every excuse possible to knock at your door."

"That's nice and creepy all at the same time." We both laugh. "Actually, I'm pretty private so even if they did come knocking, I'd just ignore it. So far it's only been a couple loud parties though."

"Lucky. Their parties are notorious. Living right next door, you can drink all you want then stumble home. No cab bill for you."

I have yet to attend, let alone drink at one of their "notorious" parties, but I don't care enough to correct Tony. Instead, I just nod, swishing my hands over the water.

He continues talking but I soon grow bored. He's cute with a decent body and a great smile. I can't help but notice he's lacking something though. Tattoos maybe? I've never liked them before, but now…

Coty's relaxing on the steps in the shallow end with a girl planted beside him. His head is cocked toward her, smiling at whatever she's saying. She has a hand on his bicep, close to his chest. There's a familiarity to her touch. She has beautiful black hair piled on top of her head with big hoop earrings framing her tan, delicate face.

Coty's eyes drift over to mine, locking me in place as Tony drones on like white noise. My heart beats faster as the seconds pass. I cut the connection by glancing at Marc. He's lounging at a nearby table with a somewhat feline quality. His shoulders draped loosely over the back of his chair, he yells something in Spanish at the girl beside Coty. I watch fascinated as she stands up, approaching him slowly with a teasing smirk playing at her full lips. Before Marc can react, she flings her hands at his face, sending streams of water all over him. He lunges for her instantly and she backtracks. Beckett intercepts her with one arm, then deposits her into the pool. When she reappears, she cusses at the cackling duo.

"Marc's sister."

I bring my attention back to Tony, raising both eyebrows.

"That's Marc's sister," he tells me. "She's off limits to all the guys but she's got a thing for Coty. Always has."

"Have they ever hooked up?" I hold my breath awaiting his answer.

Snorting, he says, "No, nobody crosses Marcos."

"I thought he hated me when I first met them."

"He doesn't like most people. He's ride-or-die for his close friends and family but that's it. His family's fucking loaded so he's suspicious of everybody. Don't take it personally."

I consider what Tony just shared, looking Marc over again. He exudes such a fuck-the-world attitude with his sleeves of tattoos and general detached attitude that I never would've guessed he grew up rich. It's not fair to judge but other than his custom BMW, he seems just like his roommates. I mean he shares an apartment with two other guys. Their apartment is definitely nicer than mine but not fancy by any means. There has to be a bigger story there. I tuck that tidbit away for later.

Tony surprises me by reaching out to brush my shoulder. I quickly push his hand away with the flick of a wrist and a scowl on my face.

"Sorry, you had-"

He's cut off as I'm yanked forward by a hand on my ankle causing me to yelp. Coty surfaces right in front of me, gliding his body up mine as he stands, water cascading down his stormy face. He pins a hard stare at Tony, then grabs my waist, pulling me to the deep end. The movement is so fast I wrap my legs around him to keep from going under. He drags me from the middle of the pool to the ledge. I squeeze my knees around his torso when my center gets too close to his naked stomach, allowing me to hang a safe distance from his hard body. He spins us so I'm blocked from the others then puts his hand behind my back effectively saving my skin from the rough cement lip.

"Let me down. You should know better than anyone how good of a swimmer I am." I pop an eyebrow, daring him to argue.

He only shakes his head. "You'll run."

"Do you need something then?"

"I didn't want you talking to him anymore."

Oh, here we go. "Why not? Your friend seems cool." *Ish.*

"I didn't want his hands all over you."

The roll of my eyes does nothing to faze him.

"Do you see yourself right now? You literally just manhandled me."

He drops his gaze between us, dragging his eyes up my body until they hit mine. I clear my throat, fidgeting in his hold. "Go riding with us tomorrow."

"No."

"Why? You didn't like riding with me?"

"You should take whatever flavor you were testing last night riding instead."

"Jealousy looks good on you, babe. What about that prep-douche you had over, huh?"

Gripping his shoulders, I bring my face forward, shortening the distance between us. "And yet…here we are." He growls when I sit back again.

"I know." His frown returns. "Look, I'm sorry. For the second time. I want to make it up to you."

"You don't owe me anything. I told you I just want to be civil."

He looks down at our compromising position.

I remove one of my legs but he shoots his hand back to grip my knee, wrapping it tighter around his waist. The jostling makes my arms slide around his strong shoulders.

"I want you to ride with me tomorrow."

I bite the inside of my bottom lip. "I can't."

His eyes catch on my mouth while his hand leaves the wall. Before my back touches the edge though, he drags his hand slowly up my spine pushing my chest forward until our faces are mere inches apart. My nipples pebble beneath my top as my breath catches.

"I want you with me."

His whisper is louder than the commotion going on outside the pool, hitting me right where it shouldn't. Drops of water drip from his flattened hair, slowly traveling down his forehead. Watching them, I have the urge to catch the errant drops with my mouth, kissing them away before they reach his eyes. I lick my bottom lip on reflex.

A large splash to our left has him spinning to glare at the culprit. With him distracted, I slip out of his grasp, bracing my arms on the pool ledge and pushing out of the water before he can stop me.

I collect my belongings, ignoring his frustrated sigh as I dash out of the gate.

On shaky legs, I make it back to my balmy apartment and immediately jump in the shower. Somehow, I feel hotter now than I did after being in the blistering sun for hours on end. I turn the water to cold, then slump against the wall.

He's pushing closer and closer. The more I try to block him the more he just keeps coming. He's under the impression I'm with Drew one way or another and yet he still acts interested at every turn. Drew, Beckett, and now Tony, he doesn't want anyone else playing with the new girl, like I'm some prize. What will he do when he discovers I'm closer to trash than treasure though? Throw me away like yesterday's garbage? It's what my mother's been trying to do since I was born.

I'd be lying if I said I didn't feel something for Coty, too. He lured me in with that sexy body that he carries with such an easy swagger. His beautiful face lights up with such wonder while his coffee-like eyes hold the more concealed emotions. His affectionate gestures are slowly becoming my undoing. He's absolutely hypnotizing. And him living right next door…could end badly. I just don't know for who exactly.

◆ ◆ ◆

The next morning, I find Beckett sitting just outside our apartments eating a doughnut. He offers one to me as I pass, so taking the step below him, I sit and weigh my options. This is the third time he's tried to offer me food and I still owe him for that chocolate bar. When he insists it'll just go to waste, I make an exception to enjoy the jelly-filled goodness I didn't pay for while he sips his coffee.

"Work?"

Mouth busy chewing, I nod. "You?"

"I go in later. Marc and Coty had some paperwork so they left earlier." I take a sip of water, watching him closely. "Where *do* you work anyway?"

I point to the logo on my shirt.

Laughing, he says, "I never even noticed. Do you like it there?"

I shrug. "I like the tips. Lots of drama lately though."

After regaling me with some work stories of his own, my cell rings with another UNKNOWN caller and I ignore it just like the others, wishing they'd take the hint already.

"Lover boy?"

"Nope." I shake my head, twisting my hair into a ballerina bun then adjust my visor over my eyes. With the temperature spiking again today, I'll need my long hair off my body.

"What's going on with Coty?"

"You tell me, he's your boy."

Beckett studies me for a minute, his crystal-clear blue eyes looking for something. Something I'm sure he won't find.

"You need to be careful with him."

I scoff. *What the hell does that mean?* "In case you haven't noticed, I'm trying to keep as much distance as this six-foot hallway will allow. I live next door, that doesn't mean I'm up for grabs. You guys need to be careful, how about that? Just because a woman is within reach doesn't mean you have a right to touch." I stand, descending the stairs in a huff.

"Angela."

I stop, surprised he's using my actual name and not his usual nickname for me.

"I mean it. I've never seen him like this. He's all over the place ever since you showed up. If you are serious about that fucking nerd-twat, then you need to make that clear to Coty."

Sarcasm laces my every syllable. "I'll get right on that."

Choosing between my stepbrother and a guy I barely know. *Yeah, right.*

"Are you two serious?"

I shake my head at his question, at this conversation, at the entire situation.

"I gotta go."

"Just give him a chance then."

"Bye, Beckett."

CHAPTER 14

Angela

ANOTHER CRAPPY SUNDAY. THIRD ONE IN A ROW TO BE exact. An hour into my shift I was told to go home—by Joe. He's back from vacation along with the unease his presence brings. It was busy but he still sent me away, making me question what I did to earn his sudden spite. The uncertainty turns to irritation and I drive away fuming.

Halfway home, my phone rings but this time I answer it without even checking the screen.

"Where have you been?" My mom's screech fills me with immediate regret. *Why did I choose today of all days to pick up?*

"What are you talking about?"

"You think because you move out you don't have any responsibilities here anymore?"

Yes. "And what responsibilities are those?"

"Rent!"

I bark out a disbelieving laugh. "You've got to be kidding me. I pay rent where I live, which is at my apartment, away from you."

"I raised you, you ungrateful bitch!"

"Yeah, thanks for that, but I don't owe you anything. I let you keep the child support check even though you technically aren't supporting me anymore. That's more than enough."

"All you've ever done is take, take, take. Take my money, take all the food, take up space in every place I've ever scored us, you name it. Now that you're out from under my roof you think you're off the hook repaying me? I've been paying your way for years! It's time you return the favor."

Favor? Is she serious? I can't believe the crap she's spewing. I was wondering what kind of bullshit she'd pull next but I had no idea she was busy spinning out of control trying to come up with what she could hold over my head. What she could use against me. And the best she could think of was my childhood? It shouldn't shock me that she's kept tabs over the years but I never thought she'd throw it in my face as an actual debt. She's reaching, even for her. She probably knows it, too, but it's the only leg she's got to stand on so she's going with it.

I'm not though.

"You're un-fucking-believable, you know that?"

"Watch your mouth! You're still my daughter."

Don't remind me.

"That's right," I sigh. "I am your daughter. A child you didn't have to have, I know. You should've aborted me like you've told me a thousand times. For whatever reason you didn't though and here I am. Tell me how much the abortion would've been and I'll pay you that amount. Will that make things right between us?" Since not going through with it is the biggest regret of her life apparently, maybe the price tag for my birth will help her come to terms with her choice once and for all. "After that, I won't owe you anything, anymore."

I hate the tears that form so I blink them away, not ready to give in yet.

"Well, it'll help but it won't be enough. I've been carrying you for eighteen years. That's a hell of a lot more than you're offering. I gave you *life* after all."

A sob rips through me before I can stop it. "Then come and take it back!"

Hanging up, I toss my phone in the cupholder, then slam my hand down on the steering wheel. I let her get to me. I let her win.

Fuck.

She got me to lose control when I've worked tirelessly not to. It's a lonely place living without power and my mother thrives from having company. She welcomes the once composed into pure hysteria with open arms. She's been pushing my entire life to get me into her manic world. I've always been able to stay calm and wait out the worst of it, knowing there were no alternatives. I didn't have anywhere else to go, unlike my sister. I'd be just as unwanted with my father as I was with Rianne, and at least I already knew that evil. Better the devil you know than the one you don't, right?

I make my way into my apartment on auto pilot without any recollection of even getting here. Trying to rein in my emotions is like separating each one into a different jar. It must be done carefully, taking complete concentration.

With a deep inhale, I glance around the small space. I finally have something that puts me out of her reach, making this studio the most sacred thing in my life.

The crap at Hot Spots and now the drama next door has been chipping away at my façade for weeks without me even realizing it. She caught me in a moment of weakness and I won't let it happen again. I can't.

I'll rebuild what's been damaged and make myself stronger. I can be strong. I will be strong. I am strong.

◆ ◆ ◆

Groggy after being woken from a nap, I drag myself out of bed to answer my door. I'm not even surprised when I find Coty on the other side. I figured he'd come looking for an explanation for yesterday's disappearing act. I didn't expect him to show up bearing gifts though. He holds up plates full of the best food known to man—taco truck beef tacos. It's too good of an offering to send him away and judging by his smug grin he knows it.

"Are you hungry?" *Well, now I am.* "I thought I'd bring dinner to you since you won't let me take you out."

I give him a once-over and, of course, he looks good. A white tank that shows his sexy tattoos with relaxed athletic shorts. He has sneakers on though foregoing his preferred barefoot look.

I open the door wider as an answer.

"You just wake up or something?" He points at my hair when I scowl, explaining, "Bed head."

Indignantly, I continue past him to check myself in the bathroom. Seeing he's right, I unwrap my tight bun, letting my hair fall loosely around me. It's one of the rare occasions it's actually holding a curl and I ignore the frizzy pieces tickling my face to rejoin him.

"If you think this is bad, you should see my sex hair."

He just stares at me as I accept one of the plates. I thought it was a good joke. Not my best, but I'm working at half speed still. I'll try again when I'm fully awake.

He clears his throat to suggest eating outside to which I agree instantly since the only other place to sit is my bed and that's just not happening.

I don't bother showing him around since it's literally one room, so we head out on the balcony to dig through our food.

"Did you get any limes?" Pretty sure the first rule in eating taco truck fare is one must have an abundance of limes. It's downright sacrilegious otherwise.

Thankfully, Coty pulls out a takeout container with six lime wedges.

I look up at him blankly.

"What?"

"Where are yours?"

He laughs. "We can't share these?"

At my incredulous look he hands them over, wisely choosing to go without.

Coty breaks the comfortable silence after a while.

"How are you? I thought you'd still be working."

I wince, ignoring his question. "So did I. I'm not sure what's going on."

"Hey, I'm sorry about last night if I made you uncomfortable. You said you just want to be friendly, then I pressed the issue when

I shouldn't have. We like having you as a neighbor and I'm happy to be friends with you. I don't want you to feel like you have to avoid us." He smiles sheepishly. "Or me specifically."

I shrug a bare shoulder. "That's reasonable. I like living here, too." *More than you know.* "I just don't want there to be any weirdness."

"Zero weirdness," he agrees.

"You won't do your caveman routine?"

He puffs out a breath. "I'll try my best, neighbor girl." He winks, and I act like it wasn't forced.

I thank him for dinner, then shift to my back, soaking up the last rays the sun is offering up for the day.

After a few minutes, I crack an eye to find Coty biting his lip, looking at the sliver of stomach peeking out between my white cut-off shorts and off-the-shoulder striped shirt. I pull my shirt down, watching as his eyes cut to mine. *Busted.*

He stretches out next to me on his side with his head propped up.

I close my eyes again.

"Tell me something."

I hear him roll to his back. "Like what?"

"Anything you want, friend."

He chuckles, but doesn't indulge me right away.

At his prolonged silence, I open my eyes. His head is turned my way while he gazes over at me. I couldn't look away if I tried, so I greedily take my fill of his saccharine eyes.

As soon as he speaks, I'm mesmerized by his relaxed voice. The calm cadence of his words soothes me in a way I didn't realize I was craving. I never want him to stop. I tell him so and he obliges.

He tells me about his childhood. His school and the picture-perfect student he was even while riding dirt bikes like a hellion every weekend. He tells me about his job. He loves it but wants more. Something to give him more purpose.

He's just getting to romantic relationships when Beckett yells from the parking lot.

We both sit up to find Beckett, Marc, and some girl standing next to the motorcycles. The guys are wearing their jackets with jeans but the girl is wearing tiny shorts and a tight tank top. Judging by the cheesy smile Beckett's wearing, he's more than happy with her attire. She's putting on Beckett's spare helmet and it reminds me of the time I wore it.

I tilt my face down on my knees watching them.

"You in or what?"

Coty shakes his head, loosely wrapping his arms around his folded legs. "Not tonight."

My heart warms. He's ditching his friends. For me?

They look to me.

"Hey, neighbor girl."

"Hello again." To Coty I say, "You should go. I don't want you to miss out on your special Sunday night ride."

"Will you go, too?"

I shake my head. If we're going to be friends, I can't ride with him. It's too enticing. He's too enticing. The physical contact, however ordinary they try to make it seem, clouds my judgement.

Without taking his eyes from mine, Coty calls out, "Have fun without me, boys."

They, including Coty, do their usual "ride it" chant and then we listen as the bikes take off before I move to stand.

Coty looks up, curious.

"It's uncomfortable out here."

"So uncomfortable." He chuckles. "I didn't want to say anything."

I grab his hands to help him stand but once he's up, he doesn't let go immediately. When I try to pull away, he unfairly uses his superior strength, gently bringing me forward again.

"Are you okay? You're always beautiful but today you look... tired."

Just what every woman wants to hear. "You woke me from a nap."

He runs his hands up my wrists, then to my elbows, warming my skin.

"That's not what I meant," he says softly.

I quirk an eyebrow. The truth is I am tired. I'm tired of living this life that wasn't meant to be. I can't escape my mother's abuse even being out from under her thumb. I'm tired of fighting to control the constant emotions working their way out. I'm tired of having to watch my every move. The rigged game that is my life has left me worn out and reeling. I'm tired of having to justify a life that I haven't even been allowed to fully live yet.

That's what goes through my mind when I reach up and kiss Coty on the cheek. Inhaling sharply, he presses his cheek closer.

"I could use a friend."

"You got one." His eyes flick between mine. "Let's go to my place. It's empty and has lots of seating. And a TV."

"Hey." I smack his arm.

"I mean it does though. You can pick a movie and I'll make popcorn."

Well, when he puts it like that.

I choose a comedy that I haven't seen before but Coty swears will be my new favorite. Doubtful, considering I fall asleep halfway through.

I wake up to Coty holding me under my knees and shoulders. Too tired to argue, I snuggle in closer as he takes me back to my apartment, mindful not to bang my head against any doorways. Marc holds their door for us to pass through, then Beckett's at mine, unlocking it with my keys I brought over. He pushes it open for us then disappears from sight.

Coty lays me down gently, tucking me into my bed.

"Goodnight, Angela."

He presses a sweet kiss to my hair, but I'm fast asleep before I can even thank him.

What feels like only a short time later there's knocking. Or tapping. No, definitely knocking. Incessant knocking. Knocking I wish would go away. Instead it grows louder. More demanding.

I peel my eyes open to realize the sound is coming from my door.

Thinking it's Coty again, I throw it open only to find the space empty.

Maybe it was a dream?

Footsteps on the stairs catch my less-than-alert attention and I croak out, "Hello?"

The footsteps halt.

I hesitate, listening, but nothing happens. With my heartbeat in my ears, nearly blocking out all other sound, I shut my door, locking the deadbolt. If it was Coty, he would've said something, anything, and he sure as hell wouldn't have been going down the stairs at—I glance at the clock—one o'clock in the morning. None of the guys next door would've.

I grab my phone, twisting it between my hands. Who could I even call? I don't want to wake Drew. By the time he'd drive over here, the person could be gone—hopefully. And I don't have the neighbors' numbers. *Shit.* I'm seriously rethinking not having a social media account right now. Don't those have alerts like texts do?

Over at the window, I look outside, hoping to catch whoever it was coming out of the stairwell. When nobody emerges, I check around the parking lot. Living in apartments though, there's no telling which cars belong and which ones don't. Just as I'm about to look away I see taillights pulling out of the entrance. I can't tell the make and model from here but one thing's for sure, it's a truck.

CHAPTER 15

Angela

"HEY, NEIGHBOR GIRL," BECKETT SINGSONGS FROM their back balcony. "Have fun at school today. Make sure you learn something new." He laughs when I flip him off without even turning to face him.

I continue walking all the while ignoring their commentary like I've done every other day this week they've done this. Ever since falling asleep on their couch, there's been a companionable understanding between us. It's been friendly, pleasant even, and they've chosen to celebrate our newfound friendship with an embarrassing send-off each morning.

Although I'd never admit it, I look forward to our new routine. The boys have such a laidback dynamic that it's easy to get swept up in their easy ways. Plus, they make me laugh which is always a bonus, even if most of Beckett's jokes are dirty.

Peeking up at them, I notice he has one of his signature bike shirts that offers up a double entendre, this one saying *Put The Fun Between Your Legs*. He's donning work pants and a backward Seahawks hat. He's adorable. And mischievous. Always mischievous, that one. He's leaning his forearms over the railing, looking over at the school entrance. He's just as protective as Coty, I've noticed, but is more selective as to when he lets it show. He has more restraint. When he's not drunk anyway.

Coty, however, has the subtlety of a caveman banging his club over your head. I watch his eyes scour the other students before landing back on me. I smile shyly at being caught watching him. He knows the effect he has though and smiles back brightly. He's wearing a crisp, white button up shirt today with the sleeves rolled up. His hair is styled like he gave it the old college try but then said 'screw it' making it look naturally mussed. He's leaning back in one of the patio chairs with his ankles crossed on the table. His slightly distressed jeans counteract the nice shirt just enough to give him a bad-boy-who-also-means-business look. That man is yummy on a bad day and today he's downright delectable.

I trip over my own foot, producing a round of laughter from above.

A pajama bottom clad Marc silently watches the whole thing but joins in when I stick my middle finger higher for the whole group. My bratty attitude only intensifies their amusement.

After saying our goodbyes, I study my shoes as they clap across the pavement the rest of the way. The entire student body is busy thrusting their yearbooks in people's faces in hopes of getting some profound accolade they assume someone's been thinking about them but never shared due to lack of opportunity. *Eye. Roll.* I skipped out on that tradition along with the class ring. I enjoy the freedom to buy things for myself but normally only out of necessity. My two exceptions to this rule being sneakers and sugary treats.

Ever since freshman year when some asshole pointed out I had holes in my shoes, I've made it a point to never get caught in ragged footwear again. They'd been my only pair of shoes for two years in a row—even after my feet had outgrown them by a size and a half. I used a toothbrush with bleach on them every night to give the illusion they were new despite them causing painful cramps and blisters daily. When my toes finally cut through the tops, having nowhere else to go, there was no way for me to cover what they were any longer. It was humiliating to have it pointed out by another person though. It's one thing if it's something out of my control but I tried really hard to make the best out of that particular situation.

My mother refused to take me shopping for school clothes, blaming my old ones not fitting anymore on me by saying I was *"getting fat thanks to my nonstop eating."* A teenage girl going through puberty with a below average appetite from stress and lack of food available? *What an inconvenience I must've been.*

As for the sweets, well, that's obvious—they're delicious. I would spend my last dollar on a cupcake liner full of sugar topped with frosting. That's just good sense.

◆ ◆ ◆

It's not until I park next to Joe's F-250 later that I realize I forgot to grab a hat for work. *Great.*

I hop out, quickly clocking in. Joe stops me on my way to the dryer though and asks me to stay late to wash the bay windows. Groaning inwardly, I agree. Washing the windows is a bitch. It's done after hours, meaning you don't earn any tips, and takes forever. The employees take turns doing it each night. I haven't had to for a while so it's not that surprising, but I still don't like it. Especially since that puts me here alone with Joe. I shiver at that thought.

Just as a tiny hatchback rolls through, I hear Joe call my name over the dryers. A thumb over his shoulder, he shouts, "someone's asking for you out back," then takes over for me.

It's unusual for somebody to request me specifically but Drew's done it before when he's stopped by randomly. Which is why I'm even more surprised to find Beckett's large Tahoe idling on the track.

I smile as I grab the spray gun, starting at the front grill. It's not that dirty so I quickly hose it down then move up to wet the windshield. That's when I realize it's not Beckett looking back at me, it's Coty. And he looks like the Cheshire Cat as soon as I notice him. Fighting a smile, I continue spraying, moving around to the passenger side as I go. I round to the back, soaking the entire SUV then reach over to activate the track. By the time the rollers make it to the tires, I've already hosed down the side, and am finishing up at the front fender.

I place the spray wand back in its holder but when I twist back around, I almost collide with the now open driver's door. Before I can jump back, Coty darts his arms out, yanking me inside by my waist. I awkwardly land on his lap with an oomph. He closes the door just as the Tahoe begins rolling forward on the belt.

A look behind us reveals nobody's waiting to be helped. Thankfully.

I reach for the handle but Coty blocks me with his hand. *This can't be happening.* If my boss sees this, he'll either fire me or expect the same treatment and I honestly don't know which is worse.

Next, scrambling for the center console, Coty thwarts my attempt by wrapping an arm around my middle effectively gluing me to his lap. The side sprayers kick on, hiding us from view under the constant stream of water.

Barking out a humorless laugh, I lean forward so I can look at him. There's no way he could've managed this in his Camaro. He knew what he was doing when he brought Beckett's ride.

Although his outfit is still impeccable, he now has an all-black hat, slightly crooked, over his previously styled hair. The bad boy side that was merely peeking through before is currently in full view. He's wearing an unapologetic smirk and damn if I don't feel like making him sorry.

"What do you think you're doing?"

He counters my question with one of his own. "Guess who I just ran into?"

I shrug, having no idea who we could possibly have in common.

"Your boy Drew." Coty leans forward, lowering his hands on my hips, making it difficult to concentrate. "And his girlfriend."

Who? Wait, what?

"Yeah, funny story. He was all over some blonde chick and when I got in his face—you know, to defend your honor—she jumped in to explain the situation. That your *friend* Drew is her boyfriend and that you two have never even dated. Dude wasn't very forthcoming but he agreed with everything she said." He waits a beat then accuses, "You lied to me."

A harsh laugh escapes me as I shake my head, feeling my fishtail braid brush the glass from the movement.

"I never said he was my boyfriend. I went along with insinuations you guys made all on your own. I didn't disagree when you made the stupid assumptions, yeah, but I never lied. I moved in next to three grown men who party, ride motorcycles, and are always in my business. What the hell did you expect me to do? Wave a red flag in front of myself saying 'easy target here'? I don't think so."

I study the rainbow soap coating the windshield. The incredibly fruity aroma with a distinct chemical undertone—a smell I should be accustomed to, but the fresh air usually helps to cut the detergent's strength down significantly—now threatens to overwhelm my senses.

Coty crowds my back with his muscular chest, surrounding me. His signature scent overpowers the soap, helping me to easily drown in him instead.

"Bullshit. You wanted to make me jealous."

I close my eyes, trying to trick my mind into thinking this isn't really happening. Not here. Not now. "Why would you be jealous, Coty? I thought we were friends." We were totally nailing that whole friend thing by the way.

"You know why."

Fine, maybe we weren't nailing the whole friend thing after all.

"What's your plan here? To make me pay for some lie you think I fed you? You have less than a minute…" I cock my eyebrow in the rearview mirror, letting that thought sink in.

"Babe, I'd close this whole fucking place down if I wanted to teach you a lesson." I could call his bluff but I'm not out of moves yet. "Go for a ride with me."

His breath fans across my neck, producing goose bumps. Everywhere.

"No."

Coty stomps on the brake just as the mitter curtain covers the entire front end, darkening the inside of the car. The tire goes over the roller, activating the alarm. The alarm is meant to stop an accident from happening if cars on the belt at the same time are close together and one jumps a roller. It shuts down the entire conveyor belt until someone can clear it for restart. He essentially just bought himself a couple more minutes, at least.

He's smart, I'll give him that.

His hands glide lower, causing me to wiggle with an ache that's settled between my legs. He pushes down on my bare thighs, groaning for me to stop moving.

"Come for a ride with me. Please," he murmurs again, this time against my cheek. He's now wrapped around my entire back until I don't know where I end and he begins. His touch is too much and not enough all at the same time, and I fight the urge to beg, shamelessly, for more. Or less. Anything to make this needy ache go away. He's everywhere but where I don't want to need him. His spicy coconut musk surrounds me much like the foam still surrounding the vehicle and I can barely function at this point.

"Why?"

"I want to show you something," he pleads. Massaging my inner thighs brings me in even harder on his erection. *At least I'm not the only one affected by this grinding.*

Friendsville made for a nice rest stop and all, but it looks like we're back on the road to something much, much more intimate.

I'm damn near panting as I try to clench my thighs together, however the steering wheel in the way forces my legs to stay spread apart. I scoot forward, anything to get some control back—if I ever had any to begin with—but Coty holds me firmly in place. I shift again because he's right *there* and it's taking everything in me not to start this ride he keeps asking for here and now.

"Stop. Moving."

BOBI ANDONOV's voice drifts through the car speakers, the alarm still blaring outside.

"I'm not going to have sex with you," I rasp out, not even convincing myself.

His snicker comes out somewhat strained as well. "Who said I want to have sex with you?"

Fingertips dance across my thighs, igniting a fire that I know can burn him, too. I roll my hips achingly slow once on his lap, barely stopping when my whole body is dying to repeat the movement. We both groan at the friction. The sound alone has me dying to rub on him like a cat in heat but somehow, I manage to remember my original point.

I turn my head to the side, and lips against his, I ask, "You don't?"

"Brat."

"I've been called worse." I shrug lightly.

His eyes bounce between mine. "By who?"

Cupping my jaw with his hand, he prevents me from turning away. Softly stroking my cheek, he closes his eyes then I feel his tongue ever-so-gently lick my top lip. It's such a sweet gesture, almost like he's asking for permission. My moan being the only sign he needs, he seals his lips to mine. The contact is thrilling yet unnerving all at once. The car wash is forgotten, the boundaries I've been setting all along are forgotten, hell, I'm pretty sure my own name is forgotten in that twinkling of time.

Tilting his head for better access, the alarm shuts off and the Tahoe jerks forward again. The sudden movement breaks both the kiss and the moment. I fly forward, trying to clear the fog Coty's enveloped me in.

The final rinse showers the Tahoe from all angles, ridding the colorful foam along with the barrier it provided.

Coty doesn't get the memo regarding space, however, as he runs his hand up my spine all the way to my hairline, then gently grips the back of my neck. He caresses the spot below my ear, pleading, "Say you'll come with me."

Afraid to use my voice, I nod.

Once the driver's door clears the nozzles, I step out. I don't know where Joe is but I don't want him to see me on a customer's lap. I won't risk losing this job even if Coty is more than just some customer. I'll use the alarm as an excuse for my absence, should he bother asking.

Skirting around the dryers, I'm relieved to find my station Joe-free. The alarm should've kept him plenty busy. No business wants a lawsuit on their hands, not even a mismanaged one like Hot Spots.

Towels in hand, I dry the Tahoe off, feeling the weight of Coty's gaze the entire time. Saving his door for last like usual has my stomach in knots though. *What if he tries to tip me?* That alone would dirty something that already feels pretty damn risky.

When I'm done wiping the doorjamb, I see him reach in the back. Swiftly, I move to close the door when he catches it, presenting a takeout bag—not money.

"I brought you dinner. That's what I was doing when I saw Drew and his girl. That was my plan from the beginning. I was going to bring you food for your break, that's all." He smiles, hands up in innocence. "I swear I didn't have any ulterior motives."

"You don't need to buy me anything. I can pay for my own food." I toss the towels in the hamper.

"Just take it. I already ate mine and it'll go bad before the others get home."

I purse my lips. His excuse is flimsy at best, but he did go through the trouble of getting me dinner, knowing I had to work.

On a sigh, I take the bag. "Thank you."

"No problem. Where's your hat today? Don't you usually wear one?"

He takes his off, tossing it to me when I explain I forgot mine. I catch it easily but his eyes harden at something over my shoulder the next minute, then he's pulling out.

Careful of my helix piercing, I put the hat over my head, pulling my braid through the back. Turning around, I jolt finding Joe a few feet away, arms crossed, eyes narrowed. *How long has he been there?*

I bypass him, hoping to skirt by without incident. Joe's been so unpredictable lately. Luckily, he lets me go unbothered. I chance a look back from inside only to find Joe still staring after Coty.

I hear the dryers come on, so I hurry to drop off my dinner before I miss the car and the chance for a tip. Luckily, Joe's gone when I return.

I'll have to stay alert tonight. If there's one thing I learned from my mother, it's to never be an easy target. Judging from Joe's lazy authority, his aim probably isn't very good anyway but you never know. Even lightning can strike twice.

Just a little bit longer.

CHAPTER 16

Coty

I LOOK THAT FUCKER RIGHT IN THE EYE BEFORE LEAVING.
I see you, asshole.

As soon as he walked up to my window, I knew I recognized him. I just wasn't sure from where exactly. It wasn't until I asked for Angela and he started acting cagey as fuck that it hit me. He's the guy I've seen cruising through Creekwood. More than once, too.

Maybe it's work-related. Some car wash emergency.

Yeah. Right.

No, dude looks like a real piece of work. I've been to this car wash a few times over the years and it's never been short on hot, young girls as employees. It's not hard to guess he uses his bogus authority to his advantage.

I'll put an end to that shit if I see him creepin' again though. I doubt Angela even knows he's been pulling drive-bys right outside her open windows at night.

Jumping on the highway, I take the long way back to the shop.

I'm so wired right now, I need the extra time to work out some of this energy.

Damn, that girl is fiery.

She set my whole body ablaze in less than five minutes. I haven't felt anything like that in a long time, if ever.

She pushes me every step of the way, refusing to give in and fuck if it doesn't make me want to fight that much harder. I don't want her to give in though. That's who she is. Who she needs to be for whatever reason. I'm not trying to break her. No, I'm trying to bow with her. She's got to realize she can bend without snapping first though.

My mind flashes to having her on my bike. She was molded to me like a second skin and I loved every minute of it. When we tore around that hairpin, she let me take over, trusting me to guide us safely through the curve. It was beautiful. I worried she would fight for control like she's been doing since I met her. When she didn't, it was like taking a hit of the most potent drug. *Addictive.* Getting her to let go, even for a second, was heady shit.

For her, letting go means giving someone else power. She's made it obvious she's not letting that power go either, no matter how small it might be. Angela keeps everything in her life wrapped up tight to ensure that power can't be taken, so for her to hand me a small piece for those few moments meant something. Something significant.

She just needs to learn it's okay not being so headstrong all the time, and I want to be the one to teach her. Show her what it's like to let loose a little. Explain she's worthy of more than just existing. Prove that life can be more than working to just work some more.

I'm not gonna lie, seeing her come close to losing her shit back there was one of the hottest things I've ever seen. The fact that she kept her head while I was losing mine shows just how much restraint that girl possesses.

Damn.

I had no intention of pulling her inside the car today. I really did just want to drop off some food for her. Getting a good look around her place the other night, I could tell she doesn't cook much. Beck mentioned the way she devours the food he's gotten her to eat, almost like she's not used to having any. She makes it clear that she won't accept a handout, so we've been trying to find excuses to feed her without her taking offense. A fine line to walk, but I think I can manage. Hopefully anyway. So far, it's worked out.

After my meeting, I was near someplace she'd talked about wanting to try, so I stopped off to grab her some dinner. Little did I know I'd be the one ending up ravenous.

My car getting new tires today ended up working in my favor and Beck's SUV gave me just enough room to work up my own appetite.

Angela can get me hard with only a few smart-ass comments, never mind the grinding on my dick she was doing. I adjust myself again, groaning from the stiffness in my jeans.

Drew and his actual girlfriend eating at the same place wasn't what I would call luck, but I'm glad it worked out that way. Once I found out she wasn't really with the dude, I couldn't resist teasing her. She may not have lied about him being her boyfriend, but she knew damn well what she was doing not telling us the truth. I should've known though. When we pushed, she shoved right back, never backing down.

When I pulled her onto my lap, I thought I would give her shit for trying to make me jealous. We haven't been the best neighbors so far, so I understood when she explained why she let us believe she did have a man.

She's had me tangled up since I first saw her. I tried to tell myself to stay away if Drew was in the picture, but then I'd catch sight of her and that effort flew right out the same window I would see her from. I've been going crazy with this friend-zone bullshit. Truth be told, I'd take whatever she's willing to give. I look forward to any interaction I have with the girl. Her smile alone pulls me in and wraps me up like a hard-won victory. She doesn't give them freely, so when she lets one loose it feels like an accomplishment.

Every exchange I have with her is better than the last. I thought riding with her plastered to me was pretty fucking incredible, until I felt her in the pool. It would've been too easy to push against her in that sexy bikini and show my appreciation for her swimwear. I was already so worked up from seeing her swimming that I almost lost it when Tony touched her. Dude pissed me off. She's too good for a loser like him. Fucker deserved the jab he got to the jaw that night when he bragged about the easy access Angela could provide. Not to that asshole. Not to any asshole—if I can help it.

Then today having her so close, breathing her in—strawberries mixed with sunscreen—almost proved to be too irresistible. It took everything in me not to take a bite to see if she's as sweet as she smells.

That kiss though.

That kiss will haunt me. Plain and simple. It was over before it even started and yet I felt more passion in that small taste than I would've thought possible. All that sass could have Angela flaunting her sexuality with pride, instead she tucks it away to wield as a weapon when needed. Funnily enough, I never saw myself as a masochist—until now.

The urge to wait at her door to finish what we started has me getting off at the closest exit.

Sam Tinnesz's "Play With Fire" infuses the interior making me long for open air. *Fuck it.* I'm not going back to work today. I need to ride.

I voice out a text to Beck, asking him to drive my car home. He'll talk shit but whatever. He can kiss my ass. Beckett's always teasing, always picking at weak spots, hoping nobody can turn the spotlight on him, but he's kicked it up a notch since Angela moved in. I swear the dude is trying to rile me up.

I haven't even tried to hide my attraction for her. They see the way I'm drawn to her whenever she's near. Hell, I think we all are. All three of us can admit she's hot.

Even Marc. Oh, I've seen him looking. He's cautious around her like he is with everyone but I've caught him checking her out just the same.

Where Marc feigns indifference, Beck all out plays with her. The thing is he likes to play with every chick. Raised by a single father for most of his life, he thrives off female interaction. He craves it. Any and all. Only on his terms though. He's careful to keep his playful demeanor front and center around the opposite sex. He never keeps them around long enough to see his other personality traits. Hell, he barely lets us see them.

The other night in the hallway he came close to revealing some of his more prominent childhood issues though. At first, I thought Beck hated Drew because he was interested in Angela, but after seeing him almost pummel the guy, I figured it out—Drew reminded Beck of the asshole that stole his mom away from him and his dad when he was ten years old. He doesn't talk about her or the fuckhead she ran off with, but the constant stream of women in his life says enough. He'll never let a woman close enough to do that kind of damage again. Doesn't stop him from basking in their affections though.

With Angela, it's different. Before we even realized it, it was starting to feel like she belonged. And not just with me, but with all of us. While we were busy trying to crack her barriers, she slipped past ours. So, when another man threatened to take her away, memories flared and Beck lost his shit. I can tell it took everything in him not to straight drag the dude. Luckily, his love for hybrid drinks won out and Angela's friend lived to see another day.

Pounding up to the apartment, I pause when a woman passes by, going the opposite direction. She's older, late thirties or early forties, and beautiful. Something about her has me doing a double take. She holds herself with a faux superiority that screams insecurity. She's wearing a black tank with no bra, her nipples almost piercing through the thin shirt. Her short, wavy auburn hair mixed with her provocative shirt makes her appear younger than she is. Her flashy flip-flops slap against the concrete as she makes her way past. She looks up, our eyes connecting for a split second. The color immediately reminds me of Angela's, having just spent time gazing into her stunning hazel eyes. The most mesmerizing eye color I've ever encountered and now I'm seeing it on somebody else.

Ready to ask who she's here for, I frown catching her already crossing the lot to a shiny, red Honda Civic.

I catch a whiff of an unfamiliar scent, floral and nauseatingly strong. It's extremely unpleasant and has me quickening my steps just to avoid it.

There are only three apartments on the top floor of this building: mine, Angela's, and old man Gary's. I think I know exactly who she was here for though. Those eyes were too familiar to ignore. I should know, they've had a starring role in my dreams for weeks now.

In my room, I change into some jeans with the knees blown out and a white tee with my moto jacket thrown over top. Once my boots are laced up, I hurry out to my first true love—my R6.

On my baby while adjusting my helmet, I turn the key and rev the throttle, feeling my bike come to life. I never get tired of this. The loud purr of the exhaust, the rumble of the engine, the wind against my front, floating over the road, feeling untouchable and exposed at the same time. Out of the lot, I ride to the middle of nowhere, ready to lose myself in more ways than one.

I fell in love with riding at a young age when my dad first introduced me to dirt bikes. That was when I was still naïve and didn't know he was only spending time with me to appease his guilt. Back then I thought my mom and dad were happy. In love. How stupid I was.

Eventually I caught on, albeit too late, a fact I feel guilty about to this day. I wish I could've been there for my mom sooner but she chose that life. She chooses it even today. She's always been okay with turning the other way when my father pulls late nights with his students. Always female. Never the same one twice. Always the same story though—they're lacking inspiration and don't know where to find it. Dad, playing the compassionate professor, is always there to lend a hand for the good of the arts.

Right.

Over the years I've begged my mom to see what he's doing. To leave him. I've even offered to help support her just to get her out of there, but she won't. She's too afraid to change what's always been her normal—the only life she's ever known. I thought after the university stepped in with disciplinary action, she would finally be forced to acknowledge his habitual cheating, but no. She's weak.

Not me though. I don't have to sit there, watching that piece of shit make a mockery out of his marriage, out of my mother, out of our family. I've stayed away for years, making it clear if my mother wants to see me she's welcome, as long as she doesn't bring him along. I refuse to be around the guy anymore.

Learning my father was banging his students made me pull away more and more until the dirt bikes became my cherished reality rather than the childish escape they started out as.

I learned to lean on others when I couldn't handle the tension at home. Beckett and Marc were both dealing with their own issues but out there we could leave it all behind. We could be strong. We could be brave. We could push ourselves past the point of fear until we lost all the other worries trying to drag us down. We could laugh, forgetting our home lives had lost humor long ago. We could be young and stupid, ignoring the demand from our families to grow up.

My dad was no longer welcome at the track the second he made the mistake of inviting one of his conquests to pose as a spectator. My mom might've turned a blind eye but I wouldn't. Both my boys backed me when I told Dad and his side-piece to leave, then made me take it out on the track when he listened.

We all used that track as our safe place, our home away from our own dysfunctional homes. It became like a fourth friend. We needed it like we needed each other. Graduating, then moving out, gave us the freedom we'd been desperately seeking on the track. Marc and I got our street bikes first, with Beck following soon after. Dude didn't like being left out. Hell, he still doesn't. Not that I blame him. We're closer to brothers than friends, all of us still having rocky relationships with our own families but not with each other. Never with each other.

Beck at least talks with his father, having only the one parent for most of his life. However, they just keep it all surface, nothing too deep for the Meyers' boys. He and his dad have a close bond, living through what Beck's mom put them through together, but

a strained relationship all the same. They have a mutual understanding, a respect for one another, but they didn't heal together
and I'm not sure they ever will. That woman fucked them both up
when she vanished out of what seemed like thin air. Beck's always
been the most reckless of the three of us. Sometimes I thought
he pushed limits harder than anyone else hoping his mom would
come home if he did something notable, something to make him
worthy. Hell, I even held out hope for a while. She never did
though. *Good riddance.* Except, of course, at night when she returns to him in his dreams. That though, that's a different story.

I pull my front tire into a quick wheelie before coming back
down on both tires, opening her up on the deserted road ahead.
The apple orchards to my left are just showing small bits of color
but aren't quite fragrant enough to smell from here. To my right
are barren hills just begging to be developed.

When I settle down, I want a big chunk of land. Space for
kids, room for my toys, maybe even some crops of my own. The
silty soil makes for good crop-growing in this area. That's what
Marc's father figured out early on and took a huge chance on a
large piece of property. He planted every kind of crop he grew up
around and it paid off. Watermelons, cantaloupe, apples, grapes,
mint, corn, even Washington's beloved cherries. Pumpkins and
squash for the fall. His produce is the most sought after in the
Columbia Basin. He wants Marc to take over one day but that's
never been Marc's plan. Sure, he loved the miles of orchards, but
for different reasons. One being the liberation it provided from the
man who ran it. He would ride anything with an engine as far as
he could to avoid his father's overbearing presence and the sheet
of disappointment that always cloaked their labored relationship.

Cutting between the tightly lined trees over the years on our
dirt bikes, I became fascinated with the colors, the smells, the way
there was a purpose for everything. The exact spacing between
fruit trees, the perimeter of conifer trees used as windbreak to prevent fruit drop, the perfect timing to harvesting the crops. I can't

say it'd be a bad life running a family farm, but I might revolt, too, if it were forced upon me at every turn, especially given his father's heavy-handed approach.

Marc and his father don't talk at all, they yell. They cuss. They even throw blows when things get too heated. They're two hot heads that can't get along long enough to even attempt a civil conversation with each other. Marc's father has always had high expectations for his only son, never willing to let Marc forget that either. The fact that Marc walks his own path pisses his father off immensely. And the fact that it pisses his father off pisses Marc off further making them both royally pissed off most of the time. Marc's mother stays out of it, loving both men equally but separately. Marc's younger sister, Maggie, has never been held to the same standards, being treated like the princess of the family instead. It was tough for Marc constantly being put down for not meeting his father's insane criteria while watching his sister get away with damn near everything. Marc's never taken it out on her though. He knows it's his father causing all the damage and aims his rebellion where he sees fit. Joaquin's sole heir working as a part-time mechanic and semi-present manager is disappointing to say the least, never mind the fact that it's what Marc loves.

Well, working with cars and motorcycles is his passion. Managing people? Not so much. That's why he leaves most managerial obligations to me—like today's meeting.

Beyond the small orchard, I take a wide bend in the road, leaning with my bike then slowly straighten out of the curve.

The meeting was a long time coming. Working at the garage has been great for so long, especially having my best friends there every day, but something's been missing lately. It has for a while. We can all sense it. Like something major needs to happen to wake us up from the complacent life we've come to enjoy. Working, riding, the occasional race to make some side cash, it's starting to feel a bit...ordinary. We've been on this path for years, with no complaints, but what if there's more? I want to see what else there is.

Working under someone else's rules with no room for growth has become downright suffocating. That's why we set up the meeting in the first place. It's the first of many steps in the right direction for where we all agree we want to go.

As for our home life, we've lived together since graduation and it's been a fun ride all on its own. Since Angela moved in next door, the dynamic has shifted. There's an unsettled feeling that wasn't there before. Almost like that's what's been missing. Like *she's* been missing. From my life or ours, I don't know. I do know having her in our apartment—the couple times she ventured over—was peaceful, and when she left it felt like she took something important with her. I wanted nothing more than to keep her where she was the night she passed out on our couch. To keep her where I could ensure she'd be safe from everything and everyone. I ultimately moved her back over to her place knowing she'd be angry for allowing herself to be vulnerable in front of us. Angela doesn't do vulnerable. Her sleeping form in my space was a sight I could get used to though. I wouldn't be surprised if she had a rule to never sleep anywhere save for her own bed. Knowing she felt comfortable enough to sleep there makes me grow all kinds of warm and tingly. I might be breaking through some of her barriers already. And I can't wait to see how much closer she'll let me get.

◆ ◆ ◆

The sun long gone, I meander back toward town since I lost track of time a while ago. I found a few new places for us to try out on our next group ride though.

My earpiece chirps with an incoming call.

Beck.

"Yeah?"

"Still riding?"

"Yup. What's up?"

"I just saw your bike was gone and noticed neighbor girl

wasn't home either. Just seein' if my newly washed truck had something to do with that." I can imagine the shit-eatin' grin he's no doubt wearing.

"She's not home yet?"

It's dark as hell. She never works this late.

Yeah, we all know her schedule at this point. The girl's got us by the balls and doesn't even know it yet.

"I can go check her door to make sure."

Next, I hear a series of knocks that sound suspiciously like the tune of "You Are My Sunshine." *What a tool.*

I wait for his response while steadily increasing my speed. Angela could have a whole life that we don't know about. Hell, we barely know the life she has right next door. The little we've observed and managed to piece together points to her not really having anybody in her life. She walks into school with her head down, refusing to even acknowledge her classmates. She doesn't party, not even with us, which most people her age would jump on. The only person we've seen her with is Drew, but I just saw him tongue deep in his girlfriend.

"Nothin'. Did you get her number yet?"

"No. I didn't really think I'd need it." *Lie.* I tried. Many times, to be exact, but she never gave it up.

"I don't know, man. Maybe she had a school thing. Or maybe she's on a date."

Always talking shit.

"I just saw her a few hours ago. She didn't say anything," I snap.

"Uh huh. Because if there's one thing Angie's known for, it's sharing her business."

Angie? The previous warmth seeps out hearing my friend's latest nickname for her.

"What's that supposed to mean?"

"Listen, I get it, you like her, but you're gonna scare that girl off. You need to take it easy with your approach."

"Are you kidding me? You, of all people, are giving me relationship advice?"

"You in a relationship now?"

Whatever.

"Coming from the guy that has more of a relationship with the toilet than an actual woman."

"We've been over this! I like that toilet. It's the perfect fit for my ass." My lips purse at the corner. "Besides, who the fuck has time to pursue women? They come to me, bro. By the dozen."

I'm about to argue when he speaks again, saying, "Baker's dozen."

Against my will a laugh escapes. Dude never disappoints.

"I'll swing by her work. Maybe she got held up."

"Alright," he sighs.

I click off, speeding toward the last place I saw Angela, hoping she's there as much as I'm hoping she's not.

CHAPTER 17

Angela

EVERY TIME I WASH A WINDOW, HE FINDS ANOTHER excuse for me to clean it again. I've never had to wash the same window twice. Tonight though, Joe has a bug up his ass and is taking it out on me.

Sweat gathers more now that the bay doors are closed, trapping all the stuffy air inside. I toss Coty's hat off to secure my braided ponytail into a bun. I'm bending down low, stretching onto my tiptoes, pushing the squeegee with enough force to ensure there are no water spots, yet it still isn't good enough. I can feel my face growing flushed each time he points out another issue. My stomach growling, Coty's takeout eaten long ago, is the least of my concerns at the moment.

Joe keeps moving around the wash, making it hard to keep watch the entire time, no matter how I angle my body for a better view, while doing a good enough job. I'm trying to get every nonexistent spot so I can get the hell out of here already. It doesn't matter where he is though, I can feel his presence everywhere. I can feel his eyes locked onto my body with each movement I make. I want to believe this isn't what it feels like. If he'd stayed in the office like he's done in the past then I'd be done by now and wouldn't feel like I'm putting on a private show for my depraved boss.

"Looking good in here."

I can't help the scoff that comes out while shaking my head. *Really?*

"I would hope so." I put my hands on my hips, turning to face him. Joe's eyes immediately make the journey from my toes up to my chest. I cross my arms, cutting off his view. "Am I good to go then?"

He nods absently, looking around. When he steps closer, I dodge to the side, trying to escape the corner he's about to get me in. Unfortunately, he shoots his hand out, trying to stop me.

I look down at his suspended hand with as much disdain as I feel. "Joe," I lift my eyes to his, making sure he fucking hears me, "don't."

Joe lifts his face, keeping his eyes locked on mine, then puts both hands up.

"Hey, I was just wondering if you wanted more hours. Boss says to keep you part-time when you graduate but I can change that."

I cock an eyebrow. The owner doesn't even come around enough to know who I am, let alone to dictate how many hours I work. I seriously doubt he said a word about my schedule. No matter what my mother would have me believe, I'm not stupid. I see right through what he's doing here. I just need to play my cards right without giving in to his game while somehow keeping my job.

My clammy hands drag down my thighs. "Full shifts on Sundays again would be nice. Maybe add some mornings with Amity during the week once school is out?"

I drop Amity's name, hoping to distract him. If she's already taking him up on his offer for "more hours" then maybe that'll take, and keep, his focus off me.

His eyes narrow slightly before he quickly covers it with a neutral expression. "Amity is great and all, but she's not cutting it lately. Maybe you can take over all of her shifts?"

I pick up the discarded hat, careful to keep my back away from Joe.

"Sure, whatever works best. We can look at the schedule once school's done."

Hose in one hand, I rinse the squeegee, then drop the used towels in the washer. When I turn back, Joe's wringing out a towel I must've missed. He walks over to throw it in the washer, stopping next to me and tugging on Coty's hat around my wrist.

"Who's the guy? The one that came through earlier. Is he your boyfriend?"

"No." I cringe at the waver in my voice.

His interest on the hat, I try to extract it from his grasp but he yanks it forward abruptly, catching me off guard. I lose my balance from the unexpected change which unfortunately, brings me flush against Joe who wastes no time taking full advantage of the compromising position.

The hold on my wrist tightens while his left hand latches onto my other arm, penning me in. It's just shy of being painful but unwanted just the same. I can simultaneously feel his hot breath on my face that's twisted to the side, his doughy belly against my taut stomach—that's now roiling with acid—and his disgusting erection digging into my outer thigh that feels more like a rival flag pole fighting for leverage. Battling down the bile clawing its way up my throat, I try to step back but Joe holds firm.

"Get off me. Now." I grit out each word, keeping my face cranked.

"You haven't even heard the *arrangement* yet."

My stomach drops out onto the floor, leaving behind an empty shell.

"Hey, Joe, I'm heading out for the night. Do you need me to-"

My head snaps over to the man coming around the corner from detailing. Before I can utter a single word, I'm released harshly, Joe's booming voice masking any sound I might make.

"That's it for now, buddy." He steps forward, blocking my savior from view. "I'll lock up. Have a good night."

I take that as my cue to leave as well and with my bag in hand, I rush out the front door. It's fully dark as I speed walk around the outside of the building.

I'm shaking so bad when I jump in, I don't get my key in the ignition until my third try. Water collects in my eyes but I look up, blinking it back. That asshole doesn't deserve my tears. Checking in the rearview mirror to see the lights from inside, I turn the radio on full blast to silence the thoughts racing through my mind, and peel out of the lot listening to "Middle Finger" by Bohnes.

I don't stop though. I drive until my hands are steady on the steering wheel. I drive until my ears are too full of roaring lyrics to hear my own heartbeat. I drive until I can see through the tears that keep threatening to spill out. I drive until I'm at the gas station the boys took me to on our ride together. I didn't even know where I was driving but somehow I ended up here. Somewhere familiar. Somewhere that reminds me of them. Of him.

Parking, I lay my head against the wheel and take a few minutes to collect myself. Joe's rough touch was so jarring after Coty's attentive caresses. Where my body welcomed Coty's touch before my mind could even catch up, my body all out rejected Joe's without needing my brain at all.

As soon as my feet hit the ground, my stomach heaves and I grip the side of my Jeep as I double over, letting my body do what it needs to. My stomach deprived of food pays off for once and nothing comes out.

"Angela?"

Please no.

A swipe of my mouth, I straighten to find Coty staring directly at me. Helmet off, it's resting on his lap as he straddles his black bike. Worry lines every inch of his face. What the hell is he doing here?

"Yeah?" I ask, irritation clear. I'm over men today, especially the handsy ones.

He's full on scowling but I don't give a shit. I'm drowning over here, trying to keep my head above the tainted water that is my life. I can't worry about his feelings when I'm busy keeping my own at bay.

"Are you okay? I saw you pull in and it looked like-"

"Totally fine, Coty." I cut him off before I'm forced to hear what I look like. I don't need to face what's undoubtedly seeping out of me. Not now. Not in front of him.

He shakes his head, dismounting. I put my hands in the pockets of my shorts—that I fully intend on burning once I'm home, anything to rid myself of Joe's touch—and hold my ground.

Coty comes around the front of my car, propping himself against the top of the tire well. The knees on his jeans are ripped clean out with his motorcycle jacket zipped up to his chin. He crosses his boots and looks over at me, taking in too much as usual. I'm not cowering under his gaze though. Let him see. Let him see that he's not getting in.

Matter-of-factly, he says, "I'm starving."

I can't keep the surprise off my face.

"I've been out riding and it's late. At least keep me company while I eat." He holds out his hand, looking at me with more hope than I deserve.

I reach in to grab my wallet then step past him and his open hand. Relief floods when he lets me pass without so much as a touch.

We go our separate ways once inside, picking out what we each want to eat, then meet at the cash register. I make sure to pay first and grab a table while he pays for his food. I don't have much of an appetite but I want to try to get something down. The acid churning in my stomach needs something to soak it up.

We eat in comfortable silence while I occasionally sneak glances at his choice in food.

"What?"

"Nothing." I half-smile. "I didn't know you liked corn dogs." Then because I can't help it, I say, "Are you twelve?"

I release a laugh I didn't think I was capable of right now.

His eyebrows shoot up at my mood change but he doesn't comment.

"What about you? Since when do oatmeal cookies count as a meal?" He tosses his balled-up napkin at me.

I swat it away, answering truthfully, "Since that's the only thing in the house. If you're lucky."

"Your mom didn't cook?"

I snort. "Definitely not. She barely even bought food, let alone put it together into a meal." I look up, saying, "Unless she was trying to impress a new guy." Even then, I wouldn't consider that exactly cooking. More like forcing two foods that don't belong together into one dish and letting them battle it out.

Coty's eyes search mine.

I clear my throat, cleaning the table. When his hand lands on mine, I yank it away like I've been burned.

"Please," I say to the table, knowing he can hear me, "not tonight."

"Hey." He leans his head to the side, catching my eye. I slowly raise my head, meeting his brown eyes. Open sincerity the only thing I see there, I relax. Slightly. "My mom cooked dinner every night. Still does. No matter what. No matter how long it takes my dad to *tend* to a student, dinner's always on the table. She thinks the monotony masks the unpredictability that comes from having a cheating husband in the house." He pauses, glancing around before meeting my gaze again. "I get it. The destruction a parent can cause."

"He's a teacher?" My voice shakes more than I intend.

"Professor." Coty nods, clearing his wrappers as well. "Poetry in American Literature. Never a lack of females in that class. Dad lost sight of the words and started focusing more on the women writing them."

"And your mom, she knows? And stays with him?"

"To this day. I didn't though. We've always struggled to connect. Him living a slow life full of reading, me wanting a faster pace, we couldn't find a common ground. But his cheating killed any chance of us ever bonding. I lost respect for him a long time ago."

"I'm sorry. I," I shake my head, unsure how much I should say, "never met my dad."

The silence that follows clogs my throat entirely.

Coty surprises me again, saying softly, "His loss." Then, "Ready? You got school tomorrow, right?"

He stands, taking our combined garbage in one scoop. I slide out of the booth and follow him out the door. Returning to my Jeep, Coty reveals two candy bars. *Damn him*, I think ruefully.

We sit on the curb, watching the occasional car pass as we eat our desserts.

"Thank you for that."

"It was selfish really. I just wanted to watch you eat candy again. You eat it like it's the first and last time you've ever tasted chocolate. It's kind of incredible."

My face warms despite the night taking a chilly turn.

"Well, that's embarrassing, but I meant for everything. The takeout from earlier, tonight, this, now. I, uh, I needed it." I stare down at my feet, unwilling to face how much truth that sentence holds, how much I appreciate his generosity, how much I appreciate him. His gentle, yet insistent, approach he somehow knows I need. His admission about his family to take the spotlight off mine. He's perceptive. I knew that from the first time we met but I never thought he'd be able to read me like he does. He picks up on things I'm not even aware of. A fact that both pleases and alarms me. What if I don't want to be seen? The scarier question is, what if I do?

"I don't know what happened in your life," he pauses when I shift, "or tonight. And I'm not asking, Angela. Okay? I just…I want you to know I'm here. I'm here whenever you're ready to talk. About anything."

He nudges my shoulder with his.

"What if I'm never ready?" I whisper.

"Well," he blows out a breath, "I signed a contract with Creekwood, so technically I'll still be here."

I bark out a laugh, marveling at how it can feel so good at such a bad time.

"Seriously though, I'll be here. Remember what I told you?"

He stands, offering his hands to help me up. I give him one and mostly do it myself.

"You say a lot of stuff. How am I supposed to remember everything that comes out of that pretty face?"

Coty doesn't release my hand as he guides me to the driver's side. He spins around to face me. Without thought, I step back, rocking on my heels.

"Pretty, huh?"

"That's all you heard? Figures."

A charming smile splits said face. I gently pull my hand from his.

"I told you I wouldn't let you fall. I got you."

"You don't even know me."

"Then let me," he counters. "Let me get to know you." He steps closer and slowly, ever so slowly, brings his hands up to frame my face. The intensity in his eyes holds me captive as his boots brush my shell toes. "I want to know everything about you, babe, but I'll settle for whatever you're willing to give me."

I don't realize I'm crying until I feel Coty wipe a stray tear away with his thumb. The realization sends me reeling. Coty, however, senses my withdrawal and leans forward, resting his forehead against mine.

I close my eyes, willing the others not to follow their predecessors.

"Are you still going riding with me?"

I shake my head which only makes him laugh.

"Yes, you are. You already promised. I mean you basically dry humped me when I asked so that's as good as a promise in my mind."

My eyes snap open to find him smiling mischievously. He knows just when to lighten the mood. *Jerk.*

His gaze holds mine, leaving the ball in my court, and I take the moment to simply breathe him in. The hint of coconut is slightly washed out from his long ride. Nature, fumes, and unconcealed want—he smells like a man on a mission. He knows where he's going and there are only two options—jump on and enjoy the ride or get the hell out of the way. You only regret the chances you don't take, right?

I bring my hands up to wrap around the back of his neck and gently scratch his hairline behind his ears. His eyes remain open but darken to a dusky brown, almost black. Before I can overthink it, I lean in, closing the distance. As my lips touch his, he hesitates, still leaving the choice up to me. His hands twitch on my cheeks but he doesn't increase pressure. He lets me go at my own pace, not pushing me into anything I'm not ready for. My eyes flutter closed as I press my lips to his in a tender kiss. He groans out his own appreciation, but still, he doesn't move. His lips are the perfect mix of soft and strong. I know he could overtake me at any moment, yet there's something so potent in trusting that he won't.

I pull back to thank him again but Coty beats me to it.

He drops his hands from my face, avoiding my questioning stare.

"Let's get you home."

I return to Creekwood without any music, letting the calm night air fill my senses while reflecting on the unexpected turns this night took. I was close to losing my grip. The grip on why I continue. On why I keep fighting when I'm constantly reminded how easy it would be to give up. I've struggled my whole life to change the course my mother mapped out for me. Tonight felt like one wrong turn too many. Joe's callous treatment had me considering crashing the entire thing just to escape the endless obstacles.

I didn't though. Coty appearing unannounced being a big reason. His presence soothes me as much as it unnerves me. He shouldn't have the effect he does on me, only having known each other for a short time, yet he understands what I need when I need it. I'm sick of fighting the attraction I have to him, but I still need to keep some distance, at least emotionally, since living next door is proving difficult where space is concerned. I never want to leave my happiness, or sanity, in the hands of a man like my mother has spent her life doing. A little fun with Coty without a commitment might help take care of both desires. *Light and easy.* Nothing too deep.

I also need to figure out what to do about Joe. I can't let him catch me like he did again. He may get others to play his sick games but I won't be one of them. No matter what promises he makes, it's not worth selling the only thing I have left—my dignity.

There's no way I can tell Drew what happened. There's no way I can tell anyone about what Joe did. It'd be my word against his and mine already has the stench of my mother's misdeeds attached to it.

If anyone did believe me, they'd expect me to quit, but I can't. Not yet. I need the job at Hot Spots at least until graduation when I have additional availability to offer a new employer.

Just a little longer.

◆ ◆ ◆

I hear Coty enter the lot behind me. He followed me the entire way back, keeping a comfortable distance for my sake more than his I'm sure.

Climbing the stairs, exhaustion from the day settles over me like a harsh current threatening to pull me under.

As my foot reaches the top step, the boys' door flies open, hitting the wall with a metallic clang. Beckett appears in the doorway, arms crossed over his broad chest, eyes narrowed to slits. He'd be intimidating if I didn't already know what a softy he is.

"And where have you been?"

Seriously?

I bypass him and his probing stare, heading straight for my door.

"Hello to you, too."

"You never work this late, so what were you doing?"

He finally unfolds his arms only to adjust his hat, facing it backward. The move strikes me as a nervous tic but that doesn't make any sense. Why would he care whether I was home or not?

The little scruff on his face makes him look utterly adorable—as adorable as a 6'6" man can be—added with his lips turned down and I have to fight the urge to laugh. I pity his future daughters already. And he *will* have daughters. Only the baddest of boys get rewarded with daughters. It's the most surefire way to make them pay for their transgressions. To spend their life trying to protect their daughters from the same indiscretions they themselves committed to others. It's genius, really.

Obviously, my dad chose to skip his penance altogether by ignoring my existence from the start.

"I'm not the only one, you know? We were worried."

His forest green shirt reads *Ride The Beast* and I wonder, not for the first time, if he has a monthly subscription of tacky motorcycle shirts made just for giants like him.

A throat clearing has both our heads turning. Coty, jacket unzipped and hanging open with his helmet propped under an arm, approaches us with eyes glued to his roommate's. Beckett breaks into a grin, bringing his gaze back to me though.

"Looks like you found her after all."

My eyes shift between them, confusion wracking my brain. Apparently, neither feels inclined to elaborate further though because all they do is play a round of The Topic's Lava, refusing to even touch the subject.

"Well, I'm home now. Thanks for the concern?"

A chuckling Beckett leaves, giving us some privacy.

Coty meets me at my door instead of going to his own like I knew he would.

He leans his arms against my doorjamb, taking up the frame like I hoped he would. I peruse his body, from his badass boots up his ripped jeans to the all-black jacket over his plain tee. How does he always make simple outfits look so damn attractive? His lips remind me of our sweet kiss made even sweeter by the candy we'd eaten. I reach his mocha swirl eyes that are already on mine. He was watching me check him out.

He's too tempting and I'm a mess. He's beautiful and I'm defective. I don't want to risk corrupting him which is why I close the door softly after a whispered goodbye.

Light and easy.

He's like a fantasy slowly consuming me while I'm living a nightmare I can't seem to purge. Yet.

I hear a soft, "goodnight, Angela," followed by the distinct click of a door closing across the hall.

Hitting repeat on "Head Above Water" by Avril Lavigne, I jump in the shower, hoping to scrub off today's residue. I scrub my body like a criminal cleaning their crime scene. *No fingerprints left behind.* No trace—visible or otherwise—of Joe's touch to be found, I clean my body again. And again. And again. I scour my skin, wishing a new layer would form in its place with each brush. My vulnerability combined with the vigorous cleansing leaves me feeling raw and exposed.

With scalding water pounding my chest, I lean my head against the wall, breathing through my mouth. The steam coats my throat like the heat steeping my skin. A hiccup escapes followed by another, then another.

I stay there until the water runs cold. Until Joe is no longer a phantom haunting my disinfected form.

My head, however, is a different story.

CHAPTER 18

Angela

P REDICTABLY, THE CAR WASH DOESN'T NEED MY HELP FOR
the next few days, giving me time to look for another job.
After my lengthy shower the other night, a plan began to
form. One where I take matters into my own hands before they
can fall into anyone else's.

Not wanting Coty to know what I'm up to, or why, I've been
going to the library to use the computers. Ever since seeing that
wedding, I look forward to coming here now. I even checked out
some books about ethics in the workplace. Spoiler alert! Hot
Shots is failing—miserably.

Drew calls one day as I'm leaving.

"Where are you? I don't see your car."

"Where are *you*?" My heart jumps to my throat, thinking he's
at the wash.

"At your apartment. I wanted to see if I could talk you into
some Chinese tonight."

"Oh." My pulse steadies. "I'm driving there now. I…had some
errands." It's true. Mostly. "Can we go to my place again?"

Drew groans dramatically. "Last time their sweet and sour
chicken was so dry I almost choked."

We switch between two places in town, each of us favoring
one over the other. Mine has its strengths while his has its chicken.

"But their egg rolls are so much better," I whine.

My plea goes unanswered though.

"Hurry up. I don't want to run into one of your neighbors
again."

"I heard about that," I snicker even though really, it's not that funny. I can only imagine the hell he caught not only from Coty, but his girlfriend afterward. I bet Jamie wasn't thrilled about someone mistaking Drew as another woman's.

"I figured he would tell you. Please tell me you're not hooking up with your neighbor." He laughs incredulously.

I bristle. "I'm not."

"Well, he likes you, so watch out."

"What's not to like? A broke girl with daddy problems *and* mommy issues. That's prime stripper material."

"Over my dead body," he growls, making me laugh.

"The dull new toy next door caught his attention momentarily, that's all. He'll grow tired of playing in the dirt and move on soon."

"That's the dumbest shit I've ever heard."

"Doesn't change the fact that it's true." I shrug even though he can't see me. "I'm about to pull in."

I hang up, parking next to his car. All the boys' cars and bikes are here along with several others, almost filling the lot to capacity. It's Friday night. *Party night.*

I rush into Drew's waiting arms as he leans against his silver beauty. Unable to speak, I press my face into his shoulder, inhaling his fruity musk.

"Are you ready? Or do you need to change first?"

I glance down at my outfit. My ripped-to-shreds skinny jeans hang low on my hips while my thrift store band tee is tied into a knot, showing a slice of belly. I pulled half my hair up into a top knot, leaving the bottom half straight this morning. My skater-style black and white Adidas shoes complete my look.

I scan Drew. I'm underdressed compared to him but that's nothing new. I swear he strolled out of the womb wearing Nantucket reds. His salmon-colored shorts and blue polo could get him onto any golf course in the country. Perfectly styled hair adds a genuinely charming quality that he already has in spades.

I'm so lucky to have him in my life.

He sees me smiling and returns the gesture. "What?"

"Nothing. Can we go now? If you can stand to be seen with me that is." I beam, wondering how many more times we'll be able to do this.

He catches me up on all the things. From his girlfriend to his dad. I've never had a close relationship with Drew's dad but I've never had a problem with him either. Drew works with him at some fancy building. I'm not exactly sure what they do, but I know they work hard and love their jobs. Even though I'd never admit it to Drew, I've always found it to be inspiring, their situation. Working closely with someone you love and still wanting to show up day in and day out. It can't be easy, yet Drew and his dad, Robert, make it look like a cake walk.

I grudgingly drive us to his restaurant of choice. As usual, it's not busy. Must be why their chicken tastes so good—less customers means more attention to fried poultry.

Conversation doesn't flow as smoothly as usual and I feel myself holding back on certain topics now, whereas before I was always an open book with him. I steer away from anything neighbor related, just telling him bits and pieces about my apartment life. I avoid work talk altogether, fearing I'll spill the truth about what's really going on. I'll tell him about Joe. Just not today. Or tomorrow. Okay, I don't know when I'll tell him, but I will—eventually.

I hate hiding things from him but it's for both of us. His relationship with Jamie is getting more serious by the day. I'm finding my way on my own. Slowly. I still love Drew like a brother and want him in my life; I'm just trimming some of the strings that've been tying us together for so long.

Afterward, we're met with a full parking lot when we return to Creekwood. Unable to find a spot, Drew offers up his, preventing him from coming up. We say our goodbyes and I park in his space once he leaves.

People are everywhere. Packed onto the guys' balcony. Huddled on the stairs. Some even loiter near the cars. How do the other residents not care? What about the manager? I seriously want to know what kind of deal the guys have with her that she turns a blind eye to this. She lives on the property so she has to hear at least some of this. Creekwood is broken up into three sections forming a broken U shape with the pool in the middle. Hers is in one of the outer buildings while ours is in the central hub.

A pack of guys descends the stairs as I approach. Unease slows my steps. I contemplate going the long way around to the back staircase, the one leading to the pool, but the lights there are constantly burning out, so I pull my shoulders back, walking around them as they fill the sidewalk. A few turn my way and one lets out a low, appreciative whistle. Keeping my head forward, I shoot my eyes over to the group, gauging their proximity.

"Hands off. Shit, eyes off, too."

Everyone, including me, looks up to see Coty staring down from their front balcony.

"She yours?" the whistler, I think, asks.

Coty opens his mouth to answer but I beat him to it with, "I'm nobody's," then frown realizing there's more truth to that than anything I've ever said.

All eyes return to me. I keep mine on Coty though, wishing he'd see what I'm too nervous to tell him. His eyebrows dip but rapid movement to my right causes me to break our connection. I swing my back to the wall, facing the guy—again the whistler—as he advances.

"I'm Jason."

His hand hangs between us. I glance from it to his face, letting the moment stretch until it's awkward, for him anyway. I personally don't mind. I don't want to touch him. Plus, you can tell a lot by watching someone, especially when they're uncomfortable.

I nod, then move to signal I'm leaving.

"Aww, it's like that? No name for the beautiful girl?" he teases. Before I can see it, he reaches out, hooking a finger into one of the shredded slivers in my jeans.

I yank my leg out away from his obnoxious touch, scolding, "What the hell was that?"

"Leave her alone, J." I hear Beckett warn above our heads but I don't dare look away from Jason in front of me or the group behind him in my peripheral.

"Aww, come on. I'm just having some fun. Why does it matter?"

The whining is annoying. If I didn't already find him unattractive, I definitely would now.

Beckett's chuckle comes out sinister. "You'll see."

Then Coty is there causing everything—maybe even time—to freeze. He glances over to me with an unreadable expression before posting up in front of Jason, hands clenched at his sides.

"What the fuck don't you get about 'hands off'?"

Jason shifts, his eyes darting past Coty's shoulder. Coty moves his head, blocking his view.

"She said she wasn't yours. She's free game then, right?" The crack in his voice gives away his nervousness. What he says next reveals his stupidity. "I was just going to offer her a drink. I thought we could go for a dip out back. Maybe the naked variety." He laughs, looking to his boys who are watching with mounting apprehension as Jason blunders full speed ahead, completely oblivious.

Without warning, Coty's fist connects with Jason's nose, resulting in a sickening crunch my own sinuses feel. In a blur of motion, Coty lunges at Jason, aiming for a second hit, but everyone jumps into action, separating the two. Jason doubles over, howling in pain as his nose bleeds uncontrollably.

"You're done. Don't show here again."

"What the fuck, man? What's so fucking great about her anyway?"

Beckett calls down, "Yo, J, you heard him. You're out."

Jason throws his hands up, letting the blood flow freely. "First Tony, now me? You're choosing this skank over your boys? Pussy better be fucking good if you're going through this much trouble."

Eyes widening, I open my mouth to tell this loser off but Coty lands another punch, this one across the jaw. Jason falls backward, ass meeting concrete in an almost comical slow-motion feat. Luckily for him, he stays there.

"Get the fuck out of here and don't come back. I see you near her again and you'll be cut from the races, too."

My eyebrows lurch.

"You wouldn't!"

"He would."

I jump at the thunderous tone from the step above me. Marc stands with his arms across his chest, eyes fixed on the bleeding mess in front of him.

Jason squints up at the group gathered around and jerks a nod. Some help him stand but others shoulder past, returning to the apartment, not one looking my way.

Coty, tightly coiled and unmoving, watches silently as Jason makes his way to a nearby car with help from a friend. His back tenses waiting for them to leave. Only when the car's out of sight does he breathe fully, turning to look at me. Out of the corner of my eye, I notice Beckett smiling before he goes back inside.

The stairwell finally empty, I study Coty as he slowly approaches, eyes locked on mine the entire time.

"Some party."

"Will you come upstairs with me?"

"I live upstairs."

"No, to my place."

"So I can meet more of your *friends?*" I give him a pointed look. "I don't think they like me."

"Fuck them."

"No, thanks. I'm tired." His hand—his bloody hand—shoots out, stopping me before I can even try to escape. "Oh my god. That needs to be cleaned." I grab at it but he pulls the damn thing back. The other hand snakes around my waist, bringing me against his front. His alcohol tinted breath dances over my face.

"Come upstairs with me," he pleads.

"Get one of your friends to clean your hand."

"I'll kick them all out and then you'll have to," he jokes—I think. "Come with me."

"You're crazy."

"You're beautiful," he counters, making my heart squeeze. Never getting compliments growing up has made me suspicious whenever one is given to me. The problem is Coty sounds and acts sincere and while I still wonder if he means it, I realize I *want* him to.

I push against his chest, asking him to release me. Not yet finished, he drags his hand down my arm, reaching my hand. Our fingers lace together like it's the most natural thing in the world, then he leads me upstairs.

He stops at his door and waits. He's leaving the decision up to me—again. Always.

Shaking my head, I turn the knob. "I'll help clean it, then I'm leaving."

Coty remains close behind, keeping our hands entwined as we enter. Almost instantly, there's a whoop from across the room. *Beckett.*

"If I knew that's all it took to get you to party with us, I would've been knocking people out this whole time."

"You're a moron," I joke.

He somehow disentangles the girl attached to his side and makes his way over to us. I watch in wonder as people move aside for his mountainous form.

"What can I get you to drink?"

I blanch, remembering his idea of a drink.

"I'm just here to take care of this," I say, gesturing to Coty's bloodied hand with my free one.

His eyes grow wide. "Oh, shit. I'll get the vodka."

"I'm not using vodka. I need soap and water." I roll my eyes.

"The vodka's for me." Coty grabs the bottle from Beckett and nudges me forward. "We can use the bathroom."

Oh. Yeah, I knew that.

Tucked away in the bathroom, Dermot Kennedy's "Power Over Me" drifts from down the hall. Coty closes the door, muffling the song and crowd noise significantly. Next, I'm spun and pressed against said door, Coty's face burrowing into the crook of my neck.

"Where have you been?"

Him breathing me in like a man drowning makes everything else fade away.

"Um, dinner?"

Pulling back, Coty licks his bottom lip, his eyes roaming over mine like he just remembered how hungry *he* is.

I close my eyes, counting to ten. I get to two when I feel Coty step between my legs. I raise onto my tiptoes preventing additional contact. He doesn't bother hiding his frustration, letting out a low rumble deep in his chest.

"I missed you."

"It's been two days." Before he can argue, I steer us back on track. "Are we doing this? I thought I was cleaning your hand."

Still eyeing me—rather hungrily might I add—he reluctantly nods, and sits on the closed toilet lid, holding his hand out for me to take. Careful to hold it from the bottom, I run water over the top, watching as the blood washes away. I squirt some soap from a repurposed whiskey dispenser and wash his knuckles gently but thoroughly. Coty, taking pulls from the vodka bottle, doesn't miss a second, watching every move I make. I shift the water to cold, hoping to combat both Coty's swelling and my own heated thoughts.

Finished, I gently blot dry his hand with a towel.

"I don't see any cuts." I'm almost positive it was all Jason's blood. "Does it hurt?"

He simply nods.

"Where?"

Using his good hand, he crooks a finger at me.

After a hesitant step, I halt, unsure. Unsure if this falls under 'light and easy'. Unsure if I even care.

Coty's hooded eyes travel my body head to toe and back again, leaving a storm brewing the more he explores. When he makes it back to my eyes, he nods his head, beckoning me closer. I don't move.

He tips the bottle back for another drink and I snag the bottle next. I take a sip, cringe, and place it on the counter. I step around Coty's legs in a standing straddle. His head tilts back, watching me closely, and drags his now dry hand up the back of my thigh. Never once breaking eye contact, he settles it right below my ass cheek, then does the same with his other hand. He pulls me forward, bringing his face in line with my chest.

My hand comes up to play with his hair. The areas that were sweaty from the fight have dried, making his dark brown hair soft but wild. He's wearing a black V-neck that's tight over his still-taut muscles. His jeans are slung low over his hips and tucked haphazardly into black boots. The bathroom is filled with his spicy coconut smell but it's been muddled from the party raging just outside the door.

Remembering why I'm here in the first place, I grip the strands, angling his head to the side. Coty lets out a low growl as I bring my face in close to his.

"Why are you fighting your friends?"

Coty remains quiet, looking between my eyes. Just when I think he won't answer, I relax my hold to straighten, but Coty has a different idea—one he doesn't bother running by me first. Suddenly, he lifts me up by the backs of my thighs and my arms reach around the back of his neck so I don't face-plant into his head. Placing me on his lap, he runs his hands down my legs until he hits behind my knees, then drags me forward. It's erotic and sweet and makes me want to run far, far away, however, I stay put. For now.

Pleased with our new position, Coty snatches the vodka up again. After taking his own swig, he lifts the bottle to my lips. I hesitate briefly before opening my mouth for a drink, too.

Full of liquid courage, he says, "They can't have you."

"Neither can you," I counter, just as bold, maybe even bolder. I don't drink often, so the vodka's hitting harder than I'd like to admit.

"Why not?"

Leaning in, my lips graze his ear. His hiss makes me smile.

"I'm not yours." I pull back, meeting his eyes. "It's better that I'm not."

"For who?" His grip on my thighs tightens.

I stare, willing him to see the truth but terrified of what he might discover.

"Everybody," I answer honestly, my arms falling from his neck.

Coty hauls my ass forward, placing me directly on top of his erection, saying, "Bullshit."

A small gasp tumbles from my lips.

God. Damn.

The ache that started moments ago is fully raging now, begging to be soothed.

Before I can shamelessly grind on the guy, someone knocks on the door, snapping me out of my lust induced stupor.

"Fuck off!" Coty growls.

"I need to go," I sigh, slowly getting to my feet.

Coty lets me, but follows suit, staying close.

Inspecting my appearance in the mirror, Coty steps up behind me—he's not a fan of personal space that one—and says, "Sunday."

My brain, working slower with the hormone and alcohol tornado swirling about, is struggling to keep up.

"Riding. Let's go this Sunday. Not with the guys either, just you and me."

He watches himself graze my lower back with deft fingers. I suck in my breath when his hand begins the trail up my backbone only he can blaze. My thighs clench together as I attempt—in vain—to smother the throb that's pulsing to the same beat outside, I swear.

"I have to work," I manage to croak out.

Not missing a beat, he says, "I'll wait."

My response gets lost in the haze Coty's hands are creating as he continues paying special attention to his favorite spot—my spine. Gripping the bathroom countertop, I close my eyes and drop my head, letting out a defeated, and embarrassing, moan.

"Coty."

He sweeps my hair to the side before lowering his mouth to the skin there. A murmured, "hmm," the only noise I can make out over my heavy breathing. Kisses on the back of my neck have my knees slamming into the cabinet as my legs try to buckle.

Coty encircles a hand around my front, holding me up by my quivering stomach.

"Coty?" I pant out, more desperate. Desperate for what? I don't know.

My knuckles, now white, cling to the edge—of both the counter and my sanity—while my legs shake uncontrollably.

Coty's tongue swirls lightly before closing his lips over the skin, sucking roughly. Watching him make out with my neck, I arch my back, pressing him where I really, really want him.

He releases my skin gently, almost reluctantly, to meet my eyes in the mirror again.

"What do you need, babe?" he breathes out, pained. Ever so slowly, without looking away, he leans back down, sinks his teeth into my shoulder then closes his eyes, savoring the taste. Sucking away the pleasant pain elicits loud moans from both of us. My clothes suddenly feel too restrictive. Why the fuck am I wearing pants today of all days?

My palm slams against the hard surface, wishing he'd give another place that same attention. Coty's mouth is the single best thing I've ever experienced and the rest of my body is dying to test his skills. As much as my body is screaming at me to turn around and see what else Coty can do with those lips, my overactive mind is objecting just as loud.

"Could you, uh, give me some room?" The words physically pain me but need to be said all the same.

Instantly, two tortured eyes snap open. Before pulling back, he kisses the red spot marking my skin with closed lips, then spins me to face him. Unfortunately, my body has turned to jelly and I blatantly sag against him. We're both breathing heavy but some color's seeping back into Coty's near midnight eyes.

His lips turn up into a sinful grin as his hands clasp the counter, caging me in. "Are you sleeping over?"

Hands on his chest, I push him back, gaining some much-needed air.

"I warned you about things getting messy."

"Life is messy. I can take it." He pops his shoulder up, completely unconcerned.

Although he makes a valid point, he's also been drinking and he's horny. He'd say anything right now to get laid.

I open the door, stepping into the party. Coty stays a step behind me as I make my way down their hallway. Beckett has a girl, a different one than earlier, pressed against his bedroom door with one leg wrapped around his waist. He detaches from her face, seriously that looks intense, and smiles lazily over at us.

"Neighbor girl," he teases. "Did you play nurse in there or what? I bet you fixed Coty up real good." His cackling laugh jostles his guest, causing her to glare my way.

I tsk, "Don't be jealous. Looks like you've got someone taking care of you already."

Coty wraps his hand around my middle possessively and barks, "Close the door, jackass." This only spurs Beckett on further which almost knocks both him and the girl clear over.

He murmurs something about needing to find himself a nurse before resuming his extreme make-out session.

Grimacing, I continue into the living room to find Coty's other roommate with a girl on his lap and another at his side, both peppering him with kisses. Marc looks up to Coty briefly.

Those boys have their fun lined up for the night. The thought that Coty might still find his has me bristling as I reach for the door handle.

Past the threshold, I say, "It looks like you guys have your hands all full. Have fun with that."

Coty's eyebrows furrow. "What does that mean?"

"Your roommates are taken care of for tonight. You better get back in there so you're not left out."

I hate the bite to my words revealing the jealousy that's sunk its claws into me, refusing to let up.

Coty breaks into a knowing smile and leans back, shouting, "Party's over! If your face, or any other part of your body, isn't attached to Beck or Marc, get out."

Groans erupt but people begin filing out just the same. My mouth opens and closes like a stupid fish in what I'm sure is a very impressive parting gift for the guests as they pass.

"'Night, neighbor girl. See you Sunday," the sexy jerk says before winking.

I lift a hand stiffly, then flee into my studio.

Coty's proving to be a more worthy counterpart than I originally thought. Why does he have to live next door though?

CHAPTER 19

Angela

AN OVERTLY ANNOYING RINGTONE, MY ANNOYING ringtone, wakes me the next morning. Last night took a toll on my lightweight head. I grab my phone off the small bedside table, wincing at the pain the small movement causes. Seeing another UNKNOWN caller, I curse. A press of a button and the device goes gloriously silent.

Just as my eyelids start to grow heavy, an insistent knocking startles me. It's unlike any other knocking I've ever heard. It sounds like it's from a song actually. A Britney Spears' song to be exact, circa 2000-and-late.

Grumbling across the room, I throw open the door only to find a takeout bag held up in front of my face.

I snatch it out of the abnormally large hand holding it and scowl.

"Stop bringing me food." On my way back to bed, I toss the bag on the counter, mumbling, "I can buy my own breakfast," then fall face first onto the sheets I kicked off last night. I was overheated after the bathroom incident and couldn't handle anything touching my skin. Anything other than Coty's hands that is. *Or mouth.*

I can't hide the smirk playing at my lips as I turn my head to the side, watching Beckett as he follows.

"Hey," he says, offended, grabbing the bag back. He pulls out a sugary doughnut, then proceeds to eat the whole thing in two bites. Mouth smacking obnoxiously, his eyes scan my studio. The couple steps it takes him and his massive legs to reach my bed is about how long it takes to check out my apartment so it works out perfectly.

I glance over his freshly showered appearance as he sits against my headboard beside me. He's dressed for work in dark blue mechanic pants and a stained white shirt with holes scattered throughout.

"How are you feelin' today?" I ask, breaking the awkward silence. "I would've thought you'd still be in bed." I try to wiggle my eyebrows but one is smashed against the bed so I give up, letting my suggestive tone do the heavy hinting instead.

"Ha! I don't let chicks stay over. They can play all they want but they gotta leave me never wanting more. Of anything," he adds, using his own indicative tone.

No suggestion needed, I scold, "You're a pig."

Mock horror covering his face, he scoots down to tickle me. Within an embarrassing amount of time, I'm laughing to the point of tears and screaming, "mercy," but the jerk shows none. Beckett continues his ruthless attack, so bringing my foot up between us, I kick him square in the stomach with all my strength. Wide eyed, he falls off the bed with a giant thud. Wiping my eyes, I poke my head over the side, nervous he might've left a Beckett-sized hole in my floor when he fell through to the apartment below. *That would totally kill my chance of getting my deposit back.* Fortunately, I find him lying on his back with his hands folded over his chest.

"Marry me."

I roll my eyes and drop a pillow on his face.

"You're feisty." He shakes the pillow off as he stands, climbing next to me again. "I figured you were but damn, Coty's got his work cut out for him."

"Coty doesn't have shit."

Beckett just looks me in the eye before saying, "Uh huh."

Him flopping onto his back makes the whole bed bounce and I grab the headboard to keep from flying off. On my back, we lie side by side, staring up at the ceiling in companionable silence.

A few minutes pass before he rolls his head to look at me and I do the same.

"You like him?"

"Who?"

He frowns.

"It's," I start, then turn my head, facing the ceiling again. I don't want him to see the truth. I don't want any of them to. "Complicated. He can look, I might even let him touch, but that's where it has to end."

"Parents do a number on you, too, huh?"

I look at Beckett again. He's having a rare serious moment and I don't want to miss it, but it's his turn to hide.

Face to the sky, he says, "I get it. My mom took off a long time ago. It was just me and my dad after that."

"He didn't remarry?" I ask quietly.

"No. I think we both thought she would come back to us. Hoped she would anyway."

"Did she?"

"Nope. Not once. Not even when things got really bad." His eyes close and I give him the time he obviously needs. Finally, he opens them. "No, she never showed. Left one day with some dude she'd been sneaking around with and never came back."

Without thought, I reach over to grab his hand.

"You know that has nothing to do with you though, right? That's her issue."

"Is that what you tell yourself?"

I sigh. "Yes...and no. I would've preferred my mom leave me honestly."

"Don't say that. You don't know what it's like to only have one parent. One that's running at half-speed while the world rushes past them."

I can't help but smirk. "Don't I? You have no idea what I've dealt with. You don't get close to girls because you're scared of getting hurt again. I *know* I'll be hurt again. Things don't come easy for me in this life. No one can change the shitty hand I've been dealt but me."

His blue eyes find mine.

"Does that usually work for you?"

"What?" I snap, growing more irritated by the second.

"Pushing people away before even giving them a chance."

I glance down at the steady rhythm of his chest. "Yes."

"I can tell." He slides his hand out of mine. "But you should know Coty's in. He's *all* in. I've known him for a long time now and I've never seen him like this. He's had girlfriends over the years but he's never been this irrational over them. Hell, he's so jealous, he doesn't even want me talking to you." He scoffs.

"Then why are you here? I doubt he'd like you being in my bed."

"'Cause I know you wouldn't let me try anything if I wanted to."

I cock an eyebrow. "Do you? Want to?"

He takes his time looking over my face then down the rest of my body before making it back to my eyes.

He shrugs noncommittally.

"Don't get me wrong, you're hot. Like I can't believe we get to watch you parade around in a swimsuit and not get called perverts 'cause it's in our backyard and we can't help but appreciate our amazing view." I smack his arm which only makes him smile wider.

"I don't parade around. And you're still a pervert."

"Agree to disagree." He shoots me a wink. "Anyway, even if I wanted to make a move, I wouldn't 'cause Coty is hooked and I'd never do that to my boy. I'm badass like that."

"He's not hooked. He's bored to death with the sausage fest you three have going across the hall and thinks I can give him some entertainment for a while. He'll lose interest soon enough."

"Have you seen him when you come around?" he asks incredulously.

"Yeah, he acts like a caveman that wants his way. He'll tire when he learns he's never going to get it though."

"Oh, Angie," he pats my head, "you have a lot to learn. Coty isn't looking to hit it and quit it. Dude's got feelings for you. How else do I need to say it? He likes you, okay? He doesn't sleep around like…" His eyes dart around, avoiding my gaze. "Marc." He ignores the choking sound coming from my throat. *Glass houses…* "If you really don't want to be with him, then you need to tell him, like today. That boy is one hand job short of being whipped."

"Are you done yet? Not only did you rudely wake me up but now I'm being lectured by the biggest pig in wolf's clothing I know. Worst Saturday morning ever," I grumble.

"Man, your mom really did fuck you up if you don't even know your fairy tales."

I flip him my middle finger with my eyes closed which is why I don't see the pillow coming until it smacks me square in the face.

Beckett shoots off the bed in a flash, saying, "No, please, continue your pity party."

Pillow in hand, I sit up and cock my arm back. I launch it across the room but Beckett's freakishly long body is already at the door and, quicker than I thought someone his size capable, he opens and closes it, barely making a sound. The pillow, however, smacks against the wall with a soft thump before landing unceremoniously to the floor. Okay, so my timing *and* aim were both a little off.

Next thing I know, Beckett's obnoxious laughter wakes the rest of Creekwood.

Like I said, worst Saturday morning ever.

◆ ◆ ◆

Hot Spots being slammed all day worked out well for several reasons. For one thing, I barely had enough time to catch my breath, never mind fixate on Beckett's early morning admission. Another reason being I only saw Joe once today and it was when I pulled in for my shift. Luckily, he was helping a customer so I was able to skirt by without notice. I had to take the long way around the building for breaks but the extra exercise was worth avoiding my handsy boss.

Just getting home from grocery shopping, my phone rings, cutting off the song "Won't Go Down Easy" by Jaxson Gamble. When I see UNKNOWN light up the screen, I yank it off the cord and answer it.

"What are you doing?" a male voice asks.

"Who is this?"

"Don't play dumb, Angela." Something about the voice seems familiar. Fucking rude, but familiar. "Where are you?"

The shrill ringing of warning bells fills my ears.

"Joe? I already left for the day."

He just laughs. *What'd I miss?*

"I know. Do you think you could meet me?"

The bells are now screeching full volume.

"Can it wait 'til my next shift? I have a bunch of food I need to get inside." A *bunch* is a bit of an overstatement but sounds better—more responsible. Unlike Joe's callous behavior the other night.

Out of habit, I glance around to see if the boys are home. They're not. Their bikes are gone.

The lampposts lighting the dim parking lot buzz with swarms of bugs surrounding the bulbs.

It's quiet. Too quiet. The sudden urge to get upstairs is overwhelming.

"I can meet with you when I come in tomorrow."

"That won't work. I can't talk about this there. It's about Amity."

Amity? "I don't really know her. Not sure how I'd be any help."

"I think she's stealing."

I pause, my hands full of my two reusable grocery bags. I'd already suspected Amity was the one to lift those tips that day we shared a shift but I didn't have enough proof to say anything. At the time though, it had seemed like Joe was captain of Team Amity, so now I'm wondering what happened to make him bow out of her corner. And more importantly, why is he bringing this up to me?

"That's why I need you to take over her shifts. We need to discuss the change. Privately."

Leaning against my Jeep, I kick a pebble with my shoe, sending it skidding across the deserted asphalt.

"I already said I would talk to you about that after I graduate. I can't take over Amity's shifts while I'm still in school. I'm not sure what else we would need to talk about."

"I could come to you."

What? Why the hell is he pushing this? There's no plausible explanation for us to meet after hours. Plus, he has to know I don't trust him after the shit he pulled. *Right?*

"I don't think that's necessary. I'll talk to you at work."

"You know I could just get your address from the office, don't you?"

My heart stops. My address. The day he insisted I write down my apartment number comes to mind. *Fuuuuck.*

I scan my surroundings again. I've been so busy wondering about those nosey neighbors of mine that I didn't even think to look for anyone else. Straightening, I hurry over to the building, taking the stairs two at a time.

"Actually, I need to let you go. Some friends are stopping over so I'll see you tomorrow."

I don't wait for his response before hanging up. Hopefully the thought of a crowd will scare him off. Although he seems to be growing bolder, I can only hope he doesn't get reckless. Regardless, Joe threatening to use my address has my stomach in knots. I'm not sure what I'd do if he followed through and I don't plan on finding out.

CHAPTER 20

Angela

As it turns out, Joe's dilemma wasn't all that pressing. Imagine my surprise when I found out Little Miss Thievery herself would be working alongside me today. Then to confuse matters more, Joe treated Amity much the same as he did the last time the three of us shared a shift. Flirtatious. Familiar. *Baffling.* Downright disgusting. All further proving that the crap Joe tried selling me last night was just that—shit.

The only saving grace was that with the object of his affections—and suspicions—present, it kept Joe away from me. The three of us worked well together, meaning they worked and flirted while I kept to myself in the front drying cars, washing and folding towels, scrubbing invisible stains off my shoes, pretending to tan in full view of witnesses—I mean customers—during lulls, and any other menial task I could think of.

Sadly, during one of those faux chores some tips magically went missing. It's not hard to pinpoint exactly who the thief was—their name rhymes with calamity—but I would like to know whether or not Joe knows. If he does, what's he going to do about it? And if not, am I willing to risk my job by throwing her stealing ass under the already unprofessional bus? I don't know the answers yet, but that money was earned by my hands which is where it should've stayed, damn it.

◆ ◆ ◆

Less tips means eating in, so after a measly dinner of frozen tortellini—ketchup doubles as tomato sauce, right?—I'm on my bed scrolling through new music when there's a round of four knocks at the door.

Louder than necessary, I yell, "Who is it?" Truthfully, I could've spoken normally and they would've heard me, but I want whoever is on the other side to know I can, and will, be loud. Also, I wait for an answer before opening it this time.

"Your incredibly sexy neighbor ready to take you for the ride of your life."

Despite the cheesiness, I grin and pull the door open to a drop-dead gorgeous Coty. He wasn't joking about the incredibly sexy part. I'm almost positive he wasn't kidding about the ride either.

On the verge of blushing from images his statement creates, I cross my arms, throwing on my best scowl.

"Damn, I was hoping it was Beckett."

Coty's eyebrows snap together. His roommate's earlier words about him being jealous more than ever come to mind.

I drop my arms and the act.

"I'm kidding." I roll my eyes, smiling at his resistance to budge. God, what a beautiful mess. He said he could handle messy, didn't he? I don't think he knew just how messy things could get. "What's this ride you're offering?"

"Funny girl. Are you ready?"

"Let me change and I'll meet you down there."

Coty rushes to stop me from closing the door though.

Arching an eyebrow, I watch as he reaches behind his back, grabbing something from his back pocket. Next, he presents a black hoodie—*his* black hoodie.

"Here. I grabbed this for you in case it gets cold." Quieter, he says, "It doesn't have the drawstring."

I snap my gaze back to him.

"I, uh, took it out. Last time you said yours hurt your back?"

A slow smile stretches my face. He's always protecting me, almost on instinct at times. Standing before me now is a nervous

Coty though. He's giving me a glimpse of his soft heart and hoping I don't throw it in his face. I want to show him how appreciative I am, how much this one small thing means to me, how nobody in my life has ever tried to prevent such a minor inconvenience for me—the inconvenience people usually try to avoid is me—but I don't trust myself to speak. Not right now. So, dropping my eyes from his, I take it, then close the door softly.

On my bed, I bring Coty's sweatshirt up to my face and inhale. His signature scent hits me and I'm done for. I've come to crave his smell and having it here in my apartment feels better than it should. It feels like it belongs. My fragrance and his—blended in perfect harmony, neither fighting for the spotlight, just happy to share the stage with one another.

I debate whether I should invite him in or just ditch altogether. When I hear the roar of his engine outside, the decision becomes clear. I'm already in further than I originally wanted. Turns out there's nothing light and easy about the boy next door. Some semblance of boundaries can still be set though. Establishing rules now will help if I need to push him away later—not if, *when*. When my hideous past resurfaces, it'll be easier to walk away if neither of us gets too deep. I just hope wading in won't take us both under in the meantime.

With one last creeptastic whiff, I change into warmer clothes—black leggings paired with a white tunic covering my ass finished by my all-black Adidas sneakers. I throw on Coty's oversized hoodie and look in the mirror. *I am in so much trouble.* Taking a deep breath and sending up a silent prayer, I need all the help I can get, I go down to meet my incredibly sexy neighbor ready to take me for the ride of my life.

Beckett and Marc beat me out there but Coty is quick to explain they're not joining us.

"Nice hoodie, Angie."

The appreciation in Coty's eyes matches Beckett's words. I look down at my outfit feeling my body buzz.

"Thanks. I love it." My teeth catch like part of my recent pasta just slipped out. I chance a peek at the guys but nobody seems to realize the weight of what just happened. Everyone's too lost in their own convoluted worlds to notice the turmoil in mine.

Suited up and ready to go, the roommates call out their traditional motto.

I tip my face to Coty.

"You guys are always saying that. What does it mean anyway?"

"Ride it? It means to ride life, don't let it ride you. It's a reminder that no matter what gets thrown at you, you still have the power to decide how you maneuver through it. Riding motorcycles is the truest testament to that since even a small pebble can send the strongest of riders reeling."

Already wearing his helmet, he helps me get mine on. In my Coty-induced haze I forgot to tie my hair back, so he helps to tuck it away from my face as I place the helmet over my head.

Beckett catches my eye, nodding as he passes.

"What was that?"

Coty's face has taken on a darkness that wasn't there before.

I tip a shoulder up. "Neighbor secret language. Didn't you get the memo?"

"Guess I didn't. Is that the same one that states Beck gets to wake you up with breakfast?"

Although playful, his words carry a tinge of hurt to them. Honestly, I'm surprised I didn't hear from him about it sooner.

"Jealous?"

Head dropped, his answer's immediate. "Extremely."

"Nobody gave Beckett permission to do that. And he just talked about you the whole time anyway, so you have nothing to be jealous of. Trust me."

He doesn't look up so I grab the mouthpiece of his helmet and lift until our eyes meet.

"Hey."

Lost in his thoughts, he remains quiet.

I grip the hoodie and his eyes follow the movement. "This means a lot." Finally, Coty's gaze reaches mine. "Any asshole lacking manners can interrupt a good sleep. But this, this means so much more than any unwelcome wake-up call ever will."

I lean in, forgetting I have a helmet covering my face, and bump awkwardly against his. We both laugh at my mistake, breaking the tension from a moment ago. He bends until our helmets are pressed together, face-to-face, and pauses. Our eyes flit between each other's as we hold the unconventional embrace.

"Don't be mad," I whisper.

"I'm not mad. I'm jealous as hell. I want mine to be the first face you see in the morning. Not Beckett's. Not anyone else's. Just mine."

Whoa. Coty didn't even bother checking the temp of the water before diving straight in, did he?

Unable to respond in an effective, or generally mature manner, I deflect. "You do not want to see me first thing when I wake up. You should be grateful, really. Your friend took one look at me and ran the other way. Seriously, he'll never make that mistake again."

His eyes narrow but he smirks anyway. "I doubt that."

Coty steps back and holds out his hand. I stare at his long, outstretched fingers, debating.

When I meet those chocolate eyes again, he repeats, "I'll wait."

Coty is so much more than I could've anticipated. He pushes but also pulls. He gives while taking. He knows what I need and offers me what I didn't realize I wanted. He's the wild I thought was unattainable. He's the stability I've craved for so long but gave up on. He's the wrench thrown into my simple plan, but, oh, what a delicious diversion he's been.

Placing my hand in his, I decide to swim with the current instead of against it for once. Maybe that really is the best way to get back on shore safely.

There's only one way to find out though.

CHAPTER 21

Angela

COTY'S BODY FEELS DIFFERENT. THIS ENTIRE SITUATION feels different. More familiar. More comfortable. Our bodies being better acquainted, feel more at ease against each other. We bend and shift with one another in a private slow dance while driving at dangerous speeds.

Coty's skills prove impressive again, especially as he maneuvers around every dip and curve with full confidence. It's erotic. Every now and then he reaches back to rest his hand on my thigh. Almost like he's checking on me as much as he's ensuring I'm really there. I relish the times he does.

My body molded to his isn't enough. I want more—of everything.

Stretched around him has reignited the flame that he lit the other night. The patience I've been practicing has run out and in its place is want. Pure, unadulterated want.

I keep my hands planted on the tank while Coty takes us further away from town. Miles off the lit highway, we weave through dark country roads. Just when I start to worry about where he might be taking me, Coty, of course, reaches back to hold my thigh reassuringly even as we fly down a straight path. His touch soothes me. While I haven't known Coty all that long, I've picked up on more than he's shared, too. I may not be able to trust him with my heart because of my own issues, but I know I can trust him with my body. His father's unfaithful ways caused Coty to respect women in a way most guys his age can't even grasp. Or care to. Anytime I've asked him to stop, he has. Without question. Without even a moment's hesitation. I know he wouldn't make me do anything I don't want to do which I've used as my safety net thus far. Now though, I'm having a hard time caring about the consequences at all.

Speeding through the night while wrapped in an intoxicating mixture of Coty and his motorcycle has me almost bursting out of my own skin. The combination is overstimulating in the best and worst of ways. The next time Coty squeezes my taut thigh, I groan and rest my forehead against his back, pulling in deep breaths. Coty's warm hoodie does nothing to counteract the goose bumps that've broken out across my body. There's a goddamn current buzzing beneath my skin and Coty's the one with the switch in his adept hands.

I feel like a caged animal.

"Wrong" by ZAYN filters through the Bluetooth speakers so I try to lose myself in the lyrics instead of my dirty thoughts. Coty's body tenses but he continues driving with the same precision, clearly not as affected as I am. Thankfully, one of us still has a level head. I'm itching to run my hands all over him and his steadfast restraint. If we were in any other vehicle, I'd have tested his resolve ten times over by now. Maybe. Probably.

We pass a half-open gate, slowing to a crawl, then turn onto a dirt path on an incline. My sole focus on Coty turns to our surroundings. No street signs, no lights, no indication as to where we are, my heart keeps a pace more comparable to our previous speed. We haven't passed another vehicle for miles and I couldn't pick this place out on a map in broad daylight. Vast hills line the road on each side, effectively blocking out everything but me and Coty and the brap of his street bike as it effortlessly coasts along the less than desirable terrain.

Minutes pass and suddenly thousands of tiny lights appear in the distance. Drawing closer to the ledge, my breath catches in my throat upon discovering it's our entire town spread out beneath us like a tiny replica made for our personal enjoyment.

Coty slows to a stop near the edge and kills both the engine and the only noise filling the sultry night air. Neither of us moves for a moment. Hypnotized, I dismount carefully, then spin in a complete circle while taking in the stars above, the looming mountains behind us, and the flat stretch of city below. Making it back to Coty, I find him looking at me with similar awe. He holds out his hands so he can help. I step forward and let him, keeping my eyes on his. Helmets taken care of, Coty looks back to me with an intensity that heats me from the inside out. I don't step back even as he pulls my body flush with his. I don't drop my eyes even as he brings his hands up to cup my face. I don't pull away even as I feel him seducing me with everything he's got.

Coty hesitates, giving me the option to stop. Not even close to done though, I reach my hand around the back of his head and press my lips to his. Starting out sweet, almost exploratory, it quickly turns heated, passionate. It's rough and desperate and long fucking overdue.

Coty groans and the husky sound shoots straight to my core, making me grip his hair. My other hand rests on his neck nearly covered by his leather jacket. He pulls back abruptly, unzipping his coat entirely, only to dive back in again. It's the only skin I can reach and I take full advantage. With a tilt of my head, I deepen the kiss I've been craving since he showed up at my front door offering me his modified hoodie. A hand to my ass, Coty yanks me up and over the bike, setting me on the gas tank, facing him.

I break away on a gasp. "Coty, we're on a bike. What if we fall?"

He nips at my lips, calmly. "I won't let you fall." And the way he says it, I want to believe him.

Then, like the last thirty seconds never happened, Coty's mouth is back on mine, chasing away any remaining apprehension. Our mouths continue to make love as his hands grip my hips, bringing me forward until his impressive erection rubs my center in a frustratingly erotic motion. Coty's lips wreak havoc on my mouth while his body creates utter mayhem for mine. I never stood a chance. His skills outrank mine greatly and I'm happy to let him take the lead. For now, anyway.

The ride here was the foreplay leading up to this moment. It's been building for weeks, if I'm being honest, since the moment our eyes connected really. The attraction being too great, too strong, it's damn near consumed me.

Both of us teeming with sexual tension, neither comes up for air as we pour our desire into the other. My lips match his. His tongue chases mine. When his teeth join the competition, I almost surrender on the spot. As Coty slides his hands further into my hair, his grip tightens, pulling slightly. My head bends backward trying to overcompensate but Coty's mouth latches onto my bottom lip, ensuring I can't go far. Teeth bared, he draws out my lip before closing his mouth and soothing the sting away completely. Being pulled in opposite directions makes for a luscious game of tug-of-war that'll eventually end in victory. For me.

A whimper escapes my tender lips as I bring my hand from his neck to his chin. Gripping it with my thumb and forefinger, I pull, forcing Coty to meet my mouth again.

Naturally, our bodies recline together but before I hit the windshield, Coty's hand shoots out to grip the glass acting as a cushion for my back. He leaves his other hand in my hair, helping to hold my head to his. *As if there's anywhere else I'd rather be.* I wrap my arms around his neck, arching my back. On a growl, Coty breaks free of my mouth and tilting my head for better access, starts sucking hungry kisses down my neck. The motion of him rocking into me causes the bike to shift beneath us. With each thrust, the wheels roll forward. Only once he lets up, does the bike roll my pussy directly back to where she belongs—pressed against him. The repetitive friction is borderline torture—slow and sensual and just shy of giving me what I need. What we both want.

I'm panting and groaning and losing my mind one touch at a time. When I'm fed up from being left on the side lines, I fist his hair, returning his face to mine. Ready to be back in the game, I lick his lips methodically, ratcheting up the heat factor a few more degrees.

"Damn, babe. I've been dying to kiss you again."

A breathy laugh escapes me followed by the only response I can offer—my lips tell Coty what my head can't, my tongue shows him what my heart never will, and my hands say what he's dying to hear. Not a single word is spoken, yet he gets the message all the same. I'm here. I'm yours.

For now.

Still clutching his hair, I make my way down his jaw, nibbling as I go. Coty's hand squeezes my hip roughly as he sucks in a breath. I drop one hand to explore his chest. I've seen him shirtless countless times but haven't had the pleasure of experiencing it firsthand. Until now. My fingers venture over the grooves of his strained muscles. And they. Are. Everywhere. A hand under his shirt, I trail my nails up his firm abs while keeping up my feast on his neck.

"Fuck. Angela, you're killing me."

His rough voice, the only noise besides the tires crunching the loose gravel, reminds me of our surroundings.

Close to his ear, I whisper, "Is this where you take all your dates?" The thought ran through my mind when we arrived and now I'm dying to know.

Coty pushes to standing, leaving me to lie almost flat on my back. Using his free hand, he grasps my collarbone gently before grinding his cock into me not so gently. Our groans mix into one agonized sound of desire. My thin leggings, now drenched, are as good as gone. They tried their best, really, but Coty's seduction proved too powerful for the stretchy cotton.

He throws my previous question back in my face, asking, "Jealous?"

Easy. "Yes."

He drops down and devours my mouth with his once more. My hands meet air as he pulls back sharply. "Good. I want you to feel what I feel." He nips at my lips playfully. "I want you so jealous you can't even see straight." My bottom lip gets sucked between his. "I want you thinking about me when you're in your bed, thinking about how much you want to sneak across the hall and into mine." Voice too hoarse to continue, he seals his lips against mine, then pulls back again, causing me to whimper. He's playing with his food while I'm eagerly waiting to be served. "Are you there yet, babe?"

Lips against mine, his eyes implore me to answer. Unable to, I pause. I'm not sure if I can admit what he's asking. Yes, the thought of Coty bringing another girl here makes my stomach cramp, bad, but do I have a right to covet something that's not mine? *Someone* that's not mine. Having to go without most times, I learned to deny that useless cloak of envy each time it was presented. Greed, resentment, jealousy, they never got me anywhere. Nowhere I wanted to be anyway. Avoidance became my greatest ally, my closest friend. A downright necessity at times. Of course I noticed what others had: happy families, loving parents, birthday cakes—the usual—but dwelling on the things I didn't have was a waste of time.

As for his other question though, while it's true I have fantasized about having Coty in my bed, I think I'll leave him wondering a little longer.

Eyes still searching mine, Coty straightens.

"Wait, wait, wait. Come back." I pull at his shirt and he obliges, lowering. "What was the question again?"

Mouth flattened, he stands out of reach a second time.

"You fight dirty," I accuse, placing my hands on his chest, still trying to cop a feel of his hardened muscles.

The cold air has slipped between us, clearing my head of the hormone fog it's been enveloped in since we left Creekwood.

Coty's near black eyes keep mine entranced as he drops down closer. When his lips are hovering just above mine, he whispers, "That's 'cause you've had me against the ropes since we met."

I sink my teeth into his bottom lip and, without breaking eye contact, rise with him. I watch with satisfaction as his eyes flare with renewed desire. Just before he can resume his own sweet torment, I release him and use his arms to dismount.

Coty follows, albeit slower from needing to adjust himself, and takes my hand.

And I allow it.

For now.

Hand-in-hand, we wander over to the edge of the cliff and gaze out at the cityscape before us. I watch, mesmerized, as a plane lands in the distance. I can't help but notice how small it all seems.

"How did you find this place?"

Coty swings his head to me.

"Are you sure you want to know?" He squeezes my hand, laughing lightly.

I swear my lips scrunch on their own.

Coty releases my hand, and slipping under the warm hoodie, his fingers trail my spine. I shiver from the skin-to-skin contact.

I realize then that I couldn't keep the guy off my backbone if I tried.

He turns his head forward again. "No, I found it once on a solo ride. I come out here when I need space. Living with the others is cool but sometimes I need to get away. You know?"

"The need to get away?" I can't help the sneer in my words. "Yeah, I do know. With my childhood, getting away is a luxury you pray for daily. Moving out was me getting away. And staying away." Dropping my gaze to my shoes, I quietly add, "Hopefully."

Coty's hand stills. "Why do you say that?"

Kicking a stray rock over the ledge, I listen for its descent before looking over to Coty whose sole focus is on me.

"I just can't go back to my mom's. I won't."

Something crosses his features but disappears before I can ask about it.

"Do you still see her?"

"No. We…uh," I huff out a breath, "have an agreement." *Of sorts.* "When I moved out, we made a deal so she would leave me alone."

Coty's eyes narrow suspiciously. "How's that working out?"

Turning back to the lit-up town, I tell him, "Not great. She's up to her old tricks but nothing I can't handle."

"What tricks are those exactly? Should I be worried?"

My head snaps over to him and I almost choke from what I see there.

I twist, making his hand fall from my shirt. Coty scowls.

"My problems stay my problems. I promise they won't make their way next door or to any of my other neighbors."

I throw my hands up, smirking ruefully.

Rianne will never catch sight of Coty if I can help it. She has a knack for taking anything good, anything untainted, and twisting it into something ugly with her mental gauntlet. Battering it until nearly unrecognizable. Trying to make anyone feel as lonely and scared on the outside as she does on the inside. Sinking her claws into any fresh meat she can until their need for self-preservation eventually kicks in and they can escape. I refuse to let my mother's manipulation reach Coty. Whatever he may be to me, he'll never be hers to toy with.

Coty catches me as I pass to the bike but I stand firm at arm's length. "What happened? Where'd you go? You're back to throwing this neighbor shit at me when we just…" A look over his shoulder, he says, "Angela-"

"You do know you're my neighbor, right? You and Beckett and Marc. You guys are *just* my neighbors."

"Bullshit," Coty shoots back. "That didn't feel very neighborly to me." He jerks his thumb behind him.

I, however, avoid looking at the bike at all costs. It's too soon. Instead, I shrug him off. "Well, the others haven't asked me to ride with them yet."

"And they won't."

"Oh, yeah? Why's that?" Arms over my chest, I cock an eyebrow with as much attitude as I can muster. "Because you called dibs?"

"I didn't have to, babe. They fucking know."

My arms fall to my sides and I bite out, "Know what?"

In a flash, he's there, grabbing my face between his hands. "That you're mine."

"Coty, look-"

"Don't. Don't try to deny it. I told you I'll wait and I will, but you need to stop acting like this isn't happening. Babe, you're all I think about. Having you steps away every night and not being able to touch you is killing me. The thought of one of my boys touching you is enough to send me over the edge and do something I might regret. Do you get that?"

"That you need anger management?"

Smirking, he says, "God, you've got a smart mouth." He leans down to place a soft kiss against said mouth. "I'd do anything for my boys, share anything with them, even my bike, just...not you."

Completely deflated, I gently press, "Why?"

Gaze on my lips, he says, "You tell me."

"I moved in next to three single guys but won't sleep with any of them, it's the ultimate challenge. A chase too great to turn down. It's not that hard to figure out. Anyone would want to beat the odds." Through the ache in my chest, I whisper, "You'll get over it."

"You're right, you are challenging. But you're so much more than that." Bending, he gives me a lingering kiss that I greedily deepen before he pulls away, smiling. "But you're wrong, too. I won't get over it. You're like a drug I can't quit. Each hit filling a need but never enough to fully satisfy the want. That want is you, babe. I want you. And not just your body, which I'll happily take anytime." He winks cheekily when I frown. "But the rest of you. All of you. Everything."

My eyes scan his for a hint of what I'm sure I'll find. An angle. "What do you mean?"

He sighs and leans his forehead against mine. "I mean what I said, Angela. I want you. No games, no hidden agenda, just you."

Coty is asking for more than I've ever had, never mind what

I've been able to give. Nights like tonight prove I can have some fun and let loose a little, but to hand over my heart and trust him to care for it the way nobody ever has? I just don't know if that's in the cards for me. If it'll ever be in my grasp.

"I'm not going anywhere." Coty's tongue sneaks between my lips and I moan.

"Why are you pushing this? What if something bad happens? We live next door."

His thumb pulls my bottom lip down. "It won't. If it does-"

I shake his thumb off. "If it does, I'll have to move. You guys outnumber me. Do you really not see the position you're putting me in here?"

"I've been thinking about a lot of positions to put you in."

Both hands braced on his chest, I push with all my might, making him barely take a step back.

"See? I knew you were a perv."

"Can you blame me? You show up looking like a skater version of the girl next door rocking a slippery attitude and a string bikini and you think I'm not gonna fantasize about you? Sorry, babe, but any man in his right mind would."

Didn't I just say that? *Ugh, men.* "Here I thought you were sweet." I roll my eyes, grabbing Beckett's borrowed helmet while Coty puts his own on.

"I'll be anything you want me to be, as long as you say you're mine." He then leans his helmet to mine, waiting for me to close the distance. Always letting me choose.

It's clear I have a lot to think about but he's right. There's nothing neighborly about us except our addresses. Coty's hot, sweet, patient, and drives me wild in the best of ways. All I can do is try to hold him off while I figure out how to slip a life vest over my head without him taking offense. Contrary to Coty's naivete, there *will* come a time that I'll need it.

My helmet meets his in a bobble-head-esque kiss. "I need time to think."

"Then you got it. I just need to know, when can I see you again?"

I bark out a laugh, shoving him. "You're insatiable."

The cool night air swirls around us on our ride home. Wrapped up in Coty and my thoughts, I feel lighter than I have in a while. Like maybe some of the weight on my shoulders has been lifted. Not transferred, not gone—it's still there and it's still mine—but it feels lighter, not as stifling. I just don't know if that's a good thing yet.

CHAPTER 22

Angela

WITH GRADUATION ON SATURDAY, MANY ADULT lives are set to officially begin come Sunday—the ones without severe hangovers anyway—but mine started years ago when my role switched from child to the only mature figure in the house. The one saddled with holding my emotionally immature mother together. Reminding her when bills were due. Then the one paying those bills after she chose to neglect them. Soothing her as she sobbed in a heap on the floor about the life she'd never have. The one dodging the insults hurtled my way for purportedly robbing that same unattainable life. Taking care of myself with my own earnings while she squandered away any money she could get her idle hands on. Her latest ex-husband being her most recent victim—*that I know of*—she never discriminated where she could get the money. Willing to lie, cheat, and steal from anyone to get it, Rianne would find a way.

I had hiding places all over the house for income I garnered. At first, she showed restraint, only taking small amounts so as not to alert me. Bored with not causing friction though, she grew bold and raided all my hiding places at once, leaving them bone dry.

I'll never forget the day I came home from work to find my room upturned, everything ripped from the walls, clothes thrown about, mattress flipped, shoes tossed around. Seeing the drawers to my secondhand dresser yanked clear out was what set me off though—I'd taped money under the bottoms of those drawers. I was diligent in keeping them closed whenever she was around or before I left the house. Already doing my own laundry for years, she had no reason to be near my dresser. She was never quiet about her dislike in my clothing choices either. *Too sporty. Not feminine enough.* Just the way I like them.

No, the only way she would've found the money was if she went searching. Finding the tape pockets empty was the last time I came close to losing it. My temper. My grip. My fucking sanity. I had saved hundreds of dollars. And it was gone. All of it.

The worst part was seeing her standing in the doorway with a victorious smirk on her face. Not an ounce of guilt. No shame whatsoever. Just sick anticipation awaiting a reaction. Which is exactly why I didn't give her one. I cleaned up my room with shaking hands and cloudy eyes. Not saying a single word even as she made comments from her spot at the threshold. Still, I didn't break.

With each shirt folded, I added another brick to my border. Every shoe reorganized was another wall built. Replacing the drawers, I set the armor in place. Righting my bed was attaching the final piece of defense in keeping me safe.

She could be the hurricane that destroyed everything in its path, but she'd never break me. The little bits in my life I'd mistakenly cared for became meaningless in that moment. Anything she could use against me were no longer important—memories, hobbies, interests, trinkets—they didn't lose value, they just lost value to me. Because *I* made it so, not her.

From that day forward, her attempts to get under my skin turned from childish and petty to nasty and malicious, even violent at times. She got the reactions she was looking for in the beginning. That was until I realized I had to strengthen my body, too, not just my mind. Staying composed was hard, becoming better wasn't. Rianne was willing to sink to such low depths but I chose to climb outside her reach entirely. She wanted to hurt me, I ensured she couldn't.

That's something my sister still hasn't learned. She thinks we should cater to my mom and handle her with kid gloves, where I'd rather just not handle Rianne at all. Having chosen to live with her dad for the majority of her life, she only saw the good side of our mother. She was only *shown* the good side. Our mom always behaved differently around Kelsie though, careful not to let her crazy show. Thinking Perry would come to his senses one day and take her back, she was always on her best behavior. The weekends my sister would visit were the only times I saw the kind of parent my mother could've been had I not been born. A fact she made sure to remind me of whenever Kelsie left again.

Kelsie and I get along for the most part, only if for short bursts at a time. She even gave me some old items for my apartment like utensils, cups, and a nightstand she scored at a thrift store but didn't fit her new house decor. Kelsie and her high school sweetheart got married just before she gave birth to their baby boy, Miles, in the fall. The small house they moved into has a cozy cottage style where my place has more of a I'll-take-what-I-can-get vibe, so I got a few things they found lacking.

Where we disagree is our mother which is ironic considering the very tie that binds us doubles as the noose around the neck of our relationship. Every time there's an altercation she takes Mom's side, no questions asked, no explanation needed. Of course she's never seen the ugly, sinister side I grew up with so she can't imagine the heinous things Rianne has done to me.

That's why when I met her and Miles for dinner yesterday, I tried to steer the conversation toward safer topics. I needed her help finding an outfit for graduation so I bribed her with dinner just to get her out of the house. It was worth it though. I got to spend time with my chubby-cheeked nephew while buying something nicer than cut-off shorts to wear. The outfit we picked out was flirty and fun, not exactly what I'm used to, but Kelsie swore I could pull it off. The topic of graduation obviously led to discussing who'd be in attendance. The invitation is still open to our mother. I want her to see what I've accomplished without her help. Despite Rianne having the invitation on the empty fridge for months, whether she comes is up to her. I'm sure Drew will be there, maybe even his dad since he was my stepfather for a short time. When I asked Kelsie if she'd make it, things quickly went south. She maintained she couldn't attend unless Mom went, saying it wouldn't be right to celebrate without her. Unsurprisingly, I grew defensive and things escalated from there. She left in a huff with Miles flailing in her arms. I hate fighting with Kelsie, especially when it affects seeing my nephew, but I don't understand her logic.

My world history teacher spent a summer in South Africa when he was in his teens. Mr. O'Conner's parents let him visit his cousin who had sold all his possessions to start an animal rescue sanctuary on this oasis in the South African wilderness. Anyway, he told us this story once about these Mozambican Spitting Cobras and how they would get inside the house sometimes. They're insanely venomous and a single bite could kill a human in under forty-five minutes, so it was a huge ordeal when they'd find one. They'd retrieve the snakes using special tools, including safety goggles, then release them back into the wild unharmed. Apparently, the spitting cobra—aptly named—also spits its venom at their targets. It doesn't actually do anything unless it gets into the eyes, then it can scar the cornea leaving a person blind. I can't help but wonder if this is what's happened to my sister. Our mother's poison has reached Kelsie without her even realizing it.

I came home to discover a red rose placed in front of my door. Upon finding the stinky flower, I tossed it in the dumpster outside. The boys, well Coty and Beckett, had been leaving me little notes and treats all week, so the rose was an unwelcome surprise to say the least. I'm still not sure who it was from either.

◆ ◆ ◆

Joe enters the office carrying a stack of work shirts.

"New shirts came in. Make sure you grab a few."

The last time we spoke was on the phone when he insisted I meet him for some BS excuse, yet here he stands, acting like a normal, non-skeevy boss.

Nose twitching at a strong odor, I cautiously approach the pile and take a handful. Scanning the sizes, I look up.

"They're all extra small."

"That's what everybody wears so that's what I ordered. You trying to tell me you don't fit an extra small?"

Not that it's any of his damn business, but no, I don't.

"It's hotter out there," I point to the front, "than it is back here. I like my shirts loose for a reason." Multiple actually.

Why am I explaining my clothing preferences to my manager? How is this okay?

"Well, this is the new style the boss wants everyone in so either make it work or..."

Sighing, I leave, throwing them in my locker on the way to my station. He's making it impossible to keep working here. Mandatory infant size shirts? What's next? Wet and Wild Wednesdays? Stripper Sundays?

No. Thanks.

I manage to stay busy enough that I barely notice when Coty's Camaro rolls out of the bay and into my towel covered hands.

Just as I make my way around the hood, I hear Joe call my name and glance up.

"I need you to stay late."

Shit.

"Tonight?"

He nods, sliding his hands into his pockets. He rocks back onto his heels, exposing his belly in the process. I bite back a fair amount of vomit.

"The windows need done. Nobody cleaned them last night so they're filthy. Expect to be here a while."

Double shit.

My eyes drop to the two sets locked on my every move. Coty's eyebrows snap together while Marc is sporting his usual scowl.

I dry the rest of the car in a daze, my heartbeat loud enough for them to hear through the windshield. When I open Marc's door to clean the jamb, I get an idea.

I wait until I open Coty's to put it into action.

"Hey, neighbor girl," he teases with a wink.

I peek back to find the bay empty.

"Hey, yourself. What are you guys doing here?"

They share a look before Coty answers vaguely, "Work."

Okay, then.

"What are you doing tonight?"

"Hopefully hanging with my hot neighbor."

Marc groans from the passenger side, making Coty laugh.

"I didn't realize Gary was up for visitors but I hope you two have fun."

Both guys break into laughter and I smile despite the dread simmering below the surface.

"Why? What's up?"

My gaze flits around the car, the speed of a hummingbird. "I was wondering if you could pick me up?"

Coty grows serious, immediately scanning my face. "Is something wrong with your Jeep?"

I look down to my shoe splattered in dirty water. That part was hard, but this part feels wrong. "I don't know. It sounded weird on the way here and I wanted to go to the library after work," Coty's eyes narrow a fraction and I almost lose my nerve altogether, nevertheless I persevere, "but my boss needs me to stay after-"

"Done." I don't even get to finish when Coty cuts me off. "Consider it all done. We'll take care of the Jeep. I'll be here when you get off. You can use my laptop for," his hesitation nearly ends me, "whatever you need it for. Anything else, we'll figure out later."

He glances over to Marc, jerking his chin. Wordlessly, Marc gets out and walks around the back with his hand out. "Keys?"

"He'll take it to the shop now and we'll look at it there."

My face outright ignites as I fumble for words. I didn't expect them to take control like this. I should've, but I didn't. The web I've spun can't be removed without revealing everything in the process. And honestly, that option sounds worse than asking for help—even if it did feel like exfoliating my tongue with sea salt.

I tell Marc to meet me out back, however, ignoring my wishes, he follows me through the building, hot on my heels all the way to my Jeep.

"What's his deal?"

I turn to see Joe watching from the window. Sighing, I tell him the first truth today, "I don't know."

"He looks pissed, like someone shit in his double roast beef sandwich."

I eye Marc skeptically. "Double?"

"Look at him." Marc unabashedly waves a hand in Joe's direction. I grimace but play it off as a squint. The sun *is* bright. "His sweat looks like it's a step below that pink slime shit from butcher shops." *Eww.* Actually, now that I think about it, it does. "Dude's arteries are probably working overtime."

"Maybe he's just hot?"

Marc pins me with a hard stare, making me regret I even said anything.

"Maybe he's a fucking scumbag."

Well, I can't argue with that.

With a shrug, I shuffle the keys. "Thanks for helping me. I know we don't know each other very well but Coty-"

"Coty's my boy. If he needs something from me, it's done. Period." He pauses. "He thinks you need saving."

I peek up at him. "Let me guess, you don't?"

A moment passes where neither of us says anything.

Marc takes the keys from my wavering grasp. "Is this thing going to make it to the shop okay or am I gonna have to Flintstone my ass the whole way there?"

"Umm."

I can't. I can't do it. Lies may not make your nose grow but they sure as hell make your conscience shrink.

"Watch your back tonight."

His eyes bounce over to Joe again before landing on me pointedly.

Shit.

I wait until he's gone then reach up to feel my nose, wondering if it grew after all.

◆ ◆ ◆

Luckily, by the time we switch off the sign for the night, Coty's Camaro is already backed into an empty spot. Some of the tightness in my stomach loosens when I see him there, waiting patiently. Without telling Joe, I go out to give Coty my bag and let him know I'll be a while. He assures me he's got all the time in the world making me glad he's here. Even though it felt like jumping from a cliff without knowing what was waiting at the bottom of the dark water by asking him for help, it still felt safer than swimming with a hungry shark—a shark with pink slime sweat no less.

Upon entering the office Joe starts in with the fifth degree.

"Who's that? A boyfriend of yours?"

Tracking my movements as I gather the tools needed, he crosses his arms over his chest.

"He's my ride. Car trouble."

"I could've taken you home. This isn't a place for dates."

I scoff. Loudly.

"Well, he's waiting for me." I meet his eye, hoping he hears what I'm not saying. "If you don't mind, I'm just going to knock this out and get out of here."

Not bothering to hear his response, I get to work washing the heavily streaked windows. Joe wasn't lying. They're bad. Whoever closed last night should get their ass kicked for leaving the bay in such bad shape.

An hour later, I'm surprised when I find the office empty when I finish. Joe was in and out of the bay but never stayed long. Thankfully. I don't know where he is now and I'm not sure I really care. I just want to leave already.

I wander around, listening for any sound. My steps are slow and measured as I call Joe's name.

The light from under the bathroom door, the *closed* bathroom door, catches my attention and I come to an abrupt stop. Keeping my distance, I can somewhat make out sounds like…grunting?

What the?

A knock at the office door startles me. After letting Coty in, his gaze sweeps the room. His narrowed eyes find mine, softening in the next instant. "All done?"

I nod, grateful. "Take me home."

"Yes, ma'am." His imitated southern accent makes me smile. "Hungry? I know I worked up an appetite just watching you."

"Hmm. No wonder you came early." We walk out to the black sports car with our hands clasped. "But yeah, I could eat."

Coty leans over and kisses me sweetly, tenderly.

"I've been wanting to do that all day."

Smirking, I kiss him back, my lips thanking him for things I refuse to admit. I find myself craving his presence even more since our sexy bike ride together. He calms my ever-present storms looming in the distance.

Tucked safely inside his car, Coty grabs my hand after turning up the "Too Good To Be True" remix featuring Machine Gun Kelly and takes us for a late meal.

Back at Creekwood, I grab a shower before meeting him at his place.

I'm wearing his black sweatshirt—he's never getting it back—and a pair of tight athletic shorts when he opens the door showing a living room packed with people.

"Holy shit."

He moves to block the opening.

I follow his gaze to make sure I did in fact put shorts on. My apartment's so hot, I "forget" to put full outfits on sometimes. Confirming I'm dressed properly, I look back to Coty.

"You can't wear that."

"What do you mean? What's wrong with my clothes?"

"Nothing. I like what you're wearing. A lot." His eyes darken a shade. "But I won't be able to keep my hands to myself in front of all these people behind me." He jerks his head. "Let's go to your place."

He takes a step into me but I push him back, laughing.

"Mine doesn't have anywhere to sit, remember?"

"Shit. That's right. Do you mind hanging in my room then? I want you all to myself tonight."

Eyes narrowed, I say, "Fine, but I have shit to do so no distractions."

"Babe, you *are* the distraction."

Our fingers entwined, he leads the way, making quick introductions as we go. Beckett barely looks up from the couch as a girl nibbles his ear. Marc's in the kitchen cutting up limes. He looks up and nods, saying, "neighbor girl," as we pass.

I glance over Coty's room, looking for differences from the last time I was in it. Aside from a few large rolls of official looking paper on the desk, everything appears the same. Breathing in the tropical tang, I sit on the bed and take in the beautiful picture above the headboard, reading over the quote again.

Coty closes the door, then walks over to rearrange some papers on his desk. Head down, he tells me, "We need to keep the Jeep a while longer. The part's on back-order but should be in by next week."

I couldn't keep the shock from my face if I tried. *Excuse me, what?* There was nothing wrong with my car to begin with, that I know of, so I'm completely taken aback by this information. Coty refusing to meet my eyes isn't helping.

"What part?"

"The carburetor."

This would be a great time to know something, anything, even a fun fact, about vehicles besides their make and model.

"Where'd it go?"

Coty finally looks at me, his eyebrows basically touching.

"It didn't *go* anywhere. The original one was shit and should've been replaced a long time ago. I'm surprised it didn't give you any problems." Coty coughs, adding, "Sooner."

Even though it's killing me, I bite my tongue. I'd rather him think I have car trouble than boss trouble.

"If the carburetor's still in there, then can I drive it until the part comes in?"

Coty unplugs his laptop, shaking his head. "We already stripped it. I can drive you to and from work. Or anywhere else you need to go."

My hands clench between my legs. "That won't work. I need my car back." Now.

"Babe, the guys and I already talked about it, we'll make it work. I'll put our numbers in your phone and one of us can take you wherever you need to go. All you gotta do is text a time and place and someone will show. Don't worry, we got you."

The laptop forgotten, Coty saunters over to join me. Dropping to eye level, he places his knee between my legs, placing his hands on either side of me. His advance forces me to lie back and honestly, distraction never looked so good.

Inches above my body he breathes, "Damn, I've pictured you in my bed so many times."

His fingers skirt along the skin peeking out from my shorts. Roused by the featherlight touch, I push my groin up making contact with his and he obliges by dropping his waist down to meet mine. Feeling him already rock hard makes my center throb with anticipation. With one hand holding up his torso, his other snakes around to my ass, gripping my thigh and arching it over his waist. Our groans loud and wanting, we kiss like it's the first time all over again. With new areas to reach and less clothes to restrict, we explore using our hands until soon we're both growing greedy for more.

His shirt is promptly removed and tossed across the room,

giving me free reign to explore. Pulling away from my impatient hands, he lowers to my still exposed middle and nips just below my belly button. I arch off the bed simultaneously moaning in a voice foreign to my own ears. Just when I think he's going to ask me to keep it down or leave he does it again, eliciting the same reaction.

"Coty," I pant.

"Please don't tell me to stop," he grinds out against the top of my shorts, his erratic breathing penetrating the tight material.

"I wasn't. I was going to tell you *not* to stop."

"Fuck, babe. I'm-"

The obnoxious knocking on his door that sounds like "Old McDonald" at that exact moment interrupts Coty.

A muffled groan against my shorts, my still sensitive body hums as he sits up.

"What?"

"Movie time. Are you and Angie coming out?"

Coty swings his gaze to mine, apprehension plain as day.

I shake my head gently, picking up the laptop. Coty looks at the device like he's about to throw it at Beckett. My hold on it tightens. "No, thanks."

I wait for it to fire up while propping myself against the headboard.

Flopped onto his back, Coty huffs out a breath of frustration. *You and me both, buddy.*

"I knew we should've gone to your place. How the hell can you still have homework? I thought this was your last week."

With his eyes shut, I admire his profile before answering. His dark hair, messy from our make-out session, matches his thick eyebrows. Lush eyelashes rest over those all-seeing chocolate eyes that frequent my dreams. High cheekbones and a strong jawline make his face almost too handsome, too perfect. Plump, supple lips above the slight indentation in his chin round out his nearly flawless complexion.

"It's not for school. And, yeah, Thursday's my last day."

Coty opens his eyes, holding me captive.

"When's graduation then? This weekend?"

"Saturday."

"Will your family be there?"

My mouth flattens and I look away. "I don't know. Maybe?"

"What? Your own family would miss your graduation?"

I type out a website, careful to angle the screen away from those same perceptive eyes I was just drooling over. "It's not that big of a deal. They're not really the supportive type."

Coty looks like he wants to argue but how can he? He doesn't even know my family. *And hopefully it stays that way.*

Sighing, I elaborate, telling him about my mom and sister skipping out on the big event. "Drew will be there though. Maybe with his dad since he was my stepdad once upon a time."

"That's not your sister's dad?"

Busy scanning the newest listings, I answer, "no," absentmindedly.

"You and your sister have the same dad then?"

"Uh, no. You are looking at the product of a one-night stand." I wink at him before returning to the screen. "A slip-up. I was never meant to be."

"A happy accident," Coty corrects.

"I doubt anyone sees it that way." In fact, I know they don't.

A hand to my cheek, Coty steals my attention momentarily. "I do."

My mouth twitches at the cheese factor but his serious expression has my heart picking up speed. He means it. Or at least he thinks he does. *Give it time.*

I turn my head, placing a kiss to his palm.

He continues asking questions about my past and I fill him in with the bits and pieces I'm willing to share. There's a fine line between interest and pity when revealing my childhood to others and I'm careful with the details I divulge. Always. Coty listens intently, never rushing me or pressing for answers I'm not ready to give.

At some point, I look over to find Coty fast asleep. One arm above his head, one draped over my thigh, he is the picture of euphoria. My heart squeezes watching his chest rise and fall, so steady, so sure—so fucking beautiful. It would be too easy to fall for this man. To fall for everything I've gone without.

I gently move his arm over to his stomach and return his laptop to its original spot. Bending down, I kiss his forehead before quietly letting myself out.

Beckett's closing the front door just as I enter the main room.

"You sneaking out?"

Am I? "Coty passed out, so I'm heading home."

Through the dim light from the TV, I watch his eyebrows shoot up. "Damn, Coty's gonna be pissed when he finds out you ditched him." He chuckles to himself. "Want to finish the rest of this movie?"

"Can't."

"Lame," he chides. "It's your last day or some shit, isn't it?"

"Almost."

"Come on, don't make me finish this movie alone. It's scary."

I glance at the paused screen and scoff. "*Tremors?* That movie's old as hell."

"So what? It's scary as hell, too."

Such a big baby.

"Where's that girl from earlier? She'll keep the monster worm-things away."

He plops on the couch, tsking. "You know better than that, neighbor girl. Remember? No midnight snack for her."

"Is that an apartment-wide rule or just you?"

"Why? Do you want to spend the night?" He wiggles his eyebrows as I slip my hands inside the hoodie pocket. Then, so low I almost miss it, he says, "It's just me."

His tone hints at something deeper but I'm too tired to dig, so I sit on the other side of the couch from him, stretching my legs out along his. He throws a blanket over us while I try not to gawk at how long his legs actually are.

"Can I hold your hand?"

I poke my bare foot out of the blanket in front of Beckett's face, laughing when he jerks back. He shoves my foot away playfully, mumbling something about taking his chances.

Beckett shares the story of the first time he watched the cult classic with his dad. Listening to him recall the fond memory quiets the stream of thoughts rushing through my mind and I settle in, welcoming the distraction. We fall into comfortable silence after a while. The peace it presents is staggering. Unfamiliar. Extraordinary.

My eyes grow heavy as the blanket's warmth envelopes me. With the constant heat in my apartment, I forgot how comforting a thick blanket can be.

I'm being pulled under just as I hear a whispered, "can we keep you?" but I don't remember that line being in the movie. I mean who would want to keep something around that only causes destruction anyway?

Once again, I wake to Coty lifting me. This time, snuggled against his chest, I notice him carrying me down a different hall. I vaguely recognize it as the hall to his room and not the one that leads to my apartment. Everything now dark, it's hard to be certain but his scent hits me as he swings the door shut with his foot careful not to jostle me, and I know it's his room.

"What are you doing?" I grumble.

"I fell asleep with you in my arms, I'm going to wake up with you in them, too."

Positioned in the middle of the bed, Coty follows, climbing in behind me. He wraps his body around mine and, unable to argue—physically or otherwise—I'm already drifting out to a sea of bliss.

"Shh. Sleep. I got you."

And stupid me, I listen.

For now.

CHAPTER 23

Angela

OTY'S LIPS COAXING ME AWAKE WAS A PLEASANT WAY to start the day and I've missed them ever since. He's held true to his word of being my personal chaperone, taking me to work and picking me up. I didn't realize what a relief it would be having his car waiting for me at the end of my shifts.

The morning tradition of the boys sending me off to school from their back balcony remains. Some days all three are out, other times only Coty is. Today both Coty and Beckett are sitting at their round patio table, watching me with grins plastered to their good-looking faces.

"Morning, neighbor girl," Beckett calls.

"Good morning."

"You got any errands today? I'm all yours."

Hearing an 'oof,' I look up to see Coty pulling his hand back from Beck's stomach.

"Good morning, Coty."

"I woke up alone today so I wouldn't know." His expression changes to match his glum words.

I smile anyway.

"Dude, you know I'm always up for cuddles." Beckett stands, winking as he leans his elbows against the banister.

As I cross the street over to school grounds, I can tell the moment they catch sight of the back of my shirt. I'm wearing a black racerback tank with a flowery skull on the front and my hot pink bra showing through the completely see-through lacy back. I chose my shredded white shorts to add more attitude to the already bold outfit. Today being the last day of school, I decided

I'd go out with a bang. Judging from the cusses sounding from behind me, it has the desired effect. I also filled all six of my ear piercings with small hoops instead of my usual studs, giving a bit more edge, too.

I peek over my shoulder with a mischievous smirk. The look from Coty, who's now standing with the banister in a death grip, is full of rage, heat, and, ultimately, powerlessness. I wave innocently, then continue on my way.

Only a few more steps in and I'm suddenly picked up from behind by someone who smells a lot like my favorite neighbor. Before I can react, Coty puts me back on my feet, arms wrapped around my middle.

"Are you trying to kill me with this outfit?" he says into my neck, giving me goose bumps.

"You've seen me in a bikini but this is a problem?"

"It's a problem because you're going to be surrounded by a bunch of horny teenagers."

"You're one to talk."

"Damn right."

I scoff, trying to shrug him off but he doesn't budge.

Spinning in his arms, I catch him off guard as we're brought face-to-face. My hands come up to rest on his cheeks.

"Don't you know? I'm just a horny teenager myself." I lick his lip before kissing him hard.

Close but not close enough, he presses his groin in line with mine and we both groan from the contact.

"Skip. Spend the day with me. I'll call in sick."

I push against his shoulders.

"Not happening."

I've never skipped in my life and I'm not going to on the last day of my high school career.

Plus, I've always reveled in getting perfect attendance and good grades. I never did it to prove myself to her, she doesn't deserve that kind of credit, I've always done it for myself. I take great pride in being the opposite of what she's always claimed I am—a fatherless fuck-up of a mistake. I know plenty of fuck-ups that have fathers though, proving her foolish theory wrong yet again.

Coty lets me push his body away this time.

"Do you work today?"

"No, I kept my day open for the parties."

Coty chuckles. "Sounds about right, party animal."

I roll my eyes.

He brings his face in close again, his hand smoothing over the lace to find his go-to spot.

"See you later," he says slyly then steals a quick kiss.

Releasing me, he walks back to the complex with the sexiest swagger I've ever seen. I stand here admiring the muscles in his back as they tighten from his hands in his pockets. His triceps flex, showing how strong he is. His walk is slow and relaxed, exactly how my body feels after he showers me with affection.

The fog threatening to overtake me, I spin around and walk a little faster to first period.

◆ ◆ ◆

"Will I see you at any festivities this weekend?"

"Probably not." I shrug.

"Why not? I'd pay money to see you drunk," Eli, a kid in my chemistry class, teases as we walk through the paper-filled hallway. The stupid tradition of seniors making it rain papers on the last day has left the hall a complete mess. Sheets of all sizes and colors flutter through the air around us. Eli's asked me to several parties through the years, all to which I declined, so he knows my penchant for avoiding large social gatherings. He places his hand on my lower back as we make our way out the door and into the too-bright sunshine.

I think back to the night with Coty and a bottle of vodka and my cheeks warm. "I drink sometimes."

He eyeballs me sketchily. Squeezing in closer to fit through the gate together, Eli throws his arm over my shoulder. "Well, if that's the case, maybe I'll see you Saturday night."

"Don't hold your breath," I mutter, shrugging him off just as I hear my name.

I lock eyes with Coty leaning against his Camaro, legs crossed at the ankles. His beast of a car is parked front and center at the curb, gaining interest from students and teachers alike. His eyes leave mine to shoot to Eli, who drops his arm awkwardly, before snapping his head back to me.

"Is he your boyfriend? I didn't think you even liked guys."

That makes me smile, and I give Eli a shove, then say goodbye. He chuckles as he heads toward the student lot.

Coty pushes off his car, sauntering over. His casual outfit of ripped jeans and a black V-neck tee with aviator glasses and slightly styled hair look too sexy for any sane woman to resist.

A couple feet away he stops.

"Who was that?" His head jerks toward Eli's retreating form.

My eyes stay on his with a quirk of an eyebrow. "A friend."

Coty breaks first and reaches for me in the next breath. Arms around my back, he leans in to whisper, "Babe, you don't have any friends."

I bark out a laugh. "You're starting to catch on."

He pulls back with a panty-dropping smile and grabs my hand, hauling me forward.

"I could've just walked home, you know. We live across the street, literally. You didn't need to leave work for this."

"It's your last day, of course I'm picking you up. And we're not going home."

"Where are we going then?"

Wordlessly, Coty opens the passenger door, allowing me to climb in before strolling to his side. He starts the car which draws even more attention with the rumble of the throaty exhaust, and revs it a couple more times for his own amusement.

"You'll see."

CHAPTER 24

Angela

THE OVERLOOK IN THE DAYLIGHT HOLDS AN ENTIRELY new quality than it did the last time we were here. For starters, it's off limits. The cover of night hid the tall PRIVATE ROAD sign paired with a smaller, yet just as serious one saying KEEP OUT. Yeah, Coty didn't even try to keep the smile from his face when we passed those 'suggestions' as he called them on the way up here.

Also, there are huge wind-turbines. Everywhere. The colossal white structures, a stark contrast to the olive green and muted brown terrain, essentially dominate the otherwise desolate rolling hills.

My stomach lurches, not only from the height—which is glaringly noticeable in the daylight—but also the added danger of trespassing. Like the turbines outside churning up unseen energy, unease begins to swell with each charged inhale I take.

Coty interrupts my very own anxiety tempest when he produces a large bag from the back.

"I brought extra this time."

His wink gives me pause. *Extra what exactly?*

"Limes. For lunch." With a face splitting grin, he jostles my tightly clenched hand. "Follow me."

Loosening my grip on my seat helps unfurl the knot in my chest allowing me to trail after Coty breathing a bit easier.

Evidently, he planned an entire picnic, even picking up food and drinks from the best taco truck in town, Paco's Tacos. And true to his word, he got me extra limes. And then some.

Blanket tucked under his arm, we wander over to spread it out closer to the ledge.

Once settled, we divide up the different containers and Coty happily digs in. Since I'm too hungry to nitpick about prices, I do, too.

I take in the town below as I chew. I've lived here my whole life and never saw it from this perspective. The ability to see further gives the illusion the city is bigger than it is, that it holds more opportunity than it actually does. Seeing buildings, roads—things that seem so large and imposing—appear so small and inferior, it makes me think about the issues in my life. They consume my thoughts and squash my hopes, piling up, making it hard to see past them. But if I change my perspective, maybe I'd be able to see around the problems more clearly.

"What are you thinking about?"

"How different it feels up here."

"Crazy, huh? I love being here at night but my favorite time is during the day, when I can see everything that I drive right by without ever noticing."

I glance over to watch as he takes in the scene below.

"Like what?"

He points his finger and I follow its path. "See that mountain? Years ago, when Mount St. Helens erupted, ash blew for miles and miles, even reaching over here. That mountain, standing directly in the debris' path, took the biggest blast, making it very rich in silt. There was so much ash, of course, that it spread everywhere, but that mountain has more than the rest of this entire region. Nothing's out there still, so it looks just like the others but it's not. Not even close."

Coty's eyes round as he talks.

"Will they develop it at some point?"

He shrugs a little too nonchalantly. "Probably. This area is growing every day. It'd be stupid not to use that land. The bottom is safe from the harsh winds that are infamous for wreaking havoc here. Hence." He gestures to the countless turbines spinning above our heads. "That soil's rich with nutrients you can't buy. It's where I would plant crops."

"Do you want to? Plant crops?"

He lies back and covers his face with an arm to block the sun. He pats his chest for me to join him with the other but I lie alongside him instead.

"Someday, I do. A nice piece of land where I can ride and grow things. Rugrats running around." He peeks out from under his arm at me.

I drop my eyes. I've never put much thought into my future long-term, only able to see the obstacles right in front of me. Again, looking at things from a different perspective can reveal things I didn't know were there. Hopes, dreams, goals I never realized I wanted. The way Coty describes his future makes it sound attainable, not like he just wants to get there but that he plans to. Knowing Coty's persistent ass, he probably will.

"What about you?"

Voice coarse, I counter, "What about me?"

"Do you want a family?"

Shit.

I squint at the clouds overhead and blow out a breath. "I don't know. I never really thought about it. Growing up with my mom's revolving door of men, I spent so much time resenting the pressure she put on her relationships. You know? Like her happiness depended on a man. I learned to stand on my own instead of hinging my well-being on a guy, never considering what genuine love would look like. I've never seen a healthy relationship to even want one for myself. I've just been content to survive, never bothering to strive for more. If that makes sense." A blush coats my face. "But your dream sounds nice. I hope you get it. You'd be a great dad."

I try to blink back the vision that scenario generates but against my better judgement, I don't. I imagine Coty with another woman—beautiful, happy, *loved*—standing on their porch together, watching their kids—laughing, ecstatic, *loved*—play in their expansive country yard.

That freeloader Gale, the one who showed up unannounced

the second we arrived, upgrades from a forceful wind to a full-blown fucking cyclone knocking around my chest until the rest of me is rattling in confusion.

Knowing Coty will live out his fantasy, alongside someone that deserves to share it with him, fills me with such agony I rub small circles against my sternum. On the other hand, the thought that he might not get the package deal he so desperately yearns for somehow hurts even worse.

I force myself to breathe normally even though breathing is the last thing I feel like doing.

"Hey." I turn to find him propped on his elbow gazing down at me, eyebrows pinched. "The wounds our parents make can leave the ugliest scars. But they can also teach us what not to do. If you burn your hand on the stove, do you just give up ever using it again?" The circular motion stops and I give him a blank stare. He does know cooking is not my thing, right? Luckily, he doesn't expect an answer. "No. You learn not to put your bare hand on a hot stove the next time you cook. You're more careful, more thoughtful, more prepared. Our parents influence who we are, but we choose who we become. Their mistakes don't have to be ours."

"God, I hope so."

"I know so. Look at my parents. The damage my dad's done can never be erased but that won't stop me from working my ass off being a better man, and one day husband, than him. I choose that. Watching him hurt my mom, I don't ever want to cause that kind of pain to someone I love. So, I won't." He shrugs like it's the easiest thing in the world. Like his father's ghost won't haunt him for years to come even if he's already dead to Coty.

Although, the conviction in his voice makes me believe him. He'll make an amazing husband to someone, not because he was shown how, but because he wasn't. Coty's strong enough to carve his own path, taking the road that's been hidden from him by his parents' troubled marriage and I'll bet he makes it there without incident.

With a glance down below, I can't help but wonder what alternate routes lie ahead for me. Whatever awaits me I know I have to be open to try.

A rumble in the distance has us sitting up.

"Looks like a storm's coming in." Coty gestures to the darkened horizon.

Thunderstorms don't happen often around here but when they do, they're a welcome reprieve from the constant dry heat of summer.

"Should we pack up?"

"Are you asking me to go back to your place?"

I bump his shoulder with mine.

We work together to get things cleaned up and returned to the trunk.

Before I can grab my door handle, Coty catches me by the waist and presses me against the passenger side. Gently, he brushes my hair back with one hand while I drape mine around the back of his neck, looking him in the eye.

"Thank you. You think about the little things." I've never had anyone make me feel special and Coty acts like it's his own personal mission. I hedge, "Why are you so good to me?" then hold my breath. One day he'll realize I'm just a distraction, a roadside attraction, along the carefully paved path to his highly anticipated future and he'll move on. The only thing remaining will be the footprints he left on my recklessly constructed, stationary heart.

"Because I want to." He presses a chaste kiss to my lips. "Because you're worth it." Another kiss, this one just under my ear. "Someone made you believe you're not. I'm going to show you that you are." The last being whispered against my ear melts the worry away along with the last of my resolve.

On a gasp, I draw my head back in line with his and seal my lips to his impatiently. Coty's hands drop to my ass, lifting me and I happily wrap my legs around his lean torso. I notice his hand reach behind my back just before he pushes me against the side of his car. Pinned by his waist, Coty pulls back from my mouth. My lips part, ready to beg, when his other hand grips my chin, tilting my head back against the roof of the car. He proceeds to make a meal out of my neck and chest like he didn't just fill up on lunch. I grip his hair, keeping him in place and hang on for the erotic ride he's taking me on, panting and moaning along the way.

Desperate to ease the ache his tongue on my throat is creating, I push upright using the hot metal at my back to press my waist forward, rubbing against his straining cock. Coty hisses, pulling back from my neck and catches my mouth with his before grinding into me mercilessly.

"Coty," I beg.

"I know, babe."

Both hands on my ass, he walks us to the front of his car, never once breaking our connection. As soon as I feel my back hit the unforgiving metal of the Camaro's hood though, my lips rip from his. "I'll dent your car."

"Then you better stop moving."

He elicits another moan by nipping my lips before lowering to my chest, kissing as he goes.

"I want to taste you."

"I think you got a pretty good sample already," I mutter, causing him to look up when he reaches my waistband.

One-handed, he pops the button. "I told you I had a big appetite, babe. And I'm just getting started."

My eyes go wide then both my shorts and panties are yanked down. I fist my hands by my hips, trying not to sink any lower from the movement. Now exposed, I glance around, checking that we're still alone.

Creaks under my body the only noise as Coty pulls my pathetic coverings the rest of the way down. The icy apprehension skirting across my skin quickly melts away as white hot anticipation takes over. Using my heels, I push up to help remove the material but then the metal dips, causing Coty to look at my feet. His eyes bounce back to mine and he tsks, "I told you not to move."

"You're making it kind of hard here." I resist the urge to roll my eyes. Barely.

Garments forgotten, Coty leans up to kiss me roughly. His scratchy jeans, stretched from his erection, scrape against my bare pussy as he grinds into me. My hands abandon their station at my sides to grab him. Anywhere. Everywhere. I just want more. Of him. Of whatever I can hold, if only for a moment.

"Just returning the favor," he rasps.

Once my lower half is completely naked, Coty throws my legs over his shoulders. The second I feel his lips touch my hip bone, I arch my back clear off the hood. Lips, tongue, teeth, they're all there in a tantalizing dance that I crave in a spot a little further south—a spot that's full on throbbing, awaiting Coty's touch. Swirling his tongue lower, he kisses my inner thigh and pauses. So incredibly patient at such an incredibly bad time. I'm too far gone in lust to speak, so I moan greedily instead. That's all the encouragement Coty needs before he licks up my slit then sucks my swollen clit into his mouth. I dig my heels into his back, earning myself an eager groan. The vibration rolls through my aching flesh and suddenly I'm gasping for air. Where Coty was hungry starting out, the man is downright starved now. My fists clench and unclench in his hair. Keeping my body still proves more difficult when Coty begins fucking me with his tongue. His hands wrap around the tops of my thighs as he holds me to his face. The thread holding me to Earth, to reality, to my sanity, starts to unravel, slowly at first then picking up speed with each thrust. The pressure builds until it feels like I'm riding a moving train. My lower half shakes and I know I'm close.

"Coty," I say, begging him to send me over the edge. "Fuck," I say, just because.

He returns his attention to my clit and I almost weep. Licking and sucking and stealing almost all of my breath, Coty's mouth plays me like I'm his greatest symphony.

It's not until he growls, "come for me," that I realize I still haven't. This. This is the ecstasy. The climax is just the icing on the sexual favor cake. But with one last thrust of his wicked tongue, I oblige. With my toes curled, almost painfully, and my legs frozen against his back, I'm thrown into an earth-shattering orgasm. The shaking in my waist momentarily suspended as I ride the wave of bliss Coty just coaxed from me. Coty's hunger still apparent in his groans as he guides me back to shore.

Bringing his face up to mine, he wipes his lips quickly. "That was," he kisses me deeply before breaking to finish his thought, "fucking hot."

Only able to moan my agreement, I savor the fact that I can taste myself on him.

Coty must disagree though because at that exact moment he pulls back with creased eyebrows.

"What?"

Coty doesn't answer me; however, the loud crack of thunder directly above our heads does. Before we can even react, the fast-moving cloud above us opens up, dumping rain on us.

"Shit!"

We scramble off the hood, scooping up my discarded items, then meet inside the car. The doors shut at the same time and we both break into incredulous laughter.

"I'm soaked," I declare, pulling on my shorts over my skewed underwear.

"I know. And it was the sexiest thing I've ever seen." Why is this the awkward part when I was just spread eagle in front of the guy? "Thank you."

"For what?" I may not be a pro but I do know only one of us reached orgasm—and by one of us, I do mean me.

His eyes drift down my body before returning to my flushed face. "Thanks for coming up here with me. And for trusting me."

"I wouldn't go that far," I mutter under my breath. I mean... *right?*

He grabs my hand, placing it on his thigh while he turns the key, saying, "I would." The Camaro roars to life and we leave our own little slice of heaven, riding the high of our new familiarity.

◆ ◆ ◆

I remember sitting in the back seat of one of the nicer cars my mom had finagled her way into—I was seven, maybe eight—and there was this song playing softly, the words too low for me to catch as I studied my fingers, wondering if they looked like my dad's. They were never painted, always chipped, and one curled around my fingertip if I let it grow out too long, and I thought maybe, just maybe, his were the same way. All of a sudden, the music cut off, I don't know if it actually did or if it just felt like it, but there was this moment of pure silence—utter peace, almost eerily so—just before everything erupted into total chaos. Someone had blown through a red light, nailing the front end of our car at forty-five miles an hour, causing me to slam my head into the window and shatter the glass.

Looking back, I recognize that hiccup in time as being the calm before the storm. Nature's way of preparing your senses for the bombardment of overstimulation they're about to experience.

So when Coty pulls into Creekwood and everything turns static—the song whispering into my ears, the crunch of the tires rolling across the asphalt, the swish of Coty's jeans under my palm—that's how I know, that even though there's not a cloud in sight, the storm beat us home.

In that moment suspended in time, I look over at Coty, soaking in his relaxed posture before everything speeds back up. Before the chaos descends. A hand confidently draped over the steering wheel, a smile playing at his lips, blissfully unaware. Blinded by the afterglow from the lookout, his natural magnetism threatens to pull me in as well. To shield my eyes from the impending danger.

Reluctant to tear my gaze away, I close my eyes and turn my head. A glance out my window brings reality back into focus. A red Honda—new, judging by the plates—fills the space my Jeep usually sits. When I spot familiar shag hair occupying it, my stomach clenches.

I remove my hand from Coty's thigh to shoot off a quick text to Drew, asking if he's seen my mom lately. He did spill the beans to Coty after all. Well, some of them. He wouldn't tell her where I live though.

But then, how else did she find me?

Coty's eyebrows dip as he parks. Through the mirror, I watch in horror as my mother gets out and leans against the driver's door, inspecting my new residence with an interest that makes my skin prickle.

Shit.

"Hey, is everything okay?" Coty reaches a hand out that I promptly dodge.

She shouldn't be here. She can't see him.

My phone pings with notification after notification. *Drew.* He's worried but I brush off his offers to help. I need to stand on my own or not at all. Plus, him showing up will only add to the circus currently camped at Creekwood.

On an exhale, I turn to Coty who's watching his rearview mirror closely. "Is that your mom?"

I scoff. "Kind of." *Only in the literal sense.* "Can we leave? I don't care where we go. Will you just drive me away right now?"

I look back to see Rianne zeroed in on the black sports car with a sick smirk. I know that look—well.

Beckett's Tahoe pulls up next to Coty then, the loud bass shaking our seats as we glance over at his roommates wearing matching frowns.

"Shit, shit, shit," I grit and jump out like the Camaro caught fire. Or maybe I'm the one burning up.

A breeze picks up, blowing rain-infused strands across my face, and the reminder of the earlier downpour makes me regret ever leaving the lookout. *So much for fresh starts after rainstorms.*

"Hey, Ang." I flinch at her preferred pet name. "Nice place you got here."

She straightens from the car and I pick up the pace, meeting her away from the others.

"What are you doing here?"

"I can't visit my daughter?" She holds her hands out feigning innocence and I'm guessing that's not all her hand is out for. She wouldn't risk a public scene unless she was desperate. I just need to get her inside, away from…everything.

I vaguely hear car doors slamming shut over the blood rushing to my ears.

"Are we playing the loving mother now? And I'm supposed to be the gracious hostess? Fine." I start forward. "Let's go."

"I don't know, I'm liking the view much better now."

Spinning on my heel, I watch as she locks eyes with Coty. He stands tall, his friends joining him between their cars.

No.

"You're more like me than I thought," she muses as her greedy gaze devours everyone in sight.

No.

"Angela?"

I snap my eyes shut, willing him to leave.

"Who are your friends?"

They fly open to find Coty standing at my back, too close. His gaze meets mine and he frowns. Coming up behind him are the rest of his trio.

I'm out of time.

With as much venom as I can muster, I say, "Nobody. Just nosey neighbors."

Coty's nostrils flare. I ignore him and the tightness in my chest to face my mother again.

"Hmmm. I'm not sure I believe that."

"I don't care what you believe. Let's go upstairs. I'll get you what you came for." The sooner she's paid, the sooner she leaves. All of us.

"Neighbor girl? What's going on here?"

Just enjoying a family reunion, can't you tell? "None of your business." I clench my fists, then cross my arms over my chest to hide the shaking.

"Oh, let me guess, she plays the pitiful, neglected card and you think you can save her?" She's staring at Coty but lets her gaze drift to the others. "It won't work. I should know, some things aren't worth the effort." Her eyes land on mine, making her point clear.

"The fuck?" I hear behind me but I don't dare look their way.

"Just like I thought." She laughs maliciously. "Seems like they're more than just neighbors to me, Ang." I grind my teeth as she makes a show of scanning the lot. "Where's that Jeep of yours? Don't tell me you had to sell it to make rent already? Or are they helping with that?" She jerks her head at the boys now forming a circle at my back.

I step forward, away from the safety they're trying to provide. "I don't need a man to pay my way actually. I have something called a job. A foreign concept to someone like you, but a necessity for people like me."

"Sure," she scoffs. "Tell me, how's that corrupt boss treating you these days?" When my eyes widen, she laughs. Lips curled, her eyes run the length of me, sneering, "Like I said, no better than me."

"Yeah, well, a mistake born from a mistake, right?"

"If the shoe fits." She smirks, a cruel reminder of the day I came home in tears from being teased.

Coty's hand reaches out but I shrug it off, shuffling forward.

"Bravo, Mother. I see you've been working on your insults." If only her accuracy hadn't improved as well. "How did you even find me?"

Rianne waves a hand. "I followed you after school, it wasn't that hard. I had no idea you were shacking up with three grown men though. I see you've managed to learn something under my care after all."

"I don't live with them! They mean nothing to me!" She's picking at the frayed edges of my sanity, the fibers unraveling the more she tugs.

I hear a murmured "what the hell?" through the pounding in my head.

"I didn't want you to know where I moved because of *you*. And nothing else. I refuse to be near your toxic bullshit anymore. Look at you." I gesture at her. "You think I want to be around this?"

"Oh, please. Like I'm the problem here." She steps closer, getting in my face and I hear three pairs of feet surge forward as she hisses, "Do they know what you are?"

"Leave them out of it. They're off-limits," I grit out.

The moment her eyes flash with victory I know I fucked up. I just revealed the card I'd been holding close to my chest and her triumphant smirk tells me she knows it.

"What are you doing here, Rianne?"

Both our heads jerk at Drew's voice but, she moves first, pretending to examine her hand.

"Ooh, Andrew. What a surprise. You always were jumping to be the hero," she says to her nails, then raises her eyes. "Tell me, when will you ever stop pining for Ang? From the looks of things," her gaze flicks over my shoulder, "you've been replaced."

With a growl, I lunge forward. Unfortunately, someone catches me from behind before I can make contact. I push out of Coty's arms, fighting to stay rooted.

"You shouldn't be here. Or are you all out of victims to scam so you came back for the low hanging fruit?"

"Drew," I warn, but he keeps going as he walks over to stand next to me.

"Aren't Angela's checks enough?"

"Andrew! Stop."

A peek past my shoulder reveals three sets of eyes glued to the scene, all varying degrees of interest. Coty's hard gaze flits between Drew and Rianne, then lands on mine softening significantly.

Beckett's curious stare touches everyone, never staying too long before moving onto the next. And Marc's full on glaring daggers, not giving a damn who gets cut.

Beckett steps forward, asking quietly, "You okay, Angie?"

The sympathy in his voice clogs mine. They were never supposed to see this. I shake my head at him, turning to Drew.

"Can you get me out of here? Please."

"Angela, don't." Coty's touch burns my elbow and I twist from his hold.

Unable to meet anyone's eyes, I keep mine lowered. "I have to go."

Drew on my heels, we start toward his car.

"You owe me! Don't you forget it. That debt will never be cleared."

Bright red coats my vision as I spin to face my mother again. "I already told you, you want it? Come and fucking get it! Nobody regrets you having me more than me."

A collective grumble catches my notice just before I duck into Drew's Acura. Without looking back, we speed off. Away from the only place that's ever felt safe. Away from the people that were starting to feel like family. Away from him. Away from home.

CHAPTER 25

Coty

I STEP IN FRONT OF ANGELA'S RANTING MOTHER, CUTTING her off amidst her pitiful glower. I face her, making sure she stays put, even though everything in my body is screaming to go after Angela myself. Her last words ring in my head on repeat. She doesn't really mean that, *right?*

"I think Angela's had enough," I spit.

"And if she hasn't, I sure the fuck have." Beck posts up on my side. "Damn, woman, up until today I thought I had the world's worst mom, and she abandoned me."

Angela's mom sneers, "Lucky her." *Jesus.* This bitch is evil. "You boys are wasting your time. My daughter isn't worth the trouble. You'll see soon enough."

"Leave," Beck demands.

"You've outstayed your welcome." If there ever was one.

"Excuse me? My daughter lives here. I'll come around whenever I damn well please!" She sticks her finger in my face and I rear back to avoid her talon-like nails. This demon came to play. Little does she know I'd take on the devil himself to protect Angela.

"Yeah?" I spread my hands out wide. "I live here, too, and I'm telling you to leave."

"What? Are you paying her bills or something? Wouldn't surprise me. She tries to act better than me but she's cut from the same unwanted cloth."

How can she play victim while simultaneously being the villain? I'd be impressed if I wasn't so fucking disgusted. This woman raised Angela?

"You don't even know her, do you? Angela wouldn't accept a

handout if it was her last option. She fights for her independence and refuses to be a charity case. She works her ass off, choosing to take the hard road repeatedly instead of taking any shortcuts. She's smart and tough as nails." For anyone to not see that is ludicrous. "And you're wrong, Angela isn't unwanted. I want her. I want her exactly the way she is. Which from what I've seen today, aside from a few physical features, is nothing like you." *Thank fuck.*

She barks out a harsh laugh. "Oh, really? And yet, she just left with someone else. You may think you want her, but does she want you?" She steps closer and I step back, careful not to let her too close. I don't know what this monster is capable of. "You can try to see the good in her all you want. At the end of the day she'll only ever choose herself. She'll leave this world the way she entered it, alone and completely useless."

And…wow. Just wow. No wonder Angela doesn't trust anyone. This nut job spewing her bullshit would make anybody jaded.

"It doesn't matter. I'll choose her, over and over again." I just need Angela to believe it first. Seeing where she came from shows I've got a steep road ahead but I've never backed down from digging in and pushing full throttle, and I'm not about to start now.

"*We* choose her," Beck adds firmly, nodding when I look over at him. "Every time."

"Yo, B, these new Civics are supposed to be unstealable, right?" Having stayed quiet until now, Marc steps up to my other side, surprising all of us. Beck's eyes light up like a kid on Christmas morning. "How easy would it be to reset the immobilizer?" Marc makes it a point to stay out of other people's business until he feels it necessary. Guess he's reached his limit. *Welcome to the fucking club.*

Hands rubbing together, Beck whistles, sidling up to the red hood. "Too easy, bro."

"If we see you here again causing problems, I'll personally see to it that your car goes missing." After a beat he adds, "Whether you're in it or not. Now fuck off and don't come back."

"How dare you threaten me!"

"Anyone hear me threaten her?"

"Threaten who?" Beck asks innocently, glaring at the woman in question.

"Nope. The only threats I heard were the ones you've been making toward your own daughter." I raise my eyebrows, letting the accusation linger.

Her face pales as she opens her door to climb in. "Suit yourselves. Just remember, trash can't be saved."

With that unfounded fact that I'm positive environmentalists everywhere would disagree with, we turn to watch her leave.

As usual, Beck's the first to break the silence. "Goddamn, she was nasty. I need a drink."

"Make that two."

"Three," I add.

Beck claps me on the back. "You gonna call her?"

"Fuck." I run my hands through my hair, wishing I had a hat to cover it with. "I have to. We got her car."

This makes Marc laugh. "How long 'til she figures out there's nothing wrong with it?"

I groan, turning for the stairs. "Don't remind me."

Big Mouth Beckett's laughter booms through the stairwell, bouncing off the paint-chipped walls. "You fucked yourself on that one, huh?"

Yes, yes, I did. That shit backfired big time. Keeping her car under false pretenses was meant to help Angela, not push her into some other dude's arms.

I know something weird is going on with that manager of hers. I had my suspicions before, what with his lurking around Creekwood, but driving through the wash with Marc confirmed it. Dude is bad news any way you slice it. Even Angela's absentee mom mentioned the guy being immoral. Watching him ogle Angela as she cleaned up the other night was torture. I swear I've never wanted to beat the shit out of someone so bad, but ultimately, I didn't. That job's important to Angela—after meeting her mom I can see why—and I couldn't risk her losing it over me bashing her boss's face in. With her only form of transportation taken away, I've been able to make my presence not only seen but also felt at every shift since, which seemed like a good compromise. At the time.

Angela's strong, not only physically, but mentally, too, and can take care of herself, but she shouldn't have to. Knowing she'd refuse any help I offered, I jumped at keeping her car for a little longer than necessary. It's not all bullshit—the vintage Jeep did need some repairs—but nothing we didn't already have on hand. Beck got it fixed up as best he could, practically good as new, but I've been sitting on that information, waiting for the right time to bring it up. And now she's with her boy Drew, or Drew The Douche as I like to call him—when Angela's not around anyway—after spending the day with me. Fan-fucking-tastic.

Hell, I can still taste her if I lick my lips just right, which actually is fantastic considering how incredible Angela's essence is.

I fling open our door, stalking to the kitchen to grab a sports drink from the fridge, then down the entire thing.

Today got away from me. It was damn near perfect before Satan's mistress showed up, ruining everything. Angela was just starting to lower some of her walls for me. For us. I think back to the other night finding her asleep on the couch next to Beck. She's warming up to us even if she doesn't realize it yet.

Marc takes a seat at the counter, distributing the highly desired alcohol. Three shots of Fireball poured, we wordlessly cheers, then shoot them back simultaneously. The cinnamon-flavored burn a welcome distraction from the worry coating my throat.

The kitchen falls silent, everyone lost in their own thoughts.

Family members fighting with each other is nothing new, although in Marc's family it's usually only the men that do the verbal sparring. Watching two females go at it, especially with such blatant animosity, was unsettling for all of us. The fact it was directed at the woman that had her legs wrapped around my head just this afternoon made it that much harder to witness.

My parents avoid confrontation altogether, content with pretending everything is fine. And Beck simply doesn't have any family. I can safely say none of us have ever seen anything like that before. Angela's mom was out for blood. No doubt about it. And does she really think Angela owes her for giving birth to her? I don't care how you spin it, that's not how that shit works.

Today she let her guard down, only to throw it right back up at the first sign of her past. She's strong as hell but she must be exhausted. Playing defense full time would wear anybody down. The walls Angela barricades herself behind make more sense now. It's obvious they were built out of necessity, not choice. Needing to keep yourself safe from emotional abuse like that can take a toll. Seeing her mother's cruelty firsthand gives me a whole new respect for Angela. Of course she'll probably take it as pity though. While I do feel bad—nobody should be treated like that, especially not by a parent—I admire her strength for becoming the woman she is today.

I meant it when I said I wanted Angela. My attraction to her started the minute I laid eyes on her and has grown every moment since. Each small bit she's shown, hooking me more and more. I can breathe easier when she's near, like she's the air I've been holding my breath for all my life. The air I'd go to battle for should anything, or anyone, threaten to take it away. That small taste from earlier did nothing to satisfy my hunger for her. I crave her day and night. Waking to Angela snuggled in my arms put every other morning in my life to shame. Starting a day without her in my bed lost any previous appeal and I'll do anything to make sure the next time I get her there, she stays.

"Think she'll come home tonight?"

My eyes trace the swirling pattern of the granite, considering his question. "I don't know. She has graduation in two days so she has to come back sometime, right?"

Beck rubs the back of his neck, nodding absently. Marc's lips tilt down slightly, none of us willing to voice our doubts.

"As long as that mother of hers doesn't show up. Fuck. You really want to take that on?" Marc prods.

Eyes boring into his, I challenge, "You wouldn't?"

"She deserves better than that. Shit, nobody deserves what I heard out there. I'm not even sleeping with her and I'd gladly take on that b-"

"Watch your mouth." His eyebrows nosedive until I clarify, "It has nothing to do with sleeping with her." We share a smirk.

"Coty's right. Angie's different. For whatever reason, she ended up living next door to us, the three misfits with shittier families than the next. But we get her now. We get to show her what we learned a long time ago. That family-"

"Is a choice," Marc finishes Beck's thought.

"We just have to show her that." I nod, licking my bottom lip.

Words won't work. They've been used as a weapon against her for so long, they've lost almost all meaning. We have to prove ourselves to Angela and hope she chooses us back.

◆ ◆ ◆

"Pick up," I ground out, listening to the line ring repeatedly before going to Angela's generic voice mail—again. "Shit!" I toss my cell on the bed then yank my door open.

"Hey Coty," a girl in the kitchen purrs as I pass. I jerk a nod in her direction and continue on. *No thanks.* She's cute, with her perfectly curled blonde locks draped along her tiny shirt, showing off her curvy figure, down to her skintight jeans and high heels. She's dressed to impress and usually it would. There's just one problem though—she's not Angela.

I scratch my stomach, hoping to alleviate the tightness there. It's been twenty-four hours and still no sign of her.

The packed living room sends tingles up my arms and neck, settling at the base of my skull. Rolling my shoulders, I spot my roommates out on the back balcony. As soon as I slide open the door, my eyes scan the pool, wanting to see my favorite sight back here. However, my eyebrows snap together when I find it empty. *Fuck.*

"Anything?" Beck asks, some random on his lap.

Both he and Marc look up and I shake my head in answer. We could've missed her while we were at work, but something tells me she hasn't been here. No, that girl's running. She'll return when she feels there's no longer a threat. The chance that I might be considered part of that threat is killing me.

"Want me to get Kary?" The apartment manager. She and Marc have some kind of agreement that none of us question. He keeps her happy and in return we have free run of the place. Her having keys to all the apartments is a nice perk, if needed, but I'm not ready to violate Angela's privacy. Yet.

I shake my head again. "Nah, let's give her more time."

Marc shrugs, appearing unaffected, but I know better. I take in his still form as he stares absently at the high school across the street from Creekwood's pool area and glance over to Beck with his white knuckles around a beer, ignoring the girl squirming in his lap.

The garage was nuts today, thankfully keeping us busy, yet it didn't keep my ass from checking my phone every few minutes, hoping for literally anything from Angela. A text asking for a ride. A call telling me I should fuck off already. Okay, I wouldn't have liked that last one, but at least I would've known she was alive. Not knowing is fucking torture. Her last words continue to haunt me, and with the amount of times the guys asked about her, I know they're concerned, too. Drew better be taking good care of her. The bastard.

Speaking of, what was that shit Rianne said about him having a thing for Angela? Angela said they were step-siblings at one point and have been close ever since. Was that just her mom running her mouth? Or is he really holding out for her? Thinking back to the day I saw him with his girlfriend, and how in love they seemed, I shake the notion away. Plus, Angela wouldn't stand for those kinds of games.

That level of dumbfuckery reminds me of her shitbag boss all over again.

Damn, I'm losing my mind with the scenarios Angela could be caught up in.

"Who's on the cards tonight?" I ask suddenly, earning a pair of stunned expressions pointed my way.

"Why? You want on?" Beck asks.

I shrug, crossing my arms across my chest. "It's been a while." And I could use the distraction. We all could.

"Are you sure, dude? It's been a little-"

"I'm sure." I'm well fucking aware what it's been. I swing my gaze to Marc. "Set it up."

He doesn't respond immediately, just holds my stare, then finally sighs, saying, "Alright, I'll make the call."

Beckett stands, guiding the chick off his lap. "Let's go."

"You don't have to."

"Fuck that, I'm going. I wasn't feeling this party anyway." Ignoring the protest behind him, he moves toward the door. "I could go for a race right now, too."

We watch Marc get to his feet. "I'm in, but," his eyes land on the deserted pool, "what if neighbor girl shows?"

I blow out a breath and drop my gaze, watching the calm water like she'll surface at any moment, praying she will. "Then maybe she'll stay."

She's voiced her concerns about living next to each other enough for me to know that's partly to blame for her disappearance. If me being here is keeping her away, then I can figure out somewhere else to go. I can't promise I'll stay away for good, but I can give her the space she needs to feel comfortable again.

I just wish she'd come home already.

Since she moved in, there hasn't been a single night that I didn't go to bed knowing she was asleep just next door. Tossing and turning last night, I realized how much that knowledge comforted me. Feeling her close calms me. If I lose that, I lose a piece of my mind, a piece of my sanity. I need it back. I need her back. And I'll do anything to make that happen, even if it means leaving.

CHAPTER 26

Angela

I RUN MY HANDS DOWN THE FRONT OF MY GOWN, TRYING TO smooth out the creases. Underneath is the outfit my sister helped me pick out—a peach crocheted crop top with ties at the neck and a mid-rise white skirt flowing over strappy sandals. It's fancier than my usual sporty attire, but I love it. The eye-catching colors accentuate my deep tan and toned tummy flawlessly. With a braid along my hairline, I left the rest down to accommodate the required odd-shaped cap, the one I refuse to put on until the last possible second.

If only she were coming today to see it. Yesterday, after an hour of arguing, she confirmed she wouldn't be attending. Our mom's take on my "ungrateful attitude" swayed Kelsie to skip my graduation entirely and now I've been sentenced to quarantine as punishment.

Luckily, Drew and his dad don't follow Rianne's way of thinking so they'll be there. Drew impersonating my personal chauffeur has been inconvenient, even more than when the neighbors did, so borrowing his car for the day gave me a chance to get ready at my place alone. Honestly, staying with him was a great chance to clear my head overall. Less boys occupying my doorway and headspace. More time to focus on my job search that's becoming more important as the days pass.

While there, I also found out I was approved for the financial aid I applied for months ago. Once enrolled at the local college, I'd hoped to start general classes until I could decide what career path I wanted to take, but with all the shit that's been going on at the wash, I've determined I want to become my own boss. I want to learn everything there is to know about running a business so I don't have to work for a snake like Joe ever again.

I was able to put in a full shift yesterday, too, but with the added pressure of avoiding Joe at every turn it was long and tedious. Something it's never been before he started his weird antics. Several times I stood from finishing tire polish only to find him licking his lips in my direction. I debated between punching him or quitting, but ultimately didn't do either. I can't give up the pay, at least not yet. I called my advisor during my lunch break about the possibility of starting night classes this summer but she didn't have any openings on such short notice. To top it off, Joe insisted I stay late to clean the windows knowing full well I had graduation rehearsal. I offered Zoe, a part-time newbie, twenty bucks to help so I could make it out of there in time. I wasn't going to miss out on my final high school event and I'd be damned if I'd let Joe catch me alone again.

I wasn't surprised to find the complex quiet today but I didn't expect the neighbors' bikes to be gone. I thought they'd still be sleeping off their usual Friday night party. Ignoring Coty's calls and texts has been hard, but necessary. I've been dealing with my mom's bullshit for years—it's nothing new to me—but having others see it was worse. The idea that Rianne could get her destructive hands anywhere near Coty, or Beckett, or Marc, that was downright unbearable. I'd willingly walk back into her noxious grasp before letting her poison touch the boys next door.

Some mascara and nude lip gloss complete my look as I grab my cap and clutch. I pause when I hear the voice mail notification on my phone. My mother's raspy voice fills the earpiece and I automatically recoil.

"Yeah, Ang, I just wanted to say *you're welcome.* You know if it wasn't for me having you, you wouldn't be graduating today. You wouldn't even be here, period. I'm sure you've made yourself think you got here all on your own, but it'll do you well to stop and remember who actually carried you through. Add this to the list of things you wouldn't have without me. That Jeep, your apartment, hell, the ratty ass shoes on your feet, you wouldn't have any of it if it wasn't for me."

I glance at the pair in question, my heart racing. *They're not ratty.*

"And if those thug wannabes you're hanging around with think they can threaten me, well, they have another thing coming. I will not be intimidated, Angela. Do you hear me? Maybe if you showed a little gratitude-"

I hit the delete option before she can finish. Never one to waste an opportunity to rub my face in the great sacrifice my life was to her, I should've expected this. She won't let me have anything, not even one frickin' day to feel proud of myself. Well, too bad for her, I am proud. I'm proud I was able to do it, and not because of her, but in spite of her. I dodged her jabs, ignored her insults, countered her negativity, switched my stance to block more effectively. And I did it all by myself, watching person after person turn a blind eye to the abuse, all the while learning to never depend on anyone because at the end of the day, I'm the only one in the ring with Rianne.

She said something about being threatened though. Does she mean the boys next door? Are those the 'thug wannabes' she's referring to? My neighbors definitely don't fit that description, more like male models in street clothes, but I can't imagine who else she'd be talking about. They threatened her?

I groan remembering the way I left that day. It wasn't my best work, that's for sure, but I never thought they'd continue to interfere after I left. At some point I'll have to face them, our living situation requires it, and when I do, I can only hope the pity I saw last lining their stupidly attractive faces is missing.

With one last look in the mirror, I whisper to myself, "you got this," wondering if maybe I don't.

◆ ◆ ◆

I scan the stands again, trying in vain to make out Drew's familiar face. We couldn't meet up beforehand but I told him after rehearsal where I'd be so he could try to snag a seat close by. Facing the valedictorian, Luciana, on stage, the word regret catches my attention and I tune back in.

"They say there are no regrets in life, only lessons learned and I truly believe that. Everything happens for a reason. However, we've earned a night off from lessons. Don't you think?" I clap along with everybody else. "So, give yourself the night to reflect, to revel, to slack. A night to dine, to dance, to drink…" Thunderous cheers erupt amongst the graduates, much to the dismay of the surrounding adults. The guy sitting to my left hollers incoherently making me chuckle. Once the crowd quiets, she continues, "The saying goes 'a night to remember' but I suggest it be one in which you forget. And not in the way you think either. Seriously, if there's something you're holding onto that's stopping you from being the best version of yourself, let tonight be the night you let it go. Let tonight be the night you get it all out…responsibly, of course." At her exaggerated wink, noisy laughter fills the packed coliseum. "Because come tomorrow you have the option to start fresh. The opportunity to start anew. The chance to begin the journey of becoming who you're meant to be and I, for one, am excited to see what future paths lie ahead for all of us." Luciana pauses, letting her words sink in.

I'm reminded of my time with Coty, not just at the lookout, but since our first conversation and his constant efforts to curb the reality life has laid out for him.

"In closing, whatever you do in celebration of your accomplishments both past and future, I can't imagine getting to do it with a better group of people. I'm proud to be a part of this graduating class and you should be, too. Now, let's go give 'em hell! Sorry, Mom!"

The crowd explodes into earsplitting applause as everyone jumps to their feet to give her a well-deserved standing ovation.

"Thank you, Luciana. That was truly inspiring. I'd just like to reiterate the responsible part for tonight though," Principal Reid says, as a blushing Luciana finds her seat. "When I call your name, please come forward to accept your diploma."

I zone out again as rows of gown-clad students make their way to the stage. The beaming faces filling the stands serve as a reminder of what's missing from my life. Not having a supportive family has always been my norm. I couldn't even imagine having the encouragement of others—aside from Drew, of course. Would I still be me if I had a loving, tight-knit family growing up? The kind that would fill an entire section at my high school graduation? Seeing the indifferent expressions around me, I'm guessing I'd probably take it for granted like most of my peers.

Roars of pride erupt across the arena, making it clear how loved each grad on stage is, and I can't help the ping of jealousy the cheers create. Even if my minuscule family was here, they wouldn't make a big deal like the others. The sad truth is they'll never be what I want and I'll never be what they want. The sooner we can all acknowledge that, and move on, the better. Well, for me anyway. I'm not sure my mom will ever move past her animosity toward me. Maybe it's disappointment in herself that she's projecting, but is too emotionally immature to realize. If that's the case, then I honestly don't know how to move forward. All I really want is to get on with my life without her constant insults about me not being good enough. For so long, I thought that by hiding those attachments she considers weaknesses, I was making it harder for her to strike, but the sad truth is it's never deterred her personal attacks, only lessened the inevitable blows.

The person next to me knocks my arm, letting me know it's our row's turn. We shuffle in line until we reach the side of the stage. As the girl in front of me climbs the stairs, sweat starts to collect under my arms, making me grateful for this bulky gown. My slick palms grip the railing as I follow close behind. I watch, hypnotized by the sure pace of her steps, realizing I can't remember anything we practiced last night. In slow motion she breaks away from me, walking into the spotlight to accept the rolled up mock certificate—we were all shocked to learn we wouldn't be getting our actual diplomas today but at a later date—and I freeze. *Where do I put my fucking hands again?* Without a rail to hold onto, I twist them in front of me awaiting my name. That's a normal place for hands, right? Like, people do that. Just put their hands on their stomachs. Or is that just pregnant women? *Shit.* At this point I couldn't even guess how many hands I have, let alone where I'm supposed to put them. Also, why is it so hot in here?

I somehow make out my name through the pounding in my ears.

"Angela Taylor."

The principal blurs into a faceless entity before my eyes, so I suck in a deep breath to alleviate the pressure building in my chest. Blowing it out, all I can think is maybe it's for the best my family didn't show after all. Somehow them witnessing my heinous impression of a mime stuck in a box of invisible water seems like the least preferred scenario.

Just when I start to wonder if I really am underwater, a bullhorn to the left startles me out of my trance and I look over my shoulder to find none other than my tall-as-a-redwood neighbor standing in the aisle with a frickin' megaphone held above his head, blaring a variety of obnoxious sounds including nobody's favorite—the police siren. Beside Beckett are Marc and Coty rounding out The Three Stooges Of Creekwood and my lips pull into a smile. Coty and company are making a complete spectacle of themselves. And me, of course.

"Go," the person behind me urges. A backward glance proves I'm officially holding up the line. *Great.*

"Sorry," I mutter, then stride across the stage, toward my very own fake diploma.

"Congratulations, Angela. Sounds like you've got an enthusiastic family out there." My principal half smiles-half grimaces, shaking my hand as the horn sounds again.

"I, um, thanks." I smile tightly.

The staircase at the other end of the stage feels like a torturous trek and with no one in front of me, I hesitate at the bottom, unsure which way to take. Somehow I manage to make it back okay and once seated, I spot the boys who are still planted in the aisle causing a ruckus even though other students are being called up, my turn long over.

"Way to go, Angie!" Beck yells over the speaker and I shake my head, grinning.

I mouth "thanks" to Marc as he continues clapping which is quite a feat considering he's holding one corner of a giant handmade sign. Yes, handmade. It's huge, and colorful, and I swear has glitter flaking off the bottom onto the people's heads in front of them. It's perfect.

My eyes meet Coty's and with his fingers to his mouth he unleashes a loud whistle, then winks unabashedly. Everyone in my row looks between me and my impromptu cheer section, raising more than a few eyebrows. They finally settle back in their seats, props in hand, and it's then that I see Drew and his dad, Robert, seated just behind the modern-day version of the Three Amigos. I can't keep the smile from my face as I give them each a wave. Robert beams right back while Drew points to his ears, giving me a lopsided grin.

"And with that, it is my absolute honor and privilege to congratulate this year's graduating class!"

The noise is deafening as the senior class throws their caps in the air. I'd already decided on keeping mine, so I just remove it, running a hand over my hair instead. The boys in my section rip their gowns off—thankfully they're dressed underneath—before sending them airborne, too, making everyone laugh. Beach balls and a half-inflated blow-up doll are bounced around the throng of students as families head down to reunite with their kids.

The seats the guys were previously camped in are now abandoned, surrounded by hordes of people descending the stairs. I try to focus on congratulating my classmates as they pass but my eyes keep landing on those empty seats.

I pull out my phone feeling it vibrate in my skirt only to find a text from Drew saying they're outside. His keys still in my possession, I push through the packed floor, toward the exterior doors. With the crowd thick as mud, I'm forced to pause every few steps. I text him back, letting him know which door I'll eventually be exiting.

Girls cry and hug as guys pose and laugh, all while proud parents capture every dramatic moment on their various devices. I swear someone's using a full-sized tablet to take a selfie with their kid.

Finally, the sun hits like a runaway train in the dead of night, so I use my cap to shield my eyes until they can adjust to the harsh light. My eyesight fully restored, I glance around for any of the boys, except my eyes land on something else familiar. Parked in the grass, front and center, is my Jeep. The sea of bodies parts to reveal a huge red bow on the hood. *What?* Drew steps out from behind it, shaking with laughter.

"What is this?"

"I don't know. I walked over to find you and saw it parked here already." He purses his lips, holding in another laugh. "You didn't know about this?"

"No. It's been in the shop." Why the hell would anyone bring my beat-up Jeep with a bow on it to my graduation anyway?

The revving of motorcycles, three to be exact, catch my attention and I look over to watch as my neighbors peel out onto the street. Of course. Of-fucking-course they did this.

I face Drew, then take in the gigantic bow. Onlookers share in his amusement and soon I join in, too, laughing until tears form in my eyes.

"I guess I don't need a ride to the restaurant anymore," I joke as I wipe under my eyes, careful not to smear any mascara. I hand over his keys before grabbing the massive pile of ribbon. I can only think of one colossal clown that would choose something so big. I toss it, along with my cap and gown, in the back.

"How are you going to get that out of here?"

"In drive probably," I deadpan.

"You know what I mean."

"I do. Now get in. I'll drop you at your car so you can bask in the glory of riding in this hoopty, too. I don't want to steal the show entirely."

We climb in and I start the engine, taking a moment to appreciate the obnoxious sound I've missed all week. From the way people scatter, it seems I'm the only one appreciative of such a noise. My gaze meets Drew's and we both crack up all over again. Maybe Luciana was right about letting go after all.

CHAPTER 27

Angela

"I CAN'T ASK YOU TO DO THAT. IT'S TOO MUCH."

Robert reaches out, covering my hand with his. I keep still even as my arm twitches. "No, it's not. I should've done more to help a long time ago."

At that I do slide my hand out from under his, grabbing my water instead. I study the droplets running down the glass.

"You don't owe me anything. I'm not your obligation, so please don't worry. I'll figure it out on my own."

"You're not an obligation," Drew protests harshly, earning himself a tight-lipped smile.

"It's true, Angela, you're not. You were my daughter, too, once upon a time." My heart squeezes in my chest. *Were.* So close, yet so far away. "I'd be honored to help."

Drew's been filling his dad in on my college predicament over lunch—a nice affair I also tried to get out of but couldn't—and apparently, the company they both work for has a program for their employees interested in taking business courses. The college keeps spots in certain classes at the ready as the firm offers first dibs on intern positions to top graduates. Robert offered to get me a spot in the summer course I was just turned away from.

"Thank you very much for the offer. And for the meal. It was nice to have some family," I wince when my voice cracks, "there for me today." I gulp down more water, hoping to drown the frog perched in my throat.

"You're so strong. I've watched over the years, you know?" He looks between me and his son. "Andrew used to come home upset over what your mom would do, the things she'd say. God, it must've been hell for you all those years."

"Dad."

"Hear me out. Andrew wouldn't always tell me what was going on, but having lived with Rianne myself, I could fill in the blanks." He shivers quite theatrically and I would laugh except I know he's not exaggerating. "The crap your mother put you through time and time again, and believe me here, Angela, nobody should have to go through that, especially not a child. And I am sorry that I couldn't do more for you then. I tried though." My gaze snaps to his. "Boy, did I try. A blind man could see how Rianne treated you was wrong and I may have been slow to catch on but I wasn't blind. During the divorce, I offered her a larger sum if she'd allow you to come and live with me." His sad eyes meet Drew's. "I never told you that. I know it was a tough time there for a while, you choosing to live with your mom and all. Which I understand. I know I wasn't the best father, to either of you, but I wanted to make things better for all of us." He turns to me, water filling his bronze eyes. "But she wouldn't agree."

"Why?" the frog and I croak out. Thanks to Robert's confession, the amphibian is sticking around a while longer.

"That I can't answer. I honestly don't know." He crosses his arms on top of the table. "Pride?"

I scoff through a watery hiccup. *Sounds about right.*

"What I didn't know at the time though, was that you two would find each other all on your own. You've healed each other in ways that I never would've been able to. And it turned out you didn't need anyone's saving, Angela. You just needed a friend by your side all along. I'm so proud of you both." The tears in his eyes finally spill over and I fight mine from following suit. Feeling Drew's hand under the table, I latch onto it, lacing our fingers together. "It'd give me no greater joy than to help in this one small way, if you'd let me. Just think of me as another friend in your corner."

Robert's graying hair still has bits of Drew's auburn to it and I remember when it was the other way around, only lightly salted, and in this moment all I see is his son. My best friend for as long as I can remember, for as long as I want to remember, I know everything he's done, everything he's given has only been out of pure love and selflessness. Attributes unfamiliar to the Taylors. So foreign, I'm still fighting the novelty when I do encounter them, even to this day. Which is why I nod, feeling tears escape from the movement, and say, "Okay."

Without delay, he stands, coming to my side and before I can fully push out of my chair, I'm enveloped in a tight hug. I lift my arms to wrap around him, but Drew beats me to it, wrapping his around both of us. We stand here, huddled in an amazingly awkward group hug for several minutes, letting the affection soak in.

I don't know who moves first but we eventually pull back, each of us wiping our eyes as discreetly as possible.

"Congratulations, Angela. I know you'll go far. You've already beat the odds stacked against you. Don't let anyone tell you anything different." Robert looks me in the eye.

"Thank you, Robert." I turn to Drew. "And thank *you*."

"Aww, stop, you're making me blush," he teases.

I kiss his colorless cheek.

"You heading home?" Drew asks as we make our way out the door and I nod. The high temperature from this afternoon is still holding steady and I'm glad the long gown is no longer required.

"Speaking of, those neighbors of yours certainly seemed smitten with you. They don't give you any trouble, do they?"

"Nothing I can't handle," I tell Robert honestly.

"I don't doubt that. But let me know if they step out of line. Living next to three guys could end one of two ways." *A porn or a horror movie, I know*, I refrain from saying. Wrong audience. "Really bad or really fun. I hope for your sake it's the latter. You could use some good in your life."

I attempt a salute, causing both men to chuckle lightly. *Looks like I found a new thing to do with my hands at least.*

Cringing, I promise to keep in touch, then wave before leaving.

◆ ◆ ◆

Back home, I'm too busy replaying what Robert shared that I barely notice the busy parking lot. I scoop up my discarded items and climb the stairs without a second thought.

Only when I see the cupcake bouquet in front of my door do I stop to take in my surroundings. There's loud music coming from…somewhere. People with drinks in their hands are milling about but not from any particular apartment. A glance back at the lot shows all three bikes, and cars, which means the boys are home. *Are they having a party?*

Carefully balancing the pail—the bouquet really is cute, with frosting piped petals and leaves on the miniature cakes to look like a bundle of flowers—I unlock the door and place them on the counter before discarding the rest of my stuff.

A note catches my eye as I'm drinking some ice water and I try not to laugh at the first two lines.

Swimsuits are great,
But skinny dipping is, too.
Meet us at the pool,
Or we'll come and get you.

I spot Beckett first as he rests against the fence, leaned into a girl, his usual crude biker shirt stretched across his chest, this one reading *Eat, Sleep, Ride* with swim trunks and a backward hat. He fits the party boy image perfectly. The sign from earlier is hanging next to him, tied to the fence.

"Oh, shit." He notices me and straightens, yelling behind him, "She's here!"

My eyebrows scrunch together and I peer behind me to see who just arrived. When I don't see anyone, I turn back in time to hear a sloppy chorus of "Congratulations, neighbor girl!" from the mass of people strewn around the pool area.

Beckett lunges for me before I can move and lifts me clear off my feet. "Happy Graduation, Angie."

244 | A. MARIE

"This is for me?" I take in the strangers staring my way and whisper out the side of my mouth, "Who are all these people?"

"Who cares. They're here to celebrate your huge accomplishment and that's all that matters. And yes, it's for you. I'm proud of you, our little neighbor girl."

"*We're* proud of you." Coty steps up. "Put her down. I didn't get to hug the grad yet."

"No, then I won't get her back once you get your hands on her." Coty lifts an eyebrow.

"Do I get a say here?"

I'm met with a firm "no" from each.

"Fine." I grab Beckett's cheeks and lay a close-mouthed kiss against his pliant lips. Ignoring the sharp inhale to our right, I pull back, looking him in the eyes to tell him, "Thank you." His face softens into a smile as the rest of him stays as rigid as a board. "Now, can you please put me down? The air is really thin up here." I pretend to gasp making us both laugh. "Also, there's someone else I have to thank."

"Alright," he relents, placing me on my feet, then points at Coty. "But you have to share her tonight."

"No promises." And the way Coty's staring at me, I know he means it.

"Yeah, I figured as much. Anyway, enjoy your party tonight, Angie, 'cause it's back to business tomorrow." I don't bother correcting him that it doesn't matter what day it is, this is what they do anyways. Parties are kind of their thing. I do, however, mock chide them about their embarrassing display earlier. They both grow quiet at the mention of my Jeep but have the decency to look somewhat chastised. Well, Coty does anyway, Beckett looks like he's already cooking up plans for the next prank he can pull.

"Wow." I face Coty, sticking my hands in my skirt pockets after Beckett slinks back to his female companion. "That hurt worse than I thought it would."

"What did?"

"Seeing your lips on another man."

I drop my gaze to the ground. "Would it help if I told you he had horrible breath?"

"I heard that!" Beckett shouts, then quieter he tells the girl, "I don't. She's just joking."

Unable to hold back any longer, Coty and I dissolve into a fit of laughter. It feels good to have my friend back, or whatever he is to me. Do friends give phenomenal oral?

Shaking my head, I give him a thorough appraisal. The white tank he's wearing covers the top of his black swim trunks that sit low on his hips, showing just enough skin to heat my own. I think back to when I saw him shirtless and my gaze lands on his tattoos peeking from under his shirt.

"What do those mean?"

"That's for another time."

"Like when?"

"Like when I don't still have the image of you kissing someone else."

Friends definitely don't get that jealous over a meaningless peck.

A lazy smirk makes its way across my mouth as I step closer to him. "Want me to erase the memory?" My hands snake up his chest, around his neck and into his hair. I feel Coty's fingers land on my hips and I sway from the proximity.

"If you think you can." His shrug's a little too stiff, a little too forced. It's his darkening eyes that totally give him away though. I have to bite back a smile.

"Oh, I know I can." His hands grip me tighter, spurring me on as I close the distance, crashing my lips to his. Coty's greed kicks in when my lips part, allowing his tongue to sweep inside. Mine chases his in a playful game of tag before I pull back with one last flick to his top lip.

Coty keeps his eyes closed as I watch his face. "You're forgiven," he whispers before meeting my gaze.

"For what?"

"For sharing those lips with someone that isn't me." He kisses said lips again, quickly. Too quickly. "And for ghosting me. I didn't know what happened to you, and you wouldn't even answer a single text, or come back to your apartment. I don't know, I was losing my shit."

Sighing, I drop my hands from his neck. "I know, I'm sorry." Straight off a page from Luciana's overachieving book, I'm giving myself the night off. From all of it—the caution, the guilt, the worry. Tonight, I'm letting it all go. "Thank you for trying though. I may not have responded, but I got every message and they meant a lot, along with you still showing up today for my graduation when you didn't have to. I don't deserve you."

His arms wrap around my waist, holding me tight. "You deserve more than you think. You deserve everything." Before I can disagree, he grabs my hand, saying, "Let's show you off. It is your party after all and I'm supposed to be *sharing*. Although with you dressed like that, I don't know how long my resolve will last."

"I can change," I offer weakly, not because a guy wants me to but because I have the urge to bring my hands up to cover myself without my go-to style in place.

"Don't even think about it. I'd drop to my knees right now if I thought it'd keep you in that outfit."

As he leans back showing his appreciation for my outfit, my imagination sparks, making my thighs clench.

I pull him back to me with a finger under his chin and against his lips, I whisper, "Drop to your knees and I'll be the one begging *you* to take my clothes off."

Growling, he pushes forward, crowding me again. "Upstairs. Now."

I dance out of his reach. "Maybe later. There's a party with my name on it," I say, pointing to the huge sign that literally has my name on it—aside from the bottom chunk of the L that's missing, making it look more like ANGEIA, but whatever. Arts and crafts are not these guys' strong suits. Chiseled jawlines and sculpted muscles are more their speed and that's okay. The point is they tried and this party is still for me, even if that means I have to change my name.

Coty sighs loudly. "Fine."

There are at least thirty people enjoying the early summer weather and I'm once again wondering how the guys can pull this off without management stepping in. I internally cringe, imagining all the neighbors, including Gary, listening to the loud music right now.

We make the rounds, with Coty introducing me to different people scattered around the courtyard, and I smile politely, thanking them as we go, knowing I'll never remember anyone's names. It's just too many at one time.

Coty's constantly finding excuses to touch me. Whether to tuck some hair behind my ear, hold my hand, or smooth his palm down my back—he simply won't stop.

We come to a row of tables, filled with finger foods, drinks and...sparklers? I'm not really sure honestly, but I recognize Marc's sister as she sets out more napkins, so I give her a tight smile when she looks up.

"Hi! You must be the neighbor."

Although true, there's something more to her tone, almost dismissive, that doesn't sit well. In fact, it doesn't sit at all. It's pacing like a caged animal, waiting to be fed.

I clench my teeth, taking her hand in mine for a limp shake. Coty wraps his arm around my middle, tucking me into his side. "Maggie, this is Angela. Angela, this is Maggie, Marc's kid sister." He kisses my temple which flexes with every bite of my jaw.

"Nice to meet you." It's not, really, but she is keeping the napkins stocked.

"Same." Her gaze runs from me to Coty, then back again. With a finger propped on her lip, she says, "Although, I thought you would've been here with Tony. Wasn't that who you were with last time I saw you?" She flicks her gaze to the pool.

Coty stiffens beside me.

"I live here, so that's probably why you saw me. And I wouldn't be with that guy anyway, I only met him once for a few minutes."

"Oh," her penetrating stare shifts to Coty, "then why did you give him a black eye?"

Now Coty's the one with the ticking jaw. After a long, quiet moment, he breaks eye contact with Maggie to glance down at me, cocking his head. "He deserved it."

"What are *those*?"

Our small triangle turns to see what Beckett's shouting about, then follow his outstretched finger. Realizing what he's pointing at, I pull out of Coty's grasp. My heartbeat pounds louder than the outdoor speakers, filling my ears with its brassy beat. Right away, I begin searching the new sandals for scuffs, tears, holes, anything that would give me away—that would show what I truly am— only I can't find a single mark. Nothing out of the ordinary whatsoever. What does he see that I don't? What do any of them see for that matter?

I knew I should've changed.

I pin Beckett with a hard scowl, trying to keep my voice steady. "What the hell are you talking about?"

"Those nails, girl," he says with a laugh. "You might be the only chick I've ever seen that doesn't have her toenails painted."

Oh. That. Yeah, add painting nails to the many things I never learned growing up.

My pulse slows and the music comes back into focus just before I'm scooped up from behind. With arms under my legs and back, Beckett takes the few steps across the cement bringing us closer to the pool ledge.

"Don't you do it."

His chest rumbles beneath my ribs as he advances. "What? This?" With one final step, he plunges into the deep end, taking me with him.

The chilled water slaps the part of my back exposed from the crop top making goose bumps sprout. My previously light and flowy skirt turns into a heavy, restricting weight as the water penetrates the material, pulling me down faster than the giant himself. I kick out of his arms, trying to get my legs under me before I drown in front of a party full of my closest strangers. My feet finally make contact with the bottom, and pushing with all my might, I'm able to propel upward before I run out of air. Just as I reach the surface, Beckett's hand latches onto my arm, pulling me over to the side.

"Damn, Angie, you sank like a fucking brick."

"I'm wearing a skirt, asshole!"

"A white skirt." I hear above our heads.

I was so busy trying not to die, the fact that my skirt is indeed white, therefore now see through, escaped my notice. One emergency at a time and all that, but I guess everyone's priorities are different.

"What am I supposed to do now? This thing weighs a ton." I try to drag some of the heavy material out of the water to no avail.

"Lose it."

"And do what? Swim around in my fucking panties?"

"Yes?"

"No," Coty grits, making Beckett chuckle.

"Can you grab me a towel then? I'll go back upstairs to change." Coty yanks one from a nearby chair that I'm hoping didn't belong to anyone. "You had to choose the one time I wear something nice?" I scowl at Beckett.

"Shit, sorry."

With my free hand, I splash his lowered face. "It's okay. Just help me get out of here without everybody seeing my ass."

"Can I see your ass?"

"No!" Coty and I say together.

They help me maneuver out of my skirt and into the towel with minimal flashing. I promise to return, then head up, wringing out my hair along the way.

Beckett told me, somewhat ominously, to wear my swimsuit,

so I change into my bikini before grabbing my phone so I can listen to the three new voice mails shown.

"Angela, I'm sorry I missed today. Mom called and told me what she did. I just wanted you to know I disagreed with her and stood up for you. Whatever your differences are I just wish you two could leave me out of it. I feel like crap about missing today and just thought I'd let you know I'm thinking about you. I hope you had a good day anyway. I love you."

I stare at the wall, thinking over my sister's words. They don't change what happened. They definitely don't put relatives, my real relatives, in that coliseum when it counted most. But can I really be upset about the way it all played out in the end?

I delete the message.

"Hey, grad! My dad talked to Joanna, our contact we told you about, and she found an opening for you. Call me tomorrow and I'll tell you the details. Don't call me tonight! This is your graduation night and I hope you're living it up. I just wanted to let you know so you don't have to worry. We'll talk later. Love you. Bye."

I'm squealing before Drew even finishes, then sober to listen to the last voice mail; it's from a number I don't recognize.

"Angela, hi." *Joe.* "Listen, I got you a present and was hoping to give it to you after your graduation. I can get away tonight if you want to meet up." *What?* "I'll try again later."

There's so much wrong with that voice mail I don't even know where to begin.

I click on the number to respond with a quick text, letting him know a gift isn't necessary—or wanted—and that I'll see him at work tomorrow. In other words, thanks but no thanks. *Gross.*

My phone now charging, I straighten my swimsuit top just as someone knocks on the door—four quick knocks to be exact. *Coty.* Smiling, I open the door to find him shirtless, and holding my wrinkled skirt. At least I think it's my skirt. I lost my train of thought at Coty's bare chest.

Have mercy. On what, I don't know. My sanity? My soul? I'm going with my groin since that's what's currently fighting for the most attention. To hell with the rest.

My eyes roam every inch of skin, greedily taking more as they go. His tattoos are on full display now, so I take my time studying them. I don't realize I'm touching him until Coty clears his throat.

I pull my hand back abruptly, saying, "Sorry."

He cracks a smile. "I wasn't complaining, babe. I thought I'd bring this up for you." Between his hands is a white heap of leaking skirt and it's making a puddle on my bare doorstep. My lip twitches. "I tried to squeeze out as much water as possible on my way up here. Coincidentally, Gary might be stepping in a river the next time he leaves." We glance down the hall to the quiet door. I've never seen him but the guys have told me about his, uh, habits. "And you were right, this thing's heavy as shit. You're lucky you didn't drown."

"Make sure to tell Beckett that. Let his guilt eat him alive."

He drops his face, grimacing. "That was his way of getting you back up to your place. Shitty execution, I know, but it worked." He chances another look at me and I lift an eyebrow.

"Why would he do that when you were the ones that asked me to go down there to begin with?" I gesture to the treat bouquet forgetting there's an empty cupcake liner sitting on the counter next to it. Coty notices and tries to hide a grin. The sugar helped revive me after Skirtgate, and getting sidetracked by my phone, I forgot to clean up the evidence. What else am I supposed to do with a cupcake bouquet? Plant them and hope they multiply?

"So we could prepare." He shrugs, passing me the garment, and double-handed, I throw it into the kitchen sink before returning my attention back to him.

"Prepare for what?"

Coty frowns at the neglected item over my shoulder. I'll tend to it when I take care of the cupcakes...I mean put them away, for safe keeping.

In answer, he just holds out his hand, saying, "See for yourself."

CHAPTER 28

Angela

HOLDING HANDS, WE DESCEND THE STAIRS TO THE party, only it's no longer recognizable as the party I left. The sun's gone down making it dark save for the thousands of items now aglow. The pool alone must have hundreds of glowsticks strewn about the water, some wobbling at the bottom, others floating on the top. Each person adorned with rows and rows of glowsticks looks up and cheers as we hit the bottom step.

"You did this?" I turn my head to Coty.

"We did this. For you. We wanted to show you that even in the dark there's light to be found." He reaches in his pocket and pulls out a stack of bracelets. Snapping them, he attaches several to my wrists before doing his own. "And if there isn't, then I can always make some."

I smother his grin with a pressing kiss. Unable to express the gratitude I have for this man in words, I use my lips in a more skillful way.

"Ahem, I'll have you know Marc and I helped, too."

Coty keeps my waist close to his as I twist my neck to acknowledge Beckett. Coty continues to nibble at my ear, making it hard to concentrate but I manage—somewhat.

"Where is Marc by the way?"

Coty finally pulls away as he and Beckett share a look.

"He'll be here."

"Well, thank you, both of you, for this, for all of it. I love it."

I wrap an arm around each of them, although my right arm only goes up to Beckett's chest making it an awkward embrace all around. His height is definitely a challenge. *How do girls have sex with someone so tall?* Judging by how many of them are always hanging off the guy, they find a way.

"Let's go, neighbor girl. Shots now. Dancing next."

"What about food?" Coty interjects.

Beckett waves a hand. "Sure, eat something," then like he almost forgot, he adds, "but not someone. We're partying tonight, so no sneaking off."

He points between us and my face warms. I peer over at Coty's tattoos again. My tongue wets my lip as my eyes drift lower, taking in his chiseled abs. Sucking the lip between my teeth, I ogle the deep V stretching beneath his low-slung black shorts.

"Angie!" Long fingers snap in front of my face.

"What?" I scowl.

"Did you hear a thing I said? Shots first."

My gaze returns to Coty to see he's giving me the same appreciative look I was just giving him.

Like shots will help.

We each take a shot of clear liquor, nothing mixed despite Beckett's request, then the boys take another. I check out the table filled with more goodies now that nighttime has arrived. At the other end, next to the jar of unlit sparklers, are various containers full of glowing necklaces, bracelets, and rings, along with some sort of paint.

Decked out in more glow paraphernalia, Beckett grabs my hand, leading me to the makeshift dance floor otherwise known as the grass. We dance together, mostly trying to outdo the other's embarrassingly bad moves, until a couple of girls try to steal him away. Coty's familiar hands grab my hips from behind and our little dance battle is quickly forgotten, Beckett moving onto better prospects.

I lean my head on his shoulder, close to Coty's ear. "Hey."

"Are you having fun?"

I arch back to slowly roll my hips. "Yeah. You?"

His hand slides around to my bare stomach, pulling me further into him. "I am if you are."

We continue to dance dangerously close—considering he's in shorts and only my important bits are covered—until we break to rehydrate and eat.

I'm leaning against the fence when I see Marc slip out of a door that isn't his.

Is that? Yep, that's Kary's apartment. The manager.

And it all falls into place. Where I saw him coming from that one time. The parties, the loud music, how they get away with it all. How they're getting away with this now.

I watch as he makes his way through the party, bumping fists with different people as he approaches.

"Neighbor girl," he greets quietly, tapping Coty's fist. "What did you think of your sign?"

My eyes shoot over to it before meeting his again. "*You* made that?"

"Fuck no. That shit's all Beck. I supervised."

"Which means he barked orders the entire time causing Beck to quit from the pressure, and I had to finish the damn thing myself," Coty supplies, making the group laugh. This still doesn't solve the mystery as to where the other half of the L went though.

"Well, thank you for helping make today so special for me." I glance up to Kary's place, letting him know that I know. What exactly I know, I don't know, but I thought he should know all the same.

"No problem." He nods, grabbing a pack of cigarettes from his pocket. "I've been dying for one of these for hours." Coty frowns, glancing up at Kary's, too. "Enjoy the party." And with that he walks off into the throng of people, grabbing a girl to dance with on his way.

"What just happened?"

"I...don't know." He shakes his head, ditching our plates. "Should we take another shot?"

"One more, then I'm done. I don't want to puke at my first party."

"Bullshit." His eyebrows shoot to his hairline. "This is your first party? Ever?"

I nudge a wad of grass clippings with my Adidas slide, avoiding his questioning stare.

"Shots!"

No further prompting required, Marc and Beckett leave their companions to meet us at the table. Marc pours the shots then the three roommates hold them out, so I follow suit.

"To Angela, congratulations, babe."

We clink glasses, shooting them back.

Beckett pours another round, ignoring my protests, then lifts his, saying, "To more nights just like this."

"Cheers!" we shout in unison, before I attempt to down the fiery drink. Most of it "spills" into the grass though.

And despite more groans, Marc dispenses a third round. I only quiet when he grows serious. Well, more serious.

"To family," a scowl settles on my face before I can stop it, but Marc presses on, "the one that makes you, not the one that tries to break you."

This one I do drink to, albeit much slower than my neighbors. It's clear these guys not only treat each other like family, but genuinely believe it. I observe them in their natural element joking, laughing, watching each other's backs out of pure instinct. It's inspiring, yet fills me both awe and sorrow. Awe that three rebels looking for a place of their own found each other to lean on when they needed it most. Sorrow at never having found my own spot amongst a family, whether by blood or otherwise.

Coty collects all the glasses to set them aside. The others take turns kissing my cheeks before returning to the festivities. I go to follow but Coty yanks me back into his chest. Against my ear, he whispers, "Not so fast."

Giggling, I see Coty's hand appear in front of me holding a

container of paint. He untwists the lid and dunks his fingers inside, then he does the unthinkable and smears it across my stomach.

I spin in his arms.

"You did not just do that?"

"What did you think this was for?" He laughs.

"I-" I hadn't really thought about it actually, but now that I have, I dip my fingers in and swipe it on Coty's face making two lines under his eye down to his neck.

Now it's my turn to laugh except when the cool paste is spread down my arms in retaliation, we both fall into a bated silence. Without breaking eye contact, I scoop out more with both hands, covering his abs with embellished swirls, reaching the lines of his hip bones. When his chocolate eyes darken I get those, too, leaving no stone-hard muscles left unturned. I run my hands up to rest on his chest then make the climb to his neck and clenched jaw, the paint easily forgotten. I stand back with my stained hands on my hips, daring him to make the next move.

His hand snakes out and grabs my waist, dragging me back to his chest—that's coated in a medley of colors. "Turn around," he demands huskily.

I simply shake my head.

"Have I ever told you," his hand comes up to rub my jaw, leaving a wet sensation behind, "that you look good in pink?" The hand he pulls away is covered in the color.

Damn him.

"Hmmm, I wonder if you do, too." I rub my cheek against his, returning the favor.

Before I can pull away, he reaches up to turn my lips to his, placing a hot kiss there.

I win.

"Ooh, I think drunk Coty is my new favorite."

"I missed you," he whispers against my lips, eyes at half-mast. "I'm serious, I can't sleep without you here."

"I doubt that."

"It's true," he insists. "I know how to fix that though."

I quirk an eyebrow.

"Oh, yeah? How's that?"

"With you sleeping in my bed every night." The shrug of his shoulder is flippant, his tone is not. Not getting the reaction he was hoping for, he changes tactics. "Fine, I'll sleep in yours. If I'm with you, I'm good."

"You're drunk." I shove him lightly. He doesn't budge.

"So are you."

"Maybe." *Definitely.*

"Dance with me."

"Without Me" by Halsey starts up, so we do just that. We dance with each other like we've been doing it for years. The familiarity is palpable. His body molds to mine while my body responds to his every move. Coty's hands roam my dips and curves as the music pounds across the lawn. I grow bolder, teasing him right back. The cat and mouse game we have going intensifies with each song. Stealing kisses should be listed on Coty's resume since he acts like it's his job to keep his lips on mine. Toward the end of the night, I'm so close to exploding, I start to think maybe it is.

Somebody starts a fire in the designated pit so we take a break to fill up on the gooey goodness of s'mores. Coty has a mesmerizing habit of licking the melted marshmallow from escaping between the graham crackers before taking a bite and I take full advantage of the erotic show he's unknowingly providing. Unfortunately, every other female at the party has noticed Coty's oral ministration as well which has my nails digging into my thighs.

I stand to grab a handful of sparklers from the table—I'll do anything to get away from these fiends and maybe the lit-up sticks will serve as a deterrent. The fact that I want to warn them away from Coty has me crawling back into my head. Shaking the tension in my shoulders away, I refocus on the one night I've allowed myself.

With Marc's lighter, Coty steps close to light the ones

clenched in my fist. As they catch, star-shaped sparks shoot out in all directions. They're absolutely mesmerizing. So much so that I don't even notice Coty trying to grab some for himself until his fingers loosen mine. I allow a few to be pulled from my stiff hold, then follow him closer to the pool area.

We keep to ourselves, drawing out different shapes and watching as the fire eats up the thin sticks. Each time one burns out completely, someone is there relighting more. After several moments of playing pyrotechnics, our eyes connect across the lawn, holding me hostage. Coty gives one of his signature winks, then draws out a heart with his last remaining sparkler causing my actual heart to stop, then pick back up going double, maybe triple, the rate it was seconds before. Hell, maybe it was never truly beating until that very moment. I can't tell anymore because I'll only ever remember this feeling. The sensation that Coty's drawn-out fiery heart caused my very real beating heart to respond like life just started. Coty and his damn winking having ruined all normal heart activity, and he then has the audacity to come closer.

Obnoxious laughter steals our attention so we turn in time to watch as Beckett draws a penis with his lit sparkler. It's on the large side, but then again so is he. Coty draws his heart, Beck draws his dick. It kind of makes me wonder what Marc would draw. Oddly enough, I can picture him placing it between his lips and trying to smoke the stupid thing.

I hear someone shout "cannonball" before I see, and feel, the splash. The pool party really kicks in then along with a game of Chicken—which somehow looks closer to Turducken once Beckett's enormous form joins in.

With my eyes glued to the action, I miss Coty coming up behind me, his hands sneaking around to my exposed stomach. We're both mosaics of color and with his skin on mine, I've never seen anything more beautiful.

Coty's lips touch my ear. "What about you?" I arch into him

on reflex and he groans softly, tightening his hold. "Do you want to get wet?"

I glance up at him through heavy lashes. "Are you offering?"

Eyes holding mine, he says, "Always."

First, he stole my heart, reducing the vital organ to a mere toy—one he can wind up at will. Then, he stole my breath, straight from my lungs without so much as asking. With the way my body's reacting to his now, I can only imagine it's the next to bolt, leaving my mind the only thing left intact, untouched by Coty's pilfering ways. For now.

My hand in his, he leads me to the empty stairwell. He peeks at me over his shoulder, his gaze soft, and I nod gently, giving him the permission he's always seeking. Slowly, he walks up the stairs with me trailing closely behind. Other than my hand in his, nothing else on either of us is touching, and that distance is more noticeable than the raucous noise at our backs. I bite my lip, watching his muscled back as we approach our end of the hallway. Coty veers toward my side and I open the door wordlessly.

Just as the lock twists into place again, I'm lifted and pinned against the cold metal. Wrapping my legs around him leaves Coty's hands free to roam. He frames my face before snatching up my lips with his in a soul searing kiss. His very hard, very impressive, erection presses into me earning a moan so loud it could rival the music still pulsing downstairs. The sound encourages Coty in his quest to ruin me for any other kiss in my lifetime, and he picks up the pace, rolling his tongue like waves in the sea while mine fights to stay afloat, not yet willing to fully submit. His mouth is frantic and his body matches, grinding into mine with complete abandon. Soon, my pathetic swimsuit bottom will fall apart at the seams from the friction alone. I break apart to tell him as much when his mouth drops to my jaw, kissing his way to my ear.

Lost in the feel of Coty's mouth, a weird noise from his throat brings me back to the moment and I open my eyes to see Coty lean back, eyebrows drawn low.

"Shower?"

"Excuse me?" I've been outside all day, what does he expect?

He chuckles, placing me on my feet again. "No." He shakes his head. "The paint. It's everywhere." He points to our bodies. "And it doesn't taste very good." Looking down, realization dawns and my face heats. "I was asking if you want to get a shower...together?"

Coty's nearly black eyes gaze into mine, full of so much more hope than I can handle at the moment. If ever.

He steps back, once again letting me take the lead, so I pull his hand, guiding him to my tiny bathroom wondering how we're both going to fit inside.

Coty's fingers dance over my back as I turn on the water. Finding my bikini's top clasp, he unhooks it, and we both watch as it falls to the floor. Coty climbs into the warm water first, holding a hand out for me. Only when I'm under the steady spray, does his gaze drop to my chest, warming me from the inside as the water heats my outside. His eyes collide with mine revealing even more emotion than before. I tilt my head back to soak my hair, giving me a chance to get ahold of the most important piece here—my mind. I let the water run over my face, washing away the pink paint dried there. I open my eyes to find Coty standing inches away, his breathing jagged, his fists clenched tight. Our gazes meet and then we're smiling. A moment passes before I pull him to me with shaky hands.

Bare chest to bare chest, he whispers, "Are you sure?"

My eyes flick between his. "Yes," I breathe out, more certain of this than anything else in my life.

I'm past want, I know I *need* Coty. In exactly what manner? I'm still not sure but I can figure that part out later. Tonight is about letting go. Tonight is about friends. And although that title going anywhere near Coty's name leaves a sour taste in my mouth, I'll happily leave out labels if it means he stays and finishes what he's started.

I run my hands over his body, acquainting myself with the dips of his muscles. Coty groans, pressing into me but careful to keep his hands flexed at his sides. Mine do no such thing as they trail down his taut arms ending at his clenched fingers, coaxing them open. I place his large palms on my waist then continue my exploration of the piece of art in front of me. Coty's grip tightens, but he remains still otherwise, as I take my time discovering his body under the guise of washing away paint. I'm nothing if not efficient. Every muscle tight and flexed—besides the labored rise and fall of his chest—Coty is the picture of a man in pain. If it wasn't for the rigid tent in his shorts, I'd believe he was.

Once he's a blank canvas again, he helps to rub the paint off me as well albeit at a much, much more tortuous pace. My nails dig into his shoulders as his skilled hands drive me near the brink of insanity. His special attention to my breasts in particular has me moaning and arching shamelessly. Each touch, every stroke, my greedy body chases, begging for more. Anything to help the ache in my center. When the throbbing finally proves too much, I drop my hands to his shorts, yanking at the drawstring. One frenzied tug later, they loosen and sink lower, exposing more of that delicious V I've been drooling over all night. I lick my already wet lips as I push the trunks the rest of the way down. Coty's stiff erection springs free when I slide the material down his thighs and he lets out a hiss. Like a moth to a flame, my hand reaches out to his tantalizing cock. Wrapping my hand around the base, I get one full slow stroke in before Coty catches both wrists in his hand, hoisting them over my head.

My protest is cut off as his mouth slams down on mine, backing me into the wall. With my bottoms still on, Coty's erection slides across the material, making me cry out. If I had access to my hands, I'd remedy the problem myself but Coty's taken over and is showing no hesitation whatsoever. I do what I can in chasing his member with each thrust, hoping he'll take pity on me sooner rather than later.

I smile triumphantly when Coty rips his mouth away, panting, before releasing my wrists and dropping to his knees.

The victory cheer on my tongue dies out as his thumbs slide into my bottoms, pulling them down in one fell swoop. Next, he lets out a curse and even though he's seen me mostly naked before, I still have to fight the urge to cover myself. Remembering how familiar with downtown he became during his last visit, I drop my hands to his steady shoulders instead. If he's this eager to return, then why bother hiding at all?

My heart beats erratically as I watch Coty take care raising one foot at a time to remove my bottoms. It full-on stutters as he looks up at me with those darkening eyes. Lifting my left leg again, he places it on his shoulder before finally breaking eye contact. I can practically feel his gaze as it drops along my body ending between my thighs. The tepid water is doing nothing for my overheated state.

"So fucking beautiful, babe," he whispers as he lowers his mouth.

His kiss-soaked lips graze my pussy and I jerk. Coty's hands grab my ass, yanking me forward until I'm the equivalent of a mask he's decided to wear for the night.

His mouth teases a rhythm of lick, lick, suck, repeat. His hands knead my ass cheeks as his groans vibrate my clit leaving me panting like it's the hottest new song. And honestly, maybe it is. He's that good and I'm happy to tell him. Coty turns to bite my thigh resting on his shoulder and I cry out from the sudden pain before he can suck it all away, leaving behind a faint bruise.

"So sweet," he mumbles against my skin. One of those notorious chills appears, running up my spine.

He kisses his way to my inner thigh then latches onto my clit. I drop my head back, reveling in the feel of his mouth on my most sensitive part. It's not long before the shaking starts up.

"Coty," I moan.

The rumble of his responding growl sends me crashing over the edge and happily taking flight. Riding the high all the way back to earth, Coty slips my leg off his shoulder and stands, holding my weight that even I can't support. He strokes himself with his free hand, eager to go for two.

"Condom?"

His hand stills. "Shit. I don't have one." His eyes roam over my flushed body. "Want me to go get one? I can run next door." He looks like that's the last thing he wants to do.

I shake my head. "There's some by my bed."

An eyebrow cocks at that but I ignore it and its misogynistic undertone. He doesn't have to explain having condoms and neither do I.

The water now cold, I lean over and turn the knob, shutting it off. I straighten, testing my shaky legs but Coty lifts me from the waist so I can wrap them around his, preventing me from falling and ruining the moment entirely. We both moan at the closeness, free of barriers. His head drops to my shoulder and pushes me into the wall, dragging his cock along my seam.

"Bed," I rasp out while I still can.

Secure in his grasp, he walks us out to my bed and drops down to the mattress. Now straddling him, I quickly grab a condom from my nightstand and open the wrapper with my teeth. Coty's hands caress my thighs as he watches through heavy lids, the pressure increasing once I place the condom on his tip. While he massages toward my already sensitive core, I roll the condom down his length and lean back to watch as his thumb circles my clit. Looking up, I find his eyes on mine.

"You like that?" I nod, biting my lip when his other hand joins the party. "Do you want-"

My lips crash onto his, silencing him. The answer to any question right now is yes. Only yes.

"I want you. Now," I say, lifting up from his lap using his shoulders as support.

His hands stop teasing and find my waist to help line up my entrance with his straining cock. Our gazes connect again before I slowly lower onto him. Inch by delicious inch, I glide down until he's fully sheathed, making us both groan.

"Fuck. You're perfect."

I'd disagree, stating that he's the perfect one, but words—all of them—elude me at the moment, my only focus on how full my body is. How whole it feels now.

My forehead drops to his and we sit content, relishing the feel of each other for a moment. Digging my nails into his shoulders, I drag them down his chest, leaving angry streaks behind. If it's possible, Coty grows harder beneath me. Our pants mingle in their own sultry dance, then Coty pulls me closer, rubbing my clit against his base. A loud, unfiltered moan rips from my mouth.

"Move for me."

Wrapping my hands around the back of his neck, my nails find a new home in his hairline and I lift up ever so slightly before I roll forward and down at the same time to create the perfect amount of friction. I repeat the motion, feeling my climb toward orgasm spike again. Coty groans out his appreciation as I keep the steady pace of rolling eight motions. When his legs beneath mine start to shake, I speed up with a little help from Coty's encouraging grip. He guides me even closer, hitting my clit with each rotation, but I falter when the friction becomes too much. Luckily, Coty takes over, using his hands to continue moving our bodies the way we both need. With the increased tempo, I lose sight of where he ends and I begin until we become one, joining together in perfect harmony.

"Coty."

"I know. Almost there, babe."

"Coty," I warn.

"Now."

And with one final thrust, we kiss our orgasm straight from the other's bodies, then collapse on the bed together, completely spent.

One eye cracked, I see Coty wearing the same devilish smirk that held me captive from the beginning, and I think I finally understand what that feeling people call home is.

CHAPTER 29

Angela

After cleaning himself up in the bathroom, Coty returns to my limp form sprawled across the mattress, holding a couple of towels and tries to hand me one.

"Here. Your hair's dripping everywhere."

"The whole bed is wet."

"Where are your spare sheets? I'll switch them."

I wave him off, muttering, "Don't have any." I'm lucky to have this one decent set. "Forget it, I've always wanted a water bed anyway."

He throws his head back in a laugh, moving to search for his shorts. "Get dressed and we'll go over to my place. My bed is nice and dry. Unless you're up for changing that?"

I can just make out his bouncing eyebrows and now I'm the one laughing. I roll over to my back, wanting to dry off. The water from the shower's been replaced with sweat, but my hair is still drenched and is in fact soaking everything. I've slept in worse conditions though. A little wet spot won't keep me from my bed.

Wrapping the towel around my hair, I watch Coty hold up his discarded shorts and wring out the excess water before hanging them on the shower rod and doing the same with my swimsuit.

"Sorry to break it to you, but I'm not going anywhere. My legs don't work." *Probably.* I point to the heavy towel holding my hair. "I can't lift my head." *Definitely.* "Plus, it's too far." *Eh.*

"Is that so?" he says, coming out of the bathroom. "Then I guess it's a good thing I don't have any clothes anyway."

"Good, it's settled. We'll stay here. Naked." *Forever.*

What? No. That can't happen, not only for sanitary reasons

but this is a one-night thing. Tomorrow he's back to my incredibly hot—fully dressed—neighbor again.

I look Coty over, the moonlight kissing his bare body as he moves through the dark to my tiny kitchen, almost filling the entire thing with his figure.

Glasses of water in hand, he returns to bed. To my bed. To me.

Tonight.

"What do your tattoos mean?"

Coty sets down our drinks, then joins me, lying on his side with his head propped on his hand.

He points to the birds on his chest. "These are sparrows."

I reach out a finger, tracing the wings.

"Why those?"

I'm outlining the matured flowers below the sparrows with my fingertip when he blows out a breath and moves to his back.

Taking my hand, he rests it on his stomach. "They symbolize loyalty." He turns his head toward mine.

"Loyal? To family?" My eyebrows crease and he nods.

"Among other things. Sparrows mate for life." I drop my gaze to the intricate birds. "The roses, people sometimes associate them with love, too, but they also represent passion."

That's a lot of love-talk so I focus on the last bit, asking, "What are you passionate about?" I'm pretty sure I know the things Coty's passionate about but there's something else, something he's holding back. His eyes search mine before he speaks.

"Riding. Working. My family—the guys mostly. I want to learn more about agriculture. And…"

And?

"And one day I want to settle down with a wife, and hopefully have kids after that." He finally breaks his stare, glancing away. "Loyalty isn't an option for me, it's a given. I'm loyal to those I love and ask for the same in return. I got these tattoos to remind not only myself, but those around me, of what's really important."

The one remaining piece, my remaining piece, hovers dangerously close to finishing the puzzle of this arrangement. It's statements like this that pull my mind away from everything I've ever thought, everything I've ever assumed. Coty is different from anyone I could've planned for, so even though I want to tell Coty he's nothing like his father, I don't. Self-preservation occasionally wins out, and this being one of those times makes me grateful. He's already won everything else; my mind has to remain what I've always needed it to be—mine.

He faces me again, his gaze penetrating. "I don't want you doing this with anyone else." His words come out a plea and I nod before he can finish.

"Okay," I whisper.

"Okay? That easy?"

I blow out a breath of my own and roll over onto my stomach again, hiding most of my face. The towel falls off in the process but whatever. "I mean it'll be hard, don't get me wrong, but I'll try not to talk tattoos with anyone else while you and I are…discussing body ink."

The bed shifts suddenly, then Coty's there, hovering directly above me. I bite back a smile.

"There's that sass. I knew it was here somewhere." Coty drops his mouth to my shoulder, kissing to the other side, his cool breath making me shiver along the way. "Do you have any idea what this back does to me?"

Slow kisses start their descent down my spine and judging from the hard-on pressing into me, I have a pretty good idea. Feeling his lips rise back to my neck, I arch into him, and he sinks his teeth into my flesh.

Coty groans, sucking away the pain, while his hardness teases my readily wet entrance. Leaning on one arm, he reaches over to the bedside table to grab another condom as I toss the towel away completely. He rips the wrapper open and makes quick work of rolling the rubber on.

"Jumping to conclusions, are we?" I tease.

Coty sits back and bends my leg to the side, spreading me wide open. I hear him inhale sharply before cursing under his breath. Pressing against my back again, he nips my ear as his erection rubs my seam in time with my breathing.

"Are you saying you don't want this?" My moaning is the only response he gets. "What was that?" he asks, picking up the pace.

"Maybe," I pant.

Coty pushes his tip just past my opening and pauses. Unable to control myself, I lift, trying to slide him in further, but his hands frame my hips, keeping me still. The sheet twists in my hold.

He leans in close again, his lips settling on the shell of my ear. "Are you going to do this," he pushes in fully, causing us both to curse, and freezes, "with anyone else?"

I have to focus intently on his words because common sense flew out one of my open windows and I don't expect it back anytime soon. Not with Coty's body coaxing answers from me.

He's questioning me while soaking my body in kerosene and flicking sparks in my direction, only his question holds more than he's saying. He's asking for loyalty—the very thing he prides himself on, the quality he's inked on his body for life—but I can't give him everything he wants, even if that's what I might want, too.

Unfortunately, the fire is catching and I'm out of time. I answer with the first clear thought that pops in my head.

"I only want you."

Click. Right into place, the final puzzle piece falls.

The words are out before I can consider the consequences. Fortunately, Coty's lips are on mine the next second, instantly drowning out any further thought. He kisses with reckless abandon and I greedily plead for more.

Caught up in making love with our mouths, his hands are still keeping me in place, so I swivel my hips to remind him what he started—what he's going to finish. I grind small circles on him and his head drops to my shoulder.

"Damn, babe. What are you doing to me?"

"Same thing you've been doing to me since we met, driving you fucking crazy."

His head snaps up. "Good. Give me your worst." Finally, finally, he starts to move, pulling almost completely out before pushing back in. "This is mine." Snaking a hand around to my front to circle my clit, his name spills from my mouth with ease. "And this is yours." The thrust he delivers along with his declaration sends shivers up my spine despite the sweat gathering there.

A part of me bristles at his claims. The bigger part of me, and not just the part rapidly approaching climax, knows what he said is true—it's just taken me longer to accept it. He's been weaving his way into my life from the first day, whether I've allowed it or not. Slipping past barriers, both physical and emotional, Coty's accomplished something nobody else has by making me feel wanted. He treats me like the prize I never believed I was. He's discovered the treasure I long stopped searching for. With his continued patience, maybe one day I'll see what he sees, but for now I'm cautiously following his lead.

Knowing this and admitting it to him are two different things though, so I grip the back of his neck, bringing him close as he continues to pump, saying, "Prove it."

And Coty, not one to back down, does just that.

◆ ◆ ◆

"Angela."

I turn to see Amity propped against the door. Finished with the car I was drying, I walk over and toss the towels in the washer.

"What's up?"

"Did you call Joe last night?"

"What?" I sputter.

"Joe…did you call him last night? He said you did."

Well, he lied. "No, it wasn't me."

And I never would. There's also the small fact that I was tied up with Coty all night. My cheeks heat at the reminder, so I busy myself with laundry.

When I see Amity still hovering, I turn around, bracing my hands on the dryer and cock an eyebrow, feigning boredom.

She simply shakes her head. "That's fucked up."

I don't bite.

"He was with his family. With his *wife*. You got him in trouble."

I shrug, spreading my hands out in front of me. "I don't know what to tell you. I didn't call Joe last night. Or any night. If his wife is mad, it has nothing to do with me."

Amity stands from the doorway and steps closer, pausing. "Whatever's going on here, keep it here. Don't involve his family in your drama." Her eyes cut a path across my body, making her disgust clear.

I push into her face. "Maybe it was your call that tipped his wife off."

Her nostrils flare. "Joe told me all about you. How you ask to stay after and tease him constantly. I guess you got sick of waiting for him to finally take you seriously. But you should really watch that, desperate doesn't look good on you."

Just as I open my mouth, I hear my name, making both our heads snap to the end of the hall. Joe's bulky form lingers there.

"Car's coming your way. Get out there before you miss it." His eyes cut to Amity and she looks down before slipping past.

The dryers kick on, so I grab two towels and rush outside. I'm not sure what the hell that was about but I do know I didn't call Joe. Aside from the fact that I would never want to talk to him outside of the wash, I don't even have his number. Anytime he's called me—that I know of—his number never came up. He usually doesn't even leave messages. Then it hits me. Last night. Joe did leave a message. Something about a present. I missed the call but a number did come up that time so I texted him. *Shit.* I texted him. It wasn't a call but still, I did contact him. Even though it was harmless, Joe obviously ran with it and spun the story to Amity and who knows who else—his wife, too, apparently. But, why?

Accepting the hefty tip, I spot him barreling toward me. *Great.*

"Why aren't you wearing your new shirt?"

"Because I'm a grown woman and I don't wear baby clothes."

His eyes drop to my shell toes and make their way back up to my face, stopping on my low-cut armpits. I doubled-up on bras today, so I know there's nothing exciting happening there. He's just being an asshole to be an asshole.

"I see." He doesn't, but he wishes he did. "I'll be sure to let the boss know your feelings on the required uniforms."

If Joe doesn't have to squeeze into a toddler sized shirt— gag!—then why should the female employees be forced to? People still need to get their cars washed, regardless of what size shirt the Hot Spots' girls are wearing. Detailing pulls way more money than our side does and I swear those halfwits don't even change out of their sloppy gaming clothes.

"Did you tell Amity I called you?"

Joe struggles to hide his surprise. "She shouldn't have said anything. She's on borrowed time here as it is, but I wanted to talk to you about that anyway." I lift my chin, waiting. "You can't call me at my house. I have a family that's separate from work life and I'd like to keep it that way."

"You know I didn't call you though."

"Text. Same thing. The point is you can't hound me while I'm with my family."

"I texted you once, Joe, after *you* called *me*."

"Talking about gifts and wanting to see me." He raises his eyebrows.

What the hell? "No, that's not how it went down." At. All.

"Do you think my wife read it like that?" He waits and my stomach tightens. Joe's right, my words taken out of context don't sound so innocent even if they were.

"Maybe I should have a chat with the boss instead. I'm sure I have much more interesting topics to discuss than t-shirts."

Joe crosses his arms over his chest. "And what proof do you have?"

I scramble to name something, but come up blank. Joe was careful to never leave his number, and the one time he did, I deleted it and his message before he could even say 'bye'. I could try citing the time he grabbed me when I stayed late to wash windows but I'm not even sure the cameras in the bay run after closing time.

At my fallen expression, Joe's face splits into a knowing smile. "That's what I thought. Don't rock the boat and you won't have anything to worry about. I left something in your locker by the way." He nods behind me, before leaving me there to wonder what the hell just happened. No, seriously, what was that?

Joe just threatened me but gave me a gift, too? Talk about a double-edged sword. Neither is suitable for workplace behavior and I have the book on business ethics to prove it.

My hands shake as I grab a fresh set of towels, grateful I've at least regained movement of my body that was temporarily paralyzed. I have to quit. There's no other choice at this point. Joe's pushed too far and my back is against the wall with nowhere else to go. Securing another job before I push back, or fold, is my main goal now. I'm so close to starting that class Robert lined up that I can't jeopardize the opportunity by not having the income to pay my part.

I vow to stop by Coty's after work to job hunt some more, then move to dry the Cadillac rolling off the conveyor belt.

One thing's for sure, whatever's awaiting me in my locker is going straight into the garbage.

Screw Joe's warning.

CHAPTER 30

Angela

COTY'S SPRAWLED ACROSS HIS BED, DOWN BY MY FEET, when he asks, "So, what homework are you doing this time?" I narrow my eyes at him playfully and he throws his hands up. "Don't get me wrong, you don't need a reason to come over, ever. I just want to know what you're doing."

I release a breath, considering how much I should tell him. With his sincere eyes staring back at me, I decide it's time to share what's going on—at least some of it. "I'm looking for a job." When his expression doesn't change, I continue, "I've been having some issues with my manager. He's, uh-"

"A creep?" Coty guesses, quite accurately, making my eyebrows jump. I nod, cautiously spurring him to explain. "I noticed the way he looks at you the times I've been there. Like he wants to eat you for dinner."

Personally, I identify as more of a dessert but I get his point. And he's not wrong. Joe's sick. He'd take anything he could get, maybe even some things he can't.

"Yeah, it's been hard working there. The dynamic's changed recently, so I've been looking for something else." Coty drops his gaze to the comforter, chewing on his lip before rolling to his back. I look back to the PC in my lap.

This morning in the shower I told him about the night course I'll be starting and he was supportive, but then went quiet for the rest of our time together. Leaving him to his thoughts like I did earlier, I focus on the task in front of me. Several food service options pop up, so I apply for the ones that might fit my new schedule.

Coty clears his throat suddenly, pulling me from a coffee house attendant—or barista, excuse me—application. I find myself craving the caffeinated drink now more than ever before even though I've never tasted coffee. Fucking mocha swirl eyes.

"Has he tried anything with you? I mean do you think you're safe?"

Still typing, I answer, choosing my words carefully, "He hasn't done anything." Which is true—mostly. He tried, but he didn't get anywhere. "And I don't know. Is any woman ever really safe?"

"Angela."

I look up, meeting his warm eyes.

"I'm serious."

"Me, too. You don't know what it's like to be a female. Every man poses a threat with their size alone, not even factoring in if they're aggressive. Then you add odd behavior and lewd comments and you don't know what someone is capable of. You expect the worst but hope for the best. That's just life for a woman. I have no idea what Joe could, or would, do."

Coty shakes his head vigorously. "You shouldn't have to deal with that."

"No, I shouldn't. That's why I want to run my own business ultimately. That won't happen until I can earn enough money to start one, so for now I'm looking for another job and hoping my next boss is nothing like him."

"I want to start taking you to work again." He holds up a palm when I open my mouth to argue. "The guys and I will take turns, just until you find something new. Whether you agree or not, one of us will be there every day when you get there and when you're done. Don't be difficult. Please."

"You do know I work with him, right? I mean he could do anything, at any time, not just when I show up or leave. I don't know how you being there would change that."

"I don't either exactly. This has been eating at me for a while now but I know you can handle yourself so I haven't said anything.

It kills me knowing you're there with him though. I just want to help where I can." His eyes plead with mine, but his words hint at something else, something I've been wondering.

"Was there really something wrong with my Jeep?" When his gaze drops to the gray comforter, I know I have my answer. "Coty!"

"There was." He looks back up, grimacing. "Sort of. The carburetor did need to be replaced but we got the part in much faster than I led you to believe."

I move to stand but he jumps from the bed, stopping me.

"Just listen. Marc and I were both getting fucked-up vibes from that guy, and when you asked me to pick you up, I just knew it had something to do with him. I made the decision then and there that I'd do whatever I had to until I could make sure you were safe. I'm sorry I wasn't honest with you. I should've told you upfront that I just wanted to help out."

"That wasn't your call, Coty. I needed my car."

"I know. I'm sorry, babe, especially when all that shit with your mom happened. I never meant to put you at a disadvantage, I swear."

I hold my breath, remembering that awful scene from what should've been an amazing day. The memory of Rianne spilling our dysfunction like a half ass yard sale for Coty and his roommates to judge will forever haunt me. Add that with Coty's lie, even if it was made with good intentions, and I feel a rise in the wall he's been chipping away at. It's slight, but it's there, and I'm not sure if it's a good thing or not. I already blew through my one-night attempt with him. Maybe that was a mistake after all.

"I understand you thought you were doing the right thing, but I don't like being lied to. Ever. I've spent my life with someone trying to manipulate me and I won't put up with it from you."

"Fair enough. It won't happen again." He holds his hands in surrender. "Can I ask you something though?" Lowering back down to the bed, his face tightens and I have the urge to run away. Even though I know what's coming, I'm still not prepared when he asks, "Did you mean what you said about regretting being born?" His voice softens at the end making me soften—something I thought I'd never do.

I cover my face, leaning my head back. "I really wish you hadn't seen that. Yes and no. I regret it because of what my existence has cost her. Sometimes it's easy to believe she would've been better without me. On the other hand, I'm glad I'm here." I drop my hands to find Coty watching me carefully. "I haven't had a great life, but it's mine. That's all I can really ask for." I shrug, picking at my thumbnail. "You're not the only one working your ass off to be different than your parents, you know?"

The mattress dips, then I see his hand slide over mine, ceasing my jerky movements.

"That's fucking insane that she said that to you. It's even worse that she made you think it was true. I hate that you regret being born, even if only for a minute—that's a minute too long as far as I'm concerned. And you don't owe her shit either. Parents are given children as gifts, not as obligations. If she sees it any other way, then she's the ungrateful one." His grip around my hand, and heart, tightens. "Trust me, babe, you are nothing like your mom. I only spent a few minutes in her presence, and I could tell you're miles above where she is."

"Did you say anything to her after I left?" I squint at him.

Coty removes his hand and smirks, some of his seriousness floating away. "Not really. We may have made it clear she wasn't welcome back though." Taking the laptop, he places it on the nightstand and turns back to me. "We don't take kindly to outsiders messing with our own."

"Why? Did she say something to you guys?"

"Nope, just to you." His eyes connect with mine. "That was enough to ban her from ever returning." At my blank stare, he clarifies, "That's your mom, so if you want her here then that's your choice and I won't get in the way, much," he smothers a smile, "but I don't want to see anyone treat you like that again, no matter if they're related to you or not. I'd rather watch my right arm be sawed off with a dull blade than watch someone hurt you."

His hands frame my face and I close my eyes, hoping to hide the building tears.

"Thank you," I whisper.

"Anything for you," he whispers back. "Now, will you be a good girl and let me drive you to work?"

My misty eyes open with a roll.

"How can I argue with you after all that?"

"Exactly, you can't. Plus, if he knows your boyfriend is there every day, hopefully he won't even think about trying anything stupid."

Coty leans down but before he can capture my lips, I pull back, hitting my head on the headboard. "Boyfriend?"

Not blinking, Coty replies, "Yes?"

I shake my bruised head. "I don't remember us talking about you being my boyfriend."

"That's because you were exhausted from all the orgasms I gave you." His lips meet mine with gentle pressure, then grins. "It's okay though, I remember." He even winks, making me laugh.

Bringing my arms up around his neck, I pull him closer until he's positioned between my legs.

"I don't think so."

He cocks an eyebrow above his rapidly darkening eyes. "Do you need me to refresh your memory?"

Using his words, I murmur against his lips, "Give me your worst."

He wastes no time returning the favor—multiple times.

◆ ◆ ◆

My cell rings on my way home Friday night and I answer seeing Drew's name. Just finished with an interview, I fill him in on how well it went along with the new information I've gathered from Joanna in HR so far. She's been super helpful, and easy to work with, making the whole experience a breeze. The ways I'm grateful for Drew in my life never cease, just like his knack for looking out for me.

My smile stays in place all the way to Creekwood. The interview turned out to be for a coffee kiosk, only able to serve drive-through customers, which makes it that much more appealing. The hours are perfect and the possibility for tips is great. The owner and manager—a woman, thankfully—seemed pretty laidback. The only problem is my lack of experience with anything regarding food or beverage prep whatsoever. The owner, Faye, was confident that a little bit of training would remedy that issue though. The interview went longer than expected, which I'm taking as a good sign, and she said she'd let me know her decision soon.

As much as making fifty or more drink variations intimidates me, I'm hopeful the environment will prove better than the wash. Although this week hasn't been bad—Joe's been on his best behavior, almost leaving me alone completely—I still don't trust him. His mood swings, rivaling any hormonal woman on her worst period, can change often and for no apparent reason.

The boys showing up as promised may be helping to keep Joe in line. Most days it's been Coty or Beckett but yesterday Marc showed up when Coty had a meeting. They've been having a lot of those lately but none of them seem inclined to share what they're about. Marc surprised me by waiting in the actual bay, which did a hell of a job scaring every man, woman, and child in the vicinity. Coty's been picking me up on his bike, which causes a scene no matter how low-key he's being, while Beckett's been parking in the middle of the employee lot, music blaring, and walking *into* the wash to find me. It'll be interesting to see what happens first—whether I can quit on my own accord or get fired from the guys' antics.

Pulling up, I notice a small group gathered around the boys' bikes. Coty immediately saunters over, meeting me at my Jeep and hauls me into a hug before my feet can touch the ground, kissing me thoroughly.

I can't help but laugh. "You act like you didn't just see me this morning."

We've been spending every night together, either at his place or mine. He complains about my lack of air conditioning and I dislike the nonexistent privacy at his, so we take turns to even things out. Once we fall into bed together everything melts away though, leaving us in our personal cocoon to explore and enjoy each other. I'm quickly getting addicted to him, and it sounds like he's having a similar reaction.

Today was the first day I took my own car to Hot Spots since I had the interview afterward, and I know it bothered him not having that reassurance.

"I miss you when you turn away from me. I miss you when you close your eyes at night. I miss you when your lips pull away from mine." He leans down, softly nipping at my lips. "I miss your smell."

I rear back. "My smell? And what's that?"

"Strawberries." He shrugs, then bends until his mouth teases my ear, whispering, "And cream."

I whack his arm and push him away. "I knew it. That's all you really care about, huh?"

Coty laughs lightly.

"Neighbor girl, this boy is so whipped I'm surprised you haven't found him camped out on your doormat yet." Beckett comes up behind Coty, putting his arm around his shoulders. "Don't get me wrong though, the sex does sound amazing." Beckett guffaws just before Coty shoves him off.

With a warm face, I drop my gaze to the ground, mumbling out, "I don't have a doormat."

The crowd's gone quiet with Beckett's words and is suddenly interested in what's caught Coty's attention—me. While I may have caught it, the question remains...will I keep it? If Beckett's right about Coty's feelings, then maybe I have a chance. If I want that chance is something I'm still trying to figure out.

"I'm messin' with you, Angie." He grabs the roll bar next to my head. "Anyway, come play with us." I scowl at him and he chuckles, throwing his other hand up. "Not like that. Damn, you're grouchy today. Anything happen with that needle dick boss of yours?"

"No, he was fine." I leave out the odd looks Joe was casting my way, choosing to tell them about the interview instead.

When I'm finished, Marc calls from atop his bike, "Let's go."

"Where are you guys going?"

"Where are *we* going? You're coming with." Beckett gestures toward his bike. "Want to ride with me?" His eyebrows dance with mischief. Coty threatens bodily harm. We all laugh. There's never a dull moment with these three.

After agreeing to go, I run upstairs to freshen up. I throw on a pair of shredded jeans and a black spaghetti strap crop top with some clean shell-toes. I quickly braid my hair over my shoulder before grabbing Coty's black hoodie. Coming back down, I find everyone paired up on either motorcycles or tricked-out rides. Coty's holding a different helmet than the borrowed one I've been using all week, so I cock an eyebrow, slowing my approach. Up close, it looks like it has two cat ears sticking from the top. It's definitely a girl helmet, but I'd like to know exactly which girl he got it from.

I pop my hip out and fold my arms over my chest. Coty, reading the question on my face, answers before I even have to speak.

"Don't worry, I didn't get this from anyone else. This is yours." My eyes widen. "It was supposed to be your graduation present but I kept forgetting to give it to you." I can't help the cheesy smile that paints my face. "Although I like seeing you jealous, so now I'm kind of glad I waited."

Speechless, I take the smooth black helmet to turn it over in my hands. It's sexy, I'll give him that. He's already attached a Bluetooth speaker so I can be connected to him and the others. I never pictured myself riding a motorcycle enough to own a helmet but Coty's changing that. He's changing a lot of things.

Coty teaches me how to actually put this one on by myself, and after a few clumsy attempts, I finally get it. I give him a bobble head kiss and thank him quietly, promising to show my appreciation later which earns me an enthusiastic smack on the ass.

Wrapping my arms around Coty's waist, I prop my hands on the gas tank and he squeezes my thigh before starting the engine. Daily rides together haven't changed the fact that I still feel more comfortable using my hands to support my weight instead of relying solely on him, and the stiffness in his back tells me he's noticed. I run my hand up his stomach, letting him know I understand. He catches my hand, brings it up to his helmet's mouthpiece demonstrating a kiss, then returns it to the tank in his own way of saying he understands, too. The tension in his back eases, and after losing myself in Beckett's chosen music, we sail into the night.

CHAPTER 31

Angela

THE TREELESS PLAIN WE REACH IS ALREADY LITTERED with people. Some are dancing to loud music pouring from speakers in trunks while others are showing off different tricks on motorcycles.

The boys park in perfect unison and I realize that, unlike me, this isn't their first rodeo. I suddenly want this helmet, and everything I'm pretending to be in it, off.

Coty catches my fidgety hands in his and helps untie the straps, keeping my focus the entire time. His coffee eyes help to slow my breathing from the uncertainty knocking its way around my chest. Coty's confidence quiets my apprehension as clusters of partiers pass, taking notice of the new arrivals.

Girls call out to the guys but Coty's gaze stays glued to mine, never wavering. His smile widens each time mine tightens, telling me he's aware of what's going on. He's enjoying the hell out of my reaction which only pisses me off further. Well, the girls are the real culprits for my foul mood, but still, he doesn't have to be so damn happy about it.

As it turns out 'play' means doing stunts on motorcycles. I stand off to the side, watching as different guys in helmets alternate between wheelies and what I'm learning are stoppies—a wheelie done on the front tire instead of the back. Coty's one of the more daring riders, along with Marc and Beckett actually, and they do some complicated looking tricks together in perfect synchronization much to everyone's delight. It's all very impressive. And loud. And dirty. Between the smoke and the dust, I can barely make out some of the bikes so I wander around, looking for a cooler, knowing there's no chance I'll be the designated driver tonight. The thought alone makes me smile as I reach a tub full of beers. I dig around for a hard cider, then twist the top off with my sleeve when I find one. My hands are shaking and it has nothing to do with the vibration from the ride out here.

I pass cars low to the ground with spoilers high in the sky. Racing stripes and custom paint jobs adorn imports while meaty exhausts accentuate the American muscle. I cringe, imagining all the dust collecting through the open doors and windows. *Occupational hazard.*

Different songs spill out of pulsing speakers, causing the cars to vibrate with an energy all their own. Motorcycles rev long and loud, fighting to be heard over the lyrics being belted from all directions. Clouds of smoke collect overhead in a lazy trail upward while stars blaze from above, begging for the adoration they rightfully deserve.

The backdrop, though chaotic, reminds me of the painting with the quote in Coty's room, and I reflect on how many chances I've been taking lately. Ever since graduation, there's been a shift. Not only between me and Coty, but with the other two as well. There's an attachment growing that somehow still feels like a liability—I just can't figure out for who though.

It being a hot desert night, I take the hoodie off and tie it low on my hips, then head back to where I left the boys. A white and gray bike catches my attention on my way over and something about the rider makes me stop and stare. I'm not sure what exactly makes them different from the others but I can't take my eyes off them if I tried. Not when they pull into a wheelie then step on the seat with one foot, not when they look over to pose for a picture holding the other leg up at a tricky angle, not when they land with practiced accuracy then pull over to park, and certainly not when they take off their helmet to reveal the difference between her and every other rider here. Yes, *her.* She shakes out long, wavy hair similarly colored to mine but darker with hints of red. Her smile—as big and mesmerizing as her riding skills—doesn't reach her eyes which lock with mine for a split second before glancing away altogether. Men surround her on all sides, clapping her back, ogling her fit physique. She accepts their praise without really receiving it. I don't know how to explain it, but there's a melancholy there, a sense of invisibility only other lost people recognize. Suddenly, two guys break from the rest, implementing some sort of crowd control and her whole demeanor changes. The smile she offers them is genuine, warm, and I wonder if she's in the same predicament I am.

I hear a deep voice beside me, breaking my reverie and turn to find Marc looking at me expectantly. I didn't even see him approach.

"What was that?"

"He doesn't even see them." He nods his head back toward his roommates. A handful of onlookers, mostly female, surround Coty and Beckett as they slap box each other, laughing and dodging half-strength blows. "I wonder if he ever did." Marc's eyes glaze over, deep in thought, and I hesitate, not wanting to break this rare moment.

"Maybe he should?"

He eyes me from the side. "Is that what you want?"

"I-" *don't know.* I pick at the label on the bottle in my unsteady hold, clearing my throat. "He should have a chance with someone that's worth his time."

"And you're not? Because you had a shitty childhood?"

His tone is gentler than I expected but still holds the same air of criticism I've heard a hundred times over. He doesn't get it. No one does.

I drop the cider to my side, flinching when some sloshes out the top, landing next to my feet, and stirring up dirt.

"I've never seen a stable relationship in my life. To me they're just a myth, a fairy tale for little kids who know nothing about the harsh realities awaiting them. How am I supposed to give Coty everything he wants out of life—marriage, kids, happiness—when I don't even believe in happily-ever-afters myself?"

A few minutes pass of Marc glancing around the scene while I stare at my shoelaces, willing away the muddy spots there. No matter how hard I try, I'll always be tainted.

"The first time I rode a dirt bike, I didn't know what the hell I was doing. I just wanted to get away from my dad. I used to hang out in our farm's workshop, full of spare parts and tools. It was hot and dirty and nobody wanted to spend time in it unless they had to, so my father didn't think to find me there. One day someone dropped off their kid's old dirt bike hoping we could salvage its working parts. It ran, but not well. I didn't care though. I didn't see what was wrong with it, I only saw the one thing I wanted more than anything else—freedom. I bought it on the spot with some birthday cash I'd saved and jumped right on it. No instructions on how to handle it, no rules where to go, nothing. I literally started the thing and took off, no destination in sight other than away. Far, far away."

Quietly, I ask, "Did you make it?"

Marc barks out a laugh. "Fuck no. I ate shit ten seconds in." He looks at me, a smile still playing at his lips before disappearing completely. "I was doing it for someone else. I wasn't riding with my own goals in mind, only what I knew I didn't want. So, I pushed the bike back, worked the rest of the afternoon on it and by the time I went to bed that night, I had a passion. One that gave me more than a distraction from my problems. It was something I liked, something I chose." All these choices. How do they know they're picking the right ones though? "Once I poured my heart into it, it became more than just a way to escape, it became my life. I treated that bike better than I'd ever treated anything and the next time I tested it out, I took my time. I rode my bike the way I wanted to, not the way I thought I needed to, and it worked. From then on, I rode everywhere, not just away."

I think over his words, imagining his younger self putting in long hours on a secondhand dirt bike. What started out as feeling like a necessity to him, turned into a luxury he treasured and later made a life out of. One he didn't even know anything about to begin with. While that may have worked out for his career path, and friend circle, it didn't fix his relationship issues. Unless…

"Is that why you sneak around with Kary?"

Marc's eyes narrow. "*With* Kary?" Shifting his glare above my head, he says, "You don't know what you're taking about."

Before I can apologize for sticking my dirt-covered foot in my mouth, I catch a girl breaking away from the herd going straight for Coty as he stops for a drink.

I watch as she places her hand on Coty's shoulder, the same shoulder I was sinking my teeth into just this morning to keep from waking his roommates, and my feet carry me forward without even deciding to move. Floating closer to the gathered crowd, I watch the whole thing play out while wishing I didn't have to.

Coty brushes her off, locking eyes with me, but I stay rooted. She notices the exchange and her vigilant gaze falls over my body, landing at my shoes. I bite my lips between my teeth, closing my eyes briefly, and willing myself not to fidget.

I hear her sneer, "Are you with her or something?" but miss Coty's response.

"Where'd you find that piece of trash?" My eyes pop open, knowing she's undoubtedly talking about me. "Do you and Daddy share his projects now?"

And that does it. I dart away in the next breath, getting in her face. "I found him actually. I searched 'guys that have taste' and his name popped up. Crazy, right?"

I try my hand at imitating one of Amity's trademark cheerleader smiles, leveling it directly at the girl. It feels more clownish than anything but I've always thought the two were one and the same. They both sport stretched out, borderline maniacal, smiles while performing choreographed routines. It's the visibility of the teeth that sets them apart and with the thin layer of dust settling on mine I'm hopefully leaning toward crazed cheerleader status. Either way, it's unsettling—for all of us.

Off to the side Beckett pipes up, whining, "Hey, what does that say about me?"

I wink over at him, then lean in closer so only she can hear me, and steady my voice when I say, "He isn't up for grabs." Maybe Coty should see what other options are better suited for him, but this one isn't it and I'm happy to let her know.

Her lips dip in a patronizing way that I'll never be able to unsee, sneering, "For now."

A cold sweat breaks out on my forehead watching her slink away. Isn't that what I've been saying all along? That Coty's interest would fade once he figured it out. Once he figured me out.

Marc's story was inspiring and all, but what he fails to see is some things are beyond repair. The dirt bike he acquired had good bones. All he needed to do was improve what he already had. I'm starting from square one. From absolutely nothing. These guys may be skilled mechanics, but that doesn't change the fact that you can't fix what isn't there.

Coty approaches me, eyes already in search-and-recover mode. "What'd she say to you?"

I pop a shoulder, stepping around him. "Nothing really."

His hand reaches out to stop me and I look up, focusing on his matted hairline instead. Not finding what I've tucked out of reach, he lets me go, but only after a hard kiss on the mouth—a punishing kiss because he knows I'm holding back. If only he knew exactly how much.

Only Marc and Coty resume their show while I watch somewhat distracted until Beckett calls me over to a half-circle of cars. Breaking from my frozen stance, I join him as he hands me a spiked lemonade to replace my empty bottle. I down half the tangy drink before wiping my mouth and thanking him. He makes introductions while I keep one eye on the black bike racing alongside the red accented one in the distance, the boys' bikes kicking up tails of dust as they compete heartily. I worry my lip when both brake lights disappear from sight.

I hear, "we already know each other," and turn my full attention to the man closest to Beckett.

"We do?"

After getting a good look at him, I realize his face does look vaguely familiar.

"Yeah, we work together. I'm over in detailing. Angela, right?"

He sticks his hand out and Beckett looks from the hand to me and back. I reach for it, still trying to place him. Shaking his quickly, I wrap both hands around my drink again.

"Sorry, what's your name?"

"It's all good, you're a busy girl. I'm Steve." I scowl at his comment and notice Beckett do the same.

"Working the front definitely keeps me busy," I joke, trying to keep my voice light but he shakes his head.

"I wasn't talking about that." His tone takes on an accusatory edge.

I look to Beckett again, finding him just as confused as I am. Quickly recovering, he places his hand on my shoulder, teasing, "Neighbor girl has a lot going on. It's not easy juggling us three." I slap him off which delights him immensely.

My smile falls when I see Steve raptly watch my neighbor's hand fall away.

"Does Joe know that?"

At my boss's name, Beckett stiffens.

And it hits me. Steve is the one that walked in that night in the bay. I only caught a glimpse of his face before I booked it out of there, but there's no doubt in my mind it was him. His harsh tone is as baffling as it is unappreciated.

"How do you mean?"

Steve drains his beer before carelessly tossing it aside. An asshole and a litterer. *What's his problem?* He pushes away from the car, bringing us closer. Beckett stays quiet, but inches my way, keeping his focus solely on Steve.

A couple feet away, he stops, sticking his thumbs in his front pockets. "Everyone knows who Joe's pets are. He calls dibs and we wait 'til he's done to get ours. He's been yapping about you for a while though and from the look of things," his gaze touches on Beckett before returning to mine, "he's okay with sharing this time. I'm just wondering what I gotta do to get a piece, too?" His tongue darts out, licking his bottom lip and I feel my stomach turn.

"The fuck? Angie, what's he talking about?"

"I don't know." I throw my hands up. "Joe's my boss and that's it. Whatever he does with other girls is none of my business. The sick pact you guys have with each other is news to me, but I promise I want nothing to do with Joe or anyone else at Hot Spots, so you can leave me out of your demented game."

Steve springs forward, but Beckett sticks his hand out, catching his shirt in a massive fist between us.

"Bro, you don't want to do that. Step. Back."

The tempo of "Blood In The Water" builds from a nearby car as Steve assesses Beckett, then looks back to me, a sinister smile marring his face. An engine revving cuts off, then in the next instant Coty is at my side—helmet off, fists clenched.

"Do me a favor and get the *fuck* back."

"I'm fine right here," Steve drawls lazily, raising the hairs on the back of my neck.

"I wasn't asking. Get the fuck out of my girl's face. Now."

Coty nods at Beckett so he presses on the guy's chest as a last ditch effort to move him. Steve shrugs it off, which is actually quite impressive considering the size difference, and advances on Coty. Coty pivots to face him fully while sliding me behind his back in one smooth motion.

"I thought this was a communal thing. Can't I get a turn?" Steve taunts, trying to meet my eyes.

Coty crowds him further as I hear another engine quickly approaching. "What the fuck did you just say?"

Steve never gets a chance to answer because Marc, still wearing his helmet, rushes up and head-butts him in the face, sending his ass flying to the dirt-packed ground. Guys from the other cars dash over, and Marc wastes no time punching anyone within reach. Coty pushes me away before lunging at guys in his range, taking each one down after the last. Beckett tosses a pair of friends trying to help Steve, leaving him to fend for himself.

They're all busy when Steve eventually sits up so I scramble over to lean down to his level, and with a chunk of his hair in my grasp, I force him to look me in the eye.

"What does Joe say about me?" Even though I have a pretty good idea, I still need to hear it.

Steve's face splits into a bloody smile. "That your pretty pink puss is worth the wait."

Crimson coats my vision as bile clogs my throat. Without considering the consequences, I yank his head down, slamming his face into my lifted knee, effectively cutting off his menacing laugh. The nauseating crunch causes me to gasp, releasing his hair. His nose gushes more than it already was but I refuse to feel sorry for him. Women aren't amusement rides with lines for any idiot wanting to get their kicks off for thirty seconds. We're the prize only serious prospects work their asses off to win a chance with.

I'm suddenly yanked backward and my elbow jabs into a hard side without a second thought.

"Shit, Angie." Beckett grabs his torso, scowling at me.

I shrug while muttering, "Sorry." *All's fair in mass fights, right?*

We look down at Steve's slumped form as he groans from the ground. Beckett's eyebrow raises in question, but I ignore him and the waste of space currently rolling around in pain.

"We gotta go."

He ushers me to his green bike, tossing me his spare helmet.

"What about Marc and Coty? I'm not leaving them."

"They're right behind us."

Coty peers over from holding a guy by his shirt collar and jerks his head, telling me to go. He releases the limp heap to the ground, then grabs Marc. They run over to mount their bikes as Beckett and I do the same. He tries to readjust my hands before giving up and taking off with them still on the tank. We speed off without so much as a backward glance at the shitstorm a douche named Steve created.

Fucking Steve.

CHAPTER 32

Angela

THEY BEAT US TO THE APARTMENTS AND I'M LIFTED off the bike as soon as Beckett's wheels stop moving. Coty removes my helmet, then proceeds to pat me down like an overzealous TSA agent.

Coty's head snaps to mine, his face full of worry. "Are you okay?"

The wind from the ride now gone, the stagnant hot air creeps back in. "I'm fine. You?"

He nods, pulling me to him. "I'm good."

His pounding heart slows as he tucks me against his chest and I wish I could say the same for mine.

"Bro, you were insane. Dude fucking flew!"

Beckett's voice booms through the deserted lot as he talks to Marc who's inspecting his cracked helmet. My eyes search everyone for injuries. Coty's knuckles, swollen and covered in dried blood, are worse off than the last time I saw him use them. Marc's arms have some cuts that are still wet and in need of care. Beckett has a welt across his cheek that makes him wince anytime his expressive face shifts.

Marc's gaze rises, touching on mine before making its way to his boy. "He had it comin.'"

"How do you know?" I throw out. He wasn't even there. He couldn't possibly know who Steve was or what he was saying.

Marc drops his banged-up hand, helmet gripped between scuffed fingers and looks me in the eye. "He was fucking with you, right?"

I nod once.

He shrugs lightly. "Then that's good enough for me."

I had the entire ride to Creekwood to think about what went down tonight. What's been going on since I moved here. I've spent so much time trying to avoid drama, I failed to notice it'd been clinging to me like my mother's nasty perfume. Their bruised faces and bloody knuckles, their schedules constantly being rearranged to accommodate mine, their parties now interrupted, their friends getting banned—that's because of me. I shouldn't have been out there, acting the part of something I'm not. I shouldn't be here at all. They deserve better. He deserves better.

I pull out of Coty's embrace.

"Who was that guy anyway?"

Beckett explains what happened before I can speak. While he fills them in, I notice drops of blood on my jeans and wince. I was already planning to pull out my trusty cleaning toothbrush and bleach for my shoes, I might as well soak my pants while I'm at it. Sleep won't come easy tonight. Sleep won't come easy for a while.

"I didn't know who he was before Angie came up, I swear. He didn't say anything about knowing her until she walked over. I never would've let him near her if he did."

Marc shoves him, teasing, "Nice job, asshole."

Beckett pushes him back playfully. How can they be joking right now?

We head for the stairs, our group battered but not broken. Yet.

At the top, the boys file in their door but I turn for mine, steeling my spine for what's to come. They make a great team, their unity undeniable, but I fly solo. And at the end of the day, I'll be taking on my problems the same way I always have—alone. Tomorrow I'll have to face Joe and Steve. The next day Rianne. The day after that something else, *someone* else. No matter when, or how, my problems appear next, it won't be at the boys' doorstep again. I'll make sure of it.

They left their door open—so arrogant, so foolish—so I

stand here, watching them as they move about, laughing, drinking, taking stock of their wounds.

One loose and light, holding the world at arm's length for the day he decides to hug it close like the mother he desperately misses.

One severe and deep, locking others out until he declares them worthy—ironically mimicking the impossible expectations his own father sets for him.

One balancing everything in his fingertips, waiting for the perfect moment to make his deepest desires a reality despite the shortcomings from his parents' shallow pretense. Coty thinks a woman can make that happen. He may even think I'll make that happen. He's wrong. I can only offer a short detour along the journey. I am not the destination, nor will I be just because he appreciates the temporary view.

The three of them work in perfect unison when they could fight and grate at every turn. Since I arrived, obstacle after obstacle has been thrown in their way making for an uneasy ride. I have my own path to navigate much less worry about how I can make theirs smoother. Having a neighbor to pass the time with is one thing, having to unload and store her oversized baggage is another. At some point something's got to give and fortunately for them, I know what it is.

A weight presses in on my chest as I step over my threshold. *So close, and yet so far.* Always.

"You're not coming in? Neighbor girl?"

Guilt gnaws in my heavy chest, making it difficult to speak as I stare at the floor.

I hear their door close softly and Coty's voice floats across the hall. "Keep your door unlocked. I'll be over later."

One. Just one lie and it'll be done. I don't have to hurt anyone—other than myself—to save them from future pain.

"I'm tired." It clogs my throat sooner than I expected and the words come out garbled.

"I'll be there."

The promise lingers long after I close the door with me on the opposite side.

I twist the lock with finality and strip. Climbing into bed, I stare at the ceiling, wondering how the hell I'm going to pull this Band-Aid off as cleanly as possible. They will all have a say but my voice is the only one that needs to matter. I'll just have to make it stronger than theirs, even when it doesn't feel like I can.

Hours of tossing and turning later, Coty's knock finally comes but I don't answer it. I don't answer the text or call that follows either. When the pounding turns frantic, I know.

He knows.

"Angela, open the door."

More knocks.

"Open up, babe. I know you're awake."

A thump that sounds like a head propped against the door chips at my carefully constructed resolve, cracking my heart in two. I fist my hands at my sides, wishing the pieces would just fall already.

"Why are you doing this?"

Minutes tick by, then a choked whisper that steals my own breath. "Don't do this to me. Please."

I squeeze my eyes shut, hoping he'll be gone when I open them.

The door across the hall slams shut making me jump. I let out a long breath, with it I release the hope that had crept in while my back was turned. The hope that I could be what he wanted, what they needed. Maybe I am more like my mom than I thought. I'm just as toxic to everyone that gets close as she is. A slow-acting poison that lulls you into false security until it's too late, killing everything good in its vicinity. But, no. Not this time. I refuse to cause the same damage she has. Always taking, taking, taking for herself. I'm giving them the best outcome whether they know it or not. The least hazardous track possible—the one without me on it.

CHAPTER 33

Angela

DAYS. IT'S BEEN DAYS SINCE I WORKED. JOE DOESN'T even have the balls to call me himself to deliver the bad news either. He's been making the hourly associates do his dirty work which makes it that much worse, knowing he's feeding them bullshit they're forced to regurgitate over the phone to me. My questions go unanswered just like the constant knocks at my door. By the end of the week the punishment is loud and clear—Joe's icing me out.

The irony that I'm doing the same to the boys is not lost on me, yet my hands are tied in both situations.

Coty knocks every day before leaving for work and again when he returns. I wait until he's gone to head out myself then make sure I arrive back before he does so there's no chance of collision. Texts and calls have been ignored as well. Beckett's joined in the pursuit as well but I dodge him, too. I almost had a run-in with Marc earlier in the week when I was folding laundry but I ducked down to hide like the coward they think I am.

The only thing saving me from losing it entirely is my new-found sanctuary in the local library. The extra free time has been filled with days of job hunting and nights of reading, both accessible at no cost thankfully.

My night class starting this week helped, too. Helped to pass the time and to keep my mind occupied, but useless in getting me money. I've only had a couple more interviews but no call-backs yet.

Drew, oblivious to my neighborly dilemma, invited me out to a movie tonight which I happily accepted.

The only upside in all this mayhem is I haven't heard from my mother. I'm cautiously grateful for her silence after her last nasty call but, always waiting for the other shoe to drop, I wouldn't be surprised if she chose to pop back up at the most inconvenient of times. Come to think of it, there is no such thing as a convenient time to deal with Rianne. Whatever the boys may have said to her might've actually worked in keeping her away. *Yet another problem of mine they were forced to handle.*

Exhaling, I pull into the library to dive right back in where I left off yesterday. Four hours until Coty leaves work gives me three and a half to find a new job. I just hope it's enough. Something needs to change before I end up back where I started—broke, broken, and under Rianne's cruel thumb.

I pick up my pace through the automatic doors.

◆ ◆ ◆

Husky notes bleed out of Drew's speakers as he drives me home from his friend's house. Bebe Rexha's voice gets me every time and "I'm A Mess" is no exception. He pretends not to like it but I see his head bobbing out of the corner of my eye and I crack a small smile.

I lean my head back, inhaling Drew's fruity scent. The smell saturates the confined space along with memories of our nostalgic drives together. My need for these may have subsided but the comfort they provide hasn't, and even though I'm not supposed to, I allow myself a few seconds to absorb the relief Drew's presence always offers.

The movie, an action one, was the ultimate diversion. No sappy love story. No deep family divide. Just mindless chatter between illogical carnage. Simply perfect.

Needing to stop off at a friend's afterward helped, too. The alcohol his friend supplied in the short time we were there was just what I needed to clear the remaining thoughts swirling in my head. The expensive vodka was much smoother going down and now I'm just hoping the same proves true if it happens to come back up, too.

Tipsy from the shots, I sway in the front seat singing off-key as Creekwood comes into view. I fight to keep the hazy effects present through the gloom quickly resurfacing. *Goodbye blurry edges, hello blunt reality.* It was fun while it lasted. *Kind of.* Drew, being the steadfast designated driver, proved to be a terrible drinking buddy after all. It must be nice to have a stable career you have a responsibility to.

Parked, he looks over to me with questioning eyes. Questioning and suspicious. He hasn't pushed the topic that I've deemed off limits but he didn't have to. I can feel the sadness seeping out of my pores and I know he can as well.

"Need me to walk you up?"

I groan.

That voice. The pity it holds. The worry it represents.

I thank Drew before folding myself out of his low car.

"Don't be home. Don't be home. Don't be home," I chant with each step up the stairs.

Being on the sloppier side of my night, I forgot to do a vehicle check on the way in. I *never* forget.

Coty's head snaps up from where it was resting on the door—my door to be exact—as I reach the top. So much for getting inside undetected.

His eyes travel up my body starting at my naked toes in my slides while I stand here motionless. Busy debating whether I can chase down Drew in my current state, I miss Coty getting to his feet.

"Hey."

The raw tenderness in his voice catches me off guard for the second time tonight.

I wave a hand halfheartedly and drop my gaze to his feet, landing on a brand-new doormat where Coty's perfect ass was previously parked.

"I, uh, got you one finally. I hope you like it."

The overly sweet act feels out of place compared to the amount of torture I've endured all week and irritation sours the surprise.

Pushing past, I kick it aside with my foot. "You shouldn't have done that. I won't be here much longer," I spit with as much venom as I feel churning in my veins.

Coty blocks my hands with his body but I keep my eyes locked on his rapidly rising chest, refusing to look up.

"Don't say that. Please don't say that. Whatever happened, I'll fix it, Angela. Please. Just…don't leave." At my silence he continues, "Or I'll leave. Anything. Whatever you want." His voice lowers as does his head.

What I want? I want my life to make sense. I want a life that I actually have a say over. One that happiness resides without a constant cloud of misery hovering in the distance, waiting for the perfect time to strike and ruin what I've worked my ass off for. I want a fucking chance. A chance to be who I want and not what others keep telling me I am. A chance at being the woman my mother never could be. One that loves freely without consequences coming to those who dare to love her back.

I want the boys next door to have a fraction of what they deserve without having to fight off my relentless demons in the process. I want them to know their parents are morons for missing out on some of the best humans I've ever met. I want to not only be a part of their family but to earn a spot there all on my own without their constant help. I want to stand as strong with them as I can without.

But that's not in the cards for me. It never was. They've been stacked against me from day one and I can't place that burden on them, too. I won't.

Reluctantly meeting Coty's sad eyes, I whisper, "please move," then sigh when it comes out broken just like my heart.

Holding my stare for a moment longer, I watch as a multitude of emotions pass through his eyes leaving me dizzy. Then huffing through his nose, he flies to his side of the hall, flinging the door open and closed without looking back. I don't know what hurts worse, that I pushed him away or that he's letting me. I flinch from the sound echoing off the walls and drop my head. Eyeing the pristine welcome mat, I nudge it further away using my toe. This tumultuous cycle I call life isn't accepting anymore visitors.

CHAPTER 34

Coty

Fuck.
Fuck this.
Fuck her.

Okay, maybe not Angela, but fuck whatever stupid excuse she's come up with to ghost me. Again.

Everything was fucking perfect—until it wasn't. Just like that, she ripped the carpet out from under me, taking my heart along with it.

I've replayed every minute from that night last weekend wondering where it all went wrong. It was like a switch had been flipped from the parking lot to the top of the stairs. The incredibly hot, sexy water being turned to inhospitable, freezing liquid in an instant. I've grilled the guys time and time again to see if they said something to warrant her swift change but they seem just as clueless as I am. Her cutting off any contact with them as well should make me feel better, that it's not just me, however it only gives a finality to everything somehow, causing the panic to grow more urgent with each passing day.

After seeing that fuckwad Steve crowding Angela, then hearing what her boss has been putting her through, I retreated into my own head. The guys and I have been working on a new project, one that will make us our own bosses much like Angela's striving for with her new education plan. The new shop we're currently planning was supposed to be ours—mine, Beck's, and Marc's. But lately I've been rethinking the entire plan, especially after learning more about Angela's hostile work environment. I'd been planning to redraw the blueprints currently covering my desk with an added

302 | A. MARIE

bay for a car wash. A car wash Angela would be running. A place for her to flourish without some sleazebag putting his hands all over her. Unless that sleazebag is me, of course. And it's consensual.

The layout was so clear in my mind once I had the idea that I had to get it down on paper before it left me. I wanted to be there for Angela after Steve's disrespectful mouth ruined the night but I thought I had time to sketch up something real quick. I was wrong.

"Fuck!"

I snatch my helmet off the coffee table sitting next to Angela's abandoned one. Beck attached these active cameras to all our helmets with the intent to capture our rides from now on. I'm not in the fucking mood for a play-by-play of the wreckage I'm wading through but don't have the headspace for taking the damn thing off, so I leave it and storm back into the hallway.

Automatically I notice the discarded mat and stomp over to shove it back in place. The hell she's moving. The rental agreement she signed ensures I've got at least a few more months. Hopefully. I'll check with Marc to see if he can find out the exact date her contract ends. That'll be my deadline to fix things with Angela. If it doesn't work, then like I promised her, I'll move. She's been through enough without adding getting chased out of her apartment by the dumbasses next door to the list.

Satisfied with the rug, I look up to Angela's door, surprised there's not a permanent imprint of my knuckles in the metal. My hand twitches at my side. Shaking my head, I move for the stairs. I already begged at her fucking feet tonight and look where that got me.

I mount my bike and shoot off into the veil of night. The ruthless fist that has my heart in its vise-like grip starts to loosen as I lay on the gas, giving it my all. I haven't been able to fully breathe all week, waiting for the sweet relief only Angela brings. The smallest amount of air filters in my aching lungs and I greedily gasp for more as I fly down the quiet roads. I'm panting as I round my first corner, making for a sloppy turn and I wobble from my mistake.

Fuck, that was close.

I keep to straight roads after that, fighting to even out the spurts of oxygen being sucked in through my cracked lips. Staying up late every night to perfect the design for the new shop has wreaked havoc on my body and it's showing. The guys barely even let me come into work. Not wanting to sit at home with the reminder of what I've lost in plain sight, I've begun driving around for hours on end, searching for the best spot for our new venture. Finally finding one this afternoon, I dragged the guys out to see it for themselves before revealing the newly finished draft. The proposal was a hard sell, like I knew it would be, so I pulled out my secret weapon—Joaquin. After the initial shock that I'd even consider going into business with Marc's overbearing dad, they saw the potential the collaboration offered. New businesses start and fail daily. We knew this going in, but searched for the exact thing to set us apart from the rest. The thing that would keep us up and running for years to come. And not just surviving but thriving.

With Joaquin's farm being the huge success it is, and continuing to steadily grow, if we could land him as a client then others would surely follow. Ours being the only mechanic shop with a car wash as well, we'd be able to meet all our clients' needs in one fell swoop. Farmhands drive a variety of vehicles and we could service and wash all of them with ease.

Their eyes started to open the more I talked and soon we were spit-balling other ideas so fast I had to write them down to keep track. The one issue that kept coming up was Angela. I nodded absently each time they mentioned her, even as the pain in my chest intensified. Only when the sympathy in their eyes began outweighing their concern, I closed the conversation down, claiming I had somewhere to be. And I did. I had a girl to win back.

The doormat seemed like a brilliant idea at the time. A way to let her know that whether we were together or not she still had a home she would always be welcome in. I didn't anticipate the gesture to backfire the way it did though. Her saying she was moving had all my bones feeling like molten lava, burning me from the inside out while simultaneously dissolving my entire being into a puddle of agony.

I just wish she would talk to me, tell me what changed. I can't fix what I don't know. It won't stop me from trying, damn it. Everyone in her life has abandoned her so she expects it from me, too. The problem is she has no idea how deep I already am. I'm barely breathing as it is and I'm still willing to go deeper. I'd dive into a bottomless abyss for Angela, easily. There's nothing shallow about my love for her and I refuse to give up until she knows it, feels it with every part of her existence, and only then will I walk away if that's what she chooses. It'll be hard and hurt like hell but I can offer her that respect. The kind that no one else ever has by letting her decide her fate instead of forcing some whack predisposed notions on her.

I decide to stroll by the vacant lot and put this expensive camera to use. We'll need everything perfected before approaching Joaquin, but I'm confident once we do, we'll win him over. Compared to Angela, hard-headed Joaquin might be the easier of the two to persuade but I'm not backing down from either, no matter the low odds.

After filming the site from every angle, I turn back toward home. Knowing Angela is there alone while the guys are out makes me uneasy and I want to be there should she need anything. Not that I expect her to ask for it, but still. It's like a piece of me has willed itself to her, allowing me to only feel whole again when she's near. The hollow hall between us is bad enough, but it's a hell of a lot better than what I'm feeling now. My heart is practically pleading to go back, so I do.

◆ ◆ ◆

Something's wrong. I don't know how I know, but I do.

I dart my eyes around for the threat, recognizing it immediately. The Ford. His Ford.

Even though I'm in a public space, I lay on the gas, reaching the spot faster than usual. He only rolled by like a creeper before, but now the dude's parked. That means he's either on his way up to Angela or he's already there.

Shit.

I scramble off my bike, loosening my helmet in the process and tucking it under my arm in case I need to use it. I'm not taking any chances. Running to the stairs, I take them two at a time until I hear voices. One low with malice, one rising in alarm.

Fuck.

I soften my steps, listening.

"This is too much, even for you. You need to leave. Now."

"Angela, let me in so we can talk. I think you'll like what I have in mind."

My jaw grinds to the point of pain, but I block it out.

Angela scoffs. "Are you out of your mind, Joe? You can't show up here. This is where I *live*. If you wanted to talk to me, maybe you should've let me work this week instead of taking all my hours away."

She hasn't worked this week? My eyebrows plummet. I've been so caught up in my own misery, I completely disregarded what she must've been going through. This jackass is throwing his weight around, probably as punishment for what we did to Steve. No wonder she thinks she should move; we've caused her too much trouble as it is.

"That's why I'm here now, so we can figure something out that benefits both of us. We both know you need the money. Stop acting like you're not interested."

There's a grunt then I'm moving again. A gasp has me sprinting up the last few stairs. Rounding the baluster, I find the immoral boss himself with one hand against the door, pushing to get in while Angela's frantic eyes find mine. Joe notices, relaxing his arm. Angela uses this time to block the door with her body even more.

"What's going on, Angela?"

I stare daggers at the bastard refusing to even glance my way.

"I was just saying goodbye." Her voice firms as does her posture.

Good girl.

My girl.

Opening my door, Joe relaxes, thinking I'm going inside—just like I wanted him to. I find the banged-up Easton we keep next to the door and swing around just as Joe takes another step forward. The aluminum tings against her doorjamb, halting his advance. Angela jumps back but keeps her hold on the door steady, not backing down.

"I believe she said *bye*. That means it's time for you to go." Speaking low next to his tilted head, his eyes stay glued to Angela and I really, really want him looking at me instead.

Make a move. Make a fucking move. *I dare you.*

His eyes finally meet mine and I lick my lip with anticipation. The promise of violence sits heavy in the air, light on my limbs. I've been waiting to get my hands on this asshole and my fingers twitch on the cool metal. My only concern is keeping Angela out of the way so when this bat starts flying, she's not in its path. She's a smart girl though. I can already see her inching backward in preparation, making me smile internally. Above everything, she knows I'll always protect her. My chest swells with the need to do just that as I press in closer. Joe releases the door suddenly, shuffling back, away from me, away from my everything.

I pivot so I'm now standing at the threshold, facing Joe's overly sweaty figure. Angela, behind me, settles her hand on my lower back and it takes everything in me not to lean into her touch. I'm starved for her affection but not enough to take advantage when she's scared shitless and vulnerable.

Locking my muscles, I point the bat directly at Joe, aiming for his bloated face. He stares down the cylinder at me but takes the hint, walking backward, toward the stairs.

"Let this be your one and only warning, stay the fuck away. If you have something to say to Angela, you say it to her at work and only at work. You speak to her with someone else in the room or you don't speak to her at all. You keep your hands to yourself and far away from Angela. No means no, motherfucker. Got it?"

His beady eyes shift over my shoulder but I nudge his jaw with the bat, firmly keeping his attention where it belongs. He'll probably try to use this against her all over again but fuck it, I already have a plan for that. He needs to learn a lesson and I've got some steam to blow off.

"Angela will see you tomorrow for her shift."

I have no idea if she's scheduled or not, but it sounds like she needs the hours anyway. He can deal.

Joe spins to go but Angela calls him back, making him pause. Pushing past me, she stands to my side while addressing him.

"I heard what you told detailing about me." His shoulders tense as do mine. "You'll never get so much as a look at what's under my clothes, and neither will they, so stop spreading lies about me or I'll start telling the truth about you."

Her shaky hands go to her hips and I've never seen anything sexier. Holy shit, this woman owns me.

Joe's jaw ticks but wisely remains quiet.

We wait until the sound of his engine flares, interrupting the labored silence before facing each other. I reach for her—I can't stop myself—but she dodges, still not ready to give in. Angela's like an injured bird that can still fly—not desperate enough to accept help yet, but in need of it all the same.

Her face drops, whispering softly, "I thought it was you." My stomach tightens and I prop the bat against the wall before wrapping my arm around her waist. She stiffens but allows the contact. "I opened the door because I thought it was you."

She did? She was going to open her door for me? All week I've been begging, praying for her to open that door and the one time she finally does, I wasn't even here.

"I'm sorry it wasn't." More than she knows. "I'm just glad I got back in time. Did he hurt you?"

She shakes her head, making her long hair cascade around her worried face. "He wasn't here long enough. He showed up just before you did. I didn't think he would actually come here."

I did. I knew he was sniffing around and hate that I didn't do something sooner. She should've been safe. She should've been with me.

Her hazel eyes find mine. "I don't want to be alone."

Aw, babe, if it was up to me, you'd never be alone again.

It's the closest I've heard her come to asking for help and it breaks my heart a little. Still cradling my helmet in the crook of my elbow, I drop the arm around her waist to take her hand. "You can stay in my room. I'll lock up here and come check on you when I'm done."

I'll take the couch and fill the guys in when they get home. She'll never have to worry about anyone hurting her with us around. We'd willingly give our lives to protect her—as any good family would.

She nods solemnly then passes through my partially open door. I watch as her pajama-clad body walks dejectedly down the hall. Bare feet pad across the carpet, leaving a hint of her ever-present strawberry scent as she goes. Baggy black pajama pants held up by a drawstring cover her long legs that have kept me awake in more ways than one. A matching cropped tank showing her toned abdomen flutters as she moves.

I see a beautifully broken girl that life is trying to smash but who refuses to fall to pieces. Regardless, I'll be there to help put her back together again, should she ever need it.

Tonight came close. The droop of her shoulders tells me what she won't. She was rattled. So was I. I don't know what I would've done if he succeeded in whatever his rotted brain had concocted. The thought of his hands on her has my temperature rising all over again. I wanted blood. Shit, I still do. A bat wouldn't have been enough. Not for a lowlife like that. If he's willing to prey on someone as strong as Angela, I can't imagine how he is with others, using his laughable title to make girls bend to his will. Dude deserves worse than what he got tonight. I'm not stupid enough to think a single threat will keep him honest but I can't worry about that right now. Angela's in my bed, upset. I can't take away her pain, as much as I wish I could, but I can be there for her like nobody else ever has. I can hold her as she cries. I can listen while she rants. I can help form a new plan of action. I can love her the way she's never been shown but deserves nonetheless.

I work on getting everything settled so I can finally relax knowing she's safe in my world again. And for now, that's enough. I'll figure out how to keep her there later, because there's no other choice. I've never been more certain. She's mine as much as I'm hers.

CHAPTER 35

Angela

TIMES PASSES IN A BLUR OF ENGINES ROARING, VOICES booming, and doors slamming. The general consensus is the boys are pissed. I was, too. Seeing Joe's face at my door tonight had me shaking—with suspicion and with fear. I formed it all into one easy outlet though—anger. I welcomed its sharp claws digging in, knowing I would need it if Joe thought he was getting past my door. Judging by the way he was pushing to get in, it might've even been what saved me had he succeeded.

After Coty showed up, essentially saving me—or Joe, we'll never really know now—all that rage morphed into disbelief. Disbelief in Joe's audacity to show up at my door at all. Disbelief in Coty for riding up on a white horse disguised as a black street bike to save the day. Disbelief that I had let everything get so far out of hand.

Where did it all go wrong?

When had it ever been right?

Truthfully, my time with the boy next door came as close to normal as I've ever experienced. With Coty comes Beckett and Marc, a trifecta I never could've anticipated. Even though they're not my family, they are a family, one that defends what's important, what they love most. For the briefest of moments that included me. Until I took myself out of the equation for being the biggest problem.

Returning to Coty's room, the disbelief quickly dissolved into sadness. And longing. The constant ache from the past week sparked back to life bringing along its close friend misery. The torturous combo making my chest sting from their cruel ways. The trickery they use with lies of not being good enough, that I'll *never* be good enough.

A knock at the door has me sitting up, the blanket gripped tightly between my fingers. The door cracks open as Coty's shadow falls over the beam of light cutting through the room.

"I didn't mean to wake you."

"You didn't."

With a nod, he steps inside, bringing a glass of water. He turns to me after setting it on the nightstand. "I just wanted to check to see how you're feeling. And if you needed anything else?"

Where do I start?

"Thanks. For the water. And earlier. I'm sorry you had to deal with that."

Coty sits on the edge of the bed, gazing into my eyes.

"You didn't do anything wrong. There's nothing to be sorry for. What he did was his mistake. Not yours." He sounds so sure and I want to believe him, but a part of me wonders. Wonders if I did bring this on somehow. "I'm the one that's sorry. For this whole week." His voice catches and he drops his face, hiding it from view.

I shake my head. "No, I'm the one that pushed you away. I'm the one that's been fucking things up from day one."

His stare finds mine again. Eyebrows pinched, he asks, "What do you mean? You haven't fucked anything up."

"Ever since I moved in next door you've been dealing with my shit. My mere existence brings on a certain amount of...hassle, for everyone. Trouble follows me, affecting anyone stupid enough to get in the way. My problems aren't yours, Coty, and that's not fair to assume otherwise."

"First of all, that's not true. Trouble doesn't follow you. You've encountered some awful people in your life that think you're worthy enough to go after. That's not your fault, it's theirs. And second, your problems *are* mine. We're a team. Whether you admit it or not, you belong with us."

Scowling, I turn away. "I never asked for that."

"You didn't have to. Give me your worst, babe." I scoff at his words we've thrown around in less serious times. "I got you. Today. Tomorrow. Forever. It doesn't matter. I'm not going anywhere."

I close my eyes to whisper, "How can I be sure?"

I feel the bed move.

"'Cause that's what family does. They stick it out. They laugh, they cry, they bleed for each other, but they don't walk away because things get tough sometimes." I finally look as he rises to his feet. "You should get some sleep. I'll be in the living room, if you need me."

My hand shoots out to grab his, stopping him mid-step. "Will you," I pause, swallowing my nerves, "will you stay with me?"

The corner of his mouth quirks. "Always."

I make room for him on the bed while he undresses, leaving his shorts on. Closing the door, he joins me, wrapping an arm around my middle from behind. He doesn't pull me to him though. I yearn for his touch, for his peace, so I slide closer until our bodies are molded to one another. Coty takes a deep inhale, relaxing around me, his limbs heavy on my torso. The weight, the warmth, the knowledge that Coty intends to stick it out with me even though I'm a walking disaster—it all settles over me, silencing the doubts stirring beneath.

"Sleep, babe. We'll figure everything out in the morning."

His words play on a continuous loop until my eyelids finally grow heavy.

◆ ◆ ◆

I wake with a dry mouth and pressure behind my eyes. The previous night rushes back to me. The shots with Drew's friend, Coty, Joe. Ugh. Life may very well be sucking me dry—although the shots didn't help matters in that department.

On a groan, I reach over Coty's sleeping form to grab the glass of water, letting it wash down the cotton someone obviously jammed in my mouth. Vodka can be such a bitch like that.

I roll back over to snuggle in when I feel a hard poke to my thigh. Now it's Coty's turn to groan but his grip on me tightens, pulling me closer so his erection presses against my backside. A fire ignites just below my waistband, spreading its flames up my entire body, settling on my cheeks.

Coty's husky voice croons in my neck, "Good morning."

It is now.

"Morning," I squeak out.

His head jolts up. "What's wrong?"

"Nothing. I'm…good."

His smile matches mine then he leans forward to kiss my lips softly. Just as quickly he pulls back, eyebrows tightly knit. "Sorry."

My hands come up to grasp his jaw. "Don't be."

I pull him in again to kiss me properly—thoroughly. And Coty? The guy doesn't disappoint.

Things go from hot to scorching rapidly. Two lost souls coming together to find refuge in each other's embrace, neither one willing to pull away for fear of losing the only connection that truly matters. Where he pulls, I push. When I take, he gives.

"Open."

Two fingers hover near my mouth awaiting access. I slowly obey, opening my mouth to allow entry. Coty watches as they slide between my lips. Just before he can pull them out completely, I bite the tips, making him halt. I may listen occasionally, but that doesn't mean he's in control. Keeping my eyes locked on his, I watch as they darken to almost black until I can no longer make out his pupils.

I let go, making him groan, then he returns his attention to my mouth still sucking his fingers. I swirl my tongue around his digits tantalizingly slow. Carefully—methodically—he removes them, returning his lips to mine and I feel his now wet fingers slide beneath my loose drawstring. Instinctively, I lift my top knee, allowing him better access. Finding no underwear to work past, Coty covers my center instantly and starts working me into a frenzy with his wicked fingers.

His kiss picks up with renewed vigor. His tongue, relentless in chasing mine while he grinds into me from behind, has me clawing at anything I can reach, which facing away from Coty there isn't much, so I grip the back of his neck, keeping him plastered to me. I let my body show him what my words can't. My mouth kisses away the hurt I know I've caused. I ride his hand, clearing the uncertainty I know still lies within. I moan the name of the man who's stolen my heart so completely and tenderly I didn't even notice it was gone until he already had it cradled safely in his hands.

Coty's fingers and hips take turns thrusting, causing a perfect tide, drawing me closer and closer to shore. My moans increase until I know his roommates can hear but just as I approach the coastline, Coty breaks away, sitting up. I gasp at the harsh interruption but am quickly flipped to my back and yanked to the edge of the bed, quieting my protest. I'd laugh except the seriousness on Coty's face has me staying quiet.

Dragging my pants down, Coty cusses seeing my bare pussy on display and begins lowering himself in a daze.

"Hey," I say, stopping him.

His eyebrow quirks so I jerk my chin. He obliges with a smirk, leaning up to kiss me roughly. Fully aware this is give and take, he has to give me what I need before he can take what he wants. Although, after this week the lines between want and need are completely blurred.

Coty drops his forehead to mine. "God, I missed you. Don't leave me again."

"I won't," I breathe out.

And surprisingly, I mean it. I don't want to go through this unrelenting squall without Coty as my anchor to prevent me from drifting off into the madness.

"Promise?" he pleads quietly.

My pulse quickens so I try to capture his lips but he pulls back, waiting. *Give and take.*

"I promise," I whisper, releasing the weight that's been crushing my chest for far too long. Coty's mouth crashes to mine as I guide my hands up his toned back, bringing him between my spread legs. I'm just starting to remove his shorts when Coty slides down my body, taking the unnecessary clothing with him. With a secretive grin, he throws a leg over his shoulder and dives between my thighs, causing me to throw my head back on a moan. He pushes my other leg wider while gripping where my hip meets my thigh, holding me in place. Spread so openly to him, it doesn't take long for the pressure to build. The waves of ecstasy are rolling nearer as Coty licks me with a punishing rhythm. I'm shamelessly riding his face, holding him exactly where I want him when he pulls back slightly.

My head shoots off the pillow.

"Wha-"

"I want your eyes on me."

Does he not realize how much effort that will take? I can barely remember my own name and he wants my eyes to remain open and on him. This bossy shit has to stop.

Dropping my head, a smile creeps out as I shut my eyes and lower my hand. My middle finger barely skims my throbbing clit when it's smacked away with a growl.

"God, you're a handful."

My smug laugh is smothered by another moan as Coty lowers his mouth to the spot my finger was rudely denied. Sucking the sensitive bud into his mouth, I come instantaneously—with my eyes closed, like a normal person.

Coty stands to grab a condom before dropping his shorts and boxer briefs to the floor. My eyes, now open and alert, drink him in while he rolls it on.

"See something you like?"

His head tilts to the side and he opens his arms, giving me a better view. Perfect. He is absolutely perfect. And mine.

I crook a finger, beckoning him forward. He complies, trailing kisses up my already buzzing body. By the time he reaches my mouth, I'm more than ready.

"No."

"Liar." His deep chuckle rumbles my taut belly, warming me straight through. His tip nudges against my entrance, making me gasp.

I pop a shoulder. He asked if I saw something I *like*, but that's not the word I'd use to describe how I feel about him, not anymore.

Coty, sporting the sexiest smirk, slides his swollen cock inside, letting my heat surround him fully as I cry out in pleasure. His hands frame my face, then using his thumbs he strokes my temples softly.

"I like that answer better. I don't know which one turns me on more—your moans or your sarcasm."

"Probably the one you don't have to work as hard for."

Pulling out slowly, our breaths both catch from the loss before he glides back in, hitting my walls deep within.

"Babe, you're one challenge I'll never forfeit," Coty says before gently rocking his hips in time with mine.

I hold him to me or he holds me to him, I'm not really sure, all I do know is this moment. This moment being the one that I will hold forever in my heart, taking it out to measure against any other in my life going forward because this is the moment that Coty first made love to me. And it was everything I never knew I wanted, and more.

◆ ◆ ◆

"Here, take this one. I love you in my clothes anyway." Coty's tone rises but I ignore it as he tosses a hoodie on the bed.

I scoop it up happily, taking a whiff of his spiced coconut body wash embedded in the material. Seeing it's another one missing its drawstring, I smile.

A series of knocks that remind me of a new pop song has Coty shaking his head. "I'm surprised he gave us this long."

The door opens to Beckett standing with his hand over his eyes dramatically, while also peeking between his fingers. Coty shoves his shoulder.

"It sounded like someone was dying a slow, sexy death in here. I didn't want to interrupt. Luckily, it was fast." He throws his hands up in defense, laughing, when Coty casts him a frown. "So, you're back then?" His eyes fall on me. "For good? No more of this silent treatment bullshit?"

I pick at an imaginary piece of lint on my pants. "It would appear so."

What feels like a freight train plows into my chest, knocking me backward onto the bed with a laugh. Lifting to his hands so he doesn't smother me to death, Beckett looks down with a huge grin. "Welcome back, neighbor girl. Welcome *home*. I've missed you. I mean I didn't miss hearing that sound you make right before you-"

A demanding hand grips his shoulder, yanking him upright before he can say more. "We get the point." Coty pushes him toward the door while my eyes stay on the ceiling, praying my cheeks aren't as red as I think they are.

"I'm just messing around. Anyway, you used the camera last night, man?" Beckett's change in tone has me sitting up.

"I wanted to film, uh," Coty's eyes flick to mine, "a location."

"What camera?" I bite out.

"Not that kind." Coty winks. "It's attached to my helmet for riding. Actually, all of ours have them now."

I try, but fail, to hide my grin. They were planning for my return all along.

"Well, it picked up something else I think you should see."

The dark look he pins us with wipes the smile from my face.

CHAPTER 36

Angela

M̲Y FINGERS PINCH THE SMOOTH PLASTIC IN MY pocket as I stroll across the asphalt behind Hot Spots. The boys thought they should come, too, just in case. After much deliberation, I conceded one could come but only if I got to drive my own car. I glance over my shoulder, seeing all three occupying my vintage Jeep. Well, I got part of my wish.

I round the corner to the office door swaying open and ignore whoever's spraying down the car in the bay. Joe straightens at my approach, but I bypass him completely, heading straight for the stairs. I smirk as my sneakers pound up the creaky steps. That's right, I'm going to talk to the big man. The owner. Joe's boss. Coty called him this morning, claiming he wanted to meet about a collaboration for an upcoming event. Walter basically jumped at the chance to get his name out there and promised he'd be in his office today to go over everything. I would feel bad but the dirtbag he's entrusted with running things in his long absences has shattered any sympathy I might've shown otherwise.

Walter startles as the door bounces off the wall.

"Can I help you?" he snips.

Of course he doesn't know me. Why would he? He doesn't bother himself with such menial tasks such as getting to know the faces keeping his business afloat.

"Probably not, but you will."

Bushy salt and pepper eyebrows sink as the older man's cloudy eyes narrow. Grayish blond hair feathers over his droopy ears with a rather large nose as the focal point on his weathered face while a rumpled joke of a suit hangs limply off his figure.

What size is that thing? Also, are shit brown suits still a thing? *Were they ever?*

The whole office is covered with a half-inch thick coat of dust with papers strewn about on every surface. The desk he's sitting at has an empty picture frame next to a knocked over jar of pens. The leather chair sitting opposite him has fissures like scratches covering the seat and I'm guessing they didn't come from people visiting this office, but another from a time long ago. The place has a scattered, yet forgotten, vibe.

"Tell me," I pull the flash drive from my pocket to set it on his desk, "how does a sexual harassment lawsuit against your company sound?"

As it turns out, Coty never stopped recording after his ride last night and managed to catch Joe's late-night visit on camera.

Walter's caterpillar eyebrows shoot to his hairline and I suppress a smirk, knowing I've gained his full attention. Dragging the tattered chair against the scuffed vinyl floor, I take a seat then start from the beginning.

◆ ◆ ◆

"I still think you should talk to him about going in on a promotion together. The guy's a little out of touch, but the wash is popular. Maybe it'll bring both companies more customers."

After coming downstairs to find all three of my guys standing outside my Jeep like my own security detail, we went out for a late lunch together—at their expense unfortunately, since I'm now unemployed. A surprised, but not completely shocked, Walter offered me a promotion but I refused. Joe was the biggest issue there but he certainly wasn't the only problem at Hot Spots. As much as Joe protested, you can't argue with video proof so he was fired on the spot. Steve, however, was able to keep his job even after everything I told Walter, but it was his word against mine and all that. Nothing new sadly, but disheartening all the same.

"We don't need that tool's help." Marc speaks from the back

seat. I glance at him in the rearview mirror through the stray hairs flying around my face. "Ours will be ten times better than his shit ever was."

Frowning, I turn to Coty in the passenger seat. His knuckles gripping the roll bar tighten as he stares ahead, avoiding me.

"Your what?" When he remains silent, I quirk an eyebrow at Beckett lounging beside Marc, his motorcycle tee billowing around him. Eyes the size of saucers meet mine in the mirror before snapping to Coty.

"Bro, you didn't tell her yet?"

Squinting at Coty again, I press, "Tell me what?"

Coty sighs, dropping his hands to his lap. Over his shoulder, he says, "We've been a little occupied, if you haven't noticed."

"Yeah, bangin'," Beckett accuses.

Accurate? Yes.

Crass? Also, yes.

I catch Coty shaking his head out of the corner of my eye and sing-song, "No more sleepovers at your place."

"Like that will help," Beckett scoffs. "Angie sleeps with her windows open, everybody knows that. Just like everybody knows Angie also has sex with her windows open."

Coty lunges between the seats, setting off laughs from the entire car. Marc separates the two, then Coty lands in his seat with a thud.

He notices me sneaking peeks, asking, "What?"

"I'm waiting."

Blowing out a breath, he smooths his jeans before angling his body toward mine. My stomach constricts as my left knee starts to rock back and forth. "I didn't want to do it like this." Oh, shit. Has anything good ever followed that sentence? "I was going to tell you soon." *Oh my God!* A million scenarios play through my mind as I pull into Creekwood's entrance. "But we, the three of us, are opening a shop of our own."

Parked in a spot alongside the Tahoe, the group falls silent.

So, he's not secretly married? And he doesn't have a kid hidden away that he obviously never sees, making me have to break up with him for being such a horrible father?

I'm still playing catch-up when Beckett speaks again. "Tell her the best part."

His child-like grin comes into view as I tune back in. He's literally bouncing. Whatever Coty's nervous to tell me is having the opposite effect on Beck. The guy is practically covering his own mouth to keep from spilling the beans. Marc is quiet though, giving nothing away.

"It's not just a body shop, I mean we'll be servicing everything with a motor, not just cars, but it'll have a car wash, too. It'll be built in on the side. Just one bay, but multiple electronic kiosks accepting payments, allowing for cars to go through faster."

Three sets of eyes watch for my reaction. "Okay?"

"And I, well, we are wondering if you'd run it? The car wash portion." My eyes widen and Coty rushes to add, "You know most of the positions anyway." I raise a finger in Beckett's face, silencing the remark undoubtedly perched on his tongue. "And since you're going to school for business management, we thought you'd be the perfect person." I open my mouth but he continues, "You'd call your own shots. We'd have a say over major decisions obviously, but mostly you'd be free to run the wash however you want. So, what do you think?"

I shake my head, calling over my shoulder as I climb out, "I think you're insane."

Huge arms lift me from behind. "Angie, did you hear that? You get to be your own boss. And you get to work with us every day. All your problems solved. Boom. You're welcome."

I smack his arms so he lowers me to my feet.

"You think that'll solve my problems? Working for, not with, my neighbors? One is my, I don't know, boyfriend or whatever." I look to Coty for help, but he just scowls. "One is a giant man-baby, and the other barely even likes me," I finish lamely.

"I like you as much as anyone." Marc shrugs.

I throw my hands up. "You don't like anybody."

Beckett nodding, agrees, "She has a point."

Snickering, I don't dare look at Coty. I can feel his annoyance from here. He said it himself, we haven't had much time to talk, so that leaves our current relationship without a label. If he thought differently, he should've informed me.

"Look, Coty's my brother and if my boy loves you then I'm cool with you. We're a package deal if you haven't noticed. Just don't fuck him over and we'll be good."

My head is shaking before he finishes. "He doesn't-"

"Really?" Beckett interrupts, knocking his hand in Coty's stomach. "Dude, you're slacking."

Coty ignores Beckett. "Angela."

All eyes are on me again and it's too much. The crazy job proposal. The L word. It's all just too much, especially on sweltering concrete with boob sweat pooling beneath my bra. This is not how this conversation should've gone down. After an intense orgasm would've been much more preferable, at least the boob sweat wouldn't be as embarrassing.

I turn for the stairs but Coty rushes forward, catching my hand. "You're not leaving, are you?"

"No, I'm not going anywhere." I hate the doubt I see there. The doubt I put there.

Beckett interjects, "Angie, I get it, that was a lot. We could've handled that better." I snort. Understatement of the year. "But it still doesn't change anything. Coty's crazy about you. The kid's been head over heels since you moved in. And we want you working *with* us. You're the perfect woman for the job. You're smart, damn good at what you do, and don't take shit from anyone. We'd be lucky to have you. Anyone would."

I blink away the mist coating my eyes.

"Just...don't disappear on us again. We won't pressure you. You can say no and still be in our squad."

A watery laugh escapes as I meet each boy's eye, then Marc and Beckett excuse themselves to the Tahoe, giving me and Coty some privacy.

"What are you thinking?"

"That I need to figure out how I'm going to pay my bills."

His arms snake around my back and I wrap mine around his neck.

"What do you think about the offer?"

"Honestly?" He nods, watching me closely. "It sounds great, but-"

"Then we'll figure it out," cutting me off, Coty continues, "together."

My lungs fill with more air than necessary.

"Can I think about it?"

A loose smile breaks free. "Of course." He gestures over his shoulder. "I gotta go anyway. You'll be here when I get back?"

"I might go to the library for a bit, otherwise I'll be here."

Coty reaches into his pocket and pulling out his keys, removes one, then hands it to me. "Make yourself at home. Use whatever you need. I'll see you later."

With a quick kiss goodbye, he joins the others and they peel out, leaving me alone with my thoughts, and decisions, and sweaty bra.

Walking into the boys' apartment, I spot empty coffee mugs littering the counter. The reminder of Faye heavy on my mind, I decide to call her myself about the barista job.

The adrenaline from today's events begins to fade, its absence making room for the panic at my current situation. If they're serious about their proposition, then I'll need something to hold me over until this new endeavor is a viable reality. I won't wait around in the meantime. Sharks don't stop when they're tired and neither will I.

◆ ◆ ◆

"Like what you see, Tom?" I crack an eye to see Coty standing on his balcony, grinning without an ounce of shame at being caught.

"Tom?"

"Peeping Tom," Beckett guffaws as he and Marc join him.

Coty smiles at his roommates then looks back to me, his humor suddenly gone. In the next instant he's up and over the railing—on the second level—then dropping to the ground and landing on his feet like a frickin' cat.

I scramble up from the lounge chair I've been glued to for the last hour. After taking things into my own hands and calling the coffee stand owner, she hired me over the phone. I ran right over to fill out all the necessary paperwork before she could change her mind and I've been hanging here for the boys to return ever since.

"Holy shit. Is that how you guys always get down so fast?"

"Maybe. Only for things that are really important though." He shrugs as he takes my vacated seat, pulling me into his lap.

"Things, huh?"

His lips trace the shell of my ear, tugging on a piercing he finds there. "People," he whispers. "Person. Specifically, my girlfriend."

I pull away as he travels down my neck. "Is that what I am?"

Coty's breath blows over my bare shoulder making my skin pebble. "We can use whatever term you want, as long as you're mine. And before you ask, yes, I'm yours. Have been since I laid eyes on you, babe. My beautifully broken neighbor girl."

I scoff just as his teeth make an appearance at the base of my neck. Batting him away, I sit forward to face him.

"And you want to be attached to this mess?"

Coty's face grows serious and his hands grip my thighs, rubbing soothing circles with his thumbs.

"We're all broken in some way or another. That's what binds us together, finding someone you trust enough to protect the pieces that need it most. I can't promise you perfect 'cause I'm not perfect. I can't promise you easy 'cause it won't be. But I can promise to be here for you through it all no matter what, loving you in any way you'll allow me for as long as I'm breathing. Whether that makes you my girlfriend or not is up to you, but my feelings remain the same. I see your wreckage and want to fix my own just so I can be the armor yours is missing. I love you, Angela."

His intense gaze never breaks even as mine grows blurry. The L word was tossed around earlier but this is different. There's no mistaking his intent this time. Coty loves me. The boy that taught me how to live is now showing me what it is to love. As much as my mind rejects the notion, my heart decides it's time to take control for once.

I lean my forehead against his and whisper, "I'm not making any promises either but I fell for you, I fell so damn hard I'm still waiting for the ground to catch up with me and that scares me, so much. I trust you to hold my many, many broken pieces safely while I find my way though."

"Find *our* way."

"Together," I agree. "I love you."

His insistent mouth kisses me deep and rough, claiming what's already his.

"About damn time you two make it official."

Breathless, we pull apart.

"Did you think more about what we talked about, neighbor girl?"

Marc, still in work clothes, sits on the lounger next to ours, pulling out a cigarette while Beckett stands with his arms crossed over a gray shirt that says *Does This Bike Make My Ass Look Fast?*.

I twist in Coty's arms, melting into him as he reclines. He brings his nose to my hair and kisses my temple.

"I did. But I have some concerns." The tallest of the three motions for me to continue. "This is new for me. A relationship. Friendships. Trusting anyone in general, especially men. I'm bad at it. All of it." I bite my lip, looking between Coty's friends—my friends.

"And you think we aren't?" Beckett bursts. "Look at us. We

can't rub together a healthy relationship between the three of us except the one we shaped from scratch ourselves. Nobody showed us how, we just did what felt right, making mistakes as we went. Hell, you're the first girl we've ever had around for more than just fu-"

"What he means is, this is new for us, too," Marc quickly interrupts. "But we're willing to try because it feels right. The same way it did years ago at the track, riding without a clue as to what would come next but knowing it'd be okay with these two in my corner. You're not used to anyone being in yours but know that from here on out, we are. This one's taking up the whole fucking thing anyway and where he goes, we go." He jerks his thumb behind me making Coty's chest rumble.

"I think you mean where we go, he goes." Beckett pretends to beat his fists on his chest.

Coty runs his hands up my sides before wrapping his arms around my middle. "Dude, it's where she goes, I go. I've just been biding my time, waiting for her to show up."

"So, what do you say, Angie?"

"All for one and one for all?" I joke.

"I'll settle for a foursome."

"Motherfucker."

I'm set to the side as Coty makes a grab for Beckett. Marc hops up, tossing his cigarette butt and joins the others poolside. They play fight and trash talk amongst themselves, having momentarily forgotten about me. I sit back, watching their dynamic, the ease of it all. The love, the trust. They have each other's backs, but like Coty said, it's more than that. They respect the damaged parts in one another, never using it against each other, always keeping it safe from outsiders. Each man is strong on his own but together they're a force to be reckoned with. One I've found myself in the middle of. The comfort and security I never thought would come has settled over me like a blanket on a cold night and I'm growing more and more fond of the refuge it's provided. The three nosey neighbors refusing to give up on me has generated warmth where only cold previously lived.

Fighting to constantly stand alone was necessary but has left me tired, run down. These three provide a safe place for me to take a rest—should I decide to take one.

Today, though, is not that day.

Laughing, I walk over and shove the unsuspecting trio toward the water. Three different hands shoot out, latching onto mine and together we fall in giving Beckett a version of his foursome after all.

CHAPTER 37

Angela

"THERE WE GO."

A smudge on the window's been bothering me all day but I haven't had time to properly clean it until the afternoon rush passed. I glance over as a junky car pulls in then hustle back inside to the glorious air conditioning.

It's been several weeks since I started at Latte Da Coffee Stand and I'm finally getting the hang of this barista stuff. Luckily, my excellent customer service makes up for any mishaps I've had serving less than perfect orders. I haven't lost Faye any returning customers, that I know of, so that's a plus.

Apparently with all the college kids back in town after graduation and looking for a local coffee spot—not a chain!—to support, business has been booming. It's not the easiest job for someone like me who's not food gifted in the slightest, but the schedule allows for my night course to continue unhindered and the tips are great. Although, after falling in love with a certain someone with mocha swirled eyes, I will say I've become obsessed with the drink, giving me more motivation in learning how to make it correctly.

There hasn't been a lot of alone time for me and Coty with the long hours I've had to put in, but we've been making it work. Coty's also developed a serious coffee addiction but only during my shifts coincidentally. And I'll admit that living next door to your boyfriend does have its benefits when you're strapped for time.

With the offer on the property for their garage being accepted, the guys have been laying it on pretty damn thick in trying to convince me to accept the last remaining management position—that they made specifically for me. Digging my heels in with apprehension has only encouraged their efforts, much to my immense enjoyment. I finally conceded but only under the condition that we'd all get to know each other better, both as a unit and separately. Now every Friday before their usual parties we have family dinners together. It's been going well so far—as long as I'm not the one cooking. This week I invited Drew, too, and am looking forward to seeing all the men in my life getting along.

Joe's absence from my life has helped everyone to relax. Word has it his wife found out about the video and kicked him to the curb. I also heard a very pregnant Amity let him move in with her and the two are perfectly miserable together. Karma loves a good plot twist, doesn't she?

The ding of the drive-thru sensor draws my attention to the window and I open it, ready to take the next order. Freezing in my spot, my chest tightens to almost painful and my lips clamp together. My mother's smug grin tells me this is no coincidence and I exhale through my nose.

"What can I get you?"

"Oh, don't play dumb, Ang. You're a lot of things but naïve isn't one of them. You know what I want."

I relax my hold on the counter to lean forward on a heavy sigh.

"What happened to your other car?"

She waves a hand. "This is a loaner from a…friend." I roll my eyes, knowing exactly what kind of friends Rianne keeps. "Just until I can get mine back. That's why I'm here. I thought you should help with that."

Dropping my head back, I stare at the ceiling, filling my lungs to the hilt. "And why should I help with that?" I pop up, meeting eyes that match my own in color but not in substance. "You somehow got a car that you couldn't afford and I'm supposed to pay the bill? I don't think so." Maybe her *friend* should just let her keep this one, it fits her better anyway.

The bumper hanging off the front reminds me of the fake façade my mother puts up but has been slipping more and more lately, showing the true ruin lurking beneath. The rust spots are like the holes in her armor she's spent so long using against both the world and me. Whiny clangs from the engine speak of an exhaustion her soul carries from never measuring up to society's standards.

"Where are your guard dogs? I'm surprised they let you out of their sight after threatening my life." I stifle another eye roll. "What? Did they give up on your Ice Queen act already, seeing you for the total nuisance you really are?"

Before I can respond, smoke begins to billow out from under the hood of her car.

"Shit!" Gripping both sides of the window, I jump out feet first and land on the blistering asphalt next to the driver's door. I immediately reach through her open window to turn the keys, effectively shutting off the engine. My mother, frozen from either shock or embarrassment, starts to cry.

I quickly turn away, pulling out my phone. Coty talks me through a few simple steps to open the hood, then promises to handle the rest when he gets here.

With a swipe across my forehead, I see her shaking develop into a rolling boil and stop short. Car trouble is nothing new in Rianne's life, having driven many lemons between boy-toys, but I've never seen her react like this. This is more. More than a crappy car overheating on a summer day. This is something else entirely. My heart squeezes as I push forward with a shaky façade of my own.

Even though she was just being a wretched bitch, she's still blocking the only path for actual customers and I need her to leave as soon as possible—for everybody's sake.

"Hey, it's not that big of a deal. This summer's been hard on everyone." I nudge her shoulder, then drop my hand unsure what else to do with it before blurting, "I'm thirsty."

Happy to have something to occupy my hands, I pour us frozen hot chocolates with whipped cream, making sure to put extra on mine. I inspect the drinks, then add more to hers.

Out back, I find her sitting in the shade. She accepts the frosty drink with a trembling hand. She doesn't so much as thank me as I continue to stand, taking her in. Her smudged eyes have dark circles under them and her hair is matted in places I didn't notice before. Her clothes are wrinkled and one of her flip-flops is being held together with a piece of duct tape. It's a far cry from her usual put together self. The Rianne I know would never be out in public looking like the hot mess I see before me.

Squinting, I focus on a passing car. "You doing okay?" I grimace at my warbled voice before turning back to her.

Her tired eyes meet mine as she swallows noisily. "Like you care."

"I may not like you, but I don't wish harm on you. You've been blaming me for your life going to shit for years but I think it's time you take a look in the mirror. Kelsie chose to live with her dad for a reason. And that reason sure as hell wasn't me, no matter what you say. Blaming an innocent child born from an undesirable circumstance for your fuck-ups is just shitty. Stealing anything good from your own flesh and blood is even worse. Take some responsibility already."

Her attention flits past my shoulder as I hear a few engines pull up but I don't need see to know who it is. My real family just arrived. The one I chose.

"Did they teach you to talk like that?"

My body relaxes the moment I see the boys dismount their bikes. I called one yet they all came running—for me. Warmth that has nothing to do with the blazing sun settles deep in my bones. It glides through my body, spreading calm as it goes, quieting the constant nag in the back of my head wondering if I'm enough, if I deserve them. It's amazing what love and care can do to a person, to an open wound left abandoned and exposed. Their consideration helped soothe the pain caused by others even when they didn't have to. Even when they shouldn't have. When they had every reason to walk away, they refused to give up and I'm forever grateful. When you're told you're not loveable enough, you start to believe it. They've shown me what it feels like to be loved. That's not what my mother provided me. That wasn't love. Love isn't used as a weapon. It's a gift one should offer freely and receive with humility.

After years of living with the reason for them, my carefully constructed walls came crumbling down for the boys just next door. Go figure.

"They taught me a lot actually. Mostly about family and what it means to love, not just yourself but others." I bend down to her level. "They taught me what it's like to be loved, too, something I've never felt before. Not from friends, not from a father or sister, not even from my own mom." She, of all people, should understand what that feels like.

Her eyes fill with unshed tears as she looks away. I straighten then turn to the guys, catching Coty's hand as he reaches for me. Three sets of tight eyes greet me but I usher them toward something they're more equipped to take on.

Beckett and Marc slowly walk to the front of the car while Coty pulls me against his chest, speaking low in my ear.

"What the hell is she doing here?"

"I don't know."

"I don't like it."

I peek over his shoulder to see her wiping roughly at her eyes, knocking over her drink in the process.

"I don't either."

A loud curse steals our attention.

"Fucking idiot. What is this, amateur hour?"

Beckett smacks the hood. "Fuck off, bro. I didn't bring a rag."

We rush over, finding an angry burn on Beckett's hand. He's already rubbing furiously at the wound, clearly making it worse.

"Stop that." I yank his uninjured hand away, saying, "I'll get the first aid kit."

Coty joins me in the kiosk, grabbing a towel and a cup of

water. Returning to the car, Coty and Marc confer by the hood while I treat Beckett's burn. His pinched eyebrows soften as I smooth on some of the ointment from the small kit.

"Why are you helping her?" he asks softly.

I attach a large bandage, keeping my eyes trained on my movements. "Faye won't be happy finding that piece of shit blocking her business tomorrow morning. How's your hand?"

He flexes his fingers, testing his mobility with the binding.

"Good, thanks. I still can't believe I did that shit."

"We all make mistakes. Treat it as a lesson learned and move on." I'm suddenly reminded of Coty telling me something very similar but about burning your hand in the kitchen.

"This was a lesson I've been taught many, many times though. It was just stupid."

I nod, wiping the excess goop on a towel. "Maybe, but being mad at yourself isn't going to do any good. And being angry at the car won't help matters either," I add, seeing his glare. "Don't let anger get the better of you. You're smarter than that. That thing," I gesture to his hand, "will only get infected if you don't treat it with care, then your mistake will continue to grow and won't heal correctly."

"Why are you so good to us, Angie?"

"Because you're good to me."

"We're only doing this for you. Not for her." He leans down to kiss my forehead so I lift my eyes to his, silently thanking him.

I mull over my words to Beckett while I drift toward Rianne. By staying angry at my mom—the constant analyzing, the refusing to forgive—it's kept the hurt at the forefront of my mind, preventing me from moving forward. Being mad at myself hasn't helped either. By continuously picking at the open wound she's caused, I've been prolonging the healing process all along. Just like Beckett's burn, I need to treat the injury with care if I want it to improve, for me to be free of the pain I've been living with for so long. Deciding to do the opposite of what my anger is trying to

334 | A. MARIE

trick me into, I forgive the woman who's caused the damage I've grown to resent. As Beckett said, not for her, but for me.

"Your car's almost done. You should be able to get it someplace to have it looked at. My guys are really good with cars if you want to take it to them."

She scoffs, meeting my eyes. "*Your* guys?"

My face softens. "Yeah." I drop my gaze, nudging a pebble with my shoe. "You've had a rough time, I know that. Some at your own hands, but everybody deserves love and you've been through hell searching for it. Kelsie loves you and-" I swallow down the pride trying to elbow past. "It probably doesn't mean much but I love you, too. You didn't have to have me, or keep me, but you did. You gave me a chance at life that I don't take for granted even if I've said otherwise in the heat of the moment. I wouldn't have found the happy waiting for me," my eyes touch on Coty briefly, "and for that, I'll always be grateful to you."

Each kind word spoken is a stitch in the gaping hole left behind by a negligent parent until the steady throb fades to a calm sting.

"But my love can only be from afar. We've been through too much to pretend everything's fine—it's not. I refuse to enable you or be your punching bag. I'm not sure what made you show up here today, but I'm glad you did. I want to apologize to you. I'm sorry I can't be what you want," my voice cracking, I continue, "but this is me and I'm okay with that. I wish you a happy, or at least content, life. It'll just have to be without me in it from now on."

The scar left behind will forever serve as a reminder of a hard lesson learned but I can move on knowing I kept my composure when I could've easily buckled from the pressure. I'll remember how much strength it took to show kindness in a time when everything in me screamed not to. I'll reflect back on how the grace I showed not only to her, but to myself, resulted in a healthier me overall. I'm ready for bigger and better things sans impossibly heavy baggage.

The hood slams closed and the guys round her car. My gaze follows them as they walk to their bikes, giving us a little longer. When I look back, she's watching me through watery eyes.

"Good for you. Telling off the big, bad monster, right? That's it? You apologize once and I'm supposed to just accept it?"

She stands, coming closer and once she's within arm's reach, I wrap her in a hug.

"The choice is yours. Do whatever you want, but this is my goodbye." I release her and any remaining animosity.

Halfway to Coty, I hear her say, "Do you really think they're going to stick around?"

Without taking my eyes off Coty, I smile. "Maybe." I look over at Rianne for what might be the final time. "I'm willing to take that chance though."

They're worth it. And so am I.

◆ ◆ ◆

Watching her leave fills me with sadness where only anger used to reside full time. Beckett and Marc wait until she's gone then follow soon after, calling out their typical "ride it" mantra.

Alone, Coty pulls out my helmet with a wicked gleam in his eye.

"I have my Jeep."

"I'll bring you back to get it tomorrow. Ride home with me tonight?"

Leaning in, I kiss his closed mouth chastely, grabbing my helmet from him. "Okay, but you have to help me clean first."

Together we make quick work cleaning the kiosk before locking up.

Already on his R6, Coty helps me up, too. As per usual, he pulls my thighs in closer, setting my entire front against his back, then I place my hands on the tank in front of his seat. As he starts the engine though, I bring my hands up to wrap around his middle. Coty hesitates, allowing me time to replace them to my preferred position before taking off but I squeeze, letting him know I'm ready. His head snaps to the side, his questioning eyes finding mine, so I nod reassuringly.

I trust you.

Without breaking eye contact, he leans in resting his helmet against mine while his hand squeezes my thigh—his grip as sure and steady as his hold on the part of my heart he now owns.

With a bright smile and a shake of his head, Coty pulls onto the street, leaving any previous doubt behind. Picking up speed, we race forward exactly how we're supposed to—together and with no regrets.

EPILOGUE

Coty
One Year Later

"WHERE ARE WE GOING? I THOUGHT YOU WERE taking me to lunch."

I lift Angela's hand to my mouth, placing a kiss in her palm before dropping it back to the clutch to shift into fourth.

"I am. Kind of." Her eyes grow wide, making me laugh. "You'll be fed, don't worry. I have something I want to show you first."

My sweaty hand grips the steering wheel tighter. This could go either way. With Angela, I never really know. She surprises me at every turn, which normally I love the constant mystery our neighbor girl provides, but today I really need things to go my way. It was hard enough stealing her away from the shop. With the summer weather rolling in even earlier this year, her wash has been insane. After months of overseeing every detail of the build, and high praise from her professor, she finally accepted our offer to run the car wash portion of Pop The Hood Garage. Oh, and let's not forget the thorough contract negotiations. We put up a good effort, but she had us all along, since day one to be exact. She still doesn't know that.

We opened our automotive high-performance doors five months ago and have been booked solid ever since. Landing Joaquin as our major client set us off to a great start, but we had no idea just how crazy things would get. I've been tested in ways I never was at the old place. New problems pop up daily for me to solve, always keeping me on my toes. We now service ATVs, UTVs, dirt bikes, sports cars, farm trucks, and everything in between. Basically, we fix things that go, hell, even some things that don't. I'm pretty sure Beck repaired some lady's musical jewelry box last week on one of his rare breaks.

Not even a full year in and we're already talking about expanding. Through it all, Angela's kept her cool over on the wash side. She runs it efficiently and fairly, always happy to please customers. So much so, I swear some of the farmhands come in more often than needed just to see her. Having her so close though—and with three, if not more, sets of eyes on her—I don't have to worry like I did before. Nobody can even sneeze in her direction now without someone running to check on her. Okay, it's usually me, but Beck and Marc are always waiting in the wings, ready to step in, too. At first, she worried it would interfere with productivity—us constantly looking after her—but she soon realized it was pointless to argue. Family comes first, always. It'd be the same whether she worked with us or somewhere else, but having her so close does make things easier for everyone.

On the occasional rainy day, she'll come over to the bays to help out where needed. Angela's the hardest worker there, and in a shop full of star mechanics, that's saying something. I love being able to see her every day, even if for a short break here and there. I've tried to lure her into my office with the promise of a quickie but she rebuffs me every time with some new task she's taken on. She's always thinking of ways to improve both sides of the business and has proven to be the best damn decision we've made in this crazy venture. She's also hell bent on keeping up professional appearances which just means I'll need to take her there when everybody's gone sometime.

The thought of her on my desk has me adjusting in my seat. Angela shoots her gaze to me, seeing my discomfort. The triumphant smirk she's wearing tells me she knows what's causing it.

"Are you stealing me away just to have sex? Don't you get enough at home?"

Home. Such a simple word, yet holds so much weight. We

still spend time at both apartments but most nights are spent at hers for privacy. I also put an end to her open windows rule. The truth is I don't mind sleeping in Angela's sauna of an apartment, I never did. I'd sleep on an active volcano if it meant being close to her, but I give her shit about it because I like the way her eyebrows crease when she thinks she's at a disadvantage. It's the only warning she gives before she strikes back and I love the bite to her passion, especially when I'm the reason for it. But with her new salary, I know damn well she can afford to run the air conditioning at night, which is why I pay the bill anyway—she wouldn't let me otherwise. A small price to pay, in my mind, to ensure the whole complex isn't listening to my girl scream my name every night. Not that there's anything wrong with them knowing who's in her bed—I love that part—but I know my boys giving her a hard time about it embarrasses her. I like her wild and loud, so it was an easy decision to shut the damn windows. Getting her to agree to it, while not easy, definitely added to the fun. I smile remembering how inventive I had to get with my persuasion.

"It's not to have sex," I assure her. "Although, I like where your head's at." I wink, knowing it drives her crazy.

While clenching her thighs—I knew I had her—she groans, "I don't even have time to eat lunch right now, let alone go out, so unless you plan on feeding me while fucking me, it's not happening."

Damn, she's hangry. And I'm betting a little horny now, too. This is not off to a good start. I reach behind her seat, pulling out the bag full of tacos I ordered ahead of time. With extra limes. I know better than to offer my girl anything less than a five to one ratio of limes to tacos. Her face lights up when she sees the food and wastes no time grabbing one.

I'm almost to our destination when sucking noises have my eyebrows jumping. Glancing over, I see Angela lick the juice off her fingers, probably all that damn lime juice, giving me an idea of how to satisfy her other craving.

"Unbutton your pants."

Angela's eyes bounce to mine, confused, but I'm not joking. Even though it's unbearably hot out, Angela insists on wearing pants to work every day. I usually don't complain since she slays in anything she wears, but today they're working against me. Shorts would've made this so much easier but fuck it, I'm down to try.

She cocks an eyebrow but continues licking her finger in slow, exaggerated movements. Goddamn, she's trying to kill me.

"Now," I rasp out, barely able to speak.

With a roll of her hazel eyes, she does as she's told. Knowing her though, that's not the last of it—not by a long shot. She'll get me back somehow and I can't wait to see when she does. The fire she holds within is intoxicating and I'm addicted to her flame, always daring to see how close I can get before it consumes me by burning from the inside out.

Hopped up on nerves, and feeling pretty fucking reckless, I reach over to push inside her panties, happy to find her wet and ready, despite her indifferent attitude. Taking my left hand off the wheel to shift, I quickly replace it before I begin swirling her wetness around her pussy lips with my right hand. Her whimper fills the car, turning me rock hard, and I pick up the pace, circling her entrance in preparation. I dip in one finger, testing her readiness and she shifts forward, greedily chasing the friction she loves so much.

I got you, babe.

My second finger follows as I push my palm flat against her clit, so she can grind on my hand.

"Coty," she moans.

I peer over to see her bottom lip bitten between her teeth and her eyes closed.

She's so fucking beautiful it takes everything in me to tear my eyes away but I am still driving. With an eye on the road, I keep up a steady rhythm as Angela rides my hand. I listen to her panting, committing it to memory since it's the best sound in the world. When I can safely steal a glance at her, I see she's close. So fucking close.

My turn approaches sooner than I'd anticipated and, unable to downshift in time, I end up taking it while going way too fast. I recover like a fucking champ before coming to a full stop. Yanking the emergency brake up, I face Angela just in time to see her coming and swallow her cries whole as I seal my lips to hers. My arm starts to cramp from the odd angle but I'd break the damn thing off before I'd deny my love a proper orgasm.

Her breathing mellows as I eat up her prolonged moans, enjoying the hell out of the satisfied noises. Eventually, she pulls back with a sparkle in her eye and I can't help but smile.

"Where's my taco?" she challenges, breathless.

I bring my fingers up to my mouth for a taste, hoping it'll hold me over until later.

"I was thinking the same thing," I deadpan.

She bursts into laughter.

Brat.

"Where are we?"

Her eyes bounce around the large expanse and I follow her gaze, seeing what she does. A sturdy breeze picks up, rustling the long wild grass that'll die off soon from not having a reliable water source leaving behind shades of earthy browns. Oh, and sagebrush. Lots and lots of sagebrush that will converge with tumbleweeds rolling across the land once the winds prove too fierce for their roots.

I've had my eye on this canyon in particular and now I'm finally sharing it with Angela.

This is it. Hands interlaced, I lead her up the loose gravel driveway. My chest so tight I feel like I might pass out, I turn to her when we reach the front walk, taking both her hands in mine.

"Coty, what is this?"

Angela's eyes dart between mine and the house we're standing in front of.

"For the last year I've been keeping a secret from you."

Eyes wide, Angela yanks her hands from mine, stumbling back.

What'd I say?

"No, that came out wrong." I reach for her but she shifts, avoiding me. Well, this got away from me. "Shit, babe, this is my house. This is the secret. I've been working on it for almost a year now and it's in the final stages of being finished."

Confusion still lines her face so I try again, holding my palms out in front of me. "I'm not married. No hidden family." She actually said that shit to me once, like that's something I'd ever hide. I'll be the first one to show off our family, when the time comes. "I started building this house for...us. For you." Her eyes widen as I rush to add, "After we got serious, I bought the property then hired a builder to make a home on it. I was hoping you'd want to move here with me but didn't want to pressure you, so I waited 'til you were ready." I gesture to the solid oak door I salvaged from a dilapidated barn several towns over. Beyond it lies a foyer with options to swing right to the dining room that'll hold our Friday family dinners or left to the library I've been quietly filling for Angela. Gary isn't the only one that can online shop. If she thinks she's surprised now, wait 'til she sees what those built-in bookcases hold. No more trips to the local library, unless she wants to anyway. "What do you think? Want to look around?"

I hold my breath. *Just give me a chance.*

"You're not proposing though, right?"

I smile, shaking my head. "Nah, one step at a time, babe."

Even though I fully intend on making Angela my wife someday, I'm not rushing her. Thanks to her mom, she's got a hang up about getting married too young. I knew she'd be worth the wait the moment I laid eyes on her and she's proven me right, making me work for every inch in our year together. One day this house will even be filled with our kids, but that's a conversation for a different day. Like I said, one step at a time.

"I'm not saying yes," she lowers her gaze to the ground before peeking back up at me, "but I'd love to see it."

That's all I need.

◆ ◆ ◆

"What will the guys do?"

"What do you mean?"

After giving Angela the grand tour, and some serious sweet talk, she finally agreed to make the move together next month. The word "yes" still tumbling from her mouth, I laid her out on the granite countertop to christen our new home.

Now, as we take the scenic way back, I can't help but reflect on our journey so far. Angela likes to say I'm the wrench in her plans, that I came out of nowhere to throw her off course, but I don't see it that way. I never have. She and I are a certainty, not a chance opportunity. She was on a really bumpy detour that ultimately led her right to Creekwood, right to me, which is exactly where she's supposed to be, where she was always going to end up. Life just gave her a longer route to reach me.

"Will they stay in the apartment without you there or move out, too?"

Her hand drifts lazily over my relaxed forearm and I can't remember a time I've ever felt so relaxed. I want to live right here, right now, forever.

"They're getting a new roommate. I think they're interviewing someone today."

"Wow, they move fast."

"Well, it's not like I've been there much lately. And they know where I belong."

"Going a hundred miles an hour on your black stallion?"

That is *not* what I call my bike. *Smartass.*

"With you. Anywhere."

She returns my embellished smile as we pull up.

Parking in my designated spot, Angela narrows her eyes out the windshield, saying, "That bike looks familiar."

A long, slender *female* body covered in leggings and a tight leather jacket mounts a white and gray Honda before taking off.

We get a lot of riders through here since we're the only place that offers reasonable rates to work on bikes but that Honda's one

I can honestly say I don't remember. Maybe she only went through the wash or something. Angela figured out how to clean everything we service as well so she makes more friends than ever.

We enter through the open rolling door holding hands, drawing a crowd wanting to know about the house. With the guys covering for me for the past several months, they're probably relieved to not have to lie to Angela anymore. She fills everyone in before they eventually return to their work.

Beck's been uncharacteristically quiet amongst the excitement, keeping himself busy with cleaning, and recleaning, his station. When he moves the same tool for the fourth time, I catch his eye and jerk my chin over my shoulder. "Who was that?"

Marc's the one to answer though, saying, "The hot chick with the CBR? That's our new roommate."

My eyebrows lurch up to my hat's flattened bill—professional attire isn't really my thing—and I look to Angela, finding her with a similar expression.

Well, shit, this should be interesting.

If you want more of the Creekwood Crew, be sure to check out Beckett's epic love story *Changing Lanes* available on Amazon.

Check out my website amarieauthor.com for up to date info.

Follow me on Instagram @a.mariebooks and be sure to check out the Detour Pinterest board @ambooksandtickets.

ACKNOWLEDGEMENTS

First and foremost, thank you for taking a chance on me and reading Detour. As a reader myself, I know how many books there are to choose from, so believe me when I say how truly grateful I am that you chose to spend some time with the characters that are so dear to my heart.

Next, I'd like to give a bit of an unconventional thanks. This one is for my children even though they're banned from reading this or any of Mom's other romance novels until they're over twenty years old. Maybe thirty. We'll see. You three cheered me on from Day 1, never once letting me think there was any other choice but to keep writing. Your support through this entire process was nothing short of amazing. Not once did you guilt me, judge me, or doubt me. If the world had more people like you three, everybody would be brave enough to not only chase their dreams but achieve them as well. Thank you, thank you, thank you. You hav my heart, forever and always. (Yes, hav is intentionally misspelled.)

To my hubby, thank you for unknowingly providing me with an example of the kind of man all of my male characters will strive to be. If it wasn't for you, I'd never know what unconditional love was. You're the Coty to my Angela, but without the crotch-rocket. Or the Camaro. Or the roommates. Okay, you know what? That was a bad analogy. I love you. Thank you for loving me the way nobody else would even dare to.

To my darling Shanna C., oh my gosh. Girl!! Do you realize that you singlehandedly gave me the confidence to self-publish this book? I had no idea when I asked you to be my beta the kind of support you'd provide. You encouraged me when you didn't even know what my book was about yet. Absolutely incredible. A simple thanks will never be enough but I hope you'll accept it just the same…thank you. Truly. I'm forever indebted to you. Unless this book flops of course, then that shit's all on you. Kisses!!

To Sarah P., my editor, thank you so much for your enthusiasm with this book. It was a relief to work with someone who got it. Who got me, and my characters, and where we were going, and why. You were gentle but thorough, just what I needed.

Julie D., you worked your proofreading magic and made my manuscript shine. Thank you a thousand times. Seriously, you're invaluable and I'm so glad I found/stalked you. Did I make that creepy? Sorry, but yeah, you're stuck with me.

Murphy Rae, I drooled over your book covers long before I even wrote my own. The fact that you designed my book cover still blows my mind. Your work is absolute art and I'm honored Detour served as one of your canvases. Thank you from the bottom of my heart.

Stacey B., thanks for making my book look pretty. I couldn't have done it without you. No, seriously, I took one look at formatting by myself and was like "Nope!" So thank you!

Stephanie Rinaldi, where do I start? You pushed me to admit I was a writer by inviting me to my first writing retreat. I'd never even shared my work before and you welcomed me to the writing world with open arms. I can honestly say it changed me for the better. Plus, you know, there's the other fifty-eight billion things you've helped me with since then. You do not accept the word no and I love you for that. I cannot wait for you to share your many, many talents with the world. Thank you for everything.

There are so many people from my insta-fam that I need to thank. Jessie S, love you and your I Am Woman, Hear My Roar support. Melissa Frey, you're such a wealth of information! So helpful and generous. Ellie Malouf, I had the idea for Detour swirling in my head for days but didn't tell a soul. You DM'd me randomly saying, "maybe you're a writer," and I started writing the next day. So, thanks for that unintentional nudge! Lacy, I just love you and your kindness and humor. You're a true friend. Kiss my niece for me. Toni, you've been salivating for my book without even needing the full details. That's the kind of commitment I wish everybody had in their lives because it means the world. For real, thank you. Thanks to the many authors that cheered me on when we all know it can be a cutthroat industry. And to all the others that have virtually squealed along with me every step of the way, thank you!! My book tribe may not be the biggest, but I can guarantee it's the best.

For all the bloggers, 'grammers, and readers that helped spread the word for this release-thank you so much! This was my first time with self-publishing and I'm blown away by the support you all gave an unknown like me.

To my Nantucket ladies, thank you. Always.

And lastly, a huge thank you to Jo and Give Me Books Promotions.

Made in the USA
Middletown, DE
27 September 2023